'Wangford's originality never fails to surprise and delight. Not only does he sing and look after womankind, he is the leading light in the Nude Mountaineering Society and has just written the liveliest book about Latin America to have appeared for a very long time.

'He travels from Patagonia – a place which he portrays with greater warmth and humanity than the often pretentious and self-absorbed Paul Theroux or the late Bruce Chatwin did in their books – to Texas. He takes the theme of cowboys to chat the reader fascinatingly through Latin America today . . .

'Two years ago at a friend's property in the Chilean Andes this reviewer, after decades out of the saddle, gingerly mounted the quietest horse in the country and ambled entranced in the foothills pretending to himself that he was the gallant O'Higgins of two centuries ago. The magic of that occasion, and much more, came back on reading this quirky, charming book.'

Hugh O'Shaughnessy, *Irish Times*

Hank Wangford is a doctor doing women's healthcare during the hours of daylight. A chance meeting with Gram Parsons made him a convert to country music, and his many live performances, recordings and TV and radio documentaries, notably Channel 4's *A-Z of Country Music* and the BBC's *Genghis Khan Was a Cowboy Too*, have made him Britain's most popular country singer. Hank Wangford lives in London.

Lost Cowboys

Lost Cowboys
from Patagonia to the Alamo

by
Hank Wangford

*IN*DIGO

First published in Great Britain 1995
by Victor Gollancz

This Indigo edition published 1996
Indigo is an imprint of the Cassell Group
Wellington House, 125 Strand, London WC2R 0BB

A catalogue record for this book is available from the
British Library.

ISBN 0 575 40003 X

Designed and typeset by
Fishtail Design

Printed and bound in Great Britain by
Guernsey Press Co. Ltd, Guernsey, Channel Isles

Contents

To Nicola and Mat, Harvey and Hutt,
two lights

Foreword

It was late in the autumn of 1988, with George Bush and Danforth Quayle recently destined for obscurity, that I returned to London from the States to one of the greatest requests of my working life: would I go to Central America with Hank Wangford to begin researching some films for his forthcoming television series on country music?

Having been a friend and fan of Wangford for many years, being paid to escort this tall, uncontrollable man through some of the best drinking nations known to man was a tough assignment. I reluctantly agreed and our travels through Mexico that winter led to the memorable 'South of the Border', one of the films in his Channel 4 series *Big Big Country*.

Somewhere, some time – probably at night – we had a conversation about the Spanish Conquest.

'Why,' asked Hank, 'didn't the Spanish conquistadors colonize North America?'

I couldn't answer the question because I didn't know – but I came up with an immediate reply which bordered on the logical.

'Well, they didn't find any gold and the Indians – Apaches, Comanches, Cheyenne – they were all so much more ferocious than the Aztecs. Anyway, the Spaniards liked to inherit civilizations when they conquered. It saved them having to set up a structure by which they could govern.'

I expanded into Peru and the conquest of the Incas, and Hank seemed content. It was enough to pacify his curiosity for the time I needed to get my nose into enough books to realize that we had both missed an unassailable fact – the Spaniards *had* moved into what we call the USA. Mexico used to stretch way up to California. It included Colorado, Utah, Arizona, New Mexico and Texas. Consider the names, San Francisco, Los Angeles, San Antonio . . . they were all mission towns. These conquerors had reintroduced the horse to the Americas. They had created the vaquero, the mounted Indian cattle herder, who tended millions of tons of beef from one end of South America to beyond the Río Grande. And all before the white settlers began their American Dream.

Hollywood owes us an apology. Hank and I are not the only stupid boys who have grown up with a fascination for that man on a horse who rides into town and solves the problem in the American Way. But what had happened before the white settlers? Who were the cowboys of the Americas before the silver screen gave us John Wayne and Clint, Tom Mix and the Cisco Kid? There is an enormous gap in the cowboy story and we resolved to fill it.

We made the entire trip from the bottom of the Americas to the Alamo once, but we revisited parts of the route on other occasions. This book is a product of all those journeys. If we were to do justice to this enormous subject, we knew we had to begin at the southernmost end of South America. So, early one January, we pulled on our boots and set out for the wilds of Patagonia.

Jo Tambien

Introduction

Westerns are twentieth-century fairy tales. Joseph Stalin loved to watch them alone in his private screening room in the Kremlin. We do not know if he was a Gene Autry or a Tom Mixman; or, for that matter, a John Wayne or Ronald Reagan fan.

Though never a cowboy trainspotter or a Western film buff, I was as swept up as any urban kid by the wide open spaces, the frontier lands, the lawlessness and the heroism, the Wild West and the American Way. Grown up, I accepted Westerns as mythical, even while they strove to be grown up themselves and more true to life.

While working with Jo Tambien in Mexico, I began to realize what a distortion Hollywood had presented to us. After a lifetime of believing that cowboys were Anglo-Americans, we started hearing about all the original cowboys way down south.

The peso dropped. It appeared that the American cowboy was not even the first, but the last cowboy on the continent. Clues had been lying around for years, but no one seemed to have picked them up. As kids we had all learned about *bolas*, the sort of three-stone slingshot that riders called gauchos used in South America for hunting.

So overwhelming, though, was the image of the American white cowboy as the sole true cowboy that the gauchos didn't connect. Sure, you can be a horseman, but that doesn't make you a cowboy. In our minds, gauchos were more like gypsies. They weren't real cowboys. Or so I thought until Jo Tambien found me a copy of 'Martín Fierro'. A long poem written like a troubadour's song, it is the cowboy masterpiece.

'Martín Fierro' is the story of a nineteenth-century gaucho and the loss of his freedom as the wide, empty pampas were fenced in with barbed wire and carved up by the railroads. It tells of much more. It is lyrical, cynical, political and powerful.

'Martín Fierro' opened it all up. There had to be a vigorous cowboy culture down south to produce literature like this. I decided to go to the countries where the cowboy traditions were strongest, and look at those countries and Latin America through the eyes of their cowboys.

'Martín Fierro' reminded me of an adventure I'd read as a child, a book you might still find on your grandparents' bookshelves.

Tschiffely's Ride is the true story of a schoolmaster who set out to ride the length of the Americas on two Patagonian horses. It describes his journey with his horses, from their native pampas through high plateaus and jungles, mountain passes and roasting deserts, all the way to Washington DC. People said he was mad and would never do it; but this mild-mannered teacher from a boarding school in Buenos Aires played out his dream, went all the way, and captured the imagination of a generation. He certainly caught mine, and led me to the delights of W. H. Hudson and Robert Bontine Cunninghame Graham.

Both Hudson and Cunninghame Graham wrote most of their work, which concerned South America, on the European side of the Atlantic. Some is deeply nostalgic, but they are both lyrical writers. Hudson was a naturalist born and bred in the Argentine, who wrote moving accounts of life and nature in Patagonia and out on the pampas. He left when he was twenty-seven and spent the rest of his life cramped in London, dreaming of the wide open spaces for more than fifty years. Cunninghame Graham was a flamboyant Scottish aristocrat, radical Member of Parliament, writer and gaucho who looked and acted like Don Quixote. He liked to be called 'Don Roberto'. He left florid, baroque accounts of cowboy life, minutely detailed descriptions of ostrich hunts, rodeos and trail drives. He wrote passionately of cowboy life from Argentina to Uruguay, Paraguay to Venezuela. By the time I got to Don Roberto, if I needed any convincing, he did it for me.

I owe a lot to Richard Slatta and his book *Cowboys of the Americas*. He goes into great detail about the different lifestyles of the gauchos of Argentina and Uruguay and the vaqueros of Mexico, of the *huasos* of Chile, the *gaucheiros* of southern Brazil and the *llaneros* of Colombia and Venezuela. It is the first full comparative history of the cowboys of the Americas, covering everything from the political importance of the cowboys in the Wars of Independence to the way they warm the horses' bits on a frosty morning. While I was wondering whether to use cowboys as the key to the different cultures in South America, Slatta's book became my bible.

Cowboys didn't stop south of the Río Grande – they started there. This thought was the inspiration for Jo and me to make our ten-thousand-mile journey to trace the true and magic stories of the original cowboys.

Everything started in 1494, when Columbus returned to bring the first cattle, the first horses and the first cowboys to the New World. More than anything, the horse was the defining factor. Running across the mythical wide open spaces, the fairy-tale frontiers, ridden by the good guys, the bandits, the cowboys and the Indians, there was always the horse.

The first pact man ever made was with fire. The second pact was with the horse. With fire he mastered his environment, but with the horse he conquered the world.

Cowboys, above all else, are men on horseback. So Jo Tambien and I decided to trace the arrival of the horse in the New World, the riders it brought with it, and the way it completely changed the way of life of a continent. The stories we found changed our attitudes to a lot of things apart from cowboys.

My thanks go to Jo Tambien, of course, for all his research, tolerance, Spanish and quick thinking in tight corners. Thanks to David Boardman, too, a close friend of Jo's and mine, and the world's best research consultant.

Thanks to my band the Lost Cowboys, Martin, Reg, Kevin and Jim; to the Margaret Pyke Centre; to the Williams Boys of Newmarket Street; to all the friends I ignored. To all these, thanks for putting up with me in my self-obsessed book-writing mode.

Thanks to Colonel Frank Wangford and his colleague Ian Richards at Frank Management, and to Rachel Calder, for their friendly encouragement and professional help.

Thanks to Mike Petty at Gollancz for thinking this was a good idea, and to Neil Frederick George at the BBC for the same and for producing *Wangford's Ride*. And to Kerry McGeever for convincing the BBC that Argentina was not too far away to go Down Your Way.

The sweetest circle of all has been closed. Gollancz brought my parents together. My mother, a pretty Glaswegian schoolteacher, attended a Left Book Club discussion weekend in London. One of the lecturers was my father, an eminent Communist and author of several historical works published by Gollancz. He beat a path to my mother before any of the other socialists and proposed within weeks.

Thank you, Victor.

Hank Wangford

Seven Lost Cowboy Sayings:

'Falsehood flies and truth comes limping after;
so that when men come to be undeceived it is too late;
the jest is over and the tale has had its effect.'
Jonathan Swift

'There is no mode of progression so delightful
as riding on horseback.'
W. H. Hudson

'Life is like pullin' on a mule team.
If you ain't the lead mule,
all the scenery looks the same.'
Old cowboy

'The dumb eloquence of events
reaches where reason does not.'
Cabildo of Montevideo to the Spanish King hinting at the possibility
of their freedom from Buenos Aires' hated rule, 1806

'Never start sawing the branch that's supporting you,
unless you're being hung from it.'
Old cowboy

'They tell me everything isn't black and white. Well, I say,
why the hell not?'
John Wayne

'Old cowboys never die. They just smell that way.'
Old cowboy

1. Río Gallegos – the Dying Place

The trip started strangely enough. The airport bus we were directed onto to take us out to the plane stood stock still as we walked through it, in one side, out the other and then straight up the aircraft steps. The bus didn't move an inch. Why was it there? Was it merely a symbolic bus or a piece of performance art? I was pondering this when the stewardesses came round giving out newspapers wearing surgical rubber gloves. I thought maybe a prostatic massage was on the cards but I had to make do with the BA *Herald*.

The muzak, too. Instead of the usual gloop there was some early bebop, Charlie Parker and 'Scrapple from the Apple'. Odd. Especially getting on the plane to Patagonia.

The muddy brown waters of the River Plate were speckled with small cloud shadows as we circled and climbed away from Buenos Aires. We flew out across some green pampa and started to follow the east coast down. The pampa was as flat as the sea. We were heading for Río Gallegos near the Straits of Magellan in the deep south, as far as we could go on mainland Patagonia before Tierra del Fuego. I stared out at the flatness and traced the line joining land and sea and dreamed.

Up north the land was green and the water of the River Plate brown. Later, as we crept along the coast, the sea had turned green and the land was brown. The land looked dry and scrubby and empty. I found out later it was. From thirty thousand feet there were no distinguishing features to identify the land as of this planet. A never-ending stretch of nothing. However stark it looked, it was my first sight of Patagonia; so it just shimmered. The very name held mysterious promise. Patagonia. It sounded mythological, the Furthest Place, the point beyond which you cannot go; a land of the imagination, like Ruritania or Transylvania.

Anywhere on this continent, whether they raise sheep or cattle, whether they are sheepboys or cowboys, where there are flatlands there are always horsemen. Much of Patagonia, all the way south, is flat. So it seemed reasonable to start looking for cowboys at the very bottom and work my way up. I'd heard mutterings up north about a Scottish community ranching out on the southern wastes of Patagonia. The Welsh colony is so established and so well known that people seem to think of Patagonia almost as part of Wales, more ours than Argentina's.

But the Scots? My guess was they must have come from crofters on the Falklands. My mate Jo Tambien had heard of a Caledonian gaucho by the name of Jimmy Halliday. I had heard so many unlikely things in Buenos Aires that I had no more reason to dispute this than anything else. In fact I was already prepared. As it was late January, round about Burns Night, I had smuggled a haggis, oatcakes and malt whisky across the great water. A treat from Auld Reekie. As a semi-Scot myself I had a feeling I might meet a fellow countryman, however many times removed.

Nobody seems to like Río Gallegos. Everything I'd read about the place had been pretty scathing: a bunch of corrugated shacks on the edge of nowhere at the very end of continental America. It had been a port for wool from the sheep stations and for coal brought down on the narrow-gauge railway from Argentina's main coal mine at Río Turbio on the Chilean frontier. Just a way-station, really, but one where forty thousand people now live.

As we drove into town it looked less grindingly drab than I expected. There was quite a bit of corrugated iron, some houses made of nothing else, but it was not unlike an ordinary prairie town.

But then we saw the 'front'. The town was built alongside the sulphurous mudbanks of the Río Gallegos. The front – the promenade – was like Harlow New Town at the end of the world. A sharp wind whipped round steel tubing lamp posts, through tunnels and balustrades and across ill-fitting concrete block pavements, a skateboard park with broken swings and a dead fountain. Kids without skateboards ran up and down in the skate bowls. Beside them a concrete municipal edifice, the Centenary monument, had a big clock with no hands. Scrawled across it was 'Social Security – Cave of Thieves'. There was a monument to lost airmen in the Falklands war. Río Gallegos was a big airforce base then. It all looked like it had seen better days, but maybe it hadn't.

Some girls played down at the riverside, flouncing around in the black tidal mud. They slipped and fell and shrieked and showed their muddy bottoms to appreciative boys sitting, whistling and shouting, on the yellow rails along the front.

The wind kept on blowing. The first thing you find out is that the wind always blows here. It whistles, it gusts, it whines, it bites, it whips, it erodes, it enrages. Rain or shine, it is always blowing. They used to have little policemen's stand-up huts to shield the men on duty from the incessant wind. They were like Punch and Judy stalls or portable toilets with windows. They stopped using them when a merciless hurricane blew two of them away and a policeman inside one was killed.

In the Hotel Commercio the owner was a chinless, toothy old man with the anaemic, washed-out face of one who has felt the winds of the world all his life.

'There was a time ten years ago when the Army occupied this hotel. They watched me walk from here to my little house, my *casita*, with a surveillance camera. So much security. Didn't know whether we'd be bombed or not.' Were you bombed? 'No.'

On a bus shelter was a rough painting in crude orange splashes of one of the last Tehuelche Indians. The Tehuelche were not fierce and warlike like the Mapuche. They were big people with roaring voices. Four hundred years ago Magellan thought they were giants. They were easy-going and friendly and were all but wiped out in the Indian wars of the last century. At the top of the painting it said, 'Even though the Tehuelche is no more he continues to be a part of our earth.'

The last full-blood Tehuelche had died in 1988, four years before. In the shops were Rambo and Mutant Ninja Turtle dolls. No Tehuelche dolls.

On another bus shelter, a piece of terminal Gallego humour said, 'I love you more than shit. Even when I'm having a crap.'

Tambien snorted and said that was typical of Gallegos, that this place here was well named because Gallegos, the people from Galicia in northwestern Spain, are relished in Spain for their stupidity. Gallego jokes are the Spaniard's Irish jokes. General Franco was a Gallego.

So only a Gallego would choose to settle down on the desolate, wind-whipped banks of a sulphurous river and choose to call it after himself. It was a stupid place with nothing to recommend it. Everyone but a Gallego would have passed by.

The search for the soul of Río Gallegos would seem a little fruitless. The Tehuelche are long gone and it would be hard to find anything soulful out on the gaunt wastes of the municipal promenade. But sitting unobtrusively on the main street in town behind some muted marble-style crazy-paving cladding is the best contender. On the little brass plate it says Club Britanico. Hip hip hooray!

The first settlers in southern Patagonia were English and Scottish sheep farmers. A man called Henry Reynard arrived in 1874 in Punta Arenas, a Chilean shantytown at the Pacific end of the Straits of Magellan. Despite the fact that the area was populated with Indians, pumas, guanacos, *caranchos* and ostriches, he decided it was ideal for sheep farming. So in 1877 Reynard brought over three hundred head of sheep from the Falklands and set up his operation in and around the Straits. He was so successful that word got back to the Falklands and up to Buenos Aires and settlers, mostly Anglos, came pouring in to claim land. Soon the whole area was like an outpost of the British Empire.

At the turn of the century a traveller in Río Gallegos wrote, 'The normal language seems to be English, and one has the feeling of being in Old England or at least in the Falklands. Except for the government officials, everything else is English: the money, the sheep, the language, the drinks, the ladies and the gentlemen.'

Originally the Coronation Club, the British Club was founded for these ladies and gentlemen in 1911. Nowadays a life-size picture of its founder, George MacGeorge, looks down from an imposing gilt and lacquer frame on the club wall, patrician with an Edwardian beard and a resolute stare, as stern as James Robertson Justice in *Doctor in the House*.

His only son, Jimmy MacGeorge, was last of the line. His picture on the wall shows a big fat man with an unruly pile of black fur at his feet. His dog. Jimmy drank himself into his grave, and it looks like his dog did too. That's easy to do down here because there's not a lot else going on, even for a dog.

The club was panelled in wood and tartan throughout. The billiard room had a beautiful old table shipped down in 1920. It was the most southerly billiard table in the Americas. The baize was the greenest thing in Patagonia. The cues, the scoreboard, the pictures of inept ladies being taught billiards by apoplectic gentlemen, the chintz, the wicker chairs, all came from another age.

The dining room was Terence Rattigan crossed with Fawlty Towers, and the food was as slow and as cold as Eastbourne. When I dined there one night everyone, though they knew each other and had just been drinking together, sat and ate at separate tables, just like in the film.

Maximo the waiter was Manuel in all but name. His slicked-back black hair was slightly untidy, his white jacket was crumpled and his trousers stopped well above his ankles. He had the teacloth permanently hanging over his crooked left arm. He didn't know where he was, which might have been a blessing, and didn't know who he was, a definite plus. If no one was in the club to remind him, he wouldn't know his name. He didn't know his *culo* from his *codo*. Maximo was pretty Minimo.

The club could have been anywhere. Patagonia's unhinging winds and driving rain were locked outside. Inside was the still, timeless land of the gin and tonic and the whisky.

Rheumy-eyed men with Scottish names hung over the bar. The atmosphere was quiet, near-funereal. The men drank to forget the falling world prices of wool and the murderous volcanic ash creeping across their estancias, shrouding the pitifully sparse vegetation and decimating their livestock.

An eruption in Chile six months before had already killed one and a half million sheep. Estancias had been destroyed, people had been forced out. Jars of the ash were on sale for one peso at the local airstrip as souvenirs for tourists on their way to see the Perito Moreno glacier crack and thunder into a milky lake.

I thought this would be the best place to find out where Jimmy Halliday was, surrounded by all these Scots Argentines and these tartan walls. Yes, they knew him, his estancia was not far out in the *camp*, the country. They thought, though, that he was away right now, up in Comodoro Rivadavia selling his horses.

Juan Alejandro McIntyre was in his fifties, heavy-set with greasy greying hair and a check shirt with sleeves rolled up. He had thick weather-beaten forearms, a big belly and the sad liquid eyes of a gin drinker. He talked slowly, pensively.

He talked of his sheep, the dust and his family. He talked of his estancia. He talked of horses. He talked of storms and Indians and droughts. He explained how the Scots got their lands after the terrible Indian wars. This was a story I was to hear again and again.

In the 1870s General Julio Roca embarked on the genocidal Conquest of the Desert, herding up the Araucanian Indians of Patagonia and slaughtering them. Up until then the Indians had repelled all invaders of their territory. For opening up and securing a whole new country, grateful Argentines made Roca president. He paid his soldiers according to the pairs of human testicles they brought back. He repaid his backers with generous tracts of land.

Many Anglo-Argentines had helped out. Scots, of whom Juan Alejandro McIntyre's grandfather was one, came over from the Falklands or down from

Buenos Aires inspired by Henry Reynard's success, their eyes on the endless virgin grazing land, and fought by Roca's side.

It is hard not to see this as the crofters' revenge. Having been exiled in the Highland Clearances, torn cruelly from their homeland and tossed on to the high seas, they fetched up in the Falklands, then took part in another brutal clearance at the other end of the world. They became, ironically enough, the new lairds.

The estancias were smaller now. With years of falling wool prices, and galloping Argentine inflation they had been scraping a living for a while. Things were finally stabilizing and the new president, Menem, seemed to have stopped inflation in its tracks, though nobody knew quite how.

The McIntyre estancia was small to medium, about seventy thousand acres, with nine thousand sheep and several troops of horses. Juan – John – had the volcanic dust on his land, but not thick enough to kill it. He talked with great loneliness.

'We're all interbred. My father and his two brothers married three sisters. Three McIntyre men married three Connaught women. All us children are double first cousins.'

Though the Anglos wiped out the Indians, they learned from them. They still hunt the Patagonian ostriches in the Indian way, with the *boleadores* or *bolas*. These are three round stones wrapped in rawhide tied together with three rawhide ropes attached in the centre. They are waved round the head like a lasso and thrown at the racing ostriches' legs. They spin lazily through the air then wind round the animal's legs fast and furious, stopping them dead in their tracks. *Boleadores* were always the trademark of the gaucho, the Argentine cowboy.

As a kid in Britain, the three-stoned *boleadores* were all I knew about gauchos. The lasso we understood, but the *bolas* were a mystery. It was only later I found out that the lasso was from Europe while the *bolas* were from the Indians.

The ostriches are called *ñandus* locally and are in fact rheas. They are cooked and eaten in the Indian way, too. The legs and spine are removed, and the carcass stuffed full of hot stones and sewn up. It cooks from the inside; Tehuelche microwave.

The rhea being a big runner, its rump is the best part. They have big *ñandu* feasts in February. Charles Darwin managed to get his name on this bird as he passed through on his legendary voyage in the *Beagle*: it is called *Rhea darwinii*. They say it is a strong-tasting meat.

Sitting there at the tartan bar it finally hit me that I was in a very foreign land. People were talking of mysteries – like filling a *ñandu* with hot stones out on the forlorn Patagonian *estepa* – as though they were normal day-to-day things. I felt that I was not just from the other side of the world but from the far side of the moon.

Juan told me that some other aliens, a bunch of crazed North American gringos, had fetched up here in 1905. They holed up in the mountains of northern Patagonia for a few years, hiding from the law. They were wanted for bank robberies up in the States. They were Butch Cassidy, the Sundance Kid and their beautiful companion Etta Place.

They liked to dress as Western gunslingers and ride into Gallegos firing their six-shooters off into the skies just like in the movies. They said they were looking for land. When they went into the main bank, then the Bank of London and Tarapaca, they tied up the manager and his staff and rode off with 20,000 pesos and 280 pounds sterling. The story goes that Etta Place shot out the telegraph line conductors with her little pearl-handled Derringer to stop the news passing to the next police post.

It was also said that they didn't go straight back to their mountain retreat but used the money to go to Europe. Some years before, they had gone to the Metropolitan Opera in New York, where Sundance had developed a passion for Wagner. Legend has it that they went to the Bayreuth Festival. Stranger things have happened in the land of howling winds.

There was a man at the bar, one of Juan's chums, who was of English stock. He was full of nervous energy, far more aggressive and loquacious. He had a red check shirt, white hair and a Bruce Springsteen forward-jutting low-slung jaw. He had been a diabetic for twenty-seven years and could talk the back leg off a guanaco.

He was a whisky drinker. Big whisky drinkers, the Argentines; they drop the 's' and call it *whicky*, and drink it in *whickerias*. Whisky is hugely popular throughout South America. Each country makes its own national whiskies. In the British Club they turned their noses up at the local dram, Breeder's Choice or Old Smuggler. Myself, I preferred an honest shot of Breeder's to the obscure ersatz Scotches members were flinging down their throats, like Ye Monks! or Sandy Mac.

If I saw anything in the club, it was the separateness, the loneliness of these people, as if the emptiness of Patagonia had seeped through the cracks round the closed doors and windows and had swamped the souls of the men inside. It was not just at the separate tables in the dining room but was there in Juan's empty gaze.

Before I fell into another gin, Juan's friend said he was driving out to Cape

Fairweather tomorrow and would we like to go with him? We could try and find Jimmy Halliday. Good.

In 1885 William Halliday and his family braved the 350 odd miles of South Atlantic, sailed over from the Falklands and landed on Cape Fairweather. (A sailor called Fairweather had been shipwrecked and died there in a storm.) The Hallidays had come from Dumfries to the Falklands. Like other Falklanders, kelpers and sheepmen alike, they had heard of land available and safe for sheep rearing in Patagonia.

When they landed they drew the boat up on to the beach, unpacked some things and left them beside the boat away from the voracious sea. They scrambled over the dunes to get out of the harsh wind and camped for the night.

They woke in the morning and went back over the rise to get their belongings. There was nothing. The beach was completely, mockingly empty. The second biggest tide in the world had swallowed up everything they had. Boat, clothes, tools, furniture, pots, pans, books, grain, everything. But the Halliday family were strong and Scottish and stubborn and claimed their estancia and made their new home from nothing.

William was Jimmy Halliday's grandfather. Jimmy was head of the clan now. Squeezed into the front of a pick-up truck we went out into the *estepa* – the steppe – to find him.

Jo Tambien thought it was pretty flat, and so it was, but not the billiard-table flat of the northern Canadian prairies or the pampa. The *estepa* here rolled a little, enough to make it different from the prairie's razor-slash between sky and land. It was still flat enough to have huge skies over the empty scrubland.

It was hard, stony and dusty as we set out, more like desert. The scrub was sparse and thin, barely enough to save the topsoil from wind erosion. But it did. Small yellow-green tufts of *queron*, scrubby pampa grass, held the earth together. The land was the remains of mountainsides eaten away by prehistoric oceans that have retreated and left their flat shingle bed.

Here and there were *mata negra* and *mata verde* bushes, spiky water-savers clinging tenaciously to the wind-scarred sediments of this old ocean floor. Large dark-green *calafate* bushes bore round black berries, tasting dark and sweet like blackcurrants.

Seven sharp volcanic hills, the Seven Friars, punctuated the horizon on the west. A little way out of town we crossed a bridge made in Wolverhampton in 1911, the same year the British Club was opened. As we came off the metalled road the land rolled even more into little *mesetas*. A small cliff lined a river.

The Halliday estancia was snuggled cleverly in a hollow, sheltered by poplars from the worst of the wind. It looked out over the spreading flat valley of the steppe, a fine house with corrugated-iron roofs, a Colonial frontage and neat lawns. A little blue wooden gate opened on to a concrete path. A bright-orange avenue of African daisies and marigolds marched up either side to the front door.

A smiling, stocky man stood there in light blue denim *bombachas* (the baggy gaucho pants), *alpargatas* (gaucho espadrilles), check shirt, wide cloth *faja* (the belt wound round his belly, his *facón*, the long working knife, stuck diagonally in the back), and a black beret. It was the Patagonian style of gaucho working wear. He was not duded up. He had the well-deserved belly of an active man of sixty-four, twinkling eyes and a greying moustache. He looked like a weather-beaten Jimmy Greaves.

Jimmy Halliday had not gone to the horse market yet, and welcomed us. He smiled and twinkled some more. His son Eduardo rode up. He had a spectacular forest of red beard, a gaucho Rob Roy. More dress conscious than his father, he wore a blue shirt and bandana and toning dark-blue *bombachas*. A matching red *faja* and beret set off his magnificent beard. As he was working the horses he was wearing canvas leggings and trainers, the new universal footwear usurping the traditional *alpargatas*.

They don't wear cowboy hats near the Straits of Magellan. They don't stay on in the Patagonian winds like berets do. Jimmy said they can't use ponchos in Patagonia either. The winds just whip them up into the horseman's face all the time. 'I wear my *facón* to use in my work and because it keeps my back straight. I'm sixty-four now, a bit creaky. I still ride but I don't break horses any more.'

He stopped bronco busting four years before, so he had still been doing it when he was sixty. He spoke natural English with a slight foreign cadence and a Scottish tinge. All the men in his family had been schooled at St George's – The College – in Buenos Aires. He got his accent from his father.

'My father had a strong Scottish accent. With the isolation of Patagonia you just carry on, you don't better your pronunciation. We stay as we are. It must be hereditary because I've never been to Scotland.'

Jimmy spoke English and Spanish at home.

Eduardo spoke only Spanish with his wife and two sons. They lived in another, smaller corrugated-roofed house across the hollow. The quarters for the peons (farmhands) and the *domador*'s house were round the side of the rise.

Down in front of the Hallidays' houses was the shearing shed and the stables. Jimmy's wife Christine thought they were an eyesore. She was right.

Without the buildings it would have been nothing but the *estepa*, a lot of it, stretching a very long way, right through to tomorrow.

The chief horseman and *domador* – horse breaker – was Martín from Corrientes in the north. A good man, he'd been with them for three years. He wore thick leather *guardacalcones*, chaps, and a beret unlike his native Corrientes sombrero. He hardly spoke a word.

Eduardo and Martín cantered off in a cloud of dust to round up a troop of a dozen mares two leagues away.

'Today they changed troops and we were missing one of the young mares. Apparently she jumped the fence. I saw her this morning when I went down to the shanty and they went out this afternoon to bring her in with the rest. I'm going out to see how they are doing.'

We rode out to find them.

'You have to keep your eyes open, everything is far away. We're going to see if they went through that gate. That's less than a league away.'

Everything is in leagues down here. It is just too big for kilometres or miles. A league is five kilometres. Seven league boots? Got to be twenty miles a stride. So Eduardo and Martín were just going six miles to collect the mares. Not especially far on a medium-sized estancia like the Hallidays' which covered thirty thousand hectares, about seventy thousand acres in all.

We stopped at the gate and looked for tracks.

'We read the ground the whole time. We learn to follow, to trace a trail to see if sheep or horses or a truck has passed through this way. We can see hoof marks of horses or sheep, or the tracks of a truck.'

I stared fruitlessly at the stony ground and could see nothing. I felt like a blind city boy, trying to read Braille that had been sandpapered down.

'We can see the tracks because there's a piece of grass been stood on, a stone moved. Look, there, they've been through here.' I stared some more. I put my face to the ground but knew I'd have to spend the next thirty years down there kissing rocks before I could tell whether a gate had been opened, let alone catch a stray horse.

Then, in the distance, I could see dust rising. They had rounded up the mares and were coming back this way.

I had heard tell that the cowboys up north always rode stallions and kept away from mares which would be an insult to their machismo.

'Not here. We ride mares. Of course. It's stupid not to. How do you know whether a horse is good or bad unless you ride it? Nothing wrong with mares.'

The boys came back with about twelve mares. One 21-year-old white, the bell mare, led them into the corral to join another ten already there. She was tame, they said, but useless to ride, bucked all the time. But she always led the other wild horses into the corral beautifully.

Down on their feet in the corral, Eduardo and Martín worked the horses with a lot of whistling and whirling around and rising plumes and twists of dust. They were separating the wild fillies and old mares from the riding mares they had broken that spring. They did the job quickly with a minimum of fuss.

They lined twelve of them up shoulder to shoulder with their tails backed on to the corral fence. These had all been branded and tamed. They were looking them over to see which to take the one hundred and forty leagues – seven hundred-odd kilometres – up to Comodoro Rivadavia for the sales. They got five hundred dollars a head and would take six.

'We have a small knot of horses. If we have all our tamed horses in the corral, you'll see sixty horses lined up with their tails on the fence.'

One horse had different-coloured eyes, one blue and one brown. She was La Prisoniera, daughter of La Fugitiva. The Prisoner, daughter of the Fugitive. Another had a white eye. It was *sarca*, a weak eye, and if albino it would be blind in strong light. No good.

They had cattle but had sent them sixty leagues up to Calafate near the glaciers, on the shores of Lake Argentino, for better grazing. The scrub and pampa grass are richer and denser up there and can support cattle or a greater concentration of sheep. Down here it was sheep and horses only, and even then fewer sheep per hectare than further west.

After selling the horses they were going to the mountains to pick up some merino sheep. Last year they cut the flock down to let the *estepa* regenerate. The land on the Halliday estancia was richer and less stony than south of the River Gallegos but still needed care. Now golden yellow-green hummocks of *queron* were pushing up everywhere in spite of disappointing rainfall.

Riding across the steppe with Jimmy we saw guanacos, small wild llamas, *caranchos*, large black, crested carrion hawks with big pale-blue hooked beaks, and hundreds of Patagonian hares. A long-beaked ibis flew alongside us. Jimmy said that Dominican gulls were worse than the *caranchos* and could dive straight down out of the sky and peck out a sheep or lamb's eyes.

The *carancho*, though, is the most disliked bird the whole length of the Argentine right down to Tierra del Fuego. Although mostly a carrion bird, it will attack sickly or small animals. The hare is a favourite. The *carancho* swoops and soars over the terrified victim, harrying and taunting it while the hare twists and turns, desperately trying to dodge its tormentor. The hawk sails along elegantly, hardly moving a wing feather while its prey runs in circles, in straight lines and zig-zagging as fast as it can go. As the hare tires, the *carancho* dips down and starts to peck viciously at it. Eventually the hare gives up and squats down exhausted. Its eyes are pecked out immediately.

Often a gaucho sleeping on the pampa would wake up to find several *caranchos* perched around him, hoping for a morning meal of dead meat and disappointed to see him stirring.

There are grey and red fox, and pumas come down from the mountains to live in the shade of the cliffs by the side of the river. They will kill sheep if the gulls or *caranchos* don't get them.

I saw my first *recado* or Argentinian saddle. Jimmy showed me in his stables how it was made up of layer upon layer of leather, blanket and *bastos* (leather pads), with a broad thick sheepskin on the top and all held together with a wide cinch. Jimmy likes to sit on a black sheepskin. 'It looks better.' It looks like a sofa. It is very comfortable to ride all day.

'Mine is a version of the *recado*. There are various types of saddle all around Argentina because people have their own ways of riding according to the terrain. I use a *recado* from Entre Ríos, adapted for the work down here. I think it's better than the local one.'

Jimmy bought part of the saddle but made his own rawhide tack like bridles, harness, reins and even cinches. As he fixed the last cinch round the sheepskin mat, another penny dropped: as the belt was tightened to hold everything securely in place, I understood 'It's a cinch'.

They use ferocious-looking round, swivelling pointed-rowel *espuelas*, spurs. Their whips, *rebenques*, seem kinder by contrast. They are flat, an inch or two wide, and give a light slap rather than a bite. 'You don't want to hurt the animal unless necessary.' They shoe the horses only in the winter when the ground gets hard.

Jimmy showed me his *botas de potro*, literally 'horse boots' or 'colt boots'. Which is exactly what they are. They are soft leather open-toed boots. They have been replaced by the canvas leggings and trainers that Eduardo was wearing. They are the hide of the upper part of the hind legs of a colt. The heel of the boot is the hock, the elbow of the horse's leg.

Botas de potro were the traditional gaucho boots. Bare-toed, gauchos would ride gripping the stirrups, the *estribos*, with their toes. The original stirrups were a simple rawhide rope that was stuck between the big and second toe with a piece of wood in the bottom to rest the toes on.

Botas de potro tangibly and graphically symbolized the gaucho's absorption into the horse. They were part of his feral nature, part of his life in the wild. He wore his horse's legs on his feet. His legs became his horse's legs. For these reasons they developed into a political issue. During the nineteenth century they were made illegal, ostensibly to stop the wanton killing of too many young colts. In truth, this was part of the subjugation of the wild gaucho and the denial of his freedoms, in preparation for the parcelling off of the lands he had roamed unhindered for centuries.

Jimmy Halliday, a Scottish Argentine estanciero, was light years away from the original gauchos, the lone cattle hunters roaming the pampa, as wild as the cattle they killed when they needed to eat. Even so, that tradition still found its way to the shaded hollow on the Patagonian wastes. Jimmy still had *botas de potro*.

Jimmy and Eduardo raised criollo horses, a breed internationally established and accepted in the 1920s. Criollo means creole, born and bred in Argentina, like criollo people and cattle.

Criollo horses are strong, solid and hard working, with great stamina. They are the horses Tschiffely rode to Washington. They are small and stocky, well built with thick sturdy necks. Not as fine or as neurotic as thoroughbreds, they are perfect working horses. Nothing fancy about the criollo.

They have been around for much longer than this century. Their ancestors were the original Spanish horses, an Arab-Barb mix which came over with the conquistadors. Cowboys came with the Spanish, too.

Before the sixteenth century there were no cattle, no horses and no horsemen anywhere in the Americas.

In fact, it was Columbus who brought the first. On 2 January 1494, on his second voyage, he unloaded twenty-four stallions, ten mares and an unknown number of cattle on to the shores of Hispaniola, now the island of Haiti and the Dominican Republic.

The horses and cattle multiplied, escaped and spread rapidly. Within fifteen years they had reached Panama. Not long after they were out in the wild throughout the length and breadth of the continent. Horsemen adapted the Spanish ways with horses and hunted the wild cattle. The indigenous people, the 'Indians', learned and perfected riding skills too. So 'Cowboys and Indians' were born.

Now the horsemen in the far south were Scottish, but not quite as Scottish as I expected. Jimmy had never been to the Auld Country and frankly wasn't bothered. He was Argentine, with a Scottish heritage, but was happy on his windy plain. No endless expatriate whingeing for Jimmy or Eduardo. They lived and worked and rode across this barren land just as their forebears had done in other harsh wildernesses in Scotland or the Falklands. They were happy where they were – which was as it should always be, and so rarely is.

Happy where she was, too, was Christine Halliday, Jimmy's wife. A strong woman, she was plump, fine looking with a tough complexion hardened by the wind. She was Argentine from an English family.

Fierce at first, she warmed up as she showed off her passion, her garden. It had been mollycoddled into fertility, shaded from the stinging winds so as to produce an inspiring range of fruit, flowers and vegetables from the arid, unprepossessing *estepa*.

The apple, cherry and damson trees were bare this year. A severe frost had killed their blossom. But alive and flourishing amid the bare trees was her vegetable garden. Peas, beans, Australian onions, lettuce, beetroot, spinach, turnips, swedes, a few spuds and garlic had all been goaded out of the stern earth.

She had strawberries, blackcurrants and rhubarb. With no apples, cherries or damsons I understood there was going to be a lot of rhubarb jam in Patagonia this year.

We sat in a back room. She served blackcurrant and rhubarb and strawberry jam for tea. They were delicious with doorsteps of white bread. The tea was out of a pot with a yellow tea cosy. The wind was outside. There were chopped egg sandwiches and fairy cakes. Jo Tambien said he hadn't had a tea like that since he was six. Little did he know at the time that he was just at the beginning of his Patagonian Tea Odyssey.

Eduardo was a horseman through and through. He raised sheep but the horses were his passion. He loved to train horses slowly and gently in the Indian rather than the gaucho way. He was contemptuous of bronco busters.

'Just good athletes, that's all. It's just balance between three points, two legs and the reins. Now, *training* a horse properly to work and run, to cut into cattle, to walk right, to respond, that's real horsemanship.'

It was his hobby, his love and his life.

If they loved horses that much, could they eat them? If they went lame what did they do?

'I don't care for horsemeat myself. I have nothing against it, it's not a moral problem, I just don't like it that much. It is thought to be a delicacy by many in the Argentine, a lot of people do like eating it. But I don't know how far it really goes, for some it's just part of saying, "Oh, I like *potranca* – filly – I like eating *potranca*." But for me, you can put all the meat in front of me that you want and I think the horsemeat would be the last that I'd eat.'

What do you do then if you kill a horse?

'We often have to kill horses here. If horses break their leg or knock an eye out they have to be killed, sacrificed. We put a bullet into them and give 'em to the pigs. Oh, we'll offer it to the men if the animal's fat and meaty, and they don't worry about it, they quite like it. The *domador*, the cook, the other men, they like to eat horse.'

Twice a year the sheep are herded for shearing and dipping. The shearing sheds would be hot and thick with flying wool, dust and grease. A noisy old motor turned a driveshaft from which hung the clacketing shears. They were belt-driven like old-fashioned dentists' drills. With the bleating sheep, the chugging motor, the whirring and buzzing, the slapping clattering of old machinery, it would be boisterously noisy. Bands or *comparas* of itinerant sheep-shearers, often Chilenos from over the border, travel from one estancia to the next, joining the *paisanos* for the annual shearing.

At the Hallidays' they would have eight shearers at a time. They knew what they were doing, and they could shear a sheep in two and a half minutes flat. One man, hands and pants thick and shiny with lanolin, could deal with 240 sheep a day. So about two thousand sheep would emerge from the flurry of the sheds every day, scalped and scarred with red gashes on their naked milk-white skin, ovine skinhead number ones.

When I was there the sheds were silent. A few guanaco hides and sheepskins hung drying from the rafters. Eduardo's kids kicked a dead bird around and a couple of pigs strolled through. But it was easy to believe that the place was a madhouse when the shearers came through.

In the hallway of the Hallidays' house is the map of the land given to old Guillermo Halliday by the Governor of Santa Cruz. It goes right down to the shore of Río Gallegos. Herbert Felton had the land to the west of him, Victoriano Rivera the land to the east.

Jimmy's estancia was in fact owned jointly with his brother and sister. I had asked him whether his two grandsons would want to work in the *camp*. They said they did. This would cause further division of the estancia, he said. Shareholders in the company were other members of the Halliday clan.

'There is no problem, but I'd have to work it out with my brother and sister. And all the cousins, the shareholders. As well as Hallidays there are McIntyres and Johnsons all in the family, on the Halliday girls' side.'

*

I finally produced the haggis. It was near as dammit Burns Night and I wanted to give the folks their treat. It was the first haggis they had ever seen, but they knew what it was and I told them how to cook it. They were pleased to see the malt whisky and the oatcakes, but looked blank when I mentioned Burns Night.

Not only had they not heard of his night, but they didn't know Rabbie Burns from a hole in the ground. The irony was that the Halliday family hailed from Dumfries in lowland Galloway, Rabbie's manor, where he was an exciseman for many years and did most of his writing and womanizing.

Scotland, a country steeped in the unforgiving Calvinist tradition, lionized Burns as much for his sexual conquests as for his verses – so much so that there is a stained glass window honouring the great adulterer and fornicator in one of the great kirks of Scotland, in the House of God itself. I explained all this to the Hallidays and left them to decide whether and in what way they wanted to celebrate their new friend, their unknown hero.

Another grey Patagonian day.

Far from being depressing, grey skies seem natural over the featureless waste. Sun and fine blue skies make it stand out too clearly, give it too much light and shade, rob it of some of its transcendent powers. This monotonous bleakness is an important part of the spell it weaves upon us.

W. H. Hudson, the great English writer and naturalist, born and bred on the pampa, said of Patagonia, 'It is not the imagination, it is that nature in these desolate scenes, for a reason to be guessed at by and by, moves us more deeply than in others.' Saint-Exupéry had looked down on this bare *estepa* many times from his mail plane. He too was drawn to this wasteland:

The pilot flying towards the Straits of Magellan sees below him, a little to the south of the Gallegos River, an ancient lava flow, an erupted waste of a thickness of sixty feet that crushes down the plain on which it has congealed. Farther south he meets a second flow, then a third; and thereafter every hump on the globe carries a crater in its flank. No Vesuvius rises up to reign in the clouds; merely, flat on the plain, a succession of gaping howitzer mouths.

This day, as I fly, the lava world is calm. There is something surprising in the tranquillity of this deserted landscape where once a thousand volcanoes boomed to each other . . . I fly over a world mute and abandoned, strewn with black glaciers.

Charles Darwin, back in England after his epic five-year voyage in the *Beagle*, couldn't get the *estepa* out of his mind:

In calling up images of the past, I find that the plains of Patagonia frequently cross before my eyes; yet these plains are pronounced by all wretched and useless. They can be described only by negative characteristics: without habitations, without water, without trees, without mountains, they support merely a few dwarf plants. Why then, and the case is not peculiar to myself, have these arid wastes taken so firm a hold on my memory?

I could only agree with Darwin. I had already been entranced by other great empty places like the Shetland Isles and Connemara on Ireland's west coast. Most of all, I have carried a recurring and strangely comforting memory of the mathematical flatness of the Canadian prairies, where they have neither mountains nor, in the south, trees. The locals are serious when they say, 'There ain't no mountains round to spoil the prairie's view.' Even more serious when they say down south, 'They ain't no trees around . . . '

We drove out of Gallegos on the way to Juan's estancia. On Juan's windscreen was a sticker:

SOLITARIO SEÑOR DE PAMPAS
HOMBRE ORGULLOSO DE SU LABOR
(Lone man of the Pampas
A man proud of his work)

'This town never sleeps. It's crazy! I played bingo all last night!' Juan said.

There were a surprising number of dancehalls and bars in the red light district of Gallegos. We passed the Whickeria El Escorpio Show – the Scorpion Show Bar – which looked pretty dodgy. With a dark-brown honky-tonk front and tiny windows, it looked like a place to get several incurable diseases in one go. Since the recession had bitten, many whorehouses and bars had closed. Twenty years before, there had been so many red lights on the street, aeroplanes thought it was the runway. Ten years before, the Falklands conflict brought a brisk trade to Runway Street, but now it seemed subdued. I didn't bother to check it out.

There used to be a lot of meths drinkers. And a lot of murders. William had had a peon, a farmhand, who was found with his brains blown out. Someone had tried to make it look like suicide, but in a way that would have made a Gallego proud. There was blood everywhere, a hole in the back of his head, but the killer had dressed him in fresh clean clothes – hardly the perfect crime, but the smartest victim.

We passed over the old Wolverhampton-built bridge just outside town.

'I nearly had to blow up this bridge in sixty-one/sixty-two. I was a conscript during a civil war. There were several different army factions down here. We had it all set up, dynamited, fused, connected, all ready to blow but orders countermanded it just in time. Mind you, it's so old it's falling apart. We should have blown it up anyway.'

The McIntyre estancia was further away than the Hallidays'. All along the side of the road the dark green leaves and purple flowers of alfalfa were growing, from seeds dropped off lorries. The *estepa* was studded with windmills sucking water from deep down in the hard ground.

Fragile, on tiptoes between the sheep, a few guanacos watched us. Juan said that the sheep don't eat the *queron*, leaving it to hold the land together; instead they eat the shorter rye grass in between the tufts of *queron*.

Juan's estancia was called Killi-Aike. *Killi* was an extinct flower in Tehuelche. *Aike* meant home, a place where camp is pitched. It would therefore be sheltered and have a spring or some source of water. All the places called *Aike* were in fact Tehuelche camps before Roca cleared them out.

Killi-Aike had been built up and was larger than the original land given to Juan's grandfather by Roca. Pipelines run through it now. A gas pipeline runs from John Blake's place in the south more than two thousand five hundred kilometres – over five hundred leagues – all the way to Buenos Aires. An oil pipeline runs from twelve leagues north to Río Gallegos where the crude is collected by tankers.

On Killi-Aike the talk was not of pipelines but of sheep and horses. Juan's passion was sheep, but his wife Eva could talk of nothing but pinto horses. Their interests seemed to keep them mercifully apart.

Eva McIntyre was another strong-willed Patagonian woman, big built and fine looking. She had a gap between her front teeth. Was there any Wangford in her family? She laughed. 'I suppose there could be but I don't know.'

Her mission in life was to get the *tobiano* (pinto) horse recognized as a bona fide breed. The problem was that many thought of *tobianos* as worse than shit and wouldn't be seen dead on them. I was to meet gauchos in the north who spat on the ground at the mention of pintos. 'Crap!' So Eva McIntyre had chosen herself a big heavy rock to push up a very steep hill.

The house was another traditional Patagonian pre-fab with corrugated roofing and a little garden in front. The honeysuckle needed cutting back and the grass trimming. It was all a bit unkempt, like Juan.

The windows rattled in the wind. They would have been much noisier in the standard eighty-mile-an-hour Patagonian breeze but it was less windy than usual today. Inside it was dark and sombre. I admired the sofas and sideboard, all from another time.

Mrs McIntyre didn't like them.

'Too old. All outdated.'

A cuckoo clock and a barometer hung on the wall. Juan's *rastra* was there, his wide gaucho belt festooned with silver dollars, escudos and silver chains. Beside it was a display of *facónes*, the sword-length gaucho knives. Juan's gaucho heritage had become sitting-room ornaments. The toilet cistern was a Shanks' Patent Tubal, an old favourite a long way from home.

Eva McIntyre laid out her horse albums. She was convinced the *tobiano* was the first horse in this most southerly part of Patagonia. Pinto horses were ridden by Indians as early as 1580, when Sarmiento de Gamboa saw Indians riding with dogs as he sailed through the Straits of Magellan.

Four years later Gamboa came back and founded the first settlements on the Strait of Misfortune: 'Ten naked Indians approached us and pronounced words of welcome in an unknown language. The Chief, trying to prove their friendship, took a long arrow and swallowed it till it almost disappeared down his throat. When he slowly took it out it was covered in blood.' A pity he didn't understand what a bloody arrow down the throat might mean. Two years later the settlements were in ruins. An English pirate found a few dazed survivors wandering the deserted coast. He renamed one of the settlements Port Famine.

The horses Gamboa first saw were a different breed from the criollo horses of the River Plate and the pampa. They must have arrived separately from the original strain up north that first reached Buenos Aires in the early sixteenth century.

The reason is the Santa Cruz river. No horses could have crossed it. It was very deep, cold, steep-sided and fast-flowing. Whether the water was high or low, it always flowed at a minimum eight knots. So, said Mrs McIntyre, no animal would cross that river without being pushed or pulled by men. The pinto horses ridden by the Indians in 1580 must therefore have arrived in this southerly zone some other way, probably from shipwrecks round the Patagonian coast. So the *tobiano* is a true Patagonian horse, distinct from the criollo.

It certainly is, say its detractors. Unlike the American quarterhorse, where there is no such prejudice, no criollo could have pinto colouring. The McIntyres' original *tobiano* stallion was a fine-looking horse, but was called Poca Cosa because the inspector said it was 'everything and nothing'. It had the *tobiano* blotches with a sharp line between colours. This was important because a soft, bleeding line was not *tobiano* but *overo*.

Pinto is the same as piebald, which is white and black, or skewbald, which is white with brown, red or any other colour. These have always been judged by many as mongrels, of mixed or untrustworthy character, as impure – rejects, runts, outcasts. The gypsies of the horse world. Maybe that's why the Indians like them. As far as cowboys and gauchos are concerned, well, hell, they're just plain blotchy.

Eva dismissed the ridicule heaped on the *tobiano* as stupidity and snobbism. Quite rightly, she said, like their North American cousins, the Patagonian Indians loved the pinto. As well as being fast, strong and responsive, they looked good. And the Indians knew their horses.

Criollos are hard-working troop horses – they can be ridden by anyone and don't hold a grudge. Thoroughbreds will remember abuse and wait for the chance to retaliate later. And the *tobiano* is strong and easy-going like the criollo.

While Eva championed the *tobiano*, Juan was out checking his rams. Australian Merinos and Corriedales, a Merino-Lincoln cross, were the most popular breeds out here on the *estepa*. Juan won prizes with his Corriedales. He was preparing for a show.

The rams were pampered giants. I had read about the Patagonian giant sloth and thought for a moment I'd stumbled on some who'd had Afro haircuts. They had canvas coats on, guarding their wool from damage. I had never seen sheep that size or wool that thick. It was even sprouting densely from their foreheads. Their muzzles and ears just about poked out of the great shag pile like an afterthought.

'Mas carne, mas lana,' said a peon, seeing my goggling eyes. More meat, more wool.

Each of the rams was worth ten to fifteen thousand dollars. (A criollo horse fetched five hundred.) The depth of their wool made them look as if they were wallowing through life like a bunch of self-indulgent courtiers. The wool was heavy and lanolin-rich, dirty and dark on the outside from the grease and the dust.

Juan proudly pressed his hands down flat on the coat of one of the biggest. He pulled them apart, exposing the intimate pure-white wool underneath. He pushed them together, raising two rolls of ribbed white wool with a crack down the middle, and gazed lovingly at the luxuriant white slash. It looked just like a shiny pearly-white vagina. I didn't know whether Juan was aware of this, and I didn't ask him.

Juan's mother Mary was eighty-six, small, thin and bright, and she lived in the house next door. It had a porch. Timber from a shipwreck on Cape Fairweather had been used to build part of the house but the furniture, a long oval dining-table and chairs, came from Maples in London.

Mary was one of six Connaught girls, and one of the three who married three McIntyre boys. She had been schooled in Edinburgh.

Both the teenage children were handsome and very gaucho. Enrique sat in the stables mending some *boleadores* before he brought in a troop of horses. He was wearing the standard *bombachas*, *alpargatas* and a red beret. He smiled shyly and said nothing.

His sister Maria was dressed the same but for a peaked cap. He was dark and quiet while she was blond and a tomboy. She had been painting the heels of a horse with burnt oil and worked closely with the *domador*. She followed him everywhere. A tiny man with beret, *bombachas* and *botas de potro*, he seemed to be a father figure to her. He had taught her everything she knew about horses. Soon she would break her first horse, to 'iron out the tickles'.

Juan had had the same gaucho upbringing as Maria was now getting. His *facónes*, his *rastra* were all part of this. But he had come out of the saddle finally and given up the horse for the sheep, something a real gaucho would never do. He would lose his pride. That seemed to be what had happened to Juan.

Without a word, Juan came out with some *boleadores*. He held one in his hand and dangled the other two on the ground. Slowly, gracefully he waved them in a steady circle round his head. He said that, for maximum effect, they needed to complete one and a half revolutions before hitting the prey.

His blue nylon shirt finally pulled out of its trouser moorings and his belly spilled over his belt. The shirt stuck sweatily to his chest. But he was swinging the *bolas* round his head with such grace, such delicacy, that his belly, his shirt, his drinking, his loneliness, his disappointment all faded away. As the rawhide thrummed in the air round his head, he was the Gaucho.

He let go the *bolas* and they spun away, hanging timelessly in the dusty corral air. Exactly a spin and a half later they hit a corral post and wound round it in a blur, faster and faster until with a crack the stone balls clattered on to the post.

'Not very good,' he said gloomily.

After motoring down a few long lonely Patagonian roads under the huge sky, time and space seemed to fudge together and everything slowed down. I began to understand the meaning of the Spanish verb *patagonisar*, to 'patagonize', to become slow, easy-going, philosophical, thankful for small mercies, to become Patagonian.

Yo patagoniso, I patagonize.

Estoy patagonisado, I am patagonized . . .

The real music of Patagonia, apart from the incessant wind, went with the Tehuelche. It was primitive, aboriginal music. A lot was shamanistic. To some of the deep south tribes, song was so much part of magic that the word for 'sing' and 'fall into a trance' was the same.

The Tehuelche wore belts with bell rattles on them and played a musical bow or *koolo*, the same word as the Spanish for arse. They also played a bone flute with three holes in it. It was called a *rambo*. American for arse.

German musicologists flocked over to this primitive, unexplored land at the turn of the century, collected and analysed fifty-one Tehuelche tunes and finally declared their tonal system 'problematic'. That is pretty much how things stand today.

There is a small museum in Río Gallegos. The curator was – just for a change – a cousin of Juan McIntyre. I dug around among the rock samples, arrowheads, whale vertebrae, plants and fossils to see what I could find.

There was a skull with a bullet hole in it, another with an arrowhead stuck right between its eyes. Stuffed animals abounded – eagles, owls, *caranchos*, condors, *ñandus*, armadillos, foxes, hares, guanacos. And in the middle of them was an Edwardian bicycle with a basket on the front that had been ridden the whole length of Argentina by Charlotte Fairchild, a lady from this part of Patagonia.

The museum had a leaflet about this Province of Santa Cruz in Patagonia. It claimed Argentine and world firsts:

The biggest Petrified Forest in the world!
The most fossils in the world!
Three hundred and fifty-six glaciers! !
The oldest man in Argentina, twelve thousand six hundred years old! ! !
Most exciting of all, the only covered tennis court in the country! ! ! !

It had the same partisan tone as those small American towns hyping themselves as 'Turnip Green Capital of the World'.

The leaflet also said that Magellan held the first mass on Argentine soil down here in Patagonia in 1520. In the winter of that year he was holed up, grounded on the dismal Patagonian shore. He called the place San Julian.

It was on this same voyage that they first saw giant Indians, dancing and chanting on the shore, wearing white face paint and animal masks. One kept throwing dirt over his head. According to his chronicler Pigafetta, a stunned Magellan shouted '*Qué Patagon!*' at the vision: 'He was so tall that we reached only to his waist, and he was well proportioned. His face was large and painted all over, while about his eyes he was painted yellow, and he had two hearts painted on the middle of his cheeks. His scanty hair was painted white. As the giant danced, jumping up and down, at every leap his feet sank a palm into the earth . . . '

Some say that 'Patagon' means primitive man in ancient Spanish. Bruce Chatwin, in his book *In Patagonia*, launched into a convoluted and obscure literary explanation that Patagon was the name of a giant dog-faced monster from a troubadour epic of chivalry. Others say that it meant Big Foot. It could even have come from Quechua, the language of the Incas, who called the far south *Patac-Hunia* or 'mountain regions'. Whatever the truth, Magellan was astonished by these huge savages and gave the land its name and the beginning of its mystery.

As well as celebrating the first mass, he built a scaffold and held the first executions. There had been mutiny. From the beginning, with dog-faced giants bellowing from the desolate shores and winds that blew men to the edge of insanity, Patagonia excited violent passions. Mass and mutiny. So, while the Inquisition was getting into its murderous stride in Spain, Magellan brought piety and violence hand in hand to the New World.

Born Fernao de Magalhães, Magellan was a renowned Portuguese navigator who, fed up with his measly pay at home, sought a transfer to Spain. He felt unappreciated, let down. He had navigated the Philippines, helped win Malacca for Portugal, and was paid peanuts.

In Spain, a grateful King Charles V gave Fernao, now Ferdinand, a fine new fleet of five ships. A papal decree, in a new flush of evangelical catholicism, had divided the whole as yet uncharted world between the two great exploring nations, Spain and Portugal. Left – or east – was for Portugal alone. Right – or west – was for Spain.

So along with his new fleet Charles gave Magellan orders to find a western route – the back route – to the East Indies. That way he kept the Pope sweet but didn't leave *all* the east for Portugal. Spain got her money's worth. Magellan was on his way to finding his Straits and the Pacific Ocean, when he wintered in San Julian, bringing God and the gibbet to Patagonia.

The scaffold Magellan had built in San Julian was of such high quality and so durable that sixty years later Sir Francis Drake used it in passing to execute a couple of his own mutinous men. His mission was to loot Spanish ships heavy with riches from the silver mountain at Potosi. He had made a deal with Queen Elizabeth to split the proceeds. Strictly business. But with still no silver after a long voyage, and nothing but roaring giants on a ghostly, forbidding land, mutiny was inevitable. Drake was no doubt grateful for the ready-made gibbet standing stark on the howling shore.

I asked the museum curator whether a story I had heard about the guanaco having a special place for dying was true.

'Oh, yes, it is. The guanacos around here go to the shores of Río Gallegos to die. Darwin and Hudson talked of it. They are unique in the animal kingdom in having a dying place.'

'What about African elephants?'

'Not proved. But we know for sure about the guanaco.'

W. H. Hudson watched the guanacos' last journey:

At the southern extremity of Patagonia the guanacos have a dying place, a spot to which all repair at the approach of death to deposit their bones. The best known of these dying or burial places are on the banks of the Santa Cruz and Gallegos rivers, covered with dense primeval thickets of bushes and trees of stunted growth; there the ground is covered with the bones of countless dead generations. A strange instinct in a creature so pre-eminently social in its habits.

The grey wilderness of dwarf thorn trees, aged and grotesque and scanty-leaved, nourished for a thousand years on the bones that whiten the stony ground at their roots; the interior lit faintly with the rays of the departing sun, chill and grey, and silent and motionless – the guanacos' Golgotha.

And now one more, the latest pilgrim, has come, all his little strength spent in his struggle to penetrate the close thicket; with long ragged hair; staring into the gloom out of the death-dimmed sunken eyes.

There among the stuffed animals and whale vertebrae, I caught snatches of a dark, sad little tune. It floated in and out, lying light on the breeze, nostalgic and plaintive. Was it a harmonica? No, not quite.

It hadn't the problematic tonality of aboriginal Tehuelche music, either. It was the strong plangent tones of the *bandoneon*, the tango accordion. It was a long way from home. I couldn't quite believe I was hearing it but Jo said he heard it too. I went out the door and followed the sound up a stairwell.

Sitting alone in an empty meeting-room an old man was playing some tango to himself. Manuel Ravallo – Manny Ravage – said he was seventy-six *and a half*. The half was very important, he said, we mustn't forget that.

He was bald with wisps of red hair and a freckled pate, his fair skin florid and sun-beaten. He wore glasses, a white shirt and a tie. He sweated a lot and wiped his bald head with his handkerchief constantly. He folded his handkerchief after each wipe and put it carefully back into his pocket, only to bring it out again a minute later. He said he was the only *bandoneon* player in Patagonia.

He would be the first to admit he wasn't the greatest on his instrument – said his hands were old and stiff, couldn't do what they should any more. Then he played a sad *milonga*, coaxing some nostalgic, bittersweet sounds from his old black box.

It was a big square German button accordion. The left hand played softer chords while the right punched out the harder melancholy melody. Manny's hands may have been stiffer than in the old days but they still fluttered over the buttons like bruised old butterflies.

The *bandoneon* puffed and wheezed. Manny shouted and urged it on as if he were a bystander watching the box play itself.

'Yes! Go on!! Beautiful!!!'

He played a tune of his own, *La India Trista*, 'The Sad Indian Girl'. It was a little dance, a *bailecito*, and he roared encouragement and dance directions.

'*Hay va!*'

'*Se una!* – Come together!'

'YYAAA!!'

Then he would pull out his handkerchief once again, unfold it, mop his old head, refold it and sigh, 'Ay, *que calor!*'

Did he know any Martín Fierro tunes? He had heard some but didn't know any to play.

'I will do a Piazzola song. Piazzola is dying now.'

Astor Piazzola, the greatest *bandoneonista* and *tanguero* of the Argentine, was a national treasure. He was in his sixties and dying of cancer. Manuel played Piazzola's song for the death of his grandfather.

I could still hear it on the way out of town.

2. Dai Hard

Trelew is seven hundred miles, two hundred and twenty leagues, north of Río Gallegos, with still more of Patagonia to go. After the volcano blew way down south it was dark here for two days. A little ash came over but nothing as deadly as in Santa Cruz. Eighty thousand people live in this big successful textile town in the semi-desert of the Chubut Valley. No longer entirely dependent on the wool from the Merino and Corriedale sheep of the Patagonian *estepa*, Trelew has branched out into synthetics.

The air is hotter and thicker than down south. The land is parched. Where a thousand sheep can survive on a square league down by Gallegos, here the land can sustain only two to three hundred. A wise move, the synthetic textiles, especially with all those volcanoes around.

Trelew was on the trail carved out by Welsh settlers in 1865. Like many of the settlements round here, it bears its Welsh heritage in its name. Tre- is town and Lew is of Lewis. Lewistown.

Trelew had a fine crenellated Swiss-style bandstand in the town square. It also had the Martín Fierro Grill. Having already discovered the Argentine *morcillas* – black pudding – the across-the-board, take-no-prisoners best in the world, I ate only in *parilladas*, where meat was cooked on grills and barbecues. And only if *morcillas* were on the menu. The possibility, too, of picking up gaucho trails made us jump at the Martín Fierro.

The black puddings were great. But the kerosene fumes in the air were so fierce that we sobbed on to our steaks, weeping buckets, eyes smarting and streaming over our *morcillas*.

*

At the end of July 1865, 153 dedicated Welsh pioneers were dropped by the chartered brig *Mimosa* on to the empty Patagonian coast. They had come to rebuild a new, true Welsh Wales out in the Patagonian desert. They camped in caves in the cliff with their belongings around them as they readied themselves for the last push to their new home.

This home, this wilderness that the Welsh settlers had chosen as their Promised Land, was to be in the Chubut Valley, fifty miles away across harsh uncompromising land. They had been inspired to come here by the great Welsh nationalist, Professor Michael D. Jones of Bala. There had been a huge swell of Welsh pride, cramped by a series of repressive English laws limiting their freedoms and traditions and forbidding Welsh in schools or churches. Professor Jones had been preaching an Exodus.

Three years before, their committee had sent out two prospectors. One of them, the whimsically named Sir Love Jones Parry Madryn, is remembered now in Port Madryn, a small coastal town near the original settlers' cave homes. They were looking for a part of the world remote and desolate enough to be free and empty. Patagonia fitted the bill and the Argentine government was happy to give the land to the Welsh and to allow them their religious and educational independence.

No one else would go near the land. Nothing would grow on it. And the Indians were on the warpath.

But the Welsh, poor people from the valleys, blacksmiths, boot-makers, miners, carpenters and tailors, wanted that freedom badly enough. They had looked for parts of the world untainted by the hated English, and thought of Australia, New Zealand and British Columbia. They even considered Palestine, heavy on the biblical references. But they demanded to be left alone with their language and traditions and only in Patagonia was the government happy to do that.

The Argentines didn't really expect them to survive long enough to keep their culture intact. General Roca hadn't yet wiped out the Mapuche or Tehuelche and no one else dared venture down into the Indian territories. When the Welsh arrived, Indians were still attacking up around Buenos Aires province and Patagonia was definitely no-man's-land.

So the miners, the boot-makers and the carpenters from the valleys set out with their families across the harsh *estepa*, on the watch for big ferocious Indians or dog-faced giants who might attack and consume them. Many of their nearest and dearest back home were convinced they would end up in a big bubbling pot of cawl.

As they kept a look-out for unspeakable horrors, they had to cross hard scorched dusty desert with low scrubby thorny bushes. With one wheelbarrow among them they had to carry all their belongings on their backs. Not all of them survived. The nearest thing they had to a doctor was John Williams, a bonesetter of sorts. People from the wet Welsh mountains found themselves pushing across this arid flat wasteland on the other side of the world to find a place called the Chubut Valley.

It felt biblical. A baby girl was born on the march. They called her Mary.

The Chubut was no paradise. The desert had eaten right into the green round the river banks, leaving only a few small red willows and some clumps of pampa grass. So the Welsh had to do everything from scratch, to claim this useless land, to dig it, to water it, to sow it and to cultivate it. This would have been all very well but none of them were farmers. They had no agricultural skills whatsoever. So it was not surprising that in the first year they lost all their crops.

They built a settlement at Gaiman, this time not a Welsh name but Tehuelche for 'whetstone'. Near here the Indians used to dig up stones for sharpening their arrows and spear heads.

In fact not just the first year but the first three years were disastrous – they suffered drought, floods, everything except the expected Indian raids. But they persevered and planted their crops, sang in their chapels and built their houses to shelter from the withering sun, icy chill nights and dementing Patagonian winds.

They did it all and went on speaking Welsh.

In the difficult early years they were encouraged and helped by a Doctor Rawson, the Argentine Minister of the Interior. He organized supplies for them and even sent down horses, cattle and sheep. Most of them didn't arrive. Grateful for his help, they named another settlement in the Chubut Tre Rawson, now just plain Rawson.

There are a lot of trees in Gaiman now, many willows and poplars. It is very green. An oasis stolen from the desert, it is the legacy of Aaron Jenkins.

In the third year, with the colony at Gaiman staring starvation in the face, Aaron Jenkins had a brainwave. He looked at the high water level in the winding Chubut river and then at the parched fields around. He put one and one together.

He took his spade and started digging feverishly from the river bank towards his puny scorched little plot. Foot by foot the river water followed him until it reached and fed his grateful land. He had discovered irrigation. His wheat shot up in a bumper crop and everyone else, marvelling at Aaron's idea, quickly followed suit.

Aaron's ditch has developed into an irrigation system with two main canals sixty miles long on either side of the river. About half a million acres of desert have been brought under cultivation, raising crops, fruit and livestock. It is the Nile Valley in miniature.

Through Gaiman the Chubut river flows high and fast, a pale cloudy green. Willows weep into it. With an escarpment to the north it was easy to see how the village could flood. Up on the escarpment, on the side of a slag heap, was an Evangelical mission in a tin hut.

The Chubut winds its way across the wide arid Patagonian *estepa*. *Chubut* is a bowdlerization of *chupat*. Tehuelche for 'winding', *chupat* in Spanish is 'sucking' or slang for 'boozing'. *Chupas* are lollipops. So in a fit of public decorum the name was altered. In the same way Piddletown was changed to Puddletown to save Queen Victoria any embarrassment during a West Country tour, the Argentine government changed the 'Boozing River' to something meaningless and ethnic-sounding.

Downtown, Gaiman was very neat. Small red-brick houses with sash windows and stripped pine doors, small red-brick churches and schools, all had corrugated roofs. Streets were named after Miguel D. Jones or Juan D. Evans, pioneer heroes. People's names – Lorenzo Thomas, Ruben Rogers, Jorge Jones – suggested they had not entirely withstood absorption into the Argentine.

There was a neat little square with neatly cut hedges. Borders of flowers – roses, marigolds, primulas – and a lawn surrounded the Columbus monument. On the column alongside the dedications in Spanish, Welsh, English and Italian to exploration, New Worlds and universal brotherhood is a spray-can swastika and NEONAZISMUS AHORA. Neo-Nazis now? In Gaiman? This didn't stand easy with the neatness and prim horticulturalism of this little settlement.

All the other houses seemed to be tea houses. No sign of Neo-Nazis, just *casas de te*. Behind the lace netting of their old sash windows, it said *Te Galesas* everywhere. Welsh teas.

Unfortunately I hit Gaiman in the morning and one custom the Welsh had brought out from the valleys was an acute sense of the correct time for tea. Tea time, of course. Not midday. Always and forever four o'clock in the afternoon.

Ty Gwyn, Gwyn's house with a jasmine tree in front, said *Te Gales*. It was closed. A signpost in front pointed to Bryn Gwyn – 3km, Droffa Dulog – 9km, Bethesda – 3km.

On a giant teapot sign hanging from a baroque wrought-iron gibbet, Ty Nain said *Casa de Viejas Chimeneas y Te con Sabor y Tradicion* – the house of old chimneys and tasty traditional teas. I licked my lips. Closed. I fought my way past ivy-covered houses and painted red Welsh dragons. Past the Tea Museum. The Patagonian sun beat down mercilessly. Irrigated gardens swelled with roses, gladioli, sweet peas, marigolds, delphiniums, violets, lupins, pansies and still more roses. There was Plas-y-Coed, *Casa de Te lo mas Antigua* – the oldest tea house. Sweating and parched, I knew what it was going to say. Closed.

More huge cut-out teapot signs were stuck on posts in the streets and hung from the houses, taunting me at every turn. But it was not to be. Jo Tambien said he could still taste Christine Halliday's rhubarb jam.

Suddenly I saw *Aqui Tortas Galesas*, 'Welsh tarts here', whispering dark promises through the net curtains. I pressed my nose forlornly to the window and stared the inevitable truth in the face. Closed.

God is never closed, though. He never shuts up shop. He's always got a cuppa on the go. It's tea time all the time with Big G.

On the wall of a little whitewashed Salesian church is a sign, like a celestial wagging finger, admonishing, DIOS NO SE TOMA VACACIONES. God doesn't take holidays. So watch out.

On the edge of Gaiman the desert is suddenly there, nibbling away at the village, ready to claw it all back. There are no suburbs, no gradation, just the desert at the bottom of the garden.

But the Welsh have tea on their side and God on duty for ever. They will not be moved.

In fact some of the Welsh did move. They struck out towards the Cordillera, the Andes. They rode across the desert some four hundred miles, a hundred and thirty leagues, into the foothills. I flew.

On the plane I came face to face with the good ol' USA. An American behind me was reading a brandy-bottle label.

'AYNOS, Aynos,' he barked, 'what the hell's *Aynos?*' The word he was looking at was twelve AÑOS, twelve years.

'Aynos? Aynus?'

It's where you've got your head stuck up, mate, I thought. Looked round, checked him. Confirmed blockhead. A paunchy red-faced man was sitting there wearing a bright new panama hat. Written on the front of the black hatband in large white letters was PANAMA.

I remembered the reason why rednecks in general and cowboys in particular have their names carved on the back of their belts. It is so that when they take their heads out of their arses they will know who they are.

The mountains loomed above us on the airstrip at Esquel. After straight, waist-high horizons for so long it was a shock to have the skyline towering over our heads. A jagged stickleback of a ridge ran the length of the skyline with an astonishing range of colours to the peaks, fox-red to brick to green and grey and black to fawn.

We rode into Esquel with a well-dressed, half-Polish half-Italian woman who gave us a lift then charged us four dollars each.

Esquel is the end of the line, the most southerly point on the collapsing Argentine railway system. According to the leaflet in the Gallegos museum, it was the most southerly railway station in the world, the final stop for Paul Theroux's Great Patagonian Express. The Tronchita, the little narrow-gauge train, comes and goes at irregular and unpredictable intervals. We heard it was going to leave the next morning. It didn't.

Gauchos in baggy *bombachas* wandered around this little town. They looked much more Indian than down on the *estepa* and many wore broad flat-brimmed black Chilean cowboy hats. Esquel had the feel of a border town, and it is not far from a pass across the mountains into southern Chile. Many farmers, horsemen and cowboys went across the border for supplies.

The Mapuche, the predominant Indians in this area, were shorter and fiercer, more bellicose than the easy-going Tehuelche. The Mapuche fought hard to keep a hold on the passes through the Cordillera. They said they would lose everything if they allowed the white men to find their way through the mountains. They were right.

The museum in Esquel had many Mapuche and Tehuelche artefacts. *Che* means 'people' or 'men'. Tehuelche is People of the South; Mapuche is People of the Earth.

The cultural director was Felix M. Rapido. He arranged for us to meet some local musicians. I wondered if the M stood for *muy*, very, or *mas*, more. An important distinction. For an answer I waited to see how long he would take to find any musicians.

I had already seen ten teenage kids in the street dancing a *cueca*, a lively gaucho dance that involves a fair deal of foot stamping, and I wanted to hear any gaucho and Indian music that might be around. Manuel and his *bandoneon* had not been strictly Patagonian.

The M must have stood for *muy* because within ten minutes I was talking to Eduardo Paizhacara, a young local singer who looked classically Indian – long black hair, wide high cheekbones and deep black eyes. He wore a white shirt and black *bombachas* open at the ankle.

Eduardo had a high tenor voice which fluttered with a fast light vibrato and he played guitar in a Spanish style. He sang a *milonga*, a sad song to his grandfather who had been a Mapuche chief, a cacique, known as Juan Petiso. Then he sang a song about the guitar being the only good thing the Spanish brought over. 'The guitar is as free as the wind and the flowers.' It was a bit earnest, like *Nuevo Cancion*, the Chilean agitprop/folk song movement.

The Tronchita ran to Leleque and Ingeniero Jacobacci every now and then. Usually then, not now. It was standing in the sidings at Esquel station that evening. Shadows of the mountains were draped over little grey toytown coaches. Slatted wood bench seats were the rule in the spartan second class. A small pot-bellied wood stove and armchairs nailed to the floor were the luxury of first.

The sun set black, white and grey over some peaks called the Nuns. To the west, the spiky tops of Gorsedd Y Cwmwl, the Throne of the Clouds, with sparse splashes of salmon pink, reminded me that the Welsh as well as the Mapuche and the gauchos lived there.

We stayed at the Hotel Tehuelche. Tambien wondered aloud if any Mapuche worked there and told me of a big battle at the 'Land of Death' twenty years before the Welsh arrived. The Mapuche came and pushed out the indigenous Tehuelche.

We decided the Hotel Tehuelche had to be owned by the Mapuche. It couldn't really be any other way.

Trevelin – the town of the windmill, Milltown – down the road from Esquel is set in a valley of astonishing beauty. A Welsh scout called J. M. Thomas discovered it. Having trekked up from the semi-desert of the lower Chubut Valley, he was dumbstruck by the beauty, the enchantment of the view when he peered over the last mountain top. The peak became Pico Thomas. When he went back down the Chubut to tell them what a heaven he had found up in the hills all he could mumble was '*Cwm Hyfrwd, Cwm Hyfrwd*' – beautiful valley, beautiful valley – 'we must go west. *We've got to go west.*'

An old boarding school stands on the edge of Trevelin, some prefabs past a shanty town out on a dirt road. Before I met any Welsh, I went down to the school to hear some Mapuche songs.

Felix M. Rapido had arranged for Valeriano Aviles to come over. He was chubby-faced, an Indian mestizo, with one bad white eye like Jimmy Halliday's *sarca* horse La Prisoniera. His moustache covered his mouth like a French comic. He sang a jaunty *cueca*.

Today I've got to go
Tomorrow I'll be back

Lend me your horse
Roll me a cigarette
I'll bring them back tomorrow

It was more primitive, more basic, less like *Nuevo Cancion* than Eduardo's *milonga*. His sclerotic hands just beat rhythmically at the guitar and his singing style was from way back. He sang another.

I'm a bit pissed
So let's go over to the relations
They've got some booze
And some lovely flowers
So we could all have a good time

I liked the line about the flowers.

Mary Green stood by the Methodist chapel in Trevelin. She was small, red-haired, freckled, with a sharp, narrow Welsh nose and a small mouth. Big bottomed, she wore denim shorts and a short-sleeved shirt. She spoke English with a lilting Argentine accent and a strong splash of Welsh. With her family she spoke Spanish, which was all her Argentine husband Jorge, a geography teacher, could speak. She was teaching her children Welsh.

The two kids were peas out of separate pods. The girl was dark and Hispanic like her father. The boy was blond and pale like his mother. He stayed close to her while we talked, tugging at the bottom of her shorts.

He filled my Reeboks with pebbles, which was fine by me except I was wearing them at the time. But my legs are so long and spindly that to a small boy in a beautiful valley they must have seemed to come from right out of the sky. I was just the disembodied giant way up high on top of these beanstalks.

Mary Green spoke about the Welsh exodus. She emphasized how poor and oppressed they had been, socially as well as religiously. There were no other white men in Patagonia, which is what made it so appealing. Virgin territory, the best chance to keep their traditions and culture uncontaminated.

She told us also of John D. Evans, the Juan D. Evans of the Gaiman street sign.

John Daniel Evans was a small child when his parents brought him to Patagonia with the first wave of emigrants in 1865. He was a restless lad and one of the first to learn to ride. He used to ride across the steppe for leagues. He loved to head out west. He built the mill in the beautiful valley and founded Trevelin.

In his early twenties, in 1883, he and three friends, Hughes, Davies and

Parry, rode up into the Andes. He was a scout, a *vaquiano*, and had a great knowledge of the country and of Indian ways. Some gold dust had been found in the Chubut river and it had been a bad harvest that year. He hated farming anyway so they went west looking for gold. More fun.

Up in the mountains, they crossed paths with some Mapuche who had been run off their land up north by Argentine soldiers. They were hostile and angry. They were on the warpath to save their lands. They'd never heard of the Welsh community. White men were all the same to them.

As they had always done with Indians up to then, John D. and his companions managed to pacify them. Or so they thought. They had kept their guns hidden in their packs on the horses so as not to appear aggressive. The Indians wanted to take them back to their camp but the Welsh were nervous. They told the Indians their horses needed rest first. Their hooves had split on the rocky terrain and they were limping. They would go to their camp with them, they said, if they came back and collected them the next day.

The Indians left them but they were suspicious. They thought they were spies for the army. They stayed, hidden round the Welshmen's camp, watching to see what their next move would be.

Then the Welsh made their big mistake. Worried by the Mapuches' hostility, they decided to seek safety with the soldiers who were not far away. That was it. They were liars and spies after all. The Indians gave chase. They caught up with three of them, killing and mutilating them. They left them dying, food for the *caranchos*, with their genitals stuffed into their mouths. John D.'s mustang galloped like the wind and kept ahead of his pursuers.

His horse had a white blaze on its forehead and was called Malacara, which means Badface, or Whiteblaze. John D. knew it was a good horse but was soon to find it was a great horse.

They came to a ravine with a river down below. It was an impossible jump, but Malacara flew across it in one sure-footed bound. No pause, no thought, just one mighty leap. The Mapuche stopped, esteemed their quarry a brave man and worthy of escape, and left him. Leaving nothing to chance, John D. galloped without stop for two days and two nights to get back to the Welsh colony.

The Welsh have never had an image as great horsemen. None of the original immigrants could ride or had any knowledge of horses or of the land. Everything they learned from scratch. Most of it they learned from the Indians.

The Tehuelche were always friendly to the Welsh. When they first came to the Chubut, the Welsh believed that dog-faced Indians and roaring giants would come and consume them. For a long time they posted sentries on the low hills and the escarpment day and night waiting for the onslaught.

One day two Tehuelche Indians appeared on horseback outside a Welsh cabin. They looked like the Welshman's worst dream. Big and heavy, wild and dirty, dressed only in guanaco skins, savages.

It was an Indian Cacique and his wife come to meet and greet. They were as scared as the Welshman who shuffled slowly towards them. Shaking, he put his hand out towards the Indian. The Indian took it and noticed that the Welshman's hand was trembling more than his own. It was a good start.

Later a party of Tehuelche came by with a guanaco they had killed. They were off hunting, they said. They asked the Welsh to hang the animal for a few days then to cook it in such-and-such a way and to have it ready for them to eat when they came back in ten days.

The Welsh did the business. When the Tehuelche came back, they sat down and ate Tehuelche style, hands and teeth tearing the meat off the bone. The Welsh had never seen the like but the Tehuelche were so big and noisy and enjoyed themselves so much that they all got on like a chapel on fire.

The meat was so good, so well cooked that they gave the Welsh skins, hides and ostrich feathers. From then on the Indians started to teach the Welsh the ways of the steppe and the mountains, of horses and hunting. From then on they started a friendly, symbiotic relationship with the white man that was unique in the whole continent. They never bothered each other except for the run-in with John D. Evans.

In his eighties, John D. Evans was still lean and wiry and sported a grizzled Lloyd George moustache, a style quite popular round these parts. His horse Malacara died in 1907 at the ripe old age of twenty-seven. Evans buried his old friend under a vast black boulder at the bottom of his garden in Trevelin. His garden has gone now but the rock is still there framed by the trees of a little glade. On it John D. carved.

HERE LIE THE REMAINS OF
MY HORSE, BAD-FACE, WHO
SAVED MY LIFE DURING THE
ATTACK OF THE INDIANS IN
THE VALLEY OF THE MARTYRS
ON THE 4-3-1884 AS I WAS
RETURNING FROM THE
CORDILLERA
R I P
JOHN D. EVANS

Mary's husband Jorge pulled out one of his classroom maps and explained the importance of the *salinas* and the *salineros*, the Saltmen, in the history of their country. Precious salt came from the high flat Puña plateau in the west, to the salt fields lying below sea level on the Valdes Peninsula out in the Atlantic.

Before refrigeration, the salt was essential to salt the beef for export, along with tallow and cowhides.

'Everything ties together. Nothing is wasted.'

A long time ago, when gauchos were wild roaming cattle hunters, everything was wasted. They hunted cattle with vicious hocking knives, *desjarretaderas*, brought over from Spain, semi-circular or crescent-moon-shaped blades set at right angles on the end of a lance. They would ride up behind an animal and, with the hocking blade, slice through the tendons of a galloping steer's hind legs to bring him down. Killing him, the gaucho would take only what he needed to eat right then, the tongue and perhaps the thyroid, a tasty sweetbread, leaving the rest to rot. Others, hunting for hides, would strip off the cowhide and leave the meat.

There were a lot of wild cattle on the pampas. Three million hides were exported in 1880.

Mary gave us pasta. Jo Tambien said that pasta was brought back from China by Marco Polo – the first Chinese take-away. So we were sitting in Cwm Hyfrwd in the Andes, eating Chinese-Italian food cooked by a Welsh woman and with a Spanish Argentine companion. On the mantelpiece was a north Wales water jug from Bala with a map on the side. There was no Welsh dresser.

Mary Green looked me dead in the eye when she talked. She said her father who lived further up the valley knew a lot more. I kissed her goodbye. Once, Argentine style, not twice like they do in Transylvania.

Federico Green had just come back from Chile. With him were two younger lads and a mad volunteer Welsh language teacher from Cardiff who burned with the zealous fire of an apostle.

Fred Green was a small, wiry, foxy-faced man. His lower teeth were conical in the front. They were all his own. He wore glasses, he was balding with red hair and he was seventy-nine – and a half.

'They call me the Red Fox.'

He was wearing a grey cardigan, pink-brown check shirt, grey flared trousers, brown suede chukka boots and a red cowboy bootlace tie, a bolo.

'I don't like wearing ties – what gaucho does? So I wear a bolo.'

We had tea. Like many of the community, his wife Vera spoke only Welsh and Spanish, no English. She brought the tea out on an English Grindley tea set. A nice flower pattern. We had cup cakes and bread with red gooseberry jam. Vera couldn't explain why it was red and not green. It was delicious. Like Christine Halliday's rhubarb jam, it was the taste of exile.

Fred perked up and became his usual sparky self after tea. We went outside and talked of Indians and gauchos and saddles.

His two white and black spotted puppies played round his feet. They were Casey ('Casey Jones, good Welsh name, see') and Malvinas. He hadn't called it Falkland.

'Of course this land belonged to the Indians. We always lived happily by them and worked with them. But it was very rough going in the old days between the Tehuelche and the Mapuche. This land below the Río Negro to the south was all Tehuelche. Then the Mapuche were forced down by the Spanish, the Spanish civilization (heh, heh!) up north and in Chile. The Spanish warred on the Indians so the Mapuche came down seeking land. They pushed out the Tehuelche. Now it's Mapuche round here but it always has been ever since I was a boy.'

Were the Tehuelche not such good fighters?

'They weren't so well organized and were more easy going. They moved around all the time, they lived by hunting from day to day. The Tehuelche had his horses tied up at night. At first light he would ride out and his breakfast would be the first animal he killed. Heh, heh! Exactly so.'

Were they good horsemen?

'I suppose they were good horsemen. Of course, they lived on a horse. But today I don't see very many good Mapuche riders around. I don't know them.'

What about the Welsh?

'Usually we are better horsemen. Oh, yes, better. The Welsh treat the horses better, train them better. Oh, yes.'

You've always worked with horses?

'I've always worked with horses.'

He has. The saddle he rode seventy-four years ago as a five-year-old was Chilean. In miniature. It was very old and the pommel was rotting away. It had a high wooden frame, high front and cantle, heavily ornamented in black and white wooden stirrups inlaid with silver. It was a good shape for the mountains.

Since then Fred has always preferred a Western saddle.

'It's better for the horse, much better. You'll never spoil a horse's back with a Western saddle. The Western saddle was brought from the States originally by an American, the manager of the Leleke estancia. The gauchos use the *recado*, all those carpets and blankets and leather *bastos*. So heavy. I prefer the Western.'

The sound of a piano being played badly rolled up from the living-room. Then voices singing together. It felt like a hymn and was certainly in Welsh.

Sure enough, there at the piano stool was the crazed evangelist from Cardiff. He had been here for five months, a kind of Welsh VSO, teaching Welsh language and literature in Gaiman. He was singing the loudest and the most out of tune.

He glowed with the joy of glad tidings, the joy of doing good and knowing about it. Short, bullish and bull-headed, ruddy-faced and beetle-browed, he talked loud, fast, very very Welsh and all the time.

He had a serious Bobby Charlton haircut, a tight teeshirt that showed his nipples, and a wild evangelical smile. Not the sly patronizing smile you get from the Jesus Army as you pass their minibus on the motorway at three in the morning coming back home from a gig, more of a crazed, teeth bared, in-your-face kind of smile. The Welsh accent lent itself to his kind of threatening jollity.

As we left Trevelin the fields were full of plovers, some ibises and *bandurrias* which looked like small curlews. When the Welsh first stumbled on Cwm Hyfrwd, these fields weren't there. It was all forest, all wild, all yet to be tamed.

We came to an Army checkpoint and were flagged down. Tambien got very edgy.

'They're bastards, the military. Everything is fine and fairly sweet in Argentina right now. But they're telling you that's only because they're letting it be that way. They're just tapping you on the shoulder to remind you that they're *there*. And that Menem and all those civilians are only there 'cos they let them. But they'll be back. That's what this little tap is about. When they're needed they'll be back. *Para limpiar* . . . to clean things up. Bastards.'

3. Looking for Butch

Esquel may have been the end of the line for the Patagonian railway but for us it was the beginning of the trail.

As we set off in our hire car it was oozing a light misty rain. The mountains looked very Irish, what I could see of them, covered in a shifting quilt of cloud and mist. Now and then a break in the clouds would move across a mountain top or fleetingly reveal a high jagged ridge.

The road out of Esquel wasn't paved. The road in on the other side was. Above us was Lago Zeta, Lake Zed, which fed the Percy river. I idly wondered who Percy was but never found out. We crossed the river. *Bridge Over the River Percy?* No, no ring to it.

We started to climb, twisting up into the mists and the mountains, rattling up the unpaved road. It was well cambered, so that if heavy rains turned the stone and dust into mud, it would do great as a bobsleigh run. I didn't fancy that sort of excitement in a stressed-out Renault 11 so I was glad the rain was more like falling mist than a subtropical downpour.

The cloud and mist kept swirling and breaking and covering again. More outcrops and ridges flashed tantalizingly through the gaps with fierce haloes of blue sky that would scud out of sight as soon as I spotted them.

Stones smacked the bottom of the car. Now the mountain tops I glimpsed winking through the mist were covered in snow that sparkled in the veiled sun. Still the mists kept everything silvery grey and brown down here, shrouded from the bright blue and golden day above. The day hadn't yet lost its Irish feel. And still rocks and stones bashed and thumped and cracked and smacked and pinged and banged the floor of the car. We shook our way up the scree-surfaced road. I could see why they had put *two* spare wheels on board.

For a moment Jo and I were overcome with Elvisness. We sang a chorus of 'All Shook Up':

Uh huh huh, Uh huh huh, whoa yeah yeah
Uh huh huh, Uh huh huh, whoa yeah yeah

At the side of the road grew five-foot-high thistles and some strange phallic hairy-leaved plants with yellow flowers which must have grown up the shaft and then fallen out. There was always one or two of these yellow flowers left at the top, looking like a buttercup sticking out the end of someone's knob. It reminded me of the Love Years when hippies put flowers into the barrels of soldiers' guns.

We levelled out and looked down into a green valley. The mist was thinning. Two gauchos were moving a dozen head of sleepy cattle past a small lake. They were wearing the wider-brimmed flat black sombrero of the Chileans, not the beret of the wind-whipped southern Patagonian *estepa*. They looked like they were riding the high-framed Chilean saddles like Fred Green's. The mist started lifting above and below. Then in a flash it had gone completely.

The mountains towered around us. High and jagged, they had a sharp treeline like a carefully trimmed beard. The peaks were a pale creamy pink that bled down over the grey rock below. It looked like the mist had condensed into *dulce de leche* (caramel condensed milk), had been poured over the mountain tops and was dripping down the sides.

Whatever my botanical shortcomings, Jo Tambien seemed to know the lot. We were driving through an enchanted wood full of ancient larches and *coi-huê*. *Coi-huê*, the southern beech, is a round wispy tree. Many were bearded with Spanish moss, veiled in a shadowy sadness. Fluffy bamboo bushes tumbled out of roadside banks like green ostrich feathers. Red, orange and caramel-coloured flowers glowed wet from the rain. The drizzle had stopped and I'd had enough of jolting and dicing round potholes. We walked into the wood.

The smell of fresh morning rain on a warm mountain forest cleared the head. Endorphins surged and vertebrae snapped back into place. Jo told me the larches were three hundred years old and that this forest was a living national treasure. I believed him.

We came on to a bluff where the woods opened out and looked down on a long lake with turquoise green water. It was crystal clear, not opalescent and filled with glacial silt like the lakes at the other end of the great American spine up in the Rockies. Predictably the green lake was Lago Verde.

The mountains still had spiky teeth, craggy with a pink cream topping. I wondered whether this part of the Cordillera was volcanic or moulded from the crashing and crumpling of tectonic plates. Jo said it was both – without blinking an eye – but I knew he didn't know what he was talking about.

We drove on and on. Unpaved roads are a lot longer than paved ones. More mountains, more gauchos in small valleys, more lakes, more larches. Then we started to descend and suddenly everything changed completely. The mountains slipped behind us and the land opened out into a broad flat valley. It felt like coming out of the Andes and into Wyoming or Montana.

It was called Cholila. It was like a fertile prairie. There were horses and cattle grazing peacefully on lush green pasture land. Gauchos worked in corrals. Wooden fences, barns, wood cabins, fields of daisies. Lines of poplars suggested windier times. De luxe grazing land. The mountains were still all around us but they had fallen back and shrunk on to the horizon like some distant memory. We had stumbled out of the high southern peaks into cowboy country.

We swopped the winding mountain road for the old straight track of the prairies. There was a smell of cattle, wet hay and horses on the breeze. The high clear mountain air etched out the scene as sharp as a picture postcard. In the meadows plovers and *bandurrias* pecked around. Jo said they were ibises. I couldn't argue with him even though I wanted to. I was still transfixed by the Western movie stretched out in front of us.

It *was* Wyoming. Which is exactly what an American called Mr Preston thought when he first saw this beautiful valley, coming in at the opposite end from us, from the north. Mr Preston liked it so much he put roots down. Here where the Andes opened out to the skies he could feel the unbridled wildness of Wyoming in the 1870s.

He had spare money so he bought an estancia by an idyllic river. He bought horses and cattle. He started with three hundred head of cattle, fifteen hundred sheep he acquired from an English neighbour and twenty-eight good working horses. He bought twelve thousand acres. He had two men working for him. This valley was heaven. It reminded him of his native Utah but without troublesome police or Pinkerton's men.

Mr Preston's real name was Robert Leroy Parker but he used to call himself Butch Cassidy.

A young horseman, long hair and beard, rode past and told us how to find the old Preston-Cassidy estancia. A league or two on, over the river and up a dirt road just before a *casa de tê galesa*. Even here in the middle of the Wild West, with no other evidence of Welsh colonization, there was a tea room. More *tartas galesas*, Welsh tarts, in another Beautiful Valley. Maybe not very gaucho but I was all for it.

It was called Casa de Piedra, Stone House. It had a neat square hedge round a lush garden with a close-clipped lawn and shady trees. The house had a fine porch and on it stood Señora Tolly with her hair in curlers. She was mestizo and spoke only Spanish but said her grandmother and mother-in-law were both Welsh so she was fully grounded in the art of Welsh tea-making. She wasn't kidding.

It was the best grown-up tea I'd ever had. It got close to challenging my aunt Jean's high tea in Glasgow that I used to have as a kid.

As the five-thirty from Glasgow to Edinburgh rattled past the bottom of the garden, aunt Jean would throw a ceaseless barrage of griddle scones and pancakes at Uncle Jim and me. That was after the broth and the mince and tatties and the two veg and the rich solid fruit cake and all kinds of pies and sandwiches and biscuits and shortbread and oatcakes and gallons of tea. And then more scones and pancakes. But up here in the Andes Aunt Jean's teatime reputation with the griddle and the pan was to get its first real test ever.

Jo and I went for the full Welsh tea ceremony.

Señora Tolly began to swamp our table with food and she piled reinforcements – seconds, thirds, serried ranks of bread and cakes – on the Welsh dresser beside us. Tea was served in flower-patterned bone china. Food was served in excess.

Fat slices of bread with homemade raspberry and sweet cherry jam came and went fast. Then four slabs of cake each – coffee cake, chocolate cake, madeira and fruit cake – and two huge wedges of gooseberry tart and *dulce de leche* tart. Not for the faint-hearted or the diabetic.

It was macrobiotic hara-kiri.

We guzzled away in front of a fine old wood-burning pot-bellied stove, an Astor Oak Junior from the Union Stove Works in New York. It was heavily embellished with an ornamental skirt and shiny silver fitments. It had come from a Welsh colony somewhere else in Chubut.

Yes, Señora Tolly's grandfather knew that nice Mister Preston and his lady companion who was *muy linda* – very beautiful. We were getting closer.

Back up the road and four hundred yards down a dusty track was Butch's old house. Bellies awash with Welsh tea, we walked alongside sprays and groves of bamboo and trees weeping into a sweet murmuring river. Billowing clouds hung motionless in the broad blue skies. The mountains off in the distance were turning blue and looked more than ever as if they had caramel dripping down over their peaks.

I wondered if Señora Tolly's sugar overdose had induced some kind of terminal saccharine hallucination.

It was a soft afternoon, hot enough but balmy, full of bird calls and rustlings. The river babbled on in a quiet summer way. The ground was scrubby and rough. We walked on down the dirt track, following a tatty fence to a clump of trees.

Behind the trees was an old log cabin, a tumbledown shack surrounded by a sea of knee-high daisies and fences throttled with creepers. Its roof was a ramshackle counterpane of tar paper, tin and rotting wood shingles.

There were piles of wine bottles around the house, in the fields, under the trees, by the walls. Rudimentary garden borders around the shack were marked out with lines of wine bottles driven neck down into the ground instead of bricks. A bleached-out barn had a dead eagle crucified on one end, wings and legs splayed out over the gaping wall. Flies buzzed lazily behind the barn door. Knotted grubby sheepskins hung stiff and stinking from the rafters.

A dog that had seen better days poked its nose round the door. An outside privy, not very private with gaping holes in its walls, rose out of a mountain of wine bottles. Whoever lived here liked a drink. The whole back wall of the privy was made of wine bottles. Its rudimentary seat was a broken vegetable box. I pulled down my pants and sat on Butch Cassidy's lavvy. I always was an incorrigible tourist.

Butch came here in 1902 to hide from Pinkerton's men. He came with the Sundance Kid and his fierce and beautiful girlfriend Etta Place. They rode the thoroughbreds they had used for the quick getaways, not the Argentinian criollo. He was Mr Preston and they were Mr and Mrs Harry A. Place.

Señora Tolly's grandfather had liked the friendly Mr Preston and the beautiful Mrs Place but couldn't get on with Mr Place. Not surprising since Mr Place – Harry Longabaugh, a cold-eyed German – was the killer of the three. And he had a vicious temper. They never got caught even though they couldn't give up the habit of bank robbing. They did a few jobs round Patagonia in the five years they were based in Cholila.

No one knows for sure what happened to them after they left in a hurry in 1907. There are stories of dramatic Che Guevara deaths, gunned down in the Bolivian jungle, and there are reports of sightings in advanced old age somewhere in middle America. I prefer the vision of Butch and Sundance in wrinkly retirement in suburban San Diego.

I was woken from the dream I had fallen into on Butch Cassidy's vegetable-box lav by the lazy sound of a horse slowly drawing near. I rushed outside and saw an old man riding up slump-shouldered on a well spavined nag. I went up and said hello.

He said hello. The horse stopped and stood there.

That was as far as we got. Jo had wandered off and I couldn't find the Spanish to speak to the old boy. He just sat there on his horse, expecting little and seeing less through his rheumy old eyes. He sat and I stood and we looked through each other while the hot summer sun beat down.

He had a week's white beard growth and watery drunk eyes. He was wearing a fuzzy beret, a dark bomber jacket over a grubby shirt and jersey, *bombachas* and ten-hole lace-up work boots.

We could have been there for weeks, the old man and I, except Jo turned up and took control of the situation. The old man swung his leg over and slid off. He hitched the horse under a shady tree.

Off his horse he was a small man, bandy-legged and hunched with his arms hanging lifelessly at his sides. I understood the wine bottles. He was the owner of the cabin. His name was Aladdin Sepulveda.

I remembered Bruce Chatwin talking with Señora Sepulveda in his book *In Patagonia*. Aladdin was mentioned lying pissed in a heap by the stove. She died eight years ago and Aladdin, now sixty-eight, had lived alone ever since, building his empty bottle walls. People in glass houses shouldn't get stoned.

Yes, he said, he lived there alone but often had visitors from all over the world who came to see the famous bandit's estancia. Yes, his father knew Mr Preston and bought the cabin from him when he left in a hurry eighty years before. The rest of the estancia, the land and stock, had been bought by a beef syndicate.

The dishevelled half-dead dog I'd seen in the barn came sniffing round the corner. If it had been wearing a beret it would have looked the spitting image of Aladdin.

Although the old house, the old dog, the old man and the eagle nailed to the barn had all seen better days, it was transparently a special place.

Surrounded by fairy-tale mountains, prairies so fertile you could grow crops or raise livestock with abundant ease, shaded by trees, calmed by the scurrying waters of the river, it was very seductive. Easy to understand why Butch came. No one knows why he left.

I left to go to El Bolson.

Tambien said El Bolson is Spanish for the Bag which must have appealed to the hippies who came here and set up a community in the sixties. It appealed so much that the entire Buenos Aires cast of the musical *Hair* retired to El Bolson for the age of Aquarius.

As we drove into the long valley of El Bolson a massive jagged grey-brown ridge that sawed into the clouds towered over us on the right. It was spectacularly high and long, a mighty knife-edge of rock. I promised myself a look up there. I figured we were heading directly north, the way Butch did when he left, so the ridge was to the east.

The Bolson valley is unique. It is the only valley in these mountains that runs north-south instead of east-west. This means that it misses all the Pacific weather, which is changeable, much wetter and windier than on the Atlantic side. So El Bolson has a warmer, more constant climate than other parts of the Cordillera. Winter is a spring-like fifteen degrees below freezing. Not far away it goes to thirty-eight below. So the hippies were nobody's fools.

Much more fertile than Cholila, it is a big berry and fruit-growing area. Great. Argentina grows its best hops there. I was happy for them. Cherries, hops and raspberries were all very well, though, but where was the sensimilla?

As a card-carrying ex-hippie myself the least I expected was to be greeted at the town limits by a reception committee with a tray of spliffs and locally harvested sensi buds and lambsbread. But it was not to be. Not only no spliffs, but no hippies. We searched all over for even a suggestion of patchwork jeans or headbands, but nothing. I saw no one with long hair. No Hell's Angels or bare-assed bikers. No macrobiotic food store or head shop. No bongs in the corner stores or the newsagents. No Crosby, Stills and Nash, no Grateful Dead. No incense or tie-dye shirts. The only suggestion of counter-culture was a sign which said A *Favor de la Vida*, In Favour of Life.

We went to three camping sites and hung out but everyone was perfectly straight. Not a rattle of beads, not a tinkle of bells, not the slightest whiff of patchouli. We drank local beer made with local hops.

I kept muttering to myself, 'It's in the Bag, man, it's in the Bag,' but it was a mantra of desperation and sounded increasingly hollow. I could see I was not on to a winner.

Heading up here I had been so sure that Bolson would be the Amsterdam of the Andes, that the air would be sticky with the smell of resin wafting across from the pot plantations. Down near the end of the world, on the wind-stripped steppes of the south, El Bolson had been the Promised Land, the Eldorado of Indian Hemp, the El Stonado. It was hard to believe how wrong I could be. I wondered if Blow, the great god of cannabis, was angry with me. What had I done wrong?

On the road was a sign saying Nuclear Free Zone, normally a bit of a giveaway in these circumstances. 'Grass free zone,' I snorted.

'Forget it, man,' said Jo Tambien and we turned in without turning on.

*

Before the futile search for reefer that night I had spent a good long time looking at the great ridge as the sun hung low over the western heights of the Cordillera. Clouds still stuck to its jagged peaks and it reminded me a lot of Aonach Eagach, the Notched Ridge, in Glencoe. It was called Piltriquitron, which is Mapuche for Peaks-Stuck-to-the-Clouds.

In the light of the setting sun Piltriquitron got more wrinkled and cleft, its contours carved out by the end of the day. It looked more and more uncannily like Aonach Eagach even though it was a different shape and colour and rock. There was something about its lie that brought back that side of Glencoe. Maybe because it lay on the east of the valley it had a similar quality of light. I decided to investigate the next day.

It was a dusty climb up the *cerro* Piltriquitron. On the lower slopes were bushes and trees, hot and dusty in the sun. There was fuchsia way past its best, muted shadows of the burning reds and purples of its offspring on the bogs and boreens of the west coast of Ireland. It was from here and further west in Chile that the dancing bells originally came. We climbed through pale ghostly groves with bone-white skeletons of burned-out trees. There were a few little more leafy, bosky glades as a shelter now and then but the trees thinned out as we got higher.

El Bolson was quite low at five hundred feet. At four thousand feet we came to a *refugio*. People were inside, some sort of canteen was happening, but we moved on up. It got rockier, some wasteland of a plateau. Tight little alpine bushes clung on for dear life. Black lichens covered some of the rocks.

When we got to the top the peaks weren't stuck to the clouds at all. The clouds were above us in the blue sky and below us in the blue valley. Right on the rocky top was a clump of bizarre triffids. They looked like stinkhorns wearing Afro wigs.

They didn't put me off my pressing duty as President of the Nude Mountaineering Society, one of the few things in life I take seriously. As my tribute to this great mountain chain and in reverent memory of George Mallory and other legendary naked mountaineers, I stripped off.

George Mallory, one of the greatest skinny-scramblers of all time, was a charismatic war veteran and ex-public schoolmaster of dashing good looks. He was one of the media heroes of the twenties. Those were the days when men were men, not just climbing Everest without oxygen but climbing Everest *without clothes*.

I have long treasured a picture of Mallory and two of his colleagues in the early stages of an attempt on Everest in 1922, two years before he died near the summit. All three are wearing trilbys. George has his well-stuffed rucksack on his back, boots on his feet and nothing else. Starkers, bollock naked. One of his companions, obviously not one of the chaps, has kept his shirt and shorts on. The other, even more bizarrely, is fully clothed, hatted and jacketed but he is not wearing *any trousers*. Probably just an Associate of the Society. Not yet a Full Member.

I struck a modestly heroic pose gazing over the panorama of South America's backbone of mountains and clouds and sky. I kept my socks and boots and hat on and stood on the peak with the triffids. I looked west at the western Cordillera and Chile. I was standing at six and a half thousand feet right on the forty-second parallel. The great peak of El Tronador, the Thunderer, was to the north and the glistening white cap of the Osorno volcano in Chile over to the west. The western mountains were snow-covered and greener, wetter than the brown and pink-grey rock of the Peaks-Stuck-to-the-Clouds.

I snapped Jo reclining on the summit. He said his subscription to the NMS had lapsed and insisted on hanging on to his Fred Perry and practical shorts.

As we came down from the heights the valley became bluer and bluer. We walked through a thin layer of cloud that had drifted in below us. Still it got bluer. It was like walking into a lake except it grew hotter as we got deeper into the valley. And we realized too late that we had picked up some good blotchy sunburn.

Jo was driving us out of town fast. We were heading straight for an enormous slab of rock, looming higher over us than Piltriquitron. It was calling us. Suddenly with no warning the paved road ran out.

'Jesus, hold on!' Tambien shouted, braking violently and flinging his arm across me. Back to the bangs and lurches and potholes and dust. Back to trees on the roadside caked thick with dust above the height of a man.

The mountains stayed craggy and spiky with high ridges, bare rock and scree. Jo said it was bandit country. They like their roads wide and dusty. They need them wide because big lorries go along them all the time.

Jo and I were constantly winding the windows up and down. Down to get fresh air on this hot day and up whenever a car or lorry passed us churning up a twister of dust. Worse still was drawing up behind a lorry and trying to pass it with the desert storm it was throwing out making all the axle-crunching ruts and rocks and holes in the road invisible.

There were a lot more *dulce de leche* mountain tops. The rock became more pastel coloured, a fine pale grey-greenish blue. Road works were carving into the mountain sides all the way, major roads, huge roads but still unpaved. They were like long slashes of open pit mines, a swathe cut randomly through the great range.

Seventy miles later we hit paved road. Amazingly, the tyres were fine; we were the ones with the punctures. A few more twists and turns, another craggy pinnacle or two and we were looking at a deep dark lake, bigger than anything we'd seen before. And then in the blink of an eye we had arrived in a small town that felt like a Swiss mountain village.

We were in the land of fondue. All we could see were chocolate shops. We were in Bariloche.

About the same time John D. Evans rode into the high country looking for gold with his friends, Eduardo O'Connor, a vice admiral in the Argentine navy, decided to sail upriver to the Andes. He was looking for land but was better in a boat than on horseback. He sailed from the Atlantic up the Río Negro then branched off up the Río Limay, right across the Patagonian *estepa* and into Lake Nahuel Huapi, the Lake of the Sleeping Tiger. Eduardo O'Connor had sailed right into Argentina's southern Lake District where a string of deep dark icy lakes, gouged out by pleistocene glaciers, meander through the high peaks and forests at the top of the Cordillera.

It was, like the Welsh Cwm Hyfrwd, another side of paradise. The word got out that, with or without gold, there was some kind of Eldorado high up there in the southern spine of the country.

The alpine delights of Admiral O'Connor's discovery called to a lot of Swiss, German and Austrian immigrants who raced up there, found themselves in a home-from-home and built a Tyrolean village on the dark shores of Nahuel Huapi. With them they brought the secrets of fondue and chocolate making. The village they built was San Carlos de Bariloche and it is still the chocolate, fondue and cuckoo-clock capital of the Americas.

Towering above the lake and the wooden houses, cabins, barns, gates and sheds of Bariloche, and surging out of the thick evergreen forests that skirt their lower slopes, are the peaks of the Patagonian Andes. The great mass of the Cathedral has three twisted jagged peaks splashed with snow like church spires contorted by acid. I walked up Mount Otto, the most accessible at 4,500 feet. I figured that Otto was unlikely to be Mapuche and remembered Pico Thomas.

As I looked down from the heights on to Nahuel Huapi's dark, unfathomable waters, speckled white by the wind, there looming over me, sitting on the Divide and rising from both sides of the frontier, was the Big One. I had seen it from Piltriquitron, the Peaks-Stuck-to-the-Clouds, over El Bolson, but now I was under its very nose. It was El Tronador, the Thunderer. The rumbling and roaring that gives it its name is caused by the frequent avalanches from its permanent snow cap. At 11,550 feet it was still a mile higher than I was on

Mount Otto. It didn't thunder that day. I went back down to town. Bariloche has grown since the last century, of course, and now is a big holiday and tourist centre. It still boasts more chocolate shops than bars in an Irish village, and yodelling buskers in lederhosen.

In the town square, St Bernard dogs sit beside the statue of General Roca the Indian slayer. Roca helped clear the way to put the fondue into Bariloche. He did the spade work for Sarmiento's favourite dictum 'To govern is to populate'. An army chief fighting with Roca in these parts and down in the foothills of the Cuyo went by the name of General Ignacio H. Fotheringham.

I hailed a taxi. The driver leapt out. An exile in the land of exiles, as out of place in this displaced slice of Switzerland as the Swiss were in the old Mapuche hunting grounds, he was dressed from head to toe as a gaucho. He had the sombrero, *panuelo*, *bombachas*, boots and a wide chain-covered *rastra* round his waist. He was even wearing spurs. I clapped my hands.

'Hey! Bravo! And the *facón?*' He turned round proudly, arms held high, and there was his gaucho knife stuck through the back of his belt. This showed dedication. A *facón* was fine riding a horse but it must have been pretty uncomfortable in the front seat of a taxi. It turned out that the only thing he could ride was his cab. He was a would-be gaucho. He loved the gaucho and all that he symbolized but he'd never sat on the back of a horse in his life.

He was the first Argentine I had met who identified so strongly with the myth of the gaucho. I didn't yet realize that this was a national obsession. By wearing his baggy pants, in themselves exiles from another uncertain country, the cabbie was identifying himself as Argentine, as from around these parts – even though in the end he was just a cowboy in cloud-cuckoo-clock land.

He took me out along the shore of the Lake of the Sleeping Tiger to meet a woman who lived her life in the saddle, the granddaughter of the Texan called Jared Jones.

Life was hard in Texas for Jared Jones. His family was poor, barely scraping a living, struggling with mean harvests and having problems with Indians. He heard about good money to be made mining for precious stones down in Brazil. He decided to go south. He took off with his friend John Crockett, went to New York, got a boat that went via London and on to Brazil. He stayed there for a month or so and hated the hot, humid weather. He heard of another country even further south, full of rubies and emeralds and silver, and moved on to Argentina.

The rubies and emeralds proved to be thin on the ground so Jared got a job as a peon on a ranch. All Jared had with him was his saddle. It was a Western saddle – heavy leather and with a pommel – not like the kind they used down here.

Jared was pretty heavy leather himself, a tall, lean and rangy Texan of doubtful ancestry with a battered Norte Americano sombrero, and the local gauchos and cattlemen were a bit wary of him at first. They weren't keen to let him on a horse. They would decide if he could ride or not. The conquistadors never allowed Indians or blacks to get on the back of a horse. Only real or royal men. Jared started out as a peon *de pala*, working with tools, saws, hammers, nails and fencing wire, not with a horse. It was like being ground crew in the air force. Jared persevered until the gauchos dropped their guard and found out he was a fine horseman.

He worked hard in the saddle and saved enough to open a general store and saloon bar on Nahuel Huapi's shores. Then he started a ferry service to get to and from his store across the Limay river that Eddie O'Connor had sailed up long before. Finally, in 1889, he bought land and started the Estancia Nahuel Huapi where he raised cattle, sheep and horses.

He began with the sturdy Argentine criollo horse and interbred it with the agile Chilean mountain pony. Once he had added a thoroughbred strain his horses were fast, strong and sure-footed, ideal for Jared's dangerous passion, hunting wild boar in the mountains. He had a pack of American deerhounds and was still hunting, jumping fallen tree-trunks and dodging branches, in his seventies.

His granddaughter spoke of his dark secret. 'I can't be certain – we couldn't get any papers, you know – but I was told his father was Welsh but his mother was Cherokee. When I tell that to my aunts, they think it's terrible to have Indian blood so they say, "No No No, it's not true!" But my grandfather, in pictures, he looks Indian. Dark with big high cheeks.'

Carol Jones (they say Jon-ess down here) had the same high cheekbones and more than a whisper of her Cherokee great-grandmother's blood in her face. She was small, sparky and wiry, full of nervous energy. Her fair hair was pulled back in a single plait. She looked like a blonde Loretta Lynn, the country star, the coal-miner's daughter, herself a quarter Cherokee. She was in her thirties, tomboyish, and spoke the English of someone thinking in Spanish – very fast, and with a lot of 'buenos' and 'claros'.

She was wearing grey *bombachas* and *alpargatas*, a check shirt and a weather-beaten, flat-topped, low-crown, lived-in cowboy hat. It came from Buenos Aires, was a pampa hat and looked Australian with a wide brim bent over the eyes. She was a working horsewoman, *muy gaucha*.

Gaucho is an adjective as well as a noun. If someone is *muy gaucho*, they have all the qualities of the wild cowboys – fierce, strong, proud, brave, they go their own way, take orders from no one. *Gauchismo* is close to *machismo* but with an extra dollop of pride and a lot more style.

Gauchismo is so ingrained in the Argentine soul that a *gauchada* is a favour. The original word is thought to come from *gu-acho*, an old Indian term for 'orphan'. Wild orphans of the pampa. But 'orphan' could also be 'bastard'. We're getting closer.

Carol Jones took people horse trekking through the mountains. She was called 'Tomato Tin Jones'. When she was out in the wild, she always left a fresh tomato tin when she struck camp so people knew it had been her passing through that way.

She called her saddle a *recado* too, but it was not the *recado* of Jimmy Halliday, the great gaucho bed of the flat *estepa*. She didn't ride the Western saddle like her grandfather or Fred Green either. Her *recado* is built with a *cangalla*, a type of high Chilean frame made of wood, metal and leather: 'Then you have to put also the sheepskin and all the mattress underneath and with this saddle you are quite far from the horse, you are more standing up.' This high frame keeps the rider's weight off the horse's kidneys and tires the horse less. It's ideal for the steep mountain sides round these parts.

Was it hard being a woman in a gaucho's world?

'Bueno, I think it is harder to start with, but now the people know me for many years. At the beginning, many times when we go into the little houses where the gauchos live everybody looks at me like, you know, she's crazy being always outside with horses, by herself, doing a man's work, claro.'

Are gauchos difficult to get along with?

'Bueno, they're very proud. Very proud. I work with them on my rides, my expeditions. It's hard. Claro. Many times they get mad and I know they get mad because they don't talk any more or they don't want to eat dinner, things like that. Now they know me they will try to tell me what is wrong. And if I want something, I have to ask them how should we do this and how should we do that? And not tell them what to do. Claro. *Orgulloso*. Very proud.'

In the old days when gauchos were gauchos, it would have been ruinous to have a woman ride your horse. Even if she was your own woman, your *china*, the horse would be finished, spavined in a stroke. A menstruating woman sitting on your *recado* doesn't bear thinking about. The horse would have to be shot immediately.

It may no longer be so, but if Tomato Tin Jones needs one, the gauchos she works with will still bring her a separate horse and keep their own to themselves.

Just in case. In the same way my Scottish granny, a non-Christian non-believer, still put regular money in the Co-op church fund. Just in case.

On the other hand, there is no taboo on riding mares up here. Like the Hallidays said, 'A good horse is a good horse, and you won't find out how it is unless you ride it.'

Gauchos used to be very superstitious about many things. To the old gauchos out alone in the wild, superstition was an important part of life. So, too, was a knowledge of the land and a knowledge of the sky, for they were like the Indians in many ways.

They rode their horses very differently, true, but they slept under the same stars and drank the same bitter green maté before saddling up and riding out into the same dawn to hunt for the same breakfast. They all lived completely in the natural world that spread out for ever around them. They all felt those spirits that came through the veil.

'Superstitious? Yes, of many things, but they don't say much, they don't talk about it. But out in the mountains they might say, "No, don't go there because there you can sometimes see the White Light." And the White Light is something they see at night, coming out of the ground. I think it must be bones, old bones with some light, but I don't know. Like this cave where they told me that you can hear music from an accordion at night. There used to be a family lived here and once they had a party and two of them picked a fight and one killed the other one and the one who was killed was the musical one. So since then you can hear the accordion singing at night.'

When did knowledge of the land become superstition and superstition become religion? Under the big southern skies it was always so easy to feel a God, to touch heaven. For some Christian gauchos, heaven was above or all around. For most gauchos, heaven was in the west.

Like the cowboy riding off into the sunset, the gaucho saw his heaven over the western horizon, in the bleeding reds of the dying day. There is a long long trail far beyond the setting sun that winds off west to the Last Corral. Once on this sunset trail there is no turning back. The trail comes to a high mountain which opens up to let the rider through, bathed in sunlight. The mountain closes behind him and he smells the sweet cool air of Trapalanda.

In truth, Trapalanda is a paradise for horses, not for us. The only humans to get there will be those gauchos who treated their horses with tender loving care, like brothers and sisters.

In Trapalanda the prairies are open, unfenced and full of sweet green grass. The horses are young again, shedding their saddle sores, spavins, ring bone, spur marks and splints. All the ill-treatment they have suffered from men hell bent on conquering other men is forgotten. And good, kindly gauchos are their dear and constant companions.

When he was eighty years old, preparing for Trapalanda, Tomato Tin's grandfather Jared Jones left his wife. She was seventy-six and they had been married for sixty years.

'But they still asked after each other, how they were getting on.'

It reminded me of the story about the old couple who got divorced in their nineties. They had promised each other to stay together till the children died.

Carol Jones had no intention of marrying for sixty years and was fiercely single.

'I always say it's Señorita Jones for ever. Yes, forever Señorita. I don't want to get married.'

Her mother Edith was born a Jones and married Jared Jones's son. She was headmistress of an English school in Bariloche. Her daughter sent her grumbling outside the house to smoke a cigarette.

Edith lived in Jared's old log cabin on his ranch, the Estancia Nahuel Huapi round the foot of the lake. Tomato Tin drove us there in her big Ford four-by-four pick-up, nearly sweeping another car into the ditch as we barrelled down the highway. *Muy gaucho!*

A fisherman in waders stood in the icy black waters funnelling out of Nahuel Huapi into Eddie O'Connor's Limay river. We roared over the bridge that finally put paid to Jared's ferry-boat business in 1938. His old saloon and country store is a *parrilla* now.

His log cabin was a good size and felt like Montana at the turn of the century. Which is exactly what it was. If Cassidy had stayed, settled down and started a family in Cholila, this was how his estancia would look. The walls were rendered and plastered now, but the predominant feel was of wood and metal.

A small wood stove, beaten by hand out of old tin plate by Jared, stood in the corner. It still works and works well. A Winchester rifle and some North American Indian jewellery hung on the walls. A miner's lamp dangled from one of the beams. A chair with a plaited rawhide seat and back had been carved with a penknife out of cherry wood by old Jared. Shelves crammed with reference books placed the schoolmistress in her cowboy father's cabin.

Edith Jones lit another cigarette. In her own home this time.

'Horrible,' said Tomato Tin turning up her nose. We went outside to commiserate about the hardships of having a schoolmarm mum who knows she's always right.

4. Over to Osorno

The Puyehue Pass winds through thickly wooded slopes as it approaches the frontier. In no-man's-land at the top of the pass are the whitened bones of ghost trees, covered with filigree shrouds of Spanish moss. Years earlier I had seen these curtains of moss sold by kids on the roadside in Mexico as Christmas decorations.

Outside the Chilean customs shed, overlooking a small river, was a tiny al fresco basilica. Built on cracked concrete blocks with breeze-blocks walls, it was topped with a semi-circle of corrugated iron piping with large whitewashed pebbles stuck to the outside. Under this makeshift cupola were two madonnas, one with child, surrounded by baby milk and tomato tins full of flowers. It was an *animita*, a 'little spirit'. These shrines are built all over Chile to quieten the souls of people who died violently nearby. Some *animitas* are miraculous and are festooned with gifts from grateful supplicants. Up here high in the mountains right by the border was a shrine for travellers.

Three lines of rough benches stood in front. Must have been for parties praying that customs wouldn't search their luggage.

Outside, the dense green forest full of giant rhubarb leaves, explosive clumps of bamboo and creepers like kudzu all over the trees opened out and gave way to rolling green fields. Above them a couple of spectacular snow-capped volcanoes – Osorno with the perfect symmetry of Mt Fuji, Puntiagudo ('sharp-pointed') like a crooked witch's hat – scraped more than eight thousand feet up into the sky.

In the fields, lush green pasture land, Friesian dairy cattle were grazing.

They looked well settled in, like they had been there for a long time. It was like Kent with volcanoes.

The cattle were only the beginning. Chile felt more and more European as we rolled out of the mountains. The Friesians were joined by Herefords.

The fields were small, intensely green, with hedgerows and wood fences. A place where it rained a lot. *Alamos* (poplars) and weeping willows were all round. Wooden clapboard houses had red-hot pokers and fuchsia bushes out front.

Osorno is a German cattle town in southern Chile. The population of about a hundred thousand all arrived since the last half of the nineteenth century. The intractable Araucanian Indians had kept everyone at bay before that. There are Hispanics, Lithuanians and Latvians in Osorno, but mostly Germans.

Look in the cemetery. Few were buried much before the twentieth century. All German. Heinrich Hott. Albina Stumpful. Gustav and Oswaldo Wanger. Adolfito Engelberg. The graves and mausoleums were solid and German. They were neat and well tended and had fresh flowers.

An old man with the dropped face and silent arm of a stroke was wheeled round the corner of a mausoleum by a nurse with the full nurse's bonnet and starched apron. He had on a panama hat, thankfully without 'Panama' on the hatband, and an uncreased light beige linen tropical jacket. It was the same colour as his skin. His brown shoes shone.

'Buenos tardes,' he said warmly from the good side of his old mouth.

Tambien noticed the Riga guesthouse and we checked in. It was surrounded by ranks of fuchsia. Behind the flowery hedge was a fierce black dog. When we came to the Riga's door it flew snarling through the air and sank its teeth into the nine-foot-high metal fence rising up reassuringly behind the fuchsia hedge. Probably a legal requirement. The hound hung quizzically from the fence like a wet rag, clamped by its monstrous jaws, until it realized it couldn't eat high tensile steel.

The Residencial Riga was established by a German who arrived from Latvia in 1946. He could have been anyone, was probably a soldier. Maybe SS. Who knows? When he arrived he said his name was, erm, Neumann. Ja! Herr New-man.

He must have been all right, though. The breakfast buns had *amor* baked into them.

I left the Riga for a stroll through the faded wooden clapboard streets of Osorno. On O'Higgins Street, I saw a sign for Gymnasio O'Higgins. In front of Banque O'Higgins was a bust of a broad-faced man with a long Irish nose and a fine pair of muttonchop sideburns. It was Bernardo O'Higgins, Chile's liberator, the illegitimate son of an obscure Irishman who became Viceroy of Peru.

In 1751 Ambrose Higgins from Ballinary, a village in Sligo, turned up in Cadiz. The Irish had always been welcome in Spain; they had full rights of citizenship and could rise to any post in the military or government. The Foreign Secretary at the time was Irish.

Five years later, Ambrose sailed for the New World to try his luck. He finished up a street seller in Peru. Keen on a career in government, he went back to Spain, where he got a job as an engineer's draughtsman with a friend and fellow Irishman and set sail back West again.

He surveyed sites throughout Chile, laying out plans for settlements and military posts. He went to the palavers the Spaniards held with the Mapuche, hopeless attempts at pacifying them. Bishops and dignitaries would urge all the Indians to adopt a settled, monogamous, God-fearing way of life. They would assure the Indians of their deep friendship, and the Mapuche chiefs would affirm their good intentions. They would all have a party and eat cakes. Then the Spanish would build another settlement and the Indians would wipe it out. Higgins noted it all, the colonists' duplicity as much as the Indians' untrustworthiness.

He noted, too, the value of the Chilean cowboys. Five years after he came back, Spanish troops were being decimated by wild, screaming Araucanian horsemen with lassoos and lances, and there was a shortage of officers in the army. Higgins, now fifty years old, was commissioned as a Captain of Dragoons. He organized a thousand cowboys into the Frontier Dragoons. With a series of audacious sorties against the Mapuche, Higgins and his cowboy cavalry changed the nature of the war. Ambrose, now Don Ambrosio O'Higgins, rose through the ranks and became Governor General of Chile.

He was not an imposing figure. Small and stout, with a long foxy nose and a florid Irish complexion, he looked like he'd just come from the Galway races.

The Creole aristocracy called him '*el Camaron*' the Shrimp. But the Shrimp was not simply a figure of fun. He was a common little upstart who threatened the Creoles' jealously guarded privileges. Under the infamous *Encomienda* system, the colonists had been awarded grants of land with the accompanying Indians to work on it without pay as the owner wished. The Indians would be baptized to have a shot at heaven. It was, of course, slavery, and Don Ambrosio abolished it.

To add insult to injury, he had saved the pride of the Spanish army with a bunch of rough-riding cowboys.

*

On market day in Osorno, men walk along the rickety wooden walkways above the *corrales* in the market and pick out the livestock they want down below. The walkways tremble and shake as cows and horses and pigs bang into the supports below, and as bulls mount each other in their frenzy.

Every market day two thousand head of pigs, cattle and undocked sheep pass through. And these are all driven through by cowboys. They aren't gauchos here in Chile. They are called *huasos*.

They were working hard, the *huasos* in Osorno market, organizing the whole sale, moving lots from corral to corral and into the auction ring. Sheep and pigs in the morning, cattle in the afternoon. The *huasos* whistled and shouted and prodded the animals along. In the corrals they moved cattle around by riding into them and pushing them with the horses' forequarters, chest-butting them. *Huasos* on foot in blue overalls painted blue or red marks on the cattle and hosed the ground.

There were some very big bulls, looking all the bigger from my teetering vantage-point right over them. There was a huge snub-nose black bull and an enormous Red Point German bull under me. I silently hoped the walkway had been built as sturdily as Magellan's Patagonian gibbet.

Many of the cattlemen moving round the walkway were smartly dressed, clean striped ponchos over their crisp shirts and silk pin-striped trousers. Their black pointed boots were almost ladylike and had high heels. Their sombreros were broad-brimmed and flat in the Zorro style. Some were immaculate black or grey felt. Most were finely woven straw, still flat, but with a dipped crown and a small rim.

The *huasos* on horseback below were grubbier. They had the same black felt or straw flat-crowned hats the gauchos in Esquel had been wearing. They wore working shirts and jerseys or cardigans against the cool early-morning air – no ponchos today. Instead of the billowing gaucho *bombachas* they had jeans under high black-leather gaiters that went right up to their thighs. The gaiters covered their dainty Cuban-heeled boots and had intricate quilting and leather thongs and laces down the side. They looked just like the conquistadors' high thigh boots. The wooden *estribos*, stirrups, that the foot hides inside came straight from the early Spanish too. They were big, triangular pointed wooden half-clogs, often intricately carved. They had large three-inch-wide sharp rowelled spurs. Their whips were flat straps of leather similar to the gaucho's *rebenque*. Their reins were of plaited rope and they sat in the high-framed Chilean saddle I had seen so much of in the mountain regions on either side of the Cordillera.

*

Chilean rodeo is unique. Argentine and Uruguayan rodeo is all bronco-busting. North American rodeo traditionally involved many skills – bull-dogging and bull-riding as well as bronco-busting – but has lost touch on many levels with working cowboys. Chilean rodeo is something else.

The rodeo was in town that night.

The circular arena was split into two by a white wood fence down the middle. At each end of this big corral the wall was thickly padded and covered with leather. The *huasos* rode in. They were in their rodeo best. Their white shirts were crisp and starched, their pin-striped pants freshly pressed, their quilted gaiters, *polainas*, shiny and black and with extra long fringes and buckles glinting down the sides, their short bolero-style *chaquetas* and ponchos immaculate. They were all duded up. Most important of all, their sombreros were perfect.

Like the North American cowboys, *huasos* seem fetishistic about their hats to the point of obsession. They iron the brim freshly outside the ring to achieve the perfect straight line. They are awarded points for every part of their rigout – and extra special points for the brim of their sombreros.

The Chilean horse is sturdy and looks like a close cousin to the Argentine criollo. Some horses would have come down from Peru. Spanish settlers brought over more and by 1545 had established a stud farm in Santiago with fifty breeding mares. The horse, with its speed and nimble turns in the corral and the rodeo, is called a *corralero*. Many look as if they have some thoroughbred mixed in.

The rodeo started with *huaso* dressage. First they walked the horse on a loose rein; points were lost if it broke into any kind of trot. Next they would make the horse go into a gallop from a standing start, then skid to a halt at the other side of the corral by thrusting its hind legs forward and under, its arse nearly touching the ground. Digging its heels in. It spun round on its hind legs and galloped back to do the same routine at the other end of the corral. This happened a couple more times until the *huaso* knew the speed and responsiveness of his *corralero* had been judged.

Then, just as the horse had been worked up into a good lather, he pulled to a halt and jumped off. His huge gleaming rowel spurs clanked and jangled as he walked a few paces and stood still. The horse didn't move but for an occasional flick of its flanks. Any more movement than that lost points.

This was the most spellbinding manoeuvre of all, coming as it did straight after the crazed galloping and skidding halts. The crowd fell silent and held their breath. That was it. The *huasos* all rode out.

What came next was at the heart of the *huasos'* and *corraleros'* working skills, the pushing and corraling of the animals we had seen in the ___ that day.

A young steer raced into one side of the ring. Two smartly ponchoed *huasos* rode in together and herded the steer through a gate into the part of the ring with the leather padding. They guided him round the corral then suddenly they swerved and drove the steer straight at the padded wall.

They worked in close co-ordination. One chased the steer towards the wall while the other hemmed him in. Then they rode right into the steer with both horses, raised him off his feet and *whack!* smacked him into the padded wall. They held him there for a second then let him go. This technique is called *pechada*.

The steer, with the wind knocked out of him, trotted slowly, gingerly across the corral. The *huasos* pulled their horses' heads up, wheeled round and bore down on him again, pushing him towards the next padded wall, butting him closer with the horses' chests until *whaamm!* up he went again. This time only his front legs came off the ground.

He tottered away looking glazed and dozy. Before he could gather himself, the two riders were on him again, driving him over to the first padded wall, pushing him closer and closer until *whooomm!* he was pinioned on the corral wall, four hooves in the air, two foot off the ground. After shaking his head a couple of times in disbelief, the steer ambled out of the corral not knowing what the hell had just happened to him.

I wondered whether this was where the word 'bulldoze' came from. Jo Tambien said it was.

Then the process was repeated with different teams. Always two riders, always different-striped ponchos, the whole thing was a refinement of their day-to-day corraling or rodeo work. For rodeo is work, not just a carnival contest. In Spanish *rodeo* means the round-up.

Points were awarded for cleanness of drive, of hit, catching the bull at his centre and shoulders and how many of the steer's hooves were raised off the ground. And of course the beauty and style of the whole thing.

Beauty and style are important to *huasos*, though not as much as to gauchos. But for gauchos and *huasos* alike, superstition is a big part of life. Chile itself has a deep tradition of myth, superstition and magic. The sweetest *huaso* superstition involves spellbinding a girl with a view to friendship or marriage. It is so simple:

> To get your girl, go and smoke a cigarette with
> her mother. It is important to share the
> same cigarette and then to stick

etween the second and third
toes of your left foot.
When the object of your affections
mes through the door you must lean over and
beat the floor three times with your right hand.
With the bare left foot and the fag end still
smoking between the toes. And that's it.
She's as good as yours. She's in love.
She certainly won't be able to
take her eyes off of you.

It is not recorded whether it was the fag end between the toes or the allure of Ambrosio O'Higgin's exalted position as Governor that persuaded young Isabel Riquelme, from a wealthy Creole family, to take him into her arms. It must have been strong magic, for Doña Isabel was beautiful and nearly fifty years younger than the Shrimp. She fell pregnant and was sent to the hills. Don Ambrosio denied the boy publicly until his deathbed, but privately arranged for his care and education, and had him secretly baptized O'Higgins when he was four. Isabel was married off to a respectable neighbour.

It was Don Ambrosio's burning ambition that kept him aloof from his son. Stung by taunts about his common origins, he spirited up a title. He had Sir Chichester Fortescue, Knight Ulster and King-of-Arms of Ireland, send a document which showed that he was descended from the sixteenth King of Connaught and Sean Duff O'Higgins, Baron of Ballinary. Needless to say there is no such title, but Sligo is a long way from Peru. So Don Ambrosio became *El Baron Vallenar*. Finally, against all comers, amid a shower of abuse from the Creoles, he was appointed Viceroy of Peru.

He had made it right to the top, and now represented the King of Spain in South America. This meant effectively that the Shrimp, Don Ambrosio O'Higgins, Baron of Ballinary, Marquess of Osorno, was now the King of Spanish South America. He ruled from Panama to the south of Chile. The Sligo cowboy had become, as they would say back in his hometown in Ireland, the Head Bollocks.

In spite of the style of the *huasos* at the rodeo, they don't have as important or mythic a place in the Chilean consciousness as the gaucho does in the Argentine. Gauchos, like *huasos*, are workmen, peons, ranch hands now. But in the past the *huaso* was never as politically, historically or spiritually important as the gaucho. They were always more peasants on horseback than the wild gods of the Argentine pampa. Many Chileans, particularly *huasos* or members of *huaso* clubs, will of course dispute this. The meaning, too, of *huaso* depends on your point of view. Some say it comes from the Mapuche for 'shoulder' or 'haunch'. From Mexico to Chile, when the Aztecs or the Mapuche or the Guarani or the Incas saw the first conquistadors, they thought the men on horseback were a single animal, the rider simply a part joined at the 'shoulder' of the horse.

Others say *huaso* derives from the Quechua word meaning an unpolished bumpkin, lacking grace, rough and ready. Quechua, the language of the Incas, is still spoken around Peru, Bolivia and the upper parts of Chile and Argentina. Another, similar derivation comes from the old Spanish, Andaluz, word *guasa* which is 'no grace'. Peasants on horseback.

I'd been to the cattle market. I'd seen the Rodeo. Time to move on.

The Hotel Continental in Temuco was all wood. The floors, the walls and the high ceilings were all made of wood. There was a high wide walkway round a central wood-walled courtyard, with a wood-panelled restaurant and a wide wooden bar. Tables in the bar had small shelves built under the corners for drinks. The table tops were worn hollow with seventy years of dice playing. On the pine walls of the bar were mounted stags' heads and antlers.

By the bar was a big old white 1950s commercial Kelvinator with a circulating motor on top and huge worn chrome hinges and handles on the two doors. It was almost the only thing *not* made of wood in the room. Its motor may have circulated noisily but the beers that came out were good and cold. Real *American* cold.

In the foyer was a Spanish-style tapestry with flamenco dancers. The woman had her arms aloft. I was intrigued to see a dark bush of hair sprouting out of her armpit and marvelled at the trouble taken to weave it into the design. I went up closely – only to find it was a badly placed and poorly woven castanet.

An old leather sofa and some worn-out armchairs hunkered down in the foyer. On a wall was a faded poster of Vaucluse, France. Dusty dried blue hydrangeas stood on the reception desk. Some gold-sprayed dried hydrangeas sat in a vase down the hall. It felt still and slow. It didn't feel German at all.

Warm, brown, wooden, fading and dusty, shafts of light cutting through the dark of the bar, it had the air of an old Western hotel. It felt like Kerouac or Lowry or Henry Miller had stayed here. Or Zane Grey.

My room was ancient pink- and grey-painted tongue and groove. An old wooden wardrobe was drawn across a door, blocking the way into the next room. Bolted to the floor and hanging on the wall right by my first-floor

window was a coiled length of thick rope with knots in it at regular intervals.
I threw it out of the window and it just reached the ground. It made good sense
with the dice players downstairs. A suspect throw of the dice, an argument, a
bad fight and someone torching the place, all that wood would go up in a flash.
Always makes a man feel safe, a spare length of rope in the room.

Definitely Zane Grey.

In the plaza there is a monument: Homage to Araucania. Two figures at the
base are a settler sowing corn and the Mapuche chief Kallfulifan. He has long
hair and a headband, as in all the paintings or statues of Indians I have seen,
and he looks like Willie Nelson. On the next level are a conquistador in full
armour and tin helmet and a soldier from the 'pacifications' of the 1800s. On
the top, above all these men, is a women wearing a cloak with her arms raised.
In her hands is a round drum like an Irish *bodhran* which she is beating with a
stick. The drum is a *kultrun* and as she plays it she calls to the skies – for she is
a *machi*, a shaman, a holy person, a witch-doctor. In the Mapuche tradition the
shaman was always a woman. It is a woman who calls down the spirits, who is
the contact with the other, the magical side.

Mapuche music is aboriginal. I met Ernesto, a musician who showed and
played me the different instruments. As well as the *kultrun* and gourd rattles,
they play the *trutruca* for tribal and religious ceremonies. This is a long bamboo
pole with an ox horn on the end, used for praising the chief, the cacique, and
praising the gods. A *kullkull* is the ox horn without the long bamboo pole.

Most ancient music has things to beat and things to blow. Ernesto beat and
blew, gathering tunes, calling tunes, dance tunes, songs of praise. It is simple,
unsophisticated music, mostly a single note repeated in different rhythms. An
overtone is thrown in now and then for added excitement. The Mapuche
have various whistles and flutes. A *pifilka* is a one-note flute of wood or stone.
The *silbato* is a small round stone or clay flute. Ernesto played a little dancing
serenade on the *silbato*, a song from a lovesick Mapuche. If the girl moves her
hips to the rhythm of the song, he knows he's getting through.

An indoor market is full of mass-produced Indian crap, worse than anything
Nashville could sell at Conway's Twitty City or Johnny's House of Cash. Kids'
bows and arrows, feathered headbands, phoney *kultruns* to hang over the
fireplace. Temuco has all the signs of a tourist trap. A man with a market stall
called a *silbato* an ocarina. So much for ethnic authenticity.

Several stalls had those cheap copper plates with portraits of famous people
and a famous quote from them. Along one counter was Victor Jara, heroic

left-wing singer, who was killed by the Generals, Pablo Neruda the great Chilean poet, Violetta Parra, another heroic singer of the people, Salvador Allende, heroic President killed by the Generals, and Jesus Christ the Saviour.

Next in line was John Lennon. His quote was

> Ellos atras se pueden aplaudar
> Los ricos mas cerca del frente se pueden
> temblar sus joyas
>
> (The ones at the back can clap
> and the rich ones at the front can
> rattle their jewellery)

Tambien said that quote would appeal particularly to South America.

By this stage of the journey Jo Tambien and I had found the best place to eat in any town was usually the Municipal Market. In Temuco the Municipal Market was a lot more inspiring than the Municipal Culture Centre, which was more of a culture cemetery. The markets were often old British cast-iron structures with the cafés and restaurants around the sides and the food stalls in the central hall. That way you could see the food before you ate it – not always an advantage.

After a full-blooded Argentinian diet of red meat, innards and organs, Chilean fare was more often taken from the sea. But some of the seafood here made the stuff we had been gorging on seem like fairy cakes.

One stall was a solid black mountain. A man behind it, slushing around in rubber boots, was taking foot-wide pieces of this black stuff and sawing through them. Black, gnarled lumps, hairy looking without having any hair, accretions of hard core from the abyss, they should have been on a building site, not a food market. When the top of the lump was sawed off the man stuck two fingers into half a dozen holes and, with a slurp, gouged out the sloppy orange shellfish that had been living there. He flung them a long way into a bucket on the floor. He went rasp-rasp-rasp-rasp, slurp—splosh, slurp—splosh, slurp—splosh, slurp—splosh. I may never know what those shellfish were.

Gratefully I recognized the more familiar horror of sea urchins. A woman tapped the tops of them with a knife, like topping a boiled egg. Four thin pinkish tongues waved about from inside but I couldn't understand what they were saying.

The greatest nightmare was still to come. When I looked round at the next stall I suddenly knew the meaning of fear. It looked like another mountain of accretions, a pile of aggregate, grey and crusty rather than black, a bunch of rocks with holes, little caves in them. I moved closer and flinched. Something was moving in there. Something very very ugly. Gripped with morbid fascination – I always feel like a child in a slaughter house at times like this – I peered into one of the holes. In the depths, a diaphragm pulsed and a beaky thing clacked.

As a doctor and a member of the Institute of Psycho-Sexual Medicine I cannot recommend too strongly that men with paranoid sexual fantasies about the vagina never look inside these rocks. Looking would only confirm their most hideous fears about razor-sharp teeth waiting in the depths to devour them. I peered right up close.

A grey-pink pearly diaphragm was throbbing and a vicious curved beak clawed out from the centre. It opened and uselessly jabbed at the air. A nasty sliver of tongue darted out. I jumped back, my jaw on my chest. I pointed at the nightmare and looked pleadingly at the woman beside it. I could find no words. I might have frothed a little, but not aggressively.

'*Pico roco*,' the woman said smiling, seeing my confusion and terror. '*Son muy ricos.*'

We were sitting in La Caleta at the side of the market. We had decided to eat just fish, to stock up on seafood before we crossed the Andes back into meat country. We'd already sampled some of the joys of the cold-water Humboldt current – sea bass, calamares and crab. We'd filled up with several bowls of the universal Chilean favourite *caldillo de congrio*, conger eel stew.

I had another bowl of conger eel and asked about the *pico roco*. Jo said it meant 'rocky beak' and the waitress said, 'Muy rico.' They were served with soup or cold with mayo. I had both. The beaks were still there. The flesh, the muscle under the diaphragm, was thick and pink like the flesh of a big lobster claw. It tasted like strong crab meat.

It was the ugliest creature I had ever seen and one of the most delicious.

The only horses to be seen in Temuco were at the cattle market again, smaller and drier than Osorno's. More dust in these parts. The stockyards followed the same pattern of wooden corrals with shaky walkways crossing above them.

I wandered across the stockyards munching a *pastel de choclo*. *Choclo* is maize, and it's a kind of Mapuche shepherd's pie of chicken and onions with a top of sweetcorn mash. Tasty. I scoffed it down and watched the *huasos*.

They were working in just the same way as in Osorno. They had the same long leather gaiters, the same wooden stirrups, the same plaited rope reins. They were peons, farm workers. There were no strutting *huasos* downtown. None of that *gauchismo*, that puffed-up gaucho pride. None of that macho posturing and swaggering. In Chile there is no such word as *huasismo*.

5. Eat Your Heart Out, Pedro

Pedro de Valdivia was the conqueror of Chile. It was not easy. He worked hard and thanklessly at it for years. His conquest of Chile had none of the glamour or romance of Cortés in Mexico, of Quesada in New Granada or Pizarro in Peru. He had drawn the short straw with the Araucanian Indians.

Apart from Quesada and Cortes, all the chief conquistadors came to violent ends, mostly at the hands of their own countrymen. Only two suffered the poetic justice of the Indians. One was Pedro De Valdivia.

He came from Estremadura, the 'Hard Extreme' in Spain, like Pizarro and Cortés. Chile was harder than Peru or Mexico, further away from mother Spain, and the rewards fewer. They called it the Nueva Estremadura. There were no rivers of gold in the New Hard Extreme. No mountains of silver. Nothing but the rich lands and perfect climate of the Central Valley. It was a beautiful land, and Pedro de Valdivia loved it. He loved it even though he knew he was not going to get rich quick there.

Everything the conquistadors did was at their own initial expense. They had to find their own finance. The Spanish king just sat there and watched all the gold and silver pour in with no outlay at all. Unfortunately for him, he then watched it all pour straight out again to the merchant bankers who had financed the conquest. The prize for the conquistadors themselves was a piece of the action – a cut of the wealth and rights to lands. And the Indians who came with the lands, the *encomienda* that Ambrose O'Higgins abolished.

In Chile, unlike the other conquered territories, there was no settled kingdom. The Mapuche belonged to large family groups, not even tribes. In the polygamous Mapuche society a family group could be five hundred strong, but there was no central structure. The only leader was the father of the family who was the cacique, the chief. There was no emperor, establishment or hierarchy for the conquistadors to inherit. The Mapuche had no overall leaders until they decided to repel invaders. That they did very well.

The Araucanian Indians – the Mapuche – were the fiercest warriors in the Americas. How else could they keep successive waves of invaders out of the lands below the Bio-Bio for more than four hundred years? The Spanish were not the first to try. The Incas called the Mapuche 'the rebel peoples' and left them well alone.

So here was Pedro surrounded by unfriendly Indians. A previous expedition had been disastrous. No one wanted to hear any more about the New Hard Extreme. Pedro found it almost impossible to recruit anyone to attempt another journey south.

In the end he set out with no more than a dozen hardy souls and his mistress. They dropped down from the Peruvian heights, ploughed across the wasteland of the Atacama Desert, the driest place on earth, and arrived in the lovely Central Valley.

He founded Santiago in 1541. On the journey down he had picked up a hundred and forty more soldiers, mercenaries and hard nuts. Building the first settlement in the Central Valley was no picnic, with the Araucanian Indians hostile to the idea of strangers taking up residence in their land. At first Santiago was just a group wood and thatch houses with no defences. Until they erected a wooden fence around it there was no sense of a stockade. The settlers, under constant attack by the fearsome Araucanians, had to be vigilant all the time. And Valdivia was in there, day after day, sleeves rolled up, working, planting, fighting, guarding.

The conditions were often appalling. Supplies and reinforcements from Peru were always needed and rarely arrived. With disease, near starvation and incessant attacks from the Indians it was astonishing that Valdivia stuck it so long. But he loved the country and wrote enthusiastic letters back to his king.

His king, Charles V, was a Hapsburg and couldn't speak a word of Spanish. That didn't stop Valdivia writing.

In September of the first year Valdivia was away from Santiago with troops, skirmishing and looking for other sites for settlement. His mistress, the indomitable Ines de Suarez, fiery and black haired, stayed in Santiago. The settlement was attacked and the battle lasted for a whole day.

Ines wore a chain-mail jacket and fought sword in hand alongside the men. At the end of the day, so the story goes, Ines stood triumphant in the smoking ruins of the colony. Everything – houses, clothes, food and tools – was destroyed but they were alive.

They built themselves up again, and were attacked again, and built themselves up one more time. Valdivia was a stayer. News came down from the north of the fabulous riches pouring out of the silver mountain at Potosí in the Peruvian, now the Bolivian, *altiplano*. Pedro bit his lip and went on conquering. It must have been difficult, however beautiful the Nueva Estremadura, finding no significant precious metals while up north the silver just gushed out. The mountain at Potosí made possible the entire economic development of Europe.

Valdivia doggedly kept at it. As the Central Valley Indians became a bit more subdued, he moved further out. Ten years later he was founding places like Concepción and his very own Valdivia. It was there he wanted to retire with his warrior woman.

Sometimes he was so strapped for cash he had to improvise. In 1547 he was in Valparaíso, completely skint and demoralized. For too long he had heard nothing and had nothing from Spain. He had an idea.

He offered to take all the wealthy families of Valparaíso back up north to resettle in the more developed, safer northern colonies. He got the twenty richest families to load their fortunes, their gold and silver, which they had all got from exploiting the *encomienda* system, on to his ships. The night before they were supposed to set sail, he arranged a huge banquet for the families onshore. It was the oldest trick in the book. As they feasted and drank the night away, Valdivia weighed anchor and slipped off with the loot. He confiscated it as back taxes. He had taken eighty thousand *dorados*, a lot of money, in Chile's first tax swoop.

Unknown to the old Spaniard, his destiny was in the hands of a young Mapuche who knew him well. This young man had learned first hand the ways of the horse and the ways of the Spanish. Valdivia knew him as Alonso.

The young Indian called himself Lautaro.

It was the same in Mexico and in Peru. It was the same throughout the Americas. These were not mere men, they were gods, four-legged gods with the upper part joined at the shoulder. The story of the conquistadors being mistaken for gods is common knowledge. It is often quoted to explain the astonishing capitulation of highly organized peoples in the face of vastly inferior numbers. In a sense, though, the other side of the penny hasn't dropped. The reason for the Aztec and the Inca implosion was that *they had never seen a horse before*.

There were no horses at all anywhere in the Americas. There were no horses and no cattle until Columbus unloaded his twenty-four stallions, ten mares and a bunch of cattle on 2 January 1494. Then in 1519 Cortés brought eleven more stallions and five more mares to Mexico. The horses and cattle spread out across the continent. The Indians learned to ride the horses and to hunt the cattle.

The image of the Indian as the natural horseman is so strong that it is hard to grasp that, before Columbus came over, people walked. Whether hunting, or gathering, or travelling, they walked. A prehistoric horse, large by today's standards, had migrated – like the people – across the Bering land-bridge from Asia but that was a very long time ago. It had been extinct now for ten thousand years.

Alonso, also called Felipe, had been Valdivia's groom and page for some time. He had been captured as a boy. He stayed a few years and learned the Spanish ways of warfare, their tactics, weapons and language, their strengths and their weaknesses. The most important discovery he made, which affected the history of the next three hundred years, was that a man and a horse were two separate beings. He learned to ride.

When Alonso realized that horses were as mortal as men, he escaped and went back to his family, back to his Mapuche name of Lautaro. He was twenty years old. He told everyone of his discovery. He told them that horses could be slain and that they tired in the heat or in marshy land and then could not gallop. He showed them how to beat the Christians and defend their lands.

They caught horses and learned to ride them better than the Spanish. The Mapuche were at one with the horse, which is why we have such difficulty realizing that there was a time when they were without horses. The image of the Indian sliding bareback down the side of the horse, using the body of the horse as his cover under attack, is too strong, too enduring.

Lautaro showed his people two new combat tactics which were the start of a long tradition of guerrilla warfare in the continent. He introduced 'mounted infantry', with a foot soldier hanging on the horse's tail and running behind the rider. This way a lot of fighters could move very fast. A more devastating tactic was to stage prolonged attacks with successive waves of small groups, constantly replacing them with fresh soldiers and horsemen. So the exhausted Spanish soldiers in their heavy armour slogged away while wave upon wave of Mapuche, each one fresh and rested, descended lethally upon them. The Mapuche made Lautaro their *toqui*, their chief of caciques. They heard Valdivia was out on the road. As bait they burned the evacuated fort of Tucapel and waited for Valdivia to come. The men from Tucapel who escaped the Araucanian attack brought Valdivia there.

On Christmas day in 1553 they stood in the smoking ruins. The Indians fell upon them. They killed all the soldiers and finally turned on Valdivia. He was a big man, very big and fat now he was fifty-three, and with a big head. He was dragged from his horse, stripped naked apart from his helmet which they couldn't figure out at the time, his hands bound behind his back. Exhausted and bleeding from the stab and lance wounds he was led and then dragged by his feet to a waterhole.

They tied him to a tree. With him was an Indian slave and a priest, Father Pozo. His slave helped him off with his helmet. Valdivia offered to leave Araucania for ever if his life was spared. As the slave translated the message, the caciques cut him to pieces as their answer. Father Pozo knew the end was near. He grabbed two straws, held them in the form of a cross, confessed his sins and started to give Valdivia absolution. The Indians cut him down in full invocation.

At this point, like most history, things get a little hazy. It seems pretty certain, though, that it was Lautaro who ritually killed Valdivia by cutting his heart out of his chest and eating it while it was still beating. In that way he absorbed the strength, courage and cunning of the old conquistador.

It was a common ritual in many different aboriginal cultures and in no way out of the ordinary. But it probably gave great personal satisfaction to Lautaro. It would certainly have shouted a fierce message to those in Chile and other would-be settlers. Another version of Valdivia's execution has it that Lautaro poured molten gold down the conquistador's throat. It has an obvious ironic symbolism that would have appealed to the Mapuche.

'You want gold, old man? Then chew on this . . .'

But most people discount it in reality. Eat your heart out? That seems more likely.

Santiago is Saint James, the patron saint of Spain. He helped the Spanish Christians finally to chase the Moors out of Spain in 1492. Flushed with their success, later that same year the victorious Spanish sent Columbus out across the great water with cross and sword to find more lands to conquer in the name of God.

Statues of Santiago always show him on horseback, usually with a lance and often in full armour with a helmet. He looks like a young Pedro de Valdivia.

Parque O'Higgins and Avenida O'Higgins are the two biggest O'Higgins manifestations in Santiago. On the edge of Parque O'Higgins is El Pueblito, a small historic leisure centre, an early colonial Disneyland.

Kids go there for a day out. It is a half-adobe genuine reproduction Chilean village, conveniently built right beside a larger, gaudier fairground, Fantasilandia. The Little Village has several cafés and bars *típicos*, a chapel, shops and two museums. One is the Snail and Insect Museum: 'See Chile's Largest Fly – See the Mummified Child.'

Apparently the Pope himself, the Holy Father, felt compelled to come to the toy village in the park to bless the little ersatz chapel. Why here? And why not bless the Snail and Insect Museum while he was at it? The answer is simple. Right beside the adobe-clad Capilla del Carmelo is the Museo del Huaso. The cowboy museum.

I had suspected John Paul of having secret cowboy leanings for some time. A couple of years before I had been given a picture of the Pope's cowboy boots, blown up to life size. They had been presented to him on his visit to Texas by the Economy Boot Company of El Paso, Texas. They take pride of place on my mantelpiece.

They are grotesquely overdecorated, with 24-carat-gold piping, crossed gold keys, a three-tier gold papal mitre encrusted with rubies and a blue and white appliqué Vatican shield. Around all this swirls multicoloured stitching in the Mexican style, a cross between eagle feathers and flames, like a vision from the more hallucinatory sections of the Book of Revelation.

The boots themselves are tastefully fashioned from black lizard, presumably of a suitably threatened species, in a surprisingly round-toed design. I thought John Paul would have gone for the proper Texan needle-point, the serious Western winkle-picker. But what do I know about celestial cowboys? It's a journey of discovery after all.

His boots were the only Texan artefact I knew he owned but I was certain there must be more. It was inconceivable that he had waltzed across Texas and got no more than a pair of boots. Surely they had presented him with a religiously ornamented Western saddle with gold inlay sacred hearts, crucifixes on the pommel and bordered with masonic symbols? I've always maintained that it's better to have bad taste than to taste bad and I feel certain the Holy Huaso himself would agree.

'It was so beautiful. It was the most beautiful thing ever to have happened here.' Señora Norma, curator of the museum, paused as the memory made her eyes glisten with a shroud of holy mist. 'He wanted to hold a Mass here and everybody was so moved.'

It must have been wonderful having Juan Pablo ride into town to do a spot of blessing and to choose the chapel next door to sanctify with a mass. It didn't matter that the whole purpose of this bizarre detour to the kitsch settlement beside Fantasilandia on the edge of Parque O'Higgins was not to hold a Disneyland Mass, but to bless the *huaso* museum and check out the Chilean cowboy gear. It all sounded faintly surreal and I wished I had been a fly on the little Carmelite-style chapel wall.

I was carrying my picture of his Poliness's cowboy boots. I wondered if, possibly, J. P. had asked after any other particular item down here?

Señora Norma took me triumphantly round a corner and there was a picture of the man himself. In it he is looking pretty infallible in a *manta*, the shorter dress poncho as worn by the smart *huasos* at the rodeo. It is waist-length with broad white and red-black check stripes bordered with white and black zig-zags. He has it on over his white papal robes and is looking down at it with a satisfied smirk playing round his lips. What a score! Even his autograph is there, a small price to pay for the best *manta* in town. Behind him, beaming, is one of his staff cardinals, Monsignor Francisco Javier Cox – Frankie Cox – encouraging his boss and hoping against hope for a poncho for himself.

Did they know his Holiness would want to see the cowboy museum after blessing the little chapel?

'Oh, yes, the Vatican arranged it all beforehand. And they gave us the Holy Father's measurements and told us he would be glad to graciously accept an item of our national *huaso* dress.' Her eyes gleamed some more.

In the picture it is impossible to tell whether or not he is wearing his cowboy boots under his robes. As always they go right down to the ground. All I can say is, for a small man Juan Pablo sure walks tall.

As an aficionado the Pope must have been impressed with the collection of *huaso* artefacts and memorabilia in the little museum. They had everything. There were high-backed Chilean saddles like the one I'd first seen the other side of the mountains in Fred Green's tack room, and black leather leggings from the corrals of Osorno. Along with the big wooden clog-like stirrups, the leggings seemed to be a key to the *huasos'* story. They were completely different from the gauchos' gear.

There were two kinds of leggings and they both came directly from the conquistadors. One kind, *perneras* or *botas corraleros*, went from waist to ankle, while the *polainas* were like thigh-length boots. Both were quilted on their upper parts and fastened with straps and buckles of varying ornamentation. They did the same job as chaps, protecting the rider's legs as he worked horses and cattle, but they made them look more like sixteenth-century Spanish horsemen than cowboys. The wooden *estribos*, the stirrups, had silver inlay and intricate Spanish or Moorish carving. None of the equipment had changed radically in the previous four centuries. Compared to the gaucho gear, which was much more a mixture of European and Indian styles, this stuff was pure Spanish.

Chile's history is written on the *huasos'* legs. Given the intransigence of the Mapuche and the lack of integration by the conquerors, it is easy to see why the *huasos* stayed among their own. There are not the wide open spaces, the pampas, in Chile as in Argentina. *Huasos* did not develop as the gauchos did. They didn't disappear into the high pampa grass and hunt wild cattle, killing when they were hungry. They didn't interbreed as much with the Indians, or learn the native ways like the gauchos. They remained outsiders, more like the North American Anglo cowboys. Their leggings reflect their colonial Spanish roots much more clearly than any of the gauchos' paraphernalia which, like their whole way of life, was far more Indian.

In the same way, the Chilean rodeos show off their corraling skills, their working and moving of cattle with their horses. They don't have the gaucho charisma of the wild and lawless frontier man, the man who faces daily dangers alone. They are simply working horsemen.

Even so, the *huasos* still like to dress up. As well as their impressive leggings, they have three kinds of poncho. There is the poncho itself, the largest and a working garment, the *chamanto*, medium-sized and dressy, and the *manta* that I had seen at the rodeo and on the Holy Shoulders. They wear a bolero-style *chaqueta* or jacket over the *chaleco*, waistcoat. Like the gauchos, they have a *faja* or belt and *panuelo* or bandana. Like the old Spanish, they have *manguillas* or cuffs. They don't carry a long-bladed *facón* stuck into the back of their belt but wear one piece of machismo that eclipses even the gauchos. Their spurs, *espuelas*, are gigantic.

I had seen the *huasos* clanking away from their horses in the rodeo dressage but the spurs in the museum were even bigger. These ones were six inches across with a sharp *rodaja* or spiky wheel. Why so big? Why so fierce?

'In the beginning,' said Señora Norma, the spurs were much smaller, but as the riders wanted more speed from the animals, wanted to be more in charge of their horses, the spurs became bigger and more adorned with spikes.'

The line about being more in charge of their horses was significant. Like the gauchos, the *huasos* trained and worked their horses by conquering them, by being their master. The Indians, of course, were the opposite and trained wild horses with love, slowly and caringly; they were their brothers.

'The spurs also became bigger as part of the *huaso's* ornamentation and now they are also important for dancing the *cueca*. They ring nicely as the *huaso* stamps his feet and he can clack them together for an extra special noise.'

What a lovely pair! I could see myself falling flat on my face if I tried a *cueca* with those killers on.

Have you listened carefully to his Holiness walking in procession lately?

The fantasy that everything in the southern hemisphere is upside down, down under, materializes remarkably often.

The very British habit of elevenses must have come down with the nineteenth-century poachers – the railway builders, nitrate men, meat merchants – and refracted sideways like everything that hits this continent. Elevenses became literally *onces* in Chile.

Somehow, from tea and biscuits at eleven in the morning, *onces* has mutated into two fried eggs at five o'clock. Significantly, the two fried eggs are often washed down with the local firewater. Some more nationalistic Chileans maintain that this late afternoon pick-me-up is not called *onces* because of any British connection but because the *aguardiente* they toss down at this time is spelt with eleven letters. A likely story.

Elevenses is just one of the British legacies. The Brits realized as early as 1807, after two unsuccessful attempts at invading from the River Plate, that there was no point in blasting their way in. The future lay not in armed occupation but in *business*. Better, cheaper and more profitable. Leave the army at home. With the whiff of independence in the air it was time to encourage and congratulate. It was time, perhaps, for a bank loan to help with the struggle. It was time for the diplomats, the bankers and the merchants.

The central market in Santiago is another British legacy, bigger than the one in Temuco, a beautiful example of Victorian filigree cast iron. Made in England, as everything was, and shipped over piece by piece, it was opened by Vicuña Mackenna in 1872 when business was really booming.

The high roof flies over fancy leaf and intricate plant designs. Light pours through iron lattice-work windows high under the roof. Pillars rise into soaring arches. The ironwork's delicacy is untarnished.

Under the huge roof, noises mix as richly as the smells from the grills and ovens. Most of these markets are filled with buskers, musicians and vendors with flashing yoyos, battle-attack noise keyrings and salad shakers.

Sitting at a table and inspired by the discovery of the nefarious but delicious *pico roco*, I asked what *pejerreyes* were. Were they bony?

'You wouldn't like them.'

'Why not?'

'You wouldn't like them. Try the salmon or the sole.'

'Why wouldn't I like them?'

'We haven't got any.'

We chomped through some chicken stew and *aggregado*. I always thought aggregate came out of a cement mixer and was half expecting a little pre-columbian pre-cement pile. But *aggregado* was a mix of spicy potato, rice and veg.

Three guys came up and sang to us. Jo said they called themselves the Trio Frenesi, the Frenzy Boys. They sang sweet. They sang us love songs and cowboy songs. They gave us a song, a *tonada*, full of aching and vibrato, full of longing. They sang about the moon washing its face in the dark limpid waters of the beautiful Rio Calle Calle.

Then they played us a couple of *cuecas*, Chile's lively national dance – the *huasos*' dance. The Spanish feel is strong. The *cueca* started in Peru, out of the old *fandango*, and came south early in the nineteenth century. The Chileans quickly took the *cueca* to be their own. When they declared war on Peru at the end of the century, in a fit of pique the Peruvians changed the name of the dance to the *marinera*, the sailors' dance.

In Chile it remains the *cueca* and is a classic courtship dance. Lots of circling and puffing up by the man, lots of retreating and modest downcast eyes from the woman. It is the rooster stalking the hen. The dance of the mating chickens. Very Spanish.

Most importantly, handkerchiefs are pulled out and held high in the air. They are waved and flipped and flicked, shaken round in a hundred different ways. The hankies flick commandingly, proudly, dismissively, seductively, compliantly as the couple keep eyeballing and circling round each other.

The crowd urges them on. The tension mounts. The pair go on shuffling, preening and puffing out their chests, waving and flicking their handkerchiefs more and more urgently. They get closer and closer. They do everything except cluck and peck at the ground.

It is a very macho dance. It is easy to understand the *huasos* liking it. If the man is a *huaso* and he's wearing his serious *espuelas*, he can top the whole thing off at the right moment with a dramatic ringing clack of his rowels.

Cueca!

The Frenzies sang and played us some *cuecas*. One was about a *huaso* called Manolo who borrowed my horse and my hat and my lasso and some cigarettes and said, 'I'm the *huaso* round here.'

Sounds like I've heard that song before, somewhere along the line.

*

About the same time the *cueca* was coming down from Peru and being taken up by the Chilean cowboys, the illegitimate son of the Viceroy of Peru was sailing home to claim his inheritance. The Baron of Ballinary, Don Ambrosio O'Higgins, Marquess of Osorno, had ridden across his final frontier. On his deathbed he had officially recognized his son and left him large parts of his estates in Peru and Chile.

For Bernardo O'Higgins this was a godsend. He had been languishing in England for some time, desperate to return to Chile or to get some kind of military commission. He had been sent overseas by his father who, though he had refused to acknowledge him, had at least ensured that the boy had proper schooling.

It was a difficult time for Bernardo, still insecure about his illegitimacy and his lack of rights. He had grown up short, broad-shouldered and deep-chested, with small hands and feet. He had thick curly chestnut hair, Ambrosio's long, pointed Sligo nose and a lot of his pink, shrimp-like complexion. He had small blue eyes that he kept screwing up in a restless sort of way, as though he were waiting for a clip round the ear. His good-natured, slightly daft look was redeemed by a sensitive mouth and finely chiselled chin, but he never had his father's natural doggedness and determination.

Bernardo wrote constantly to his farther, pleading for help and encouragement, but never received any reply. As luck would have it, his maths tutor turned out to be Francisco Miranda, a Venezuelan revolutionary and a charismatic surrogate father-figure. Bernardo was no good at maths but ready to hear about insurrection and independence. Miranda taught him of the iniquities of Spain and the Spanish establishment in South America, the exploitation of his native Chile and of the battle for independence that lay ahead.

Bernardo remembered his Araucanian school friends and their tales of heroic battles against the conquistadors. He thought of his mother and her suffering because of a hypocritical society which branded her a fallen woman. He discovered which side he was on. He got revolution.

Madrid knew of Miranda's conspiracy all along. They found a memorandum with names and Bernardo Riquelme, natural son of Don Ambrosio O'Higgins, was on the list. The Viceroy was not happy and Miranda was forced to take early retirement.

When Bernardo heard that his father was deeply displeased with him, and he was to be thrown out of his lodgings, he didn't understand that the Viceroy might not go along with plans for his own overthrow. Bernardo thought his day-to-day conduct was under scrutiny.

He wrote to his father:

Don Nicolas has always reported well of me to you and has justly written of my conduct and honourable behaviour in his house. If in the past, being misinformed by the London agents, two miserly watchmakers who were swindling me, he wrote that I had been spending much money, he later realized what sort of men those agents were and changed his view . . .

I am my own barber and hairdresser; I do my own sewing and mending, and I have not wasted a single farthing, not for lack of friends willing to lend me money . . . but because I did not wish it to be said that I was acting improperly . . .

For this reason I have suffered the torments of martyrdom in this house, scorned and treated like the meanest servant, with no more clothes than the modest suit which I have been wearing for the last four years, without even an overcoat in this cold winter weather, though only just recovering from yellow fever, a severe illness in which I nearly lost my life.

Bernardo hardly paused for breath once he got started. But this last letter didn't reach its addressee, if indeed any of them had. Ambrosio ascended to viceregal heaven, and the young Bernardo was released from British purgatory. By this time he was so fired up by Miranda that when he sailed back to Chile to claim his inheritance as the Viceroy's son he had a copy of an inflammatory, revolutionary letter from Miranda sewn into his coat lining.

He was still naive. Bernardo saw no conflict of interest between being the Viceroy's son, and a good loving son to his father, and his revolutionary insurrectionist ideals. He hadn't worked it out.

Bernardo was a good Irish son to his Catholic creole mother. He looked after her and built her a lovely home. He formed another deep attachment to his half-sister Rosita who had grown into a buxom girl, plump like himself.

He so doted on his mother that he took her and his sister everywhere with him. His mother had a parrot and a parakeet which went everywhere with them too. They would sit either side of him at the table as he ate. He would chatter chidingly with them, talking to them as messengers of his mother.

His other constant companion, strange to tell, was his accordion. He loved to play the box and, like any Irishman, enjoyed a good session.

Early morning on the road north out of Santiago. A pink brushstroke of sun broke through the clouds and smog over the foothills of the Cordillera. Tambien and I were racing, half asleep, through the dawn across the fertile

Central Valley in an old black Falcôn, heading for the hills.

Outside, people and dogs were waking up, stretching and scratching themselves, getting ready for another day. Some were out blinking in the fields, pulling themselves together, ready to gather vegetables in the dawn's tentative light. Inside the car, I was aware of a strong smell of petrol. The penny dropped. We were leaving Chile, leaving the *huasos* and going for the gaucho heartland on the other side of the Great Divide.

The old Falcôn was Miguel's taxi. It stank of petrol – dangerous, solvent-abuse levels. Miguel stopped regularly to have his papers checked at police posts along the road. He had been doing this run through the high Uspallata Pass, Santiago to Mendoza in Argentina, every day all summer long. There and back, six hours each way, every summer day for the last fifteen years.

Maybe the petrol fumes helped numb the pain. Certainly they had made him a man of few words. In fact only one: in six hours all he said was 'Frontera'.

Suddenly we lurched right, turned east and plunged straight into the Cordillera. We followed the pinky-brown froth of the Rio Aconcagua's rushing waters as we climbed upwards. Mists still hung around and hid the best of the hills. Now and then they would lift briefly for a glimpse of a scrubby mountainside with big candelabra-shaped cactuses. An old railway line, out of use for ten years, ran along the other side of the steep pink valley. Its tunnels of corrugated iron had collapsed. Then the mists swirled back and impossibly high ridges teased us from above the clouds; but you couldn't see where they came from.

A watery sun started to seep through waves of mist and I caught sight of snowy peaks. As we got deeper into the mountains, the road did not disappoint, but wound backwards and forwards on itself like a tarmac cat's-cradle. And then suddenly, in the middle of see-sawing our way up this twisting skein of road, the clouds and mists evaporated.

Under a mackerel sky, huge mountains thundered out from above. Massive, gaunt and craggy, more monolithic than the alpine peaks further south, they loomed right over us. Very, very high. I craned my neck to try to see up above us as Miguel twisted and turned, wrestling like a contortionist with his old friends the bends.

By the time we got to the top of the pass, Miguel had carried us up to eight and a half thousand feet. At this point the modern traveller drives through the Cristo Redentor Tunnel, crossing into Argentina underground.

'Frontera!'

Out the other end of the tunnel, five thousand feet above us at the top of La Cumbre pass, is the statue of Christ the Redeemer. It was put there in 1904 to celebrate a final frontier agreement, proposed by the English King Edward VII, and the undying friendship between Argentina and Chile. Just like the undying friendship between the English and French which produced the Entente Cordiale.

The statue may be huge. It may have been fashioned from melted-down cannons. But dwarfed by the massive backdrop of the great mountains it looks like a free gift in a cornflakes pack.

When Bernardo O'Higgins and José de San Martín came across the Andes to liberate Chile there was no tunnel. And they climbed a lot higher than eight thousand feet.

They crossed near here with the Army of the Andes, gathered together methodically by José de San Martín. San Martín's genius was above all as a careful planner. Everything he did throughout his career was thought out, calculated and meticulously executed. He never took any risks. This meant that he might occasionally miss out on an inspired leap into the unknown, but any progress he made was always sure and certain. Anything he won he usually hung on to.

Not like the impulsive warring factions in Chile. Ever since they had declared independence in 1810 the place had been a complete mess. They were so busy fighting among themselves that they didn't put up a united front and kept getting reconquered by the Spanish. By 1816 the whole of South America apart from Buenos Aires had gone back to Spain. But up in the Cuyo area, in the foothills of the Andes around Mendoza, General San Martín was organizing things.

His other great talents were his political sense and his ability to see the larger picture. He knew that Argentina or Buenos Aires could not stay independent as long as the Peruvian viceroyalty existed. Lima was still the main seat of Spanish power and needed to be taken. Until Chile and Peru had been liberated the whole movement was built on shifting sands.

San Martín became Governor of Cuyo province, not on the face of it an ambitious career move. But Cuyo is just the other side of the Cordillera from Santiago. It used to be part of the Chilean territories until it was absorbed into the new viceroyalty of Buenos Aires. Old Inca roads cross the mountains here. Old Inca roads went right up from here into Peru. San Martín knew exactly what he was doing.

Mendoza became a second home for battle-scarred revolutionaries from the other side. As they fled to safety, San Martín looked them over to see who he could trust with his vision, who was dangerous and might imperil it, and who he would invite into his secret society.

He started a masonic lodge early on in Argentina to keep control in the newly emerging lands. He called it the Logia Lautarina, after the great Lautaro who taught his people to ride horses, who led the Mapuche to victory over Valdivia's forces and who ate the conqueror's twitching heart. The Logia Lautarina, like all masonic lodges, held on firmly to the reins of power.

This society has been established . . . grouping together American gentlemen who, distinguished by the liberality of their ideas and the fervour of their patriotic zeal, shall work together systematically and methodically [San Martín again] for the independence and well-being of America, devoting to this most noble end all their strength, their influence, their faculties and talents, loyally sustaining one another, labouring honourably and proceeding with justice under the following conditions.

The conditions stipulated that if one of the brothers should become head of state, he had to consult the lodge on matters of grave importance and all senior appointments in the offices of state, judiciary, Church and army. Betrayal of lodge secrets was punishable by death. San Martín had it all sewn up.

Of all the Chilean revolutionaries, San Martín took a liking to O'Higgins, knew he would work hard and honestly for the cause, and admitted him to the lodge. He did not admit José Miguel Carrera, a hot-headed Galician hussar who had been locking horns with everyone in Chile. He was Chile's first dictator, another crazed Gallego and a natural-born despot. Together with his family, his two brothers and his sister, he seized power by force. Twice he suspended Congress by marching in at the head of an armed mob. He created the dangerous precedent of armed coups in Latin America. San Martín was rightly wary of him, saw him as arrogant and reckless, and would not be wooed by any of the Carrera family.

Another Irishman joined the lodge. An able soldier and administrator, Juan Mackenna had been made governor of Osorno by Don Ambrosio years back. He had always been an admirer of the old Viceroy's political acumen and soldiering skills and became Bernardo's adviser, helping him with his political and military training:

If you study the life of your father, you will find in it military lessons which are the most useful and relevant to your present situation . . . Your venerated father possessed these military qualities more than any man of the century with the exception of Frederick the Great. He had a clarity of intelligence which simplified the most complicated and difficult problems . . .

The life of your father, faithfully related, would present one of the finest moral lessons in the history of humanity . . . the inestimable value of inflexible honesty, indefatigable work and immovable firmness.

The Carreras hated and feared Mackenna. Luis Carrera finally managed to goad Mackenna into a duel and kill him outside the gates of Buenos Aires. He was shot through the neck and his body dumped outside the prison. The Carreras had been stung by their lack of influence on San Martín. By this time, still gathering and training his Army of the Andes in Mendoza, the Great Liberator had made O'Higgins Commander-in-Chief of his forces – under himself of course.

By the end of 1816 San Martín had assembled an army of four thousand highly trained men. It was nothing short of miraculous. In morale, discipline and equipment it was superior to anything that had ever been seen in South America. The daily training had been constant and arduous. No other army of liberation had ever been disciplined to this degree, and it had been done with all the care and attention to detail for which San Martín was famous. More surprisingly, he had managed to equip this large army with the help of the citizens of his province. He had so infected the province with his enthusiasm and a fervent belief in their mission that they cheerfully bore the taxes and levies raised to build up the army.

Only a tenth of the army was Chilean, the rest was Argentine. San Martín made Bernardo a Brigadier and kept him low profile so as not to antagonize any of the Argentine officers or any pro-Carrera Chileans. He had plans for him.

Pueyrredon, the Supreme Director of the United Provinces, sent his friend San Martín two thousand sabres and two hundred tents.

'I send you the world, the flesh and the devil,' he said, 'and dammit, I send you no more because there is no more.'

As well as four thousand soldiers, cavalry and infantry, San Martín had a detachment of miners. They were to repair the roads and passes for the passage of artillery which was transported on sleds and carts with anchors for steep descents. To pull these carts, to carry equipment as pack-horses and even to use as mounts, they brought *nine thousand mules*. That way they kept the cavalry's horses fresh for the battles on the other side.

In January 1817 the Army of the Andes was split into three divisions ready for the epic crossing. Las Heras went south across the Uspallata Pass with instructions to join the main body of the army at Los Andes in Chile. The timetable was carefully worked out and no deviation from the plan would be tolerated. O'Higgins and San Martín took the other two divisions north over the Los Patos Pass, the old mountain trail the Spanish called the Camino de Los Andes. They pushed across a wild, bare undulating plain, surrounded by the grey, gaunt, unforgiving mountains. They climbed higher and higher, four thousand men and nine thousand mules, guns and horses, following the plan to the letter. They kept to the timetable.

During the crossing San Martín was a sick man. He had not been in the best of health for some time, prone to sudden attacks of physical and nervous prostration. A hardy, ascetic, abstemious man he pushed himself beyond the limit. On the journey he had acute rheumatic pains, sudden vomiting and severe haemorrhages. He had been relying on opium for some time and this was the only thing that kept him going. At the top of the pass – a height of twelve and a half thousand feet – he had to be carried. Yet by the time they descended into Chile and dealt with the first wave of Royalist troops, he was back in the saddle.

Amazingly, they lost no men and no guns at all on the crossing. San Martín again was ready for anything. He had prepared for mountain sickness and they gave onions and brandy to any sufferers. The only casualties were among their four-legged friends. They lost a large number of horses and mules, but with thousands of them to start with they had prepared for that too.

San Martín's plan was scrupulously observed. On 8 February, the three divisions met and rested down in the Chilean valley. The artillery train joined them. They pressed forward and won a decisive victory over the Royalists at Chacabuco. After that there was nothing between them and Santiago. The rebels entered the city on 10 February 1817 to frenzied acclaim as heroes and liberators.

San Martín wrote in his official despatch to Buenos Aires: 'In the space of twenty-four days, we have crossed the highest mountain range in the world, overthrown the tyrants, and given liberty to Chile.' A week later, Bernardo O'Higgins was declared Director Supremo of Chile.

The enthusiastic multitude thronging the plaza, and a newly proclaimed assembly, were unanimous in their choice of leader. It had to be the victorious C-in-C of the liberating army, General San Martín. But the Logia Lautarina had other ideas. San Martín had strict instructions to refuse political office and to stay in the military driving seat.

The rest of Chile had to be cleared of Royalists and, most important, Lima and the viceroyalty of Peru still had to be conquered. San Martín had a lot on his plate. So he demurred and strongly suggested the Chileans should choose Bernardo – the lodge's man, the hero of Chacabuco. The citizens were glad to go along with anything San Martín suggested.

The Carreras never stopped causing trouble but never got back into power. In fact they hardly got back into Chile. Two of the brothers were shot by the Argentines in 1818. Three years later José Miguel was shot in Mendoza. It is said that their executions were ordered by the Logia Lautarina.

Bernardo O'Higgins was Director Supremo for six years. During that time the Spanish were finally defeated and thrown out of South America.

His mother and sister and his mother's parrot and parakeet never left his side. Wherever he went, his mother and her birds went too. The parrot learned to say, 'My son the Director Supremo.' But even as head of state he never could get himself legitimized.

In 1823 Bernardo ran into harsh opposition from the powerful land-owning creole aristocracy, the same kind of difficulties his father had had with the creoles in Peru. They just didn't like the Irish.

So Bernardo went into retirement. He gave up on Chile, hoping to come back some day but knowing in his heart that he wouldn't. Disillusioned, he went to live in Peru, with his mother and his sister, his mother's parakeet and her parrot, and his accordion. He never came back.

All we see of Aconcagua, the highest mountain outside the Himalayas, is the twenty-three-thousand-foot peak nudging over a closer hill. Even with my dodgy guts, I'm ready to hike in a bit to take a better look at the great mountain. I had heard that a complete Inca mummy had been found buried way up at seventeen thousand feet. I wanted to see if I could see it. Miguel is unmoved and hurries us back into the Falcón after our thirty-second view at the roadside.

Further down the road is a cemetery. It is small and full. They say it is for the people who have died on Aconcagua. I think it is for the people who have asked the taxi driver to wait an hour while they get a closer look at the big mountain.

The mountains become redder on the Argentine side. As well as a terracotta pink they have red and purple blotches. There are screes everywhere. Immense, three-thousand-foot screes.

It is like badlands on the Argentine side, scrubby useless land, rolling hills and steep escarpments, craggy pink-red rocks getting redder all the time. My guts are complaining and I think I'm hallucinating from the petrol.

Even through the fumes, Bernardo was still with me. How did he feel exiled from his own country? Did he feel he'd achieved what he wanted? Was he a winner or loser? I couldn't figure it out.

6. Back to the Gauchos

Whether it was seven hours of petrol-sniffing across the Andes or the last twist of some Chilean bug, I was feeling pretty rough as we tumbled out of Miguel's fume-filled Falcôn into Mendoza airport. My Glaswegian mother called them the back-door trots.

We were heading for the far north-west, for Salta, a gaucho heartland. I left Jo to wrangle our way on to the waiting list for flights to Cordoba. I was too distracted by anxious runs to the gauchos' room.

Hablando con el Tigre – Talking to the Tiger – is what the Spanish graphically call these explosive moments on the roaring porcelain. Tambien had been bleating on that Mendoza was Argentina's best wine country and the epicentre of a massive earthquake in 1984. I couldn't have cared less.

To take my mind off my guts I tried to read some 'Martín Fierro' and get back to those mythical days of freedom on the wide open spaces. After Chile, I needed some of that straight-backed steely-eyed pride, some true gaucho grit. Everyone said Salta was the place for gauchos and I wanted to be ready for them.

> This is my pride: to live as free
>   As the bird that cleaves the sky;
>   I build no nest on this careworn earth,
>   Where sorrow is long and short is mirth,
> And when I am gone none will grieve for me,
>   And none care where I lie.

*

There was also the cholera. An epidemic in Peru had spread down through Bolivia into Jujuy and now Salta, just as the epidemic of conquistadors had done four centuries before. It had got as far as Buenos Aires province. An Argentine flight to Los Angeles had recklessly taken on food in Lima, the cholera epicentre. By the time the plane arrived in California there were ten cases of cholera on board. One died four days later.

Panic swept the country. The Argentine President Menem advised calm and asked people not to leave if it was not absolutely necessary. As an example, he was very calm and didn't go. In my gut-wrenched state, cholera just sounded like icing on the cake. A dose could be almost homeopathic.

I hung on through the flight up along the Cordillera's rocky spine. The plane's tyre burst on landing and with a sickening lurch Jo and I and everyone else on the aircraft went one way as my guts went the other. But we survived and arrived in one shaky piece in Cordoba. We headed for the bus station while I silently cursed that it wasn't the railway terminus.

Months before, leafing through my various South American handbooks, I had dreamed of taking El Condor or El Libertador, steaming across the pampas in an old pullman, wolfing massive amounts of red meat in the luxury of a restaurant car full of antimacassars and tinkling chandeliers. It was the vicarious enjoyment of a vanished colonial style that I had never known.

But the great British legacy of railways to Argentina had long since fallen apart. When Perón nationalized them in 1948 British shareholders the length and breadth of the Home Counties breathed a sigh of relief, for they were on their last wheels and in need of serious overhaul. The stock was scarcely rolling any more.

The overhauls never came and by the time we got to Argentina timetables had become fairly hypothetical. With trains leaving four days late and lucky to arrive within the week, they made British Rail seem punctual to the point of obsession.

Now everyone takes the bus. And when I saw it I understood why: a massive gleaming coach, great antennae sticking out of the wheel arches, its shiny sides all chrome and green and yellow. Could be Norwich City fans? Stranger things have happened.

It was the Pan American El Gigante. It was big and brash, reassuring and daunting at the same time. We were going to be with it right through the night – it's a long drive from Cordoba to Salta. I looked forward to the luxurious reclining seats, the stewardess service and the video. It didn't let us down.

The video was inspirationally bad but the stewardess was simply inspirational. I suppose it was just the Argentine way, for she treated the central aisle of the coach as a fashion show catwalk. She had dangerously high stilettos and a rude red microskirt that made the slightest gluteal whisper of her buttocks shout out the whole length of El Gigante. She teetered up and down between banks of seats, shimmying her stuff from customer to customer.

She fluttered her false eyelashes and pouted her blood-red lips as she daintily served us our 'hot food'. Though it was the worst I'd had for a good long time, she held it in her scarlet-painted fingers as if Anton Mosimann himself had knocked it up round the back of Cordoba bus station. He hadn't but I ate it all the same. And drank all the cheap *gaseosa* she kept pressing on us. Replacement therapy.

There were two drivers, one to drive and the other to talk to him constantly to see that he hadn't fallen asleep. I can't be sure whether they changed places or whether they stayed the same all through the trip.

Then the video. Now I'm a veteran of cheesy film classics like *Godzilla v. Smog Monster*, but even I couldn't get to grips with *I'll Go – I'll Kill Him – And I'll Come Back*. Whatever country you see them in they are always dubbed, these films, and seem to have been made in no original language at all. I thought I could daydream about gauchos and muse on the Argentinian version of the Italian version of the American version of what cowboys were all about. I decided to fall asleep instead.

We stopped at a raw neon-lit bus station. It looked like every other bus station everywhere, whatever the town or the country or the hemisphere. Same diesel, same smell, same litter, same loneliness. I squinted at it through the window. It looked more bleary-eyed than me so I left it alone.

El Gigante plunged on through the desert wasteland of Santiago del Estero. The stuff of the Wild West, it is an arid, dusty land punctuated with huge cactuses. In places the dust is made of saltpetre and looks like snow. The desert's flaming sunsets are from heaven and its scorching days are from hell.

We raced through the darkness past unseen snakes, lizards, parrots and desert goats. Out there in the desert beyond the coach's lights, they eat *charqui*, sun- and wind-dried goat. Up in North America the cowboys eat dried beef, *jerky*, same thing.

The only wildlife I saw, apart from our scarlet stewardess, was in El Gigante's headlights, swarming suicidally into the twin suns barrelling their way down the desert highway. As carapaces smashed to pieces out front I fell into a fitful sleep. At least my guts were leaving me alone now.

At one-thirty I was awoken by an electrical storm in the west. Cactuses, arms thrown up accusingly at the black sky, stood shocked and frozen in the lightning flashes. El Gigante shuddered, I turned over and sank back into my own storms.

A while later Jo nudged me. We were at a truck stop in the middle of nowhere. Getting out of the coach I was taken aback by the abrasive dryness of the desert night, an intense airless heat. The stop was a diner out in the wilderness, miles – leagues – from any town. Yet we weren't the only ones there. It seemed like locals, folks from nowhere, came for a night out. It was surreal.

The building was a big wooden chalet and the car and coach park a vast parched bowl of cleared field. It was more tropical now, with tall palms rustling in a scorching breeze and rough roadside grass looking as sharp and lethal as a Stanley knife.

Round the back the light pouring out of the windows was muddy with thick swirls of flying insects. There were the usual moths the size of bats, and midges and mosquitoes and gnats. Those I expected. But they didn't warn me about the Big Ones – *Los Gigantes*. Flying beetles with bellies bigger than a hot dog. They were a real horror show and made locusts look the size of a flea.

A lone floodlight over the dust bowl pinged out a bizarre rhythm as these kamikaze crustaceans manically head-butted its rusty shade. When a couple of these whirring crackling bastards bounced off my face I jumped out of my skin and sprinted straight back inside the chalet. I wasn't feeling very gaucho.

At the bar I had a large comforting glass of Breeder's Choice and told Jo of the prehistoric wildlife outside. I chewed on a spicy strip of *charqui*. In here the place was jumping. The bus crew were swapping gossip with the staff. A lot of waitresses in odd little-girl outfits, blouses with puff sleeves, dirndl skirts and white ankle-socks, hurried between the customers with their orders. Busy busy.

Hard to believe that outside lay the Cursed Earth, the land of the holocaust. The espresso machine hissed and backfired. The drivers drank brandy and, reassuringly, black coffee. Then they signalled that it was time to go and we crashed off into the black hole of night down the highway through the alkaline desert snow.

The desolation of this desert was the first great barrier for Tschiffely and his two beloved creole horses. After this the doubters and cynics began to take him seriously.

My faithful horses stuck to their work like heroes, and in spite of the fact that they had eaten next to nothing for several days, and the lack of water, they seemed as fit and willing to move as they had been in the fertile sections far behind us.

I felt like spurring the horses to a fast gallop when we entered the first forest land, for now we were out of Santiago del Estero and our first real victory was won.

My face was scorched and burnt, and my lips cracked with the salty sand and dust, but I was happy and proud, for we had crossed the region experts had told me no horse could cross from end to end, unless it be an animal raised and trained in this part.

My lips weren't cracked with salty sand. I was asleep again.

As we got nearer to the heartland of the horsemen, I must have been dreaming of wild cowboys galloping through the night under the Southern Cross. For as I came to in the dawn, waking into another dream, I had the opening verse of 'The Gaucho Martín Fierro' cantering through my mind:

> I sit me here to sing my song
>> To the beat of my old guitar
>>> For the man whose life is a bitter cup
>>> With a song may yet his heart lift up
> As the lonely bird on the leafless tree
>> That sings 'neath the gloaming star.

El Gigante ploughed on into the wakening day. Outside its windows, the dawn warmed its way through seas of ground mist that swelled round harsh dark thorny bushes and scrub. As the mists evaporated, more dense woods and green plantations softened the subtropical landscape.

We were in the foothills of the Andes, nudging the Tropic of Capricorn and only a gaucho's spit from Salta.

I surfaced at noon in the Hotel Crystal. It was clean, it was noisy and it had an epic poem, a kind of 'Martín Fierro' of tourism, on the reception wall. It was in the heart of the city, on a busy street. There was a kids' fairground on the opposite corner with a couple of rides and a carousel. I'd crashed off the bus but felt much better now. Hungry again. What a relief.

We looked for the nearest food. I needed to get some *morcillas* inside me. Always good to start the day with a bit of black pudding, especially in Argentina. The first restaurant we walked into this morning was dark and deserted. The air hung thick and weary. A dead-eyed waitress leaned on a bar looking bored, searching the ends of her fingers for her fingernails. I stood in the doorway.

'*Tiene morcillas?*' I felt like a pest.

No part of her face moved.

'*No se . . .*'

I don't know – I was outraged. OK not having black pudding, but *not knowing whether you had any or not . . .* ? Not a concept I could cope with first thing in the morning in what I'd been told was the cowboy capital of Argentina. I turned on my heel.

We found a place not staffed by the undead and got *morcillas* put in front of us almost before we sat down. Then I saw something new on the menu. New and fierce. Something *muy gaucho*.

Ubre, it seemed, was udder. I'd never had udder before, and the thought was more than usually cannibalistic. They didn't have *criadillas* (bull's balls) and although udder seemed somehow more shocking than balls I couldn't hold back. Heavily spiced and herbed, it was *parillada* on the grill like everything else.

I have to admit it was very tasty but I had a bit of trouble with the milk ducts that early in the day. Hard men, these gauchos.

If they eat all the other bits, I wondered aloud, is womb on the menu?

'*No, señor, no tenemos.*'

Salta is old and mostly untouched since the colonial period. It was founded in 1582 and it shows. The Spanish conquistadors had pushed into Argentina in this north-western corner, dropping down from the dizzy heights of Potosí in Alto Peru (now Bolivia), and found the eternally green Lerma valley. This was one of the first great colonial cities in Argentina and no revolution or war has left any scars across its leafy colonnaded plazas.

A couple of hundred years later, Salta was one of the first to declare independence in 1810. It didn't take long walking and talking my way through the town before I felt echoes of the independent spirit of Texas. The more I looked round the more it struck me that Salta is the Texas of Argentina.

For years I had treasured a T-shirt which said 'U.S. OUT OF TEXAS NOW!' The same independent attitude, the same arrogance, flourished in Salta. They were the first, they were out on the frontier and they were more Argentinian than all the rest of Argentina put together.

It's a seductive arrogance. Somehow they alone are the guardians of a tradition, of a national spirit, an independent pride in the face of a world that would impose itself. And this tradition, this independence, *is* Argentina. It *is* the gaucho.

In the same way, Texas would consider itself the guardian of a like-minded spirit of Americanism, of independence, of the frontier. And woven into the fabric of all this, the very stuff of frontier American independence, is the cowboy.

He was ruggedly independent and self-sufficient, he was American, he was not just on but *over* the frontier, outside the law, outside civilization. This was the man we call the Anglo cowboy, the descendant of immigrants who came to the Americas since the Pilgrim Fathers. But the tradition he was heir to as a cowboy, as a horseman, was entirely Hispanic.

Working and living with cattle on horseback was the Spanish way. To be more specific, the cattle, the horses and the horsemen originally brought over by Columbus came from Cordoba. Before that, the equestrian tradition was brought to Cordoba by the Moors. So in the beginning it was Moorish – but Moorish by way of Spain.

The gaucho saddle of the pampas and the steppes of Patagonia, the *recado*, the multi-layered mattress that makes the gaucho look like he is sitting on a well-padded dining table, comes from way before Cordoba and is just like the Arab *enjalma*. The gaucho rides like an Arab, too, but all these traditions were channelled through Spain on their way to the Americas. Even before jumping into the great melting-pot of the New World, the Spanish were already familiar with the state of being mestizo or *mezclada*, a mixture of race and traditions.

The tools of the Anglo cowboy's trade have Spanish origins and names. His lassoo is a *lazo*, his lariat *la reata*. He wears his *sombrero* on his head and his *chaparejos*, chaps, on his legs. He rounds up the cattle, *el rodeo*, into a *corral*, the pen or yard. He would vamoose – *vamos*, let's go – to escape the calaboose – the *calabozo*, jail. And so it goes.

The Texas cowboy learned everything from the Mexican vaquero, his horse sense, his language, his working methods. Trailing, driving, rounding up and branding cattle, all came from the vaquero.

Later, cattle were imported separately by the Anglos into South Carolina. Some say this formed the roots of an Anglo ranching tradition. But the cattle were raised as they were on farms in the old country. The farmers used dogs and whips, not horses, and had nothing to do with the true cowboy culture further out west. They never had the magic of the cowboys because they were on foot and not on horseback.

The first real cowboys, wild cattle hunters who later became cowhands, the *hombres* who rode the great prairies of North America, were riding across New Spain. Not just the Texans, but the men of California, Arizona, New Mexico, Colorado, Utah, Montana and Nevada. It was all New Spain. The horses they rode, and that the Indians rode in battle against them, were all descendants of the twenty-four stallions and ten mares that Columbus brought to the New World back in 1494.

As I thought of Texas the Alamo came to mind. A battle for independence in New Spain; a cowboy battle; a futile battle. I still wondered who won and who lost in the end. And was it a fight against tyranny or against the Hispanic tradition? The Alamo was an old Jesuit mission, this much I knew, and was as much part of that tradition as was Salta. Even the name had to be Spanish; alamo was Spanish for 'poplar'. 'Remember the Poplars!' sounds like a brawl over a semi-detached in Purley.

In Salta I was surrounded by grander versions of the mission at the Alamo. I'd seen cowboys with different hats, different saddles and very different pants but they were all cowboys. There was the same gently arrogant pride as the Texans, the feeling that history would be their witness.

Just as Salta had kicked the Spanish out in the Gaucho Wars – the Cowboy Wars – so Texas finally repulsed the Mexicans and was an independent republic before joining the United States. But I was still confused by the catastrophe of the Alamo. Why remember it? They were all killed, not saved, so it was hardly a Texan Dunkirk.

The Alamo, though, was at the end of the trail and right now I had to track down the Salteño cowboys and their music, to find the men who had been breaking wild horses and rounding up cattle centuries before the Alamo was even a gleam in John Wayne's eye.

⁕

'In Salta we are very proud. And very vain.'

Cuchi Leguizamon is one of Argentina's most famous musicians. Though he is from Salta, he is a revered *tanguero*, a tango player and composer. He was old and very doddery. Not too steady on his pins, he had fallen over four days before and hurt his hands. A pity, or so I thought, because he couldn't play anything for us on the Bechstein grand crammed into his tiny front room.

He was a feathery, spidery old man with mad fiery penetrating eyes, a grey beard, a big busy toothy mouth and thin delicate hands. He looked as if he had lost a lot of weight recently. He sat sunk deep in his armchair, tapping the floor, the fire and his piano constantly with his walking cane and rolling his tongue as if he were chewing coca. He wasn't, but his burly son Dolphin was. We were already in coca country, close to Bolivia.

Cuchi was my only musical contact, indeed my only contact at all in Salta. I needed to find out where the gauchos were so I could get to hear some of their music. Especially the *chacarera*, the classic gaucho dance. But not only did Cuchi not play us anything, he wouldn't send us on to anyone else who could.

He avoided references to any other musicians and got very tangential whenever I tried to press him. He obviously saw himself as the musical centre of the gaucho and tango worlds. He threw several smokescreens, starting with a rambling philosophical chat on the nature of things musical. Suddenly from left field he tossed Schoenberg at me as if he were some twelve-tone cowboy.

'Too cold and academic. I can't find his heart or his soul,' I said.

'Oh, he has it there but he's mad.' His eyes rolled dangerously, his teeth came out and grinned at me and his cane tapped faster. 'Completely mad.'

He jumped up, steadied himself on the Bechstein and hammered at a picture on the wall with his cane.

'Borges. He was a friend of mine.'

'Did he play the *chacarera*?' I was losing patience.

'No, but he could recite more of "Martín Fierro" than anyone I knew.' At which he gave us a couple of stanzas in its original gaucho slang:

And every man, life teaches him
   The things that a man should know.
      The jolts of trouble and knocks of fate
      Will teach him wisdom soon or late,
For nothing can teach a man so much
   As the bitter cup of woe.

With sightless eyes man comes to birth,
   And hope deceives him quick,
      And sorrow grim it follows him,
      Till it catches and rends him limb from limb;
La Pucha! How time whacks into one
   Its sore arithmetic.

His cane cracked into the last two lines and he stared at me triumphantly as if he had written it himself. I kept pushing for more contacts but he didn't want to give me any.

'Come back in a week. My hands will be better and I will play for you.' He let go of his cane for once, held it with his knees and waved his spidery fingers. 'The left hand is worse and is the most important. The right only sings the tune. But the *left* . . . ah! the left . . . ' He winced and hugged his sore hand.

He dug out a cassette of himself playing a fairly free modern-jazz version of *chacarera*. Very Keith Jarrett. Not what I was after.

'This is the essence of *chacarera*. The piano is the best instrument for this music.' The left eye wobbled a bit but the right went on boring into me.

I meekly suggested guitar or accordion but they were summarily brushed aside. Proud – and vain. I was getting nowhere so I made my excuses and left.

7. My Maté and Martín Fierro

At 3,800 feet the air in Salta was crisp and clean. The Lerma valley was close to the sky. It was raining when we went out but then it seemed to pour down for an hour or so every afternoon and dry in minutes.

Every town has a Plaza San Martín. In Salta it had cloistered, colonnaded walkways round the sides. In the centre the statue of the Great Liberator on his majestic horse was being bleached piebald by loving pigeons. Set around the sides of the plinth were bronze groups of *mujeres*, women shading their eyes, watching and waiting for liberation. The statue was surrounded by high slender palms, the native *cuehoi*, hibiscus and roses.

Along the covered sidewalks were cafés, shops, beggars, money-changers and an army of shoeshine boys, each with his box of tricks and a stool under an arm. Beggars stuck out their hands and the shoeshine boys pointed in silent accusation at my grubby trainers. They were constant but never insistent.

I sat at a café and waved them away, dismayed that my only contact had led me away from the gauchos and up a blind modern-jazz alley. Jo and I wolfed down a couple of *empanadas*, little meat-filled pasties, and decided to trawl the travel agents. We finally struck lucky and found a tour operator with a direct line to the heart of gaucho, which I knew had to be beating somewhere here in Salta. I had already read about a local hero called Guëmes who had decimated the Spanish Army with his cowboy cavalry during the wars of independence. I could feel gauchismo in the air and wasn't going to be sidetracked by a mad old maestro.

Way back I'd heard a short verse which put Salta firmly on the cowboy trail. Some might call it doggerel but I reckon it's a classic piece of cowboy haiku:

My wife and my horse
Have gone to Salta
My wife can stay
But I miss my horse

Martín Guzman and his wife Alicia Agustoni ran horse trekking, Cabalgatas, out in the wilderness like Carol Jones did down on the Lake of the Sleeping Tiger in the mountains of northern Patagonia. Martín was small, wiry, dark full of nervous energy, with thinning hair and a neatly trimmed beard. Alicia was blonde and fair-skinned, fragile, slower and shyer than Martín. We sat in their office and talked and talked. He seemed an endless fountain of knowledge and drank an endless amount of maté.

I'd seen maté drunk all over Argentina and Chile, especially in the country areas. It was too hick for the sophisticates of Buenos Aires. Yerba maté, the herb, comes from the caffeine-stuffed leaves of the Ilex paraguayensis bush. It is related to holly and is native to Paraguay and the Parana river basin. The traditional drink of the Guarani and Charrua Indians, it was adopted by the gauchos like so many of the Indian ways.

The yerba is drunk from a gourd, a calabash, or a cup through a metal straw, the bombilla, which has a filter lying in the herb. The cup itself is called the maté. Martín's was a simple narrow wooden maté with an aluminium shell. The herb is packed into the maté with the bombilla stuck into the centre. It is topped up from a Thermos flask with a pourer usually shaped like a horse's head. Hot water spews out of the horse's mouth. This cowboy pourer sorts out the problem of how to carry a Thermos around under your arm and still stay macho.

In Freudian terms the whole thing doesn't bear thinking about. Taking the spout into the mouth, the sucking of the warm fluid through the bombilla and the often warm and breast-shaped maté gourd cupped in the hand – it's all pretty suspect. Best not to worry, though, for it keeps a lot of grown men quiet.

In the end maté is simply the way they take caffeine in this part of the world. All American cowboys, north and south, lived on a basic diet of beef and caffeine with some regional variations and additions.

Maté tastes bitter, fragrant and herby, like a cross between compost, tobacco and strong Japanese green tea. It is as chock-full of caffeine as strong black coffee. They call it mateine and it's easier to drink all the time. You don't have to stop.

If it's good enough for the gauchos, I thought, it's good enough for me. I took up Martín's offer and liked its unashamed bitterness.

We talked of gauchos, of Guëmes and of Argentinian politics. Martín said he might be able to find us the Head Bollocks in Salta, the chief gaucho. Then Alicia told us of her ancestors. It turned out that she was the great-great-granddaughter of José Hernandez, the man who wrote the epic two-volume poem 'Martín Fierro'.

The books chronicle the struggles of Martín Fierro and his friend Cruz as the rapidly approaching twentieth century erodes all the gaucho's old freedoms. The whole thing is written in archaic six-line stanzas in mid-nineteenth-century gaucho slang. It is composed as if it were sung by a troubadour.

The greatest single piece of cowboy literature in the world, it is a sacred text to the Argentine. It is the story of a loner and his increasingly futile rearguard action against the forces of authority, bureaucracy and law and order. The story of country ways against city ways, it is set before the backdrop of the historic political struggle between the sophisticated wealthy capital port and the rough-and-ready backwoods provinces. The gaucho's freedom and the old way of life, and the loss of these are the same symbolically to the Argentines as the mythologized cowboys of the Wild West were to us.

Although we seem to be drawn to this idea of the cowboys' untrammelled existence, it may well be that subconsciously the *loss* of their freedom has more meaning for us than the freedom itself. We know only too well the loss of freedom in our urban, restricted and responsible lives. Modern metropolitan life is by definition restricted. Civilized, burdened with obligations and restless at the same time, we may also envy the cowboys their rootlessness and lack of responsibility to anyone but themselves.

Little matter that the truth was far from the reality, that when Hernandez wrote 'Martín Fierro' the old gaucho way, at its height in the early nineteenth century, was already long gone. Little matter that our view of cowboys has been sanitized out of all recognition. Cowboys and gauchos are archetypal figures. According to the myth, they are fearless, strong, ruthless, resourceful, brave, chivalrous and kind to women and children. This version comes directly from the stories of knights in armour or the Crusaders, out on the far frontiers doing battle with the unknown and with the infidel. Most potently of all, these are myths about men on horseback. The horse is the key to their magic.

Beyond myths and symbols, gauchos were a mixture of savagery and culture. They were arrogant, cruel and brutal, superstitious and religious. Their law was their long knife, their *facón*. They never used guns, which they despised as a coward's way out.

They were hard working and lazy at the same time. They hated getting off their horses to do menial work. They were taciturn, fatalistic and phlegmatic, and for all their wild independence, were easily led by authority. They bore suffering and injustice stoically. Life was cheap.

The reason the first part of 'The Gaucho Martín Fierro', 'La Ida' – 'The Departure' – published in 1872, was such a success, sold fifteen editions in the first seven years and captivated the whole nation was because it appealed to the gauchos themselves. So Hernandez brought out the sequel, 'La Vuelta' – 'The Return'. It might as well have been the Resurrection.

It was an accurate, closely detailed account of gaucho life in the good old days. The characters leapt out of the page. Fierro and Cruz were flesh and blood. They became the gauchos' personal friends and would be expected to turn up and sit down with them any time. Flesh and blood too were the soldiers and the Indians; the cattle round-ups and branding; colt breaking, drinking, fighting with the *facón*. The gauchos who read it hankered after the lost time of Martín Fierro, when all arguments were decided with the knife.

Through the narrative, Fierro and his old mate Cruz come up increasingly against restriction and corruption: the bent judge, the corrupt Alcalde, the bullying district officer, the pitiless commandant, the press gang, the terrible conditions, the uniform fiddle on the frontier, thieving officials, families like Fierro's dispersed and their goods and chattels sold. All these things the gauchos of the time could understand all too easily. For once someone was on their side, attacking officialdom and a negligent government, injustice and the exploitation of the gaucho.

Many of the scenes, like the breaking of the wild colt or the fight with the Indian, have glorious colour and movement. No wonder the gauchos loved it. No wonder they carried battered copies of it in their pockets. There was nothing wimpish or bookish about this poetry.

They themselves still held to the troubadour tradition and a lot of them genuinely sang and played guitar, unlike the Anglo cowboys who rarely did in reality. In the *pulperias* (the bars out in the countryside) they would sing of Fierro and his woman, his *china*, they would sing of Cruz's death in a fight. They would sing of Fierro for ever.

Fierro would be with them by the camp fires. He would be with them in the *pulperias*. They'd talk about whether Cruz was really dead.

It became so personal that José Hernandez became one with his hero and was known on the streets of Buenos Aires as Don Martín. Gauchos would come back to the *camp*, the country, from rare city visits and tell of how they saw Fierro himself, only now he was looking robustly healthy, well fed and in town clothes.

The others, of course, wouldn't believe a word. They knew Martín Fierro was over the border.

Hernandez was politically active, a thorn in various sides all his life. He was an estanciero, a rancher, he was a journalist, a politician and a soldier. Brought up on the family estancia, he lived and worked with the gauchos and got to know them intimately. His first journalism was on the *Reforma Politica* in Buenos Aires. Later he founded a newspaper himself, *Río de la Plata*, in which he constantly attacked the establishment.

When he wrote the first part of 'Martín Fierro' he was in political exile in Uruguay. This was simply the other side of the wide River Plate. Argentines think of Uruguay as it used to be, simply the Banda Orientale, the Eastern Territory. More pampas, more Argentina. But try telling that to a Uruguayan.

Now and then Hernandez would put his pen down, break his exile and slip across the River Plate at night to visit his wife. So one day – hop! Alicia's great-grandmother was born while Hernandez was still in exile across the muddy waters.

Martín – Guzman, not Fierro, but it might as well have been Fierro – kept refilling the maté and passing it round. I got the hang of sucking it through the communal straw. He told us more about gaucho cavalry, about Belgrano, about Roca the Indian killer, about San Martín and about Guëmes' painful death.

I asked him to define 'gaucho'.

'Gaucho? What is gaucho?? What is love??? How can I answer this?'

I wanted to look at some gaucho gear so Martín sent me over to Tienda El Gaucho. He said I'd find the man who made *bombachas* for the presidents of Argentina and Bolivia for Guëmes Day, when fifteen hundred baggy-panted cowboys rode into town.

Bombachas, big flapping oriental-looking pants, are something of a historical accident and the result of a serendipitous bit of crafty trading. Some time in the depths of the nineteenth century a merchant ship fetched up in Buenos Aires. Nothing unusual in that except it was packed to the gunwales with a maverick consignment of surplus French Zouave or Bulgarian Army trousers, baggy in the Moorish style. No one knew why they were there but an enterprising businessman decided to sell them to the gauchos.

Up until then gauchos wore the *chiripa*, a kind of nappy or large dhoti, a big square of cloth with a corner pulled through the legs and tucked into the belt. They had inherited the *chiripa* from the Indians. It was simple, rustic but getting a little old-fashioned. The man with the boatload of baggies going cheap managed to convince the gauchos that these were the modern answer to the *chiripa*. They were equally roomy, easy-on-the-go, good for riding and certain not to fall down during a knife fight – all in all, a better idea. The gauchos took to them immediately.

Which is just what I did at the Tienda El Gaucho. The guvnor, Guillermo Najjar, a fat balding man in his early forties, sweating all the time and mopping the top of his head, sorted me out. He obviously had an international clientele. He had English.

'Everything done by hand. One hundred per cent cotton. Special style this region.'

And special they were. In Salta the *bombachas* were bigger, baggier and more pleated than anywhere else. Up in the north-west the *bombachas* had six deep pleats down the full length of each side of each leg so they billowed out like spinnakers. Walking along, the Salteño cowboys often looked like they might inflate and float away into the sky. They needed their horses to keep them grounded. Other regions were more restrained, less exuberant.

I found out Señor Najjar was Syrian.

'Yes. Is true. Also our President, Menem, is Syrian. I make *bombachas* for him. Just like this one. Same. Also for other presidents. Bolivia and many other. Same this one.'

I got a pair in black from the Syrian.

Check those pleats.

General Martín Miguel de Guëmes is Salta's favourite son, a true hero with a classic riches-to-rags story. He was born in Salta in 1785 to a wealthy land-owning family. His mother was the daughter of a distinguished Spanish general. His father was treasurer in the Spanish local government. Salta at that time was a prosperous feudal state, doing business on the mule-train route between Alto Peru and Buenos Aires. Guëmes had a comfortable upbringing before he became a gaucho.

There were two shades of opinion in the town. Conservative gentlefolk like Guëmes' parents staunchly supported the King. Liberals, some Spanish but mostly creole, had an ear for the revolutionary rumblings from France and an eye for the writings of a man called Rousseau.

Guëmes' family was proud of him. He had done well at school and, with high hopes for a military or political career, they sent him to the military academy. In 1806, at the age of twenty-one Guëmes had just left the academy in Buenos Aires and had his first commission as a second lieutenant. Right then the British were making their first attempt to invade Buenos Aires.

Independence from Spain was brewing throughout the Americas and as usual the British, alert for the first whiff of a main chance, had passed by to see what might fall off the shaking tree.

Earlier that year, an English admiral called Sir Home (pron. *Hume*) Popham had sailed down to the southern tip of Africa and seized the Cape of Good Hope from the Dutch. It was so easy that, flushed with his success, Popham cast about for another territory to grab before returning home (pron. *Home*) in triumph, or so he thought. In those days there was a thin line between pirates, who were no more than cowboys in boats, and admirals.

He heard about the anti-Spanish stirrings in the New World and thought the River Plate might be ripe for plucking. Ever since he was born, his mother's twenty-first child, Popham had been an optimist and an opportunist. He felt blessed, lucky even to be alive, and always thought he would succeed against any odds. So he turned his squadron around and headed for Buenos Aires.

In June 1806, Popham landed south of Buenos Aires. A force of Scottish Highlanders advanced on the city. In BA there were calls for arming the people. Three thousand citizens were issued arms but many had no powder. Others had powder but no shot. There was chaos. The Spanish Viceroy high-tailed it out of town, for which the *porteños* never forgave him or Spain. The city capitulated.

Sir Home proclaimed the Río de la Plata a 'New Arcadia' for British merchants. He sent home boats full of booty. Chests full of the spoils of war were paraded through the streets of London in horse-drawn wagons with the word TREASURE emblazoned along the side in big gold letters. British businessmen were beside themselves with excitement. The government sent reinforcements with instructions: more treasure please.

Before the reinforcements could arrive, plans were made to retake the city. Over the next six weeks, troops were gathered from the other side of the River Plate. Hussars and gauchos were brought together. The main army was advancing on BA to attack the English, who had by now retreated to the fort in the city. On the morning of 12 August, Lieutenant Güemes went to the shore of the muddy river with a number of hussars and gauchos to investigate reports of an English ship in the area.

A thick mist swirled around them. Güemes stood in his stirrups trying to peer through the fog. Suddenly a gaucho gave the alarm.

'A ship!!'

The ship must have run aground. The English had sailed too close to the shore. There had been a wind from the east and the river had receded. Güemes realized a prize was sitting there ready for the taking. He sat back in his saddle, pulled out his sabre, waved it above his head, dug his spurs in and shouted: 'Let's go! Let's board her!'

Guëmes didn't have to repeat the order. The gauchos needed no encouragement. The regular hussars remained rooted to the spot, stunned by the absurdity of what they had just heard. But while the hussars sat there watching on their horses, Guëmes and his gauchos whooped and hollered and spurred their mounts into the mud and the swirling terracotta waters, charging straight for the shadow in the mist.

They had no idea how many men were on the ship or how well they were armed. They didn't know what kind of opposition was waiting for them. There were only thirty of them, but they didn't care. One gaucho could handle five Englishmen with a hand tied behind his back so the way they saw it, the odds were heavily on their side.

Anyway, the idea of boarding a ship on horseback, something never done before, was good enough for these gauchos. For they were the real thing, these guys, not rhinestone cowboys or dudes from the silver screen, but real wild-eyed screaming horsemen spoiling for a fight.

They were the first cowboy cavalry the British Navy had ever seen. And a marine cavalry at that.

As they half galloped, half swam out to the ship they saw it was the *Justine*, from Admiral Popham's squadron, a schooner with twenty-six cannon. It had run aground and was listing slightly.

When they got to its side everything was quiet. The ship looked empty. Had it been abandoned? There was no sign of anyone aboard, and a ship this size should have a crew of more than a hundred. It seemed like a ghost ship.

They stood up on their horses' backs ready to board, only to be greeted with a sharp volley of musket fire from the top deck. Two gauchos fell back into the river and one back on to his horse. The other twenty-seven, undeterred, leapt on to the side of the ship and clambered aboard.

The muskets were useless in hand-to-hand fighting. Although they outnumbered the gauchos at least four to one, the English soldiers had no chance. The gauchos had no guns. They never used them. All they had were their long *facóns* and their *boleadores*, which they swung in deadly circles round their heads.

Guëmes laid into a few seamen with his sabre. The gauchos screamed, spat and cursed a lot, curdled blood, cracked a few skulls, terrified the crew and killed a handful of English sailors. After a short and very violent battle Guëmes demanded the enemy's surrender. They ran the Spanish flag up the mast and took the ship and crew prisoner. It was Guëmes' combat debut and he became an instant hero.

They took their hundred English captives off the ship and back to the fort to join the rest of the creole army. When they got there, everyone was staring at the walls of the fort.

A white flag was flying. Beresford, the English commander, had surrendered.

In one magnificent amphibious charge the gauchos had let the English know in no uncertain terms that they didn't want to go out of the *parilla* into the *asado*. No more colonists. They were just trying to get rid of the old ones. Breathe the air of freedom for a bit.

They'd be happy to do business though. That was a different matter. But on their own terms.

Want to buy some beef? *Muy gaucho*. Hard.

As well as marking the beginning of the gaucho's long hard climb towards respectability and status as National Symbol, this act of defiance prompted Sir Walter Scott, erstwhile godfather of the tartan industry, to pen a few amusingly patronizing words on these wild horsemen. There were, he said, 'a sort of Christian savage called Guachos [sic] whose principal furniture is the skulls of dead horses, whose only food is raw beef and water, whose sole employment is to catch wild cattle . . . and whose chief amusement is to ride horses to death.'

When Sir Home Popham went home there wasn't the acclaim he expected. In fact, for his overt failure in the River Plate and for acting without authorization, he was court-martialled. He was found guilty and censured.

This defeat, and especially the humiliating cowboy charge on the *Justine*, was salutary and recognized as such by the London merchants. They still dreamed of more chests with 'Treasure' written along the side. The City of London presented Sir Home with a sword of honour for 'opening up new markets'. The court-martial was a technicality.

From then on the only British warships in the River Plate were waiting to give the first declaration of independence a twenty-one-gun salute and our heartiest congratulations.

By now the young Guëmes was fiercely impassioned. He returned home to the north-west and started to build up his gaucho army. He was at the heart of the struggle for independence, fighting the Spanish now, not the English. His fame spread. Horsemen from all over came to join him – men like Pachi Gorritti and his Gauchos of the Frontier.

Guëmes' father, bastion of the Salta establishment, the man with his hands on the government money, was horrified. Young Guëmes, still in his twenties, was cast out by his family and disinherited. After being cut loose he became even more gaucho, a wanderer, an outcast. This may have affected his style of fighting. With his *jinetes*, his gaucho cavalry, he harassed and gnawed away at the Spanish army.

He was one of the first creoles to use guerrilla tactics. It was the gaucho way, originally Lautaro's way, the Indian way, of fighting a war. The gauchos, like the Indians, *knew the land*, knew the distance from the river by the taste of a blade of grass. They knew their horses and rode like the Indians.

The gauchos even rode as well as the Mongols. Genghis Khan out on the Mongolian steppe rode small horses like the gauchos, and he was unquestionably the greatest cowboy of them all.

On 20 February 1813 Guëmes and his gaucho cavalry alongside General Belgrano completely destroyed the Spanish army that had come down from Alto Peru to Salta. It was a decisive victory, the most important in the north-west Gaucho Wars.

Guëmes succeeded Belgrano and went on fighting around the north-west with the Great Liberator José de San Martín until the end. It was Guëmes, more than others like Belgrano or San Martín, who gave the gauchos their first real poncho of respectability. Having fought and helped create the Argentine, they became national heroes – and finally the national symbol.

Not long before these first steps towards sainthood gauchos were shunned as wild and dangerous cattle-hunters. Throughout the nineteenth century, the gauchos' golden days, they remained a poisoned chalice embraced for different political motives by various factions. Suspect *caudillos* or dubious political parties would use them as a vigilante cavalry actually to fight or sometimes just to ride into town and put the frighteners on someone.

As time wore on they became, like the regional *caudillos*, more of a liability to the central government in Buenos Aires. In the larger battle between the powerful port-state, supported by the English, and the poorer undeveloped country, gauchos were bad news and needed to be controlled. So in the latter part of the century they became increasingly hobbled by the police, the army, the railroads and the staking out of the pampas.

Barbed wire did to the gauchos just what it did to the Anglo cowboys up north. And exactly as in North America, the more their freedom and individuality was constrained, the more the myth grew. The gaucho of myth overtook reality long before the century was out.

'Martín Fierro' saw to that.

When by favour of none the gaucho rode
  O'er the rolling pampa wide;
    But now alas, he grows sour and grim,
    For the law and the police they harry him,
And either the Army would rope him in,
  Or the Sheriff have his hide.

And give yourselves up for lost, my boys,
  If the Mayor nooses you;
    They'll drag you off with a hail of blows,
    Though why neither God nor the Mayor knows,
And they finish you quick if you stand and draw,
  As the gaucho used to do.

But Martín Miguel de Guëmes wasn't around to see all these changes. He continued to fight the Gaucho Wars up in the north-west. In the first free elections in Argentina he was elected governor of Salta in 1815. By this time he had built up an auxiliary army of a thousand gauchos. He needed them, being so close to Alto Peru and within easy striking distance of the Spanish forces.

He won battles and he lost battles. As well as the Spanish he had to face insurgents from the creole side. The same internecine squabbles, the same mess that was cooking up in Chile was happening all over Argentina.

Finally, in 1821, after a clandestine infiltration of Salta by hostile forces with the collusion of Guëmes' political enemies in the city, he stopped a bullet. He had always been advised to avoid injury as his blood did not clot well. He went on bleeding as he was carried by his followers through the forests trying to escape. He died ten days later.

He was thirty-six years old. Old enough to become a hero.

'*Diez dias de crueles podecimientos, fallecio* – after ten days of agony he died.'

Don Tito Campos stared straight ahead and upwards at some mythological sunset as he intoned these words. Don Tito was the man to tell me what gaucho really was.

'What is gaucho?' His gaze dropped and he looked me straight in the eye. 'Gaucho is a state of mind.'

Don Tito should know for he was president of the local gaucho club, the oldest and, according to him, the most respected in the country: the Agrupacion Tradicional de los Gauchos de Salta. By 1914 there were two hundred such clubs in the Argentine. Many immigrants new to the Argentine, Italian and otherwise, wanted to *belong*. So they joined these clubs and dressed as gauchos in order to be assimilated, to identify, to become Argentine. They called themselves names like 'Orphans of the Plains', 'Gauchos and Indians', 'Pampa Tiger and his Men'.

This identity problem was very real and in South America was unique to the Argentine. So many Italians and Spanish as well as Dutch, German, Russian, Syrian, English and Jews all descended on the Argentine in such a short space of time round the turn of the century that they had to look to the gaucho to have any sense of belonging at all. Gauchos were the only tradition they could catch on to.

Some Jews did not just join the gaucho clubs but went the whole hog. I heard of a community of Jewish gauchos in Entre Ríos, the Mesopotamia of Argentina. Gaucho Marx?

They say down in the Southern Cone that an Argentine is an Italian who speaks Spanish, lives in a French house and thinks he's English.

They also say that the Mexicans descended from the Aztecs, the Peruvians descended from the Incas and the Argentines descended from boats . . .

Now there are seventy-two gaucho clubs in Salta province alone which, like the gauchos of old, would be ready to step in should a breach become available.

'We are . . . *dis-pon-i-ble* . . . ready if called,' said the Don, leaning forward conspiratorially. 'Fifty men in a *fortine* – a fort. There are seventy-two reliable groups. That's three thousand men. Three thousand gauchos. *Standing by*.'

Maybe it should be Paper rather than Pampa Tiger but still the threat was there. However ineffectual, there was still an echo of the gauchos' aggressive political past. And the mighty unruly punch they used to pack.

I had met Don Tito at Martín and Alicia's office on the Plaza San Martín. A small, bald, handsome man of sixty-five, strong and lithe, he was well preserved with a shiny tan and a very black Ramon Navarro moustache. He was wearing an impeccably tailored sand-coloured gaucho dress suit: *chaqueta*, a bolero top heavily pleated on the front and with intricate lacework up the sleeves, huge, baggy, maxi-pleated *bombachas* ballooning out of the fitted black riding-boots, white shirt with black *panuelo*, bandana, his broad-brimmed flat black hat in his hands and his *rastra*, his broad clanking gaucho belt, a carnival of chains, horseshoes and semi-precious stones.

As usual in these broad-belted matters, Elvis came to mind.

We strolled through the old town with the Don He walked proud, gaucho, feet apart, back straight, red and black poncho ceremonially folded and draped over one shoulder, *bombachas* billowing absurdly in the light evening breezes. He touched his hat magisterially, acknowledging greetings and tributes.

'*Buenos noches*, Don Tito!'

Nod.

He was the business.

Then we went to his car to go to the clubhouse. The car, a dirty yellow Ford Cortina, was seriously gaucho. It was old and rusted and might have got a tenner in a breaker's yard. The doors stuck. I tried pushing.

'Fuerte! Strong!' urged Don Tito, jabbing the air with his fist in a manly I-could-give-her-one fashion.

We got in and the dust rose as the car sank into the ground. When it finally started, the terminally gaucho leaky exhaust box made the true virile roar of a Salteño cowboy. Dogs cowered in the street. I began to understand. You had to be gaucho to get into the car, gaucho to shut the doors, gaucho to get it started and truly gaucho to drive it away.

The Don was in the front, cool, calm, chin out, arm hanging out of the tatty front door, driving his roaring heap up the hill as if it were a gleaming new 1990s Lincoln Continental.

Barbaro! The man's a king with an Elvis belt. So by the time we got to the gaucho club – the Peña – the gauchismo was hanging heavy in the air. You could cut it with a *facón*. Already the Don had the *huasos* of Chile knocked into a cocked sombrero.

The Peña was on the outskirts of town, nestling into Cerro San Bernardo, the closest hill overlooking Salta, only a *bolas*' throw from a monolithic Guëmes statue. It was high-ceilinged, white-walled with dark wooden beams, chairs and tables. Spanish colonial, it was full of gaucho paraphernalia on the walls, mounted in the middle of the room, hanging from the beams, draped over the tables: rawhide *lazos*, lassoos, *Tres Marias* or *bolas*, *guardacalcones*, chaps up north, the Salteño red and black ponchos, wooden clog-style *estribos*, Chilean-style stirrups with that same intricate Moorish carving and silver inlay, and a high, wood-framed saddle similar to the Chilean saddle I had first seen in the beautiful Welsh valley down in Patagonia.

Once again the gauchos have their gear perfectly suited to the terrain. The horse is always foremost in their mind. Without the horse they are nothing.

The most bizarre piece of equipment Salteño gauchos use, to protect themselves out in the *monte* from the murderous thorn bushes they ride through while working their horses and cattle, are called *guardamontes*. Mounted on the horse's shoulders, they are enormous batwings of thick leather flapping out either side like mutant elephant ears in front of the rider's legs. The horse has another slice of thick leather over its chest so both horse and rider are shielded from the lacerating thorns.

Around the walls there were pictures of past presidents of the gauchos of Guëmes, all decked out, all handsome, all looking like a cross between screen cowboys, tango singers and Teddy Roosevelt. Don Tito posed for a photo, offered me some coca to chew, and sat down for a chinwag.

There was such a strong cowboy feel about the whole place that I thought about the Pope again. After coming across him in the Chilean *huaso* museum and still carrying my picture of his Economy Boot Company boots from Texas, I figured that if the Pope was such a cowboy aficionado, he couldn't have missed Salta, the gaucho mother lode. Did he come here?

'Yes, His Holiness Juan Pablo came to Salta.'

Don Tito was reverential, certainly, but in a more matter-of-fact way than Señora Norma, the ecstatic woman in O'Higgins Park in Santiago. She had had a religious experience but the Don was more pleased and proud. Knocked out to have the man here, of course, but somehow meeting him on a more cowboy-to-cowboy level.

'Magnificent. It was magnificent. Two columns of gauchos either side of the road, two thousand five hundred all the way from the airport to the town.'

'In full gear?'

'Oh yes, fully mounted, *guardamontes*, ponchos, the lot. The Holy Father stayed the night. We set up a twenty-four-hour guard around his residence. On horseback all night. Juan Pablo was very pleased.'

Now the crunch. Did he get any gaucho gear? Is his cowboy collection growing?

'Yes, the Vatican had made enquiries before he came. Our *agrupacion* gave him a poncho and boots. We learnt the sizes from his staff.'

'Black boots like yours?'

'Yes, just the same. And the town gave him *bombachas*, *chaqueta*, shirt, bandana and hat.'

Spurs?

'Yes, *espuelas* for sure.'

He got the lot! I was getting more and more excited and told the Don about my run-ins with the Pope out on the cowboy trail, about his holy Texan boots and blessed Chilean *manta*. So what did it all mean? Were my suspicions well founded? If anyone knew of Juan Pablo's covert cowboy yearnings, surely Don Tito did. He looked up into the distance, back at the old mythological sunset.

'Yes, I think His Holiness is a cowboy. He is truly a gaucho in his heart.'
In my heart I punched the air. *Yes!*

Later on I went to see the statue of Guëmes. Nestling in between the twin breasts of the round, thickly wooded Cerro San Bernardo, it was of heroic Socialist Realist proportions. Guëmes was sitting on his horse, of course, on a massive redstone obelisk in a commanding position at the top of Paseo Guëmes, a wide dual-carriageway avenue with flower beds down the middle and lined with exuberant Hollywood-Spanish colonial palaces. The statue was looking across the Paseo, his hand struck across his forehead over his eyes: 'Oh, no, not *another* gaucho parade . . . '

On a wall by the cathedral in Plaza San Martín was a poster for a dance in Salta. The group playing was Conjunto VICTOR HUGO & THE BENGALIS.

Outside, the cathedral was yellow ochre with a large masonic eye in a pyramid right over the main entrance. There was a rash of Gauchos of Guëmes plaques all over the front wall. Inside, the cathedral looked like the kind of venue Victor and the Bengalis would have liked to play.

Gaudy was too sombre a word for it. It fairly exploded in the face, like heavenly gold dust thrown in your eyes – which of course was the idea. A place of worship can be dark and shadowy, suitable for quiet contemplation, or bright, shiny and overwhelming, a gilded slice of heaven, a place where God is stinking rich. The cathedral in Salta went for the gold.

It had to be so, for it was built little more than a hundred years ago to house a miraculous silver icon of the Virgin Mary. The icon had 'cried tears in Salta *milagrosamente* – miraculously – for three days in August and one further day in October 1749 in the company of Jesuits'. So she and Jesus – *El Señor y la Virgen del Milagro* – became the patrons of Salta and were housed in this exuberant gilded palace.

The columns, the walls, the ceiling, all was covered in gold and white and red plush and marble and pinks as primary as they come. Angels flew across the tops of bright-tinted columns on to the vaulted aquamarine ceiling. Beyond the columns and gold chandeliers and velvet drapes were the altars. The main one was a gigantic marble and gold wedding-cake that rose up in gilded colonnaded tiers of grey marble with white marble angels fluttering around. On top was a celestial golden-domed Sun Palace with a huge golden sunburst halo behind. It was a divine Eldorado.

In these parts, God is very rich indeed. And the Pope is a cowboy, gaucho in his heart.

The Señor and the Virgin left their gilded cage once. They were paraded on the streets of Salta on 25 August 1948 and performed a second miracle, saving their beloved city from terrible destruction by a massive earthquake. So they deserved all the ostentatious interior decoration they got. Much of this ostentation embodies a peculiarly Indian view of heaven.

They both finished up in little chapels either side of the main altar. All round them, covering every inch of wall in the chapels, were shallow glass-fronted cases filled with small shiny things. I went up closer and a lot of them looked like little hearts. They were. And legs. As I peered at the cases I could see they were crammed with little replicas of different bits of the body. The first case was a random collection of hearts and legs. No sense of design. But next to it was one with a definite arrangement of an organic kind, a central diamond of hearts surrounded by assorted legs, right and left, with a border of lungs and kidneys. Closer to the miraculous Virgin were two cases crammed with a pick'n'mix of parts – ears, lungs, kidneys (one or both), stomachs, lots of hearts and legs as usual, bowels, a cow, noses, hands, heads, children and what looked like a pair of breasts or a moustache but turned out to be eyes.

All these little effigies, mostly an inch or two high, seemed to be made of silver. On one level it was extraordinary to see the pathology of an area so graphically displayed. Was there any mileage in checking the epidemiology, the distribution of disease, of Salta by studying these little silver charms, hopes and fears locked in their dusty mausoleums?

On another level these fetishes had little to do with Christianity and everything to do with the Indians. I had seen similar offerings in orthodox churches in Greece so they were not unique to the New World. It was one of many universal rituals which had been assimilated by the Christians. This conspicuous consumption of myths, symbols and images of the previous pagan religions, usurping all that came before, was standard practice by the Christian Church in the New and the Old Worlds. Conquest in the name of evangelism.

In a paradoxical way, though, the great colonial churches and the images of el Señor and the Virgin Mother gave the conquered people a space where their ancient beliefs, though masked, could go on living and breathing. Their old beliefs are hidden, protected by the modern symbols. As always, nothing is quite as it seems.

So these sad displays of forlorn dreams in Salta were hardly surprising. We were on the wayside of the Camino Real, the Royal Road of the Incas. At least ten thousand years old primitive man came down this way and settled in this area after the long journey across the land-bridge from northern Asia. Though these silver charms were closer to sorcery or shamanism than to sainthood, it made sense to offer them to the Virgin of Miracles. For the myths of the virgin birth, the holy trinity, the death and resurrection, the miracles, were all universal and not merely the prerogative of Christianity. Such symbols were well established in these Andean foothills in pre-Columbian days.

I wondered how many organs one person could have pinned up in a case and still survive. Six? Eight? A semi-blind diabetic with hypertension, an ulcer, arthritis and cancer could have ten items up there and still be ambulant - ear, eyes, head, heart, lungs, kidneys, stomach, bowels, hand, legs. With a bit of help they should be able to walk into the cathedral and pin up a couple more bits, a nose or a spine perhaps.

There were shops that sold these little silver amulets. I found one. It seemed like a general store, with everything from batteries, watches, maté and kettles to tapes, radios, woolly hats and . . . silver charms. Two women and a man, all chubby and jolly, welcomed me.

From envelopes stacked in a whole row of shoe-boxes they pulled out replicas of everything – head, tongue, eyes, mouth, left ear, right ear, nose, neck, torso, ribcage, spine, abdomen, hip bone, stomach, one kidney, the pair, knee, intestines, colon, ovary, uterus, breasts, a crawling baby looking like something from *Ghostbusters*, children, house, horse, brain, cow, car, book, soldier, families, the mum and dad with exact number of girls and boys – two boys and one girl, seven girls and five boys – hands, feet, *everything*.

Well, everything except a gaucho.

'*No tiene gaucho, huh?*'

'*Ehhhh, es otra vez, señor* – that was another time.'

The man shrugged his shoulders and looked wistful. I was surprised and dismayed to find the gaucho so out of favour, or in so little need of La Virgen del Milagro. I found a figure of a woman, very Indian looking, with the belly pushed out from behind.

'*Una mujer embarazada, señor.*' A pregnant – 'embarrassed' – woman. A pregnant woman may be *embarazada*, but in Spanish to give birth is *dar luz* – to give light.

And did they have wedding tackle, meat and two veg?

'*Tiene cojones? Huevos?*' They call balls 'eggs'.

'*Sí, señor.*' He rummaged through the shoe-boxes and pulled out what seemed like a rounded Christian cross. He pointed at the globular side arms.

'*Estos son testículos, señor. Huevos.*'

An encouraging smirk played round the corners of his mouth as he looked up. The two plump comfy women behind the counter were bright eyed, smiling expectantly.

'*Si, yo se, yo tengo ellos* – I know, I've got some.'

I glanced down at my trousers and the whole shop collapsed into shrieks of laughter at the funniest thing they had heard for years.

A fat albino man in a red baseball hat, patently woken from some lunar dream by the uproar of hilarity, came over and stuck his startling pink face an inch away from mine. He had bright orange hair, straw-coloured stubble, overalls he'd grown out of a while back, and chunky pebble glasses.

'From where you come? Oh, English! My friend, no? What now you speak?'

I avoided my usual *Vengo del otro lado de la luna* in case he engaged me in faltering moonspeak and blew my cover, exposing me as just another ordinary Earthperson. Instead, grabbing my silver embarrassed woman and genital crucifix, I ran out of the door.

I left a thought with the Virgen del Milagro. If she saved Salta from an earthquake, could she do anything for my volcanic bowels? If I have to talk with the tiger, I'd rather have a quiet chat than a slanging match.

I finally tracked down some singers. I'd heard that as well as its cowboy tradition, Salta was known for its music and the two were often intertwined. There was supposed to be cowboy mountain music and somewhere they featured high-pitched keening and falsetto singing. Always a fan of yodelling and high-pitched, high-emotion singing, I was keen to hear what they had here in the foothills.

I found the Salta Boys – Los Changos Salteños – three singers who played guitars and *bombo*, a big fur-skinned, double-ended bass drum beaten, often sombrely, with a single stick. The boys all had office jobs. One was with the Pan American bus company.

We met in the courtyard of the old Cabildo, the original town council building, by the shocking pink vulvas of hibiscus, more than life size round these parts, glowing and gleaming sensually in the sun after the last downpour. I'd been away from home too long.

Carlos played guitar and sang tenor. Guillermo played the *bombo* and had the bass voice. Daniel played guitar and leapt into the high, yodelling falsetto voice. A lot of their songs were pure Country music – like the 'Vidala del Nombrador', a deeply philosophical song from the heart of the Salta forests which sounds like 'Once upon a Time in the West'. It is the song of the *coya*, the mountain man, at one with the earth, mountains, sky, pumas, life and death. It was heavy, mournful and menacing. Backed with a slow booming funeral march of a beat on the *bombo*, the bass voice intoned dark verses full of dread. It was the lone troubadour on the dusty trail to the last cowboy shantytown on the final frontier.

Then the guitars came in and suddenly, through this ominous recitation, the high voice soared out, keening upwards, full of anguish and longing. Time stood still. My heart almost stopped.

This unearthly cry is the *baguala*. The *baguala* voice has the same eerie isolation as the Appalachian high lonesome wail. It's an astonishingly emotional sound and wrenched me, boots and all, into its solitary universe. A *bagual* in Quechua, the language of the Incas, is a bronco, a wild horse. Is *baguala* wild horse singing?

Both the Appalachian and the *baguala* are mountain music and share the loneliness of the hills, whether in a Salteño *quebrada* or a Kentucky holler. But the American high lonesome sound comes from European roots, mostly Scottish and Irish, while *baguala* owes more to the Indians.

> My name is Arjona always
> Whatever happens to me.

They sang a *zamba*, another slow, sad song. They sang another soaring *baguala* about a stone-faced man sitting in a green valley. They sang a *huayno*, a protest song called 'The Fire of Animana'. Out on the big wine estancias the peons rebelled against the owners. They brought all their belongings to the village square and burnt them. The flames and smoke could be seen for miles around. The news got through to the government, who sorted out their grievances. Once again, Daniel's mesmerizing *baguala* voice tore up into the air while Guillermo boomed away.

Finally the boys played us a *chacarera*, the gaucho standard I'd been searching for. A lively, excitable dance, this was about a ninety-three-year-old woman who still loves to dance and who does so like a young gazelle.

They sang indoors in the Cabildo. Their songs echoed round the wood and whitewash of the dark cavernous room where independence had first been declared in 1810. On the wall hung a heroic canvas of General Guëmes and his gaucho cavalry, arms raised with sabres, lances and *facóns* glinting, their horses flying across the wall under blood-red mountains. Wild cowboys, whooping and howling in the Indian way, the *baguala* way, falling murderously on a terrified unseen enemy and winning another inevitable victory.

You can read *The Gaucho Martín Fierro* in Quechua, the language of the Indians, the language of Cuzco. You can *sing* it in Quechua. The Gauchos *are* the Indians. If Don Tito is to be believed, *everyone* is gaucho.

*

It rained every night. Electrical storms and fierce downpours kept me awake. Martín and I were to have gone horse trekking but the hills would have been too muddy and uncertain underfoot. I lay awake hearing our *asado* in the mountains slipping away. Sheets of rain lashed the windows.

Above all this, even thunder and lightning, I could still hear the drip – drip – drip from the air conditioner above on to the broken one down here. *Adios caballos*.

The rain put paid to dreams of riding far. After a dry twenty-four hours we decided to trek a little way out to follow part of the Pan American Highway and find the Camino Real, the Royal Road of the Incas. And to find a town called Cowboys.

Vaqueros is Spanish for cowboys. Several thousand miles south of Texas on the old Pan American is a spot called just that.

Martín found me Rebelde, a most unrebellious criollo horse. She was sweet tempered, just what I needed after the thunderous dreams of the night before. Slow and quiet, she was what the gauchos contemptuously call '*Manso como para un ingles*' – 'tame enough for an Englishman'. I can take it.

The Salteño saddle, as I'd seen with Don Tito, was like the Chilean. Carol Jones in Bariloche had said how the high wood frame keeps the weight off the horse's kidneys and tires it less in these mountainous regions. It is to be sat in on the trot, like a Western saddle. It had layers of blanket and leather. Very comfortable, it kept the weight off my kidneys too.

We rode out into the Lerma valley and the Salta hills. The sun was high and hot. It must have been another slice of heaven for the conquistadors, coming down from the mountains and the high sierras to find the Lerma valley, this fertile valley that is always green, perpetual springtime so close to the Camino Real. No wonder they stayed.

The hills were deep dark green, densely wooded, rolling and folding over each other. Here and there they had been cleared and had bald tops like shorn sheep. River beds like the Río Mojotoro were wide and dried out, with fast brown rivulets racing through a bed of neon-white, sun-bleached pebbles. A family with three kids, one with an optimistic fishing pole, picked their way across the hot stones as we rode by on the river bank.

We passed fields of maize and sugar cane and tobacco plants going to seed. There had been a harvest and big brown-veined tobacco leaves were hanging everywhere to dry – in barns, along fences, over walls, on lines, over cart wheels. Everywhere. In pre-Columbian times the Indians in these parts used tobacco as poultices and smoked it only in religious ceremonies, when they mixed it with coca leaves.

We found Vaqueros though it was such a tiny pueblito that even sauntering down the road on a horse as placid, as *manso* as Rebel, if you sneeze it's gone. With a house or two hidden in the trees either side of the Pan American, the only proof of its existence was a couple of small signs saying *Zona Urban* – a patent lie. Oh, and a Red Cross sign in front of the Vaqueros clinic, the Puesto Sanitario. I posed in front of the sign for Jo to take a snap. Cowboy doctor in a cowboy clinic? Plenty of those at home.

Cowboys, gauchos or any kind of *jinetes* seemed thin on the ground until I came on half a dozen lads playing polo. They played very crudely, most of them bareback, but they rode and swung from their horses with thoughtless ease. I wasn't enough of a horseman to join in so I watched. One lad, a *rubio*, blond, in very flappy *bombachas*, swept so low above the ground he looked sure to fall, but would always rise back up on to the horse's back. They were all riding criollo horses, of course, the size of a pony with the stride of a horse.

Vaqueros didn't live up to its name. Not even finding the Río Vaqueros, the Cowboy River which joined the Spanish River, the Río Castellanos, made up for the anti-climax. If it were the States, there'd have been a Vaqueros theme park with gauchos, *pulperias* and staged *facón* fights. *Bolas* throwing. Catch your own ostrich or guanaco. Colt breaking, steer branding. At least a souvenir shop to buy some rhinestone gaucho gear, what they call in Nashville 'Tangible Memories'.

We rode on and came to another stretch of the dried-out Mojotoro. Rebelde was so quiet and docile, maybe a bit depressed, I thought. Perhaps she was on valium? She might not be as nimble as she'd need to be out there on the sun-scorched rolling stones. Rather than picking our way gingerly over the river bed, we crossed a bridge and rode into La Caldera.

La Caldera – the Cauldron – was a neat flowery little pueblo with an enormous statue of Christ. It was snoozing in the middle of the afternoon. Gardens were well tended and houses were clean. It was almost like a council estate, or the winner of one of those neatest village awards.

I was looking for a gaucho priest I had heard about. Jo asked about him but was told that he lived way out in the hills and had retired now, wasn't preaching any more. He was *muy viejo* and had nearly reached the end of the *camino*.

In his day, I'd been told, he wore full gaucho gear and would ride right into the church to take mass. He gave his services in the old gaucho slang, no doubt with readings from 'Martín Fierro' and a slap on the pulpit with his *rebenque*. I had wanted to ask him if he was related to the gaucho taxi-driver in Bariloche.

Right through the middle of La Caldera ran a long straight road paved with hexagonal stones. It was the royal Inca road, the Camino Real, that runs from high up in Peru – from Cajamarca to Cuzco, through Bolivia, down past Salta and almost as far south as Cordoba. Down this road came Quechua the language of the Incas. It is still spoken as a first language by many in these parts. After the Incas and after the Quechua, after the silver and the gold, the conquistadors followed this same route.

I looked down the Camino Real and watched what must have been the Inca municipal road-cleaning lorry brush away into the distance.

I thought about the earlier people who had passed this way. This was a natural route long before it became the Camino Real. The tribes before the Incas, the Wankas, or Huancas, interested me particularly. Like the Aztecs in Mexico, the Incas, who were ruling when the conquistadors arrived, had been the top dogs for a comparatively short time. True, they had a rich culture, and were powerful rulers and administrators. But before them there had been many different tribes and cultures. The Wankas were one of them.

There is now evidence that they were hunter-gatherers fifteen hundred years ago, long before they became dominant. The Wanka culture spanned a thousand years and established relations with many other peoples, like the Huari, Tarunas and Yauyos.

Their ascendancy was between 1200 and 1400, during which time they built cities like Anticuay Orcco along the Mantaro river valley. They had a clear architectural style and favoured circular buildings. You could always tell when a town had been built by Wankas. In the early 1990s seasonal rains in Huancavelica high up in Peru washed away enough ground to expose a whole Wanka citadel with rooms, burial grounds and canals. Pieces of pottery and other artefacts have added to our still inadequate knowledge of the Wanka culture.

The Wankas came face to face with the Incas in 1460. No more was heard of them. The question of how they disappeared seems to have been overshadowed by the cataclysm of half a century later. They had been a culture unique to the central sierras, and perhaps posed a threat to the more highly organized and ritualized Incas. We don't know. For whatever reason, Incas and Wankas were incompatible bedfellows.

To cast the Incas as the sole representatives of Peruvian culture is selective history – as good as we get at any English school. In Peru, far from pretending the Wankas didn't exist, they celebrate them as part of their folklore. The Wankas are a well known singing duo, a father and son pairing, Duo Los Wankas del Peru.

It's all out there. Nothing needs to be invented. Perhaps Los Wankas could do a Country crossover album of songs by the Blue Sky Boys. The Blue Skies were Bill and Earl Bolick from Hickory, North Carolina, the Bolick brothers. It would be 'Some Bolicks from Los Wankas'. Or 'Never Mind the Bolicks – Here's the Wankas'.

It turned out there was no cholera in Salta town after all, just further out in the north of the province. But I still got a bit of a gaucho thrill rinsing my teeth in tap water.

8. Grass and Sky, Sky and Grass

Jo Tambien was shaking me into the morning. C'mon, we're here. Where? Blinking at another bus station. I looked for my feet; still there, seemed to be in some kind of luxury bucket. Santa Rosa, was that it? OK, got it, left BA last night on the *expreso*.

A book on my lap . . . right, fell asleep over Cunninghame Graham last night. Not the gaudy trashiness of El Gigante, but the bus had great buckets for the feet. I sat bolt upright, grabbed Tambien by the lapels, and shouted at him, WE'RE ON THE PAMPA!

Well, not exactly, Jo said, we're in the bus station, but it won't be long.

The only mark of the pampa Indians in the whole of Santa Rosa loomed over us as we drank coffee. I fancied some maté but had no *yerba* and it was half six in the morning and the maté shops weren't open yet. So it was breakfast at the Hotel Calfucura. The cacique, the Chief Calfucura himself, was grotesquely immortalized in a gigantic mosaic on the hotel wall. Dancing on his grave with hob-nailed boots.

Santa Rosa looks prosperous, a typical spread-out single-storey agricultural prairie town. There are several two-storey houses around and Calfucura's hotel is one of the few high buildings. Still not high enough to get in the way of the sky. Although it is cloudy this morning, the sky is already looming large.

Pampa is Quichua for the space. As simple as that. You soon realize what a fine descriptive language Quichua is. There is a lot of pampa around. Santa Rosa is the capital of the La Pampa province, in the middle of some fierce flatness, some big space and some enormous estancias. I'd heard that the pampa is no longer the mystical sea of grass that Hudson, Cunninghame Graham and Martín Fierro kept on telling me about. I know that the lost cowboys, the wild bastards, the gauchos, the orphans of the pampa were lost and gone for ever. But there would still be big skies, big ranches, a pencil-sharp horizon and some bow-legged cowboys working a lot of cattle.

The shield of La Pampa is a classic piece of New World graphic heraldry. There is a straight line across the middle of the shield. Above it is solid bright blue, with a single tree growing into it from the straight line. Under the line it is green with the silhouette of a mounted gaucho riding along with a lance. When you leave the bus station and get out of town you see how true to life the shield actually is.

At the edge of town we passed a roundabout with an old Gloster Meteor in the centre. It was surprising to see a forty-year-old jet fighter stuck out here like a road sign but oddly it didn't seem out of place. It summed up the British domination of Argentine life. And we were on our way out to visit one of the old Anglo-Argentine estancias.

We had been met by Heather Randall who was taking us out into the flatness. Out to the family ranch. The morning sun, swimming up on to the horizon, flickered at us down along straight avenues of gum trees.

There is a lot of pampa around. Here, this is the *pampa semi-arida*. It is halfway between the desert of Patagonia and the wetter, thicker-grassed *pampa humida* found closer to BA. Here the soil is sandy and prone to erosion, not as rich as the *pampa humida*. They have to watch it. They long for rain.

'The sweetest sound after a drought is the sound of rain on the roof.'

A hot and dry month without a spot of rain had just been relieved by a good couple of days' downpour. Everything was encouragingly green. And the sky was turning bluer by the minute.

There is a huge prejudice against flat prairie lands. People warn you against them. Too flat, they tell you, as if to prepare you for the worst. It's like warning you that the sea is full of waves or that France is a bit on the French side. Can't they see beyond the obvious? Don't they look up into the sky? Aren't they touched by the illusory, magical quality of the plains?

The vastness of the horizon on the pampa means, simply, that whatever distance is covered, the horizon never gets closer. Out there reality and illusion ride side by side, and infinity beckons in between. Only the tired bones, the aching body tell us we have been travelling at all, for if we look, we have not moved. With infinity this close, God is tapping us on the shoulder, ready to sit down and have a chat.

In my wishful dreams I see the pampa in the 1860s or 1870s with the eyes of W. H. Hudson or the great and eccentric Robert Bontine Cunninghame Graham, Scottish laird, horseman, traveller, radical Member of Parliament, writer and Scottish gaucho. Out on the pampa they called him Don Roberto.

All grass and sky, and sky and grass and still more sky and grass, the Pampa stretched a thousand miles. Through all this ocean of tall grass, green in the spring, then yellow, and in the autumn brown as an old boot, the general characteristics were the same . . . A ceaseless wind ruffled it all and stirred its waves of grass. Innumerable flocks and herds enamelled it, and bands of ostriches ('Mirth of the Desert', as the gauchos called them) and herds of palish-yellow deer stood on the tops of the cuchillas and watched you as you galloped past . . .

Nothing but grass and sky and sky and grass and then more grass and still more sky. Nothing, for pampa means . . . a vast and empty space, empty, that is, of man and all his works, but full of sun and light . . .

It was the home of deer and ostriches, and of wild horses, dappled and pied, slate-coloured, roan, blood-bay, sorrel and dun, spotted like pudding-stone, calico, paint, buckskin, clay-bank, cream, and some the colour the Arabs call 'Stones of the River', they all were there, tossing their manes and whinnying for joy, leading their lives in that great grassy space, where there was nothing to be seen but grass and sky.

Robert Bontine loved his horses, especially out on the pampa.

Things have changed of course. On the drive out we passed enormous fenced-off pasture lands with herds of cattle grazing into the distance. In between were huge fields of sunflowers, maize, green alfalfa, occasional fields of rye and barley and the dusty burnt chocolate-brown of ripe sorghum. Most of these, apart from the sunflower oil, are used for cattle feed. Sorghum, very hardy and easy to grow, is used for commercial alcohol as well as feed. It is sometimes used in Old Smuggler. I'll stick to Breeder's Choice. It's commercial enough for me.

Heather Randall is slim and blonde and speaks with an Anglo-Argentine burr, a slight soft accent peppered with Spanish words or their anglicized equivalents. As in Patagonia, we are never in the country, always in the *camp*.

She was born Heather Dunn. The Dunn family have had the El Madroño estancia since 1907. Like all the great estancias from Buenos Aires to the southern tip of Patagonia, the land was given as a reward for help in the Indian clearances, General Roca's Wars of the Desert. El Madroño was repayment for a loan which helped finance the clearances.

It was originally presented to the Drysdale family in the 1880s. The Drysdales thought they had been ripped off, that the land was not worth a wooden peso and was poor recompense for their loan. The soil was thin and sandy, only four foot deep over the limestone bedrock, nowhere near as good as the *pampa humida*. More importantly, it was much too far from the Hurlingham Club in BA. Then Grandfather Dunn married a Drysdale and was only too happy to inherit the estancia from his wife.

It was a big one. We were back in the land of leagues. I realized I hadn't heard the word at all in Chile, even in the foothills of Salta. They didn't have 'the space' like there was here or down in Patagonia.

One hectare is two and a half acres. Five thousand hectares equal twelve thousand five hundred acres. But in the pampa it is easier to think of two square leagues, especially with the big estancias. El Madroño was one hundred and fifty thousand hectares, or three hundred and seventy-five thousand acres. Difficult to comprehend. The mind can cope better with sixty thousand square leagues.

The Drysdales and Dunns stayed in BA still convinced they had been short-changed on their loan to Roca. Twenty-odd years after acquiring the land they sent out a Mr Belcher, an Australian used to the wide spaces of the outback, to organize the estancia. He did well, building everything up from scratch: cattle, horses, barns, corrals, the estancia's hacienda, workshops, a blacksmith's forge, the peons' quarters and fences. He planted trees, started the battle against erosion of the sandy soil, and established fields and crops.

He kept a detailed day-to-day diary. He was devoted to his wife who died giving birth to their fourth child, George. The day she died was blank in the diary. He stuck a sprig of mimosa on to the page and wrote no more.

A nanny came out from BA to look after the kids. The pampa nights were lonely. He married her, had more kids and started a new diary. Later, as we were leaving, we saw one of Belcher's grandchildren arriving at the bus station.

There were more trees than I had expected. Being on the *pampa semi-arida* we were on the edge of the *monte*, the drier, thorny scrubland that takes over in the west as the pampa approaches the hills. The native trees are small, thorny, hard, twisted and with small leaves – dry land trees. *Chañar* and *calden* are the commonest. The *chañar* spreads south into Patagonia, into the semi-desert of the *chañar-steppe*. The *calden* – the Espinoso – is found to the west in the forests of the *monte*. Wild boar, pumas and deer live in the *calden* forests and wander down into La Pampa occasionally.

Calden trees have dark brown seed-pods like thin twirly carob. They are sweet and, like carob, are fed to cattle. The *calden* is also called the *chinchuline* tree because the seed pods, crisp and curly, look like well-cooked crunchy *chinchulines*, barbecued intestines, an *asado* favourite.

Other trees have been imported. Eucalyptus seem to grow higher here than in Australia. They are all over the *camp*. The cities have the English stamp on them and are full of plane trees.

The estancia is named after another imported tree, brought from Spain by Heather's grandfather. The *madroño* is the strawberry tree, *Arbutus undeo*, which has bright-red seed balls or 'fruits'. They are round, the size of cherries and the colour and texture of strawberries. They look like the small red plane-seed balls we collected in London. We used to break up the 'itchy balls' and stuff them down the neck of the kid in front of us in class to make them scratch and squirm.

The 'strawberries' of the *madroño* were traditionally used in Spain to decorate the women's dressy black mantillas. Against the dark, dense, shiny green of the foliage, the 'strawberries' certainly looked festive, as if someone had put them there to welcome us to the ranch.

Will Randall, Heather's husband, managed the estancia. A Canadian who had come down from Toronto to work on the pampa, he got a job on Ronald Dunn's estancia El Madroño, ended up managing it and married the boss's daughter. In his early forties, he moves quickly and commandingly. He has short, sturdy legs ideal for riding and seems very gaucho. He certainly looks gaucho in his working shirt, *bombachas*, *faja* and *alpargatas* on his feet. He is intensely involved in the running of the ranch and the raising of his livestock. For a city boy he is remarkably at home on the pampa.

His real passion is breeding cattle and the search for the perfect cross. He specializes in Brafords, a Hereford/Brahman cross. This cross has good size, good meat and is less hairy, with a smoother hide than a Hereford. He explained the complexities of how he matches bull to cow to achieve his aim of three-eighths Brahman, five-eighths Hereford. They have eight thousand head of cattle on El Madroño.

The horses they raise and use on the ranch are basically the short-legged, thick-necked criollos. They have fantastic stamina. Some of his horses have thoroughbred mixed in, as do the polo ponies. They are faster and more refined and they have longer legs, but they are also more highly strung and more skittish.

Recently, out of the blue, his main stud stallion was struck by lightning and killed. It was an act of God, a sign from above that he should change his breed. Now Will wants to breed in some American quarterhorse. Used by the North

American cowboys, the quarterhorse is ideal for working cattle and cuts into the herd better than either the creole or thoroughbreds.

On this part of the pampa the weather changes through the year. In spring the winds come, especially the *pampero* from the south. It is not as fiercely windy as Patagonia but then not many places are.

W. H. Hudson knew it well:

The general aspect of the plain is monotonous, and in spite of the unobstructed view, and the unfailing verdure and sunshine, somewhat melancholy, although never sombre: and doubtless the depressed and melancholy feeling the pampa inspires in those who are unfamiliar with it is due in a great measure to the paucity of life, and to the profound silence.

The wind, as may well be imagined on that extensive level area, is seldom at rest; there, as in the forest, it is a bard of many breathings, and the strings it breathes upon give out an endless variety of sorrowful sounds, from the sharp fitful sibilations of the dry wiry grasses on the barren places, to the long mysterious moans that swell and die in the tall polished rushes of the marsh.

Summer is hot, dry and dusty, when they pray for rain. Autumn, from March to May, is the most clement season, warm and pleasant, gentle and easy. In winter the temperature can drop to twelve degrees below freezing.

Last year they had a storm with hail stones as big, hard and heavy as cricket balls, four inches across, not much smaller than the biggest ever known. Windows were smashed, roofs damaged. Heather's father was caught in his car and had to sit in it while the storm passed. He was all right but the car was a write-off.

'We call this the penis.' Will fixed a long metal pole on to the front of the pick-up. It slipped on to a rod that ran underneath the length of the truck. As we drove out across the fields I saw why. We drove straight at the electric wire fences which were forced under the penis and slid under the truck as we passed over them. Prick-up truck?

We saw two of the peons, the gauchos, out riding in the fields. One wore a bright-blue crocheted tam, had heavy-lidded eyes, a poker face and a big belly. Very cool, he was called Lover Boy. He used to be slimmer and more handsome, but he had a lowering, smouldering charisma and still went into town in his pulling wagon, his Ford pick-up. He sat there silent and brooding as Will talked to them.

Will seemed as passionate about all aspects of the estancia as he was about his cattle and horse breeding. He bent my ear about the shallowness of the soil, the crop rotations needed to keep the soil nourished and stable, and his farm equipment. A second-hand articulated eight-wheel John Deere tractor had just cost them fifty thousand dollars, which was less than half price. When he started talking about the computers they were using now for farm management I tried to ease him over to the peons and their lives. Computers on the pampa I can do without.

W. H. Hudson never had a computer. In fact he probably wrote everything with a pencil, the original organic word processor. His descriptions of the tall pampa grasses, growing the full height of a man, give a good idea of the dangers as well as the joys of 'the space'.

Without his horse a gaucho was nothing. If he fell from his horse out on the pampa he was a dead man. He would drown in the sea of green and white, unable to see above the waving white heads of the pampa grass. No one would ever spot him. He would be a lost cowboy for sure. It was the same for the Indians:

I have ridden through many leagues of this grass with the feathery spikes high as my head, and often higher. It would be impossible for me to give anything like an adequate idea of the exquisite loveliness of this queen of grasses, the chief glory of the solitary pampa . . .

It covers large areas with a sea of fleecy white plumes; in late summer and in autumn the tints are seen, varying from the most delicate rose, a tender and illusive blush, to purple and violaceous . . . in the evening, the softened light imparts a mistiness to the crowding plumes . . .

The last occasion I saw the pampa grass in its full beauty was at the close of a bright day in March, ending in one of those perfect sunsets seen only in the wilderness, where no lines of house or hedge mar the enchanting disorder of nature, and the earth and sky tints are in harmony. I had been travelling all day with one companion, and for two hours we had ridden through the matchless grass, which spread away for miles on every side, the myriads of white spears, touched with varied colour, blending in the distance and appearing almost like the surface of a cloud.

Hearing a swishing sound behind us, we turned sharply round, and saw, not forty yards away in our rear, a party of five mounted Indians, coming swiftly towards us: but at the very moment we saw them their animals came to a dead halt, and at the same instant the five riders leaped up, and stood erect on their horses' backs. Satisfied that they had no intention of attacking us, and were only looking out for strayed horses, we continued watching them for some time, as they stood gazing away over the plain in different directions, motionless and silent, like bronze men on strange horse-shaped pedestals of dark stone; so dark in their copper skins and long black hair, against the far-off ethereal sky, flushed with amber light; and at their feet and all around, the cloud of white and faintly-blushing plumes. That farewell scene was printed very vividly on my memory . . .

Tambien was shaking me again. It was still dark. Time to get up to catch the beginning of the day with the gauchos.

Driving with Will in the pick-up across the estancia to the central corrals there was just enough light to see the mist. The dark uncertain outlines of gum trees were looming through the mist like threadbare ghosts. We passed close by a troop of horses, invisible until we were right on top of them, dark shapes standing stock still by the side of the track. Too early for them even to move their eyes, they gazed silently at us as we bumped and rolled past them over the ruts.

The wind was silent, still sleeping like the birds. The mists clung to the heavy dew on the ground. The wind pumps were quiet and still. As we got to the corrals a burning peach-coloured dawn was breaking, a fire smouldering behind the wispy eucalyptus and contorted *calden* trees. The wooden fences of the corral, the concrete dipping run, the barns, the stable with the men's tack, all seemed fragile and surreal as they seeped out of the mist.

Laughter, voices and the clattering of tins and kettles carried across from the bunkhouse. The peons were up, drinking their first maté, having the first smoke of the day, and talking dirty. They walked across to the tack room as silent as guilty schoolboys and saddled up, their *alpargatas* wet from the heavy dew. One brought in some cows, tied one to the outside of the corral fence and started milking it. A calf suckled on the unused teats as the man worked on the others.

The other peons rode off, their horses leaving trails of footprints in the dew. They were soon back, driving some young, year-and-a-half old bulls into the corral ready to start the morning's dipping. Full of adolescent hormones, several bulls went straight over and started urgently nuzzling the tethered milk cow through the corral fence.

Seeing a woman, especially one being milked, must have been too much for them. Maybe the sight of the suckling calf reminded them of something long forgotten. The pinging of the milk into the bucket broke the sleepy silence and marked the young bulls' eager snorting.

The fiery dawn had turned silver and the last of the mist had retreated to ground level like steam off the dew. Birds started singing. Outside the corrals the fields were suddenly full of March hares tearing around through the shallow mist.

The peons began dipping. They drove the bulls through a wooden chute which held a single steer at a time. A young man moved them through with a makeshift cattle prod, a bare wire looped over an electric wire overhead which he jabbed at the steer's rump. He was slim, fine featured and seemed a little reserved. Will told me he was gay.

'How do you know?'

'Because when he lived in the bunkhouse with the other men they all fucked him every night, passed him round like a whore.'

'And they're not gay?'

'Oh, no, no way.'

'You mean they fuck a young guy and they're not gay?'

'No, not at all. They're all real men, *muy gaucho*. Some are married, others like Lover Boy over there have women all over La Pampa. It was getting difficult, though, so now he lives with his mother and father away in the village.'

'And they know he's gay?'

'Sure, but they cope with it. And he's better off, although he's always been a quiet reserved lad. A bit repressed, I think. They've given up trying to marry him off. Still, he's only twenty-two and he's a good worker.'

The concrete trough, three foot wide and twenty yards long, was filled with a mucky brown mess, a daunting mixture of what looked like tar, shit and piss. Probably was. As the bulls came out of the chute they reared up wild-eyed, their long Brahman ears flapping and front legs flailing, and then plunged into the brown tarry shite. A dog snapped and yelped at them as they reared up and smashed down.

Four peons stood either side of the trough with long collared prongs, pushing the steers' heads right under the stinking slime as they swam for dear life to the other end and safety. I went over and took one of the prongs and had a go. Will warned me not to drop the prong into the foul mephitic mess or else I'd owe the men a *damajuana* – a demijohn, a ten-litre bottle – of wine. I held on to that prong. It was very hard work pushing those heads under, not surprisingly as the bulls must have weighed a ton each.

One young bull reared right up and over and fell backwards from a height, crashing into the dip. A hellish tidal wave of shite shot twenty foot into the air. I leapt backwards with the peons to avoid getting dipped. It just missed me.

Out at the other end, the dipped bulls stood, shaken and subdued, in a small corral. Steam rose from their humped backs as they licked the crap from the noses. They had been dipped for ticks, fleas and scab which I doubt had much chance of survival after that lot.

They dipped six hundred head of cattle that morning. Hard work if you can get it.

In a shady eucalyptus grove a steer is slaughtered. '*Carnear*', the Argentines call it, to make meat.

It is now eight o'clock in the morning. Hammer on the head, throat cut, so quick. Within minutes two peons have cut off its head and limbs, skinned it and hung it up. They winch it high on a harness hanging from a eucalyptus with its hide stretched out underneath to stop blood and guts soiling the ground as it is butchered. Up a gum tree. You could say that.

The carcase hangs from the tree by its hind legs, sinews and bones, blood on marble-white fascia, flesh hidden in its opalescent sheath. Suddenly, in one stroke, steaming guts spew out on to the hide. The estancia butcher, in *bombachas* and a baseball cap, clears the carcase and hangs out the best organs on a special bar. It's a vegetarian nightmare.

The heart, the *mollejas*, thyroid, the kidneys, the *tripa gorda*, the marrow gut from between the two stomachs, and most spectacularly the lovingly plaited intestines, *chinchulines*, all hang from the delicate eucalyptus like visceral leaves. *Chincho!* But I can't see any liver and I have noticed that liver, of all organs, is absent from most menus. Does he like liver? The butcher keeps working.

'Don't like the taste but some eat it.' Then he and his mate take turns at sawing the carcase down the middle of the spine. A few more minutes and they stagger off with the two sides of beef to the refrigerator. It is twenty-five past eight and everything has gone. There are fourteen peons working on the estancia and they make meat of one steer every week to ten days.

All cowboys and ranch hands, from Patagonia to Alberta, have a basic diet of beef, caffeine, tobacco and, when they can get hold of it, alcohol. These may take different forms in the different countries and some cowboys will have extras, but beef, caffeine and tobacco are always the bottom line.

The gauchos have the most limited of all the cowboy diets. Caffeine comes in abundance from the maté that they drink constantly. It is thought that maté must contain vitamin C, because gauchos, certainly in the past, existed on no more than meat, maté and tobacco. Like most cowboys, they never touched milk. Paradoxically, with all the cows around, milk has never been part of any cowboy diet. (The Mongols, of course, live on mare's milk, but that's another story.)

On the pampa, in the days when they wandered free, gauchos might carry some bleeding cuts of meat, and the tongue, hanging from their saddle. To cook an *asado*, they made fires with dung and dried animal bones, in the Indian way, because out on the pampa there were few trees and little wood to burn.

They were very wasteful when they were wild cattle hunters. They would kill an animal and take just the tongue and maybe some *matambre*, 'hunger killer', the meat between the ribs and the hide, a gaucho favourite, leaving the rest for the *caranchos*.

Another favourite was *asado con cuero*. For this the meat is cooked *asado*-style over a fire with the hide left on. The hide holds in the juices and flavour and serves as the plate. The *facón* is used to cut pieces of meat off the bone or the hide. It sounds easy, but to eat a meal with only a two-foot knife needs skill and dexterity.

The worst thing for gauchos was vegetables. They hated them, poured scorn on them, very like many Africans, and thought anyone who could eat them no better than an animal. Vegetables were definitely for poor people who were desperate and had lost all vestige of their pride.

Nowadays the peons, the ranch hands, still stick mainly to meat and maté, but they do have bread now. Fairly often on the estancia they will make a big stew with a lot of meat and bits, now adding some potatoes, carrots and onions. But it's still mostly meat.

By midday back at the hacienda the parrots were going great guns. Bright green and very noisy, they sometimes got too much for Will. If he was trying to have a siesta he'd go outside and shoot a gun to scare them off. Today thousands of chattering parrots clustered in the trees round the hacienda but it had already been a long day and no one had any difficulty sleeping. Insomnia was the least of Martín Fierro's worries:

> At the peaceful hour of the afternoon,
>> When everything seems to doze;
>>> When the winds lie down on the prairie's breast,
>>> And the whole wide world seems to turn to rest;
> To some swamp or brake, with his load of care,
>> The homeless gaucho goes

After a rest we went riding right round the estancia in the old family two-horse buggy. Then I swopped with Heather and rode Tracey, a light brown criollo/thoroughbred. Very sweet tempered, she cantered nicely.

'*Manso como para un ingles*' – just the way I like them.

One field we rode through had eight hundred head of cattle in it. I'd never seen so many cattle in one field. I told the others I'd catch them up.

I wanted to do something I hadn't done since I was a child. I remember sitting in a field and waiting for the cows to come over and check me out. There hadn't been eight hundred of them, though, so I tethered Tracey to a fence post and walked towards the herd who watched me silently. I sat down.

Slowly, trying to pretend they weren't moving, the cattle started to shuffle across. As I sat quiet and still, more and more joined in, faster and less surreptitiously. It was not quite a stampede, but within minutes I was surrounded. Wet noses came right up to me and then as the sky was crowding out I jumped up and went 'Boo!'

They turned and scuttled off fast, all eight hundred, and I got back on to Tracey and rode off to join the others. Simple pleasures.

I caught up with the others in a field with both the sublime and the ridiculous in the same space. Looking west, with the sun on its trail towards the horizon, are a troop of horses, mares and fillies, the criollo/thoroughbred mix again. Mostly bays and chestnuts, the sun glints auburn in their tails and manes. Slender, fine-featured and long-legged, standing quietly and gently grazing, they are beautiful, the essence of grace, delicacy and sensitivity.

Turn round from this ethereal serenity, this vision of pre-Raphaelite heaven, and there is a small herd of young bulls . . . *the gladiators*!! The bulls are fully grown, huge, monolithic two-ton beef mountains, monsters with bollocks the size of footballs. So much testosterone is pumping through these animals that they are doing what any hard man worth his hormones would do. They are eyeballing each other, head down, shoulders hunched up, puffing and snorting violently.

Several are head-butting each other. They charge and smash their heads together mindlessly. The ground shakes like an earthquake with the sound of distant thunder, and dust, sweat and steam rise up. There is something wondrous in their awesome power and something puny and laughable in their slavery to their hormones.

The dogs found a *peludo*, a hairy armadillo. They batted it around with their snouts and their paws as it curled up into a tight ball, hanging on for dear life. The dogs tore and bit at it. Every now and then, when the onslaught waned, the armadillo would uncurl and try to make a run for it. No chance; the dogs would be on to it again in a flash, attacking it savagely.

'They have fun with the *peludos*,' said Will.

We rode on.

Nearly back at the house at the end of the day the sun is sinking over my shoulder. Down on the ground by a fence post I see my first burrowing owls. It's surprising it has taken so long as they are very common and don't hide away. They live in burrows they make in the ground but they spend a lot of time standing around outside. There were two of them and the low sun caught their big amber eyes as they glared at us. They stood stock still, almost formal, standing to attention at the mouth of their burrow.

Always there are two of them. Burrowing owls are like swans, devoted and monogamous for life.

Hudson said: 'Not a retiring owl this . . . it stands exposed . . . staring at the passer-by with an expression of grave surprise and reprehension in its round yellow eyes; male and female invariably together, standing stiff and erect, almost touching – of all birds that pair for life, the most Darby and Joan like.'

I never think. I rode Tracey all afternoon without a thought. We trotted and cantered but most of the time Tracey did the Argentine criollo walk, a combination of both, a lazy and easy canter with the front legs and a trot on the rear. I sat on Heather's grandmother's old leather Mexican saddle. It was a women's saddle, too small for me, and I rode her with the stirrups too high and, worst of all, wearing nothing but my Bermuda shorts.

But excuses are like arseholes, as the cowboys always say. Everybody's got one and they all stink. By the end of the afternoon I had two fine saddle-sores either side of the bony base of my spine. They call them medallions – *medallones* – down here and Heather gave me some *bife de chorizo*, a big bleeding steak, to slap on them. It helped but was a bit ungainly.

At the end of the day Will did an *asado* with the finest crunchiest *chinchulines* I'd ever had. We talked of meat and maté and I adjusted the *bife* in my pants. *Lomo*, fillet, he told us, is the long strip of muscle inside the ribs. Why is fillet steak so tender? Because the only work the fillet does is in pissing, when the muscle arches the animal's back very slightly. Nothing else. The pissing muscle.

It was a crystal clear night. Firebugs burnt bright phosphorus in the trees and the stars were shining out. The Southern Cross pointed south, of course, Orion was a familiar shape up there, and the full moon grinned at us upside down and sideways, smiling and standing on its head, a reminder that we were on the other side of the world.

A week later they are branding younger steers. The El Madroño brand is an inverted wishbone with a D for Dunn inside it. It's called the Lucky D. They do the branding in the corral. The cattle for branding today are kids compared to the adolescent bruisers that struggled through the shite before. They ran the dip into a drain-off pit and are using the same chute. A dome-shaped kiln stands with its mouth facing the chute. Half a dozen branding irons are heating up in the furnace. Each iron is over three foot long with an eight-inch wooden handle at one end and the Lucky D glowing red at the other.

Things get pretty gaucho. The sensitive lad prods the cattle through and shuts a gate behind each one to pen him in. Another peon stands beside him up on the boardwalk that runs beside the chute. His mate is at the kiln cooking up the irons. When a steer is ready, he pulls an iron out and throws it in an arc over to the man on the boardwalk, a distance of about ten foot. One end is wooden and the other is red hot. The man catches the wooden end every time.

He turns and brands the animal, then tosses the iron back. The kiln man catches it perfectly every time. He turns and sticks the hot Lucky D end, hissing and spluttering, into a bucket of water to clean it then digs it back into the fire. In the same time they have moved the steer on and the branding man is ready for the next iron. He doesn't have to wait. It is already on its way.

The whole thing has a beautiful rhythm. And with the sound of the hissing water, the noise of the cattle and the smell of the burning hides it is as gaucho as they get. They don't wear gloves. That wouldn't be gaucho at all.

The *bombachas* and *alpargatas* seem to be the only gaucho gear the peons wear universally now. Some wear berets, and some old-fashioned peaked cloth caps. No *facón* in the belt, like the Hallidays in the deep south, but their habits were still strongly rooted in gaucho tradition. They rode all day and they used the multi-layered sheepskin-covered *recado*. Like all cowboys, they prefer to be on horseback all the time but as ranch hands they know they have to do their fair share of fencing, dipping and branding.

I drank maté with them. They drank it scaldingly hot but softened with sugar. I thought the natural unsweetened maté taste was much more gaucho, but the burnt lips made up for it in manliness.

They were proud, not light on *gauchismo* if Lover Boy was anything to go by. Any man who can look macho, hard and heavy-lidded in a bright-blue crocheted tam that resembles a tea cosy has got to have gaucho blood running thick in his veins.

Even when a gaucho had his horse out in the ocean of grass it was still easy to get lost on the pampa. It was hard to see distinguishing features. There were none. Like cowboys and plainsmen around the world, they would sleep with their heads pointing in the direction of their journey. The stars at night were essential. Martín Fierro swore by them:

> For there's never a man that rides the plains,
>> But holds the stars for friends,
>>> He's never alone 'neath the star-strewn sky,
>>> Where the Three Marias shine on high;
> The twinkling stars are the gaucho's guide,
>> When by night o'er the plains he winds . . .
>
> A great green plain ringed rim to rim
>> With a sky of unbroken blue;
>>> It's death if once you lose your way
>>> And here and there you begin to stray,
> The man who would cross it should mark this well
>> That now I tell to you.
>
> See every day, that your course you lay
>> And watch that you hold it dead;
>>> Don't loiter or waver or roam around,
>>> Just do your damndest to cover ground;
> When you sleep be sure that the way you go
>> You're pointing with your head.
>
> Mark well the place on the desert's face
>> Where the sun shows its first red rim;
>>> If there's mist or cloud at the dawning light,
>>> And you can't get a sight of the sun – sit tight;
> The desert waits for the man that strays
>> And it makes short work of him.

While some dream on misty-eyed about the old lost days, the wild gauchos and their freedom, and can recite more of 'Martín Fierro' from memory than is probably healthy, there are many who see this as nostalgic wallowing rather than going back to the roots. If you want to go forward, they say, you shouldn't look back. Certainly the gauchos' way of life, like that of the cowboys of the old West, has been grossly sentimentalized. Hindsight may be 20/20, they say, but don't use rose-tinted glasses.

This is in effect a continuation of the historic prejudice against gauchos as retrogressive, primitive and barbaric, stopping the advance of civilization just as the Indians did. They were at the heart of the battle between the wealthy European aspirations of the powerful elite in Buenos Aires, maintained by

English money, and the stubborn savages out in the *camp*. They had to be brought to heel, to be fettered, to be hamstrung like the wild cattle they hunted, in the name of progress.

For some Argentines, particularly modern estancieros like Will Randall, gaucho literature and the songs of the *payadores*, the troubadours, are anathema. I said how much I liked sad songs, how listening to a sad song doesn't bring me down at all but cheers me up. It reminds us that however bad things are looking there is always some way through.

A sad song, be it Country, Irish, Mexican or Argentine, helps us triumph over adversity rather than making us indulge our own pain, I said to him:

And now begins the saddest part
  Of my tale of trouble and grief,
    Although the whole of my life, God knows,
    Has been nothing more than a chain of woes
  Yet the suffering soul that sings its dole,
    In singing finds relief.

But like those who can't cope with what they see as the maudlin, over-emotional side of Country, Will wouldn't have it.

Sitting under the *calden* tree, fiddling with the chitterling seed-pods in the golden light of the autumnal full moon, he told me of Argentina's great and exciting future. There is no place for those old gaucho songs and those sad stories in the days ahead, he said. They don't really give us any sense of heritage, he said. All they do is pull us back into a reactionary morass of sentimentality. Good riddance to the old wild gauchos, he said, cutting a piece of beef off his *asado* with his *facón*. Who needs them?

A lot of what he said I agreed with. But I remembered the heart-stopping yodelling of the high soaring *baguala* voice in Salta, snapped a *chinchuline* pod and stared hard and long at the big yellow upside-down moon.

9. The Singing Cowboy

Will Randall was right, of course. We must go forward. The past is past and there's no point in nostalgic wallowing. But we can look at it, and learn from it, without hankering about it. As a piece of graffiti on the wall of a Texas toilet said, 'History is a vast early warning system'. I took note.

People like Will feel encumbered, held back by the past and only want to look in the one direction. Having suffered the ravages of the English educational system, I was relishing all these new stories, an innocent abroad basking in a newly revealed truth. The cowboy trail was, more through luck than judgement, taking me to the heart of hispanic America.

As we crossed the pampa on our way back to Buenos Aires I kept thinking of the gaucho singers and the pampa troubadours. Some North American cowboys did sing slow soothing songs to the cattle on a long trail drive, but not nearly as much as they did in the movies, and nowhere near as much as the gauchos.

The gauchos were much more likely to carry a small guitar and sing to each other in the *pulperias*, the Argentine equivalent of a combined saloon and general trading post. They could buy maté and tobacco, sell hides and tallow, and get drunk and sing songs. Even though the *pulperias* would be the only buildings for miles, out in the middle of nowhere, they were also called the *esquina*, the 'corner store'. They didn't have showgirls or whores, 'fallen angels' or 'soiled doves of the prairies', like they did in the western saloons, but sometimes with luck there might be one in the vicinity.

The *pulperia* was the hub of the gauchos' social life. It was a rough and rowdy place. Fights were common. Gauchos were arrogant, cruel and callous, but strangely punctilious within their own peculiar code. Life was cheap and killing was easy, even a pleasure, but only according to the rules.

They never carried guns. Real men fought with knives. Superstitious gauchos thought that some men could not be killed with guns; these invincible men were called *retobados* which meant 'wily' or 'cunning'. There was still the strict code, and any gaucho who got too drunk and pulled out his *facón* unprovoked was being almost obscene. Ezequiel Marquez Estrada said: 'The *facón* is not part of the costume but part of the body itself. It pertains more to the man than to his apparel, more to his character than to his social status. He who shows his knife when there is no need for it commits an indecent act.'

When it was appropriate and they did fight, they held their *facóns* in one hand and ponchos in the other. The poncho was used as a shield and as a weapon to blind or trip the opponent. The aim of a fight, within the gaucho code, was simply to mark someone's face, to show them you've won. Often it didn't stop at that. If it went to killing, throat cutting was the gaucho way, just as they did with cattle. Instant and certain. They called it 'playing the violin'.

Playing the guitar was a different kind of fight and one they liked as much as the violin. If a gaucho was singing, another would often pull his guitar out and challenge him to a musical duel. This sort of battle between two troubadours was common.

The troubadour tradition is very old. It comes from twelfth-century Andalucia. With that ancestry it has a strong Moorish stamp, just like their horses and saddles and *bombachas*. When they improvise their long songs, and do battle with words and music, their Arab blood is coming through.

In Spain this sort of song duel is called *contrapunto*. Here it is a *payada*. The singer, if he is worth his salt, is a *payador*. The best *payadors* make up the best verses. They must sing and play their guitar well, but the most important thing is to be sharp-witted. The battle is in the words and it all has a strict structure, rule and canon.

The singer starts by introducing himself and by making extravagant boasts – 'I'm the greatest, this guy is crap. Even without a guitar and a lost voice I'd still beat him,' and so on. This can take a long time.

Then the other chips in. They throw down musical gauntlets, verses for the other to beat or complete, riddles to trip them up or be thrown back. It is the wit of the answer, the turning round of an insult, the grace of the escape from a trap thrown down that makes a winner. They would sing of the day and the company, of mundane things, of wrongs and injustices and the hardships of life, of God and a gaucho philosophy, of the impossibility of love. And all the time they would try to stump the opponent.

The whole of 'Martín Fierro' is a long song in this style and with this archaic troubadour structure. It is full of rhyming battles. No wonder they sang it in the *pulperías*.

I am the best of my own at home,
   And better than best afar;
      I have won in song my right of place,
      If any gainsay me – face to face,
Let him come and better me, song for song,
      Guitar against guitar.

We kept on rolling across the *pampa humida*. The horizon got no nearer. It was marshy, green and flooded, with a lot of waterfowl. Snow-white egrets pecked at the pastures around grazing herds of black cattle. Feathery white-topped shocks of pampa grass, the remnants of the great sea, exploded at random out of the shorter grass like a cartoon minefield.

It was a warm autumn day in March. Sunflower and maize were growing between the pasture land. Grain silos, with a central pipe radiating out to the circular elevators around them, looked like frozen carousels. The horizon got even straighter and still no nearer.

Small identical pampa towns kept passing. I could tell they weren't the same town over and over because the names were different, Spanish, Indian, English, they went from Juan J. Paso to Trenque Lauquen to Henderson. In each little town I wondered who was the local hero. Who was the best *payador*? This part of the pampa, the old home of the Querandi Indians, used to be rich in song.

There have been some famous *payadors*. The greatest of all time was indisputably Santos Vega, one of the great homeric figures of the pampa. He is still thought of, sung about and, at times out on the pampa, still seen.

Being a *payador* was like being a notorious gunfighter, the fastest draw in the West. The word got out. All the young guys came for you. So it was for Santos Vega. Wherever he went he was constantly challenged to a *payada*. Singers came from far and wide to match verses and wit with him. It was what he did best and he was happy to take on all comers. He was so far ahead of anyone he was untouchable. He made up the fastest verse in the west.

Then one day, the story goes, he was approached by a mysterious stranger dressed all in black. The stranger kept his hood up and no one could see his face. They sang and played in the shade of an enormous *ombú* tree, a dark lowering tree with huge buttressed roots.

They threw down the gauntlets, challenged and accepted according to the strict rules. The guitars clashed. They pitched couplets of amazing simplicity and depth at each other. The songs flashed back and forth like gleaming *facóns*. The onlookers gasped. Santos Vega was struggling and looked like he might have met his match. They rhymed and riddled, they lunged and parried with their verses. They tossed subtle shades of meaning like ponchos into each other's eyes.

Finally the black-robed stranger drew back and put his guitar down. He had beaten Santos Vega. He turned on his heel and left and still no one saw his face. All that remained in the dark shadow of the *ombú* was a strong whiff of sulphur hanging in the air.

They say it must have been the Devil.

Whoever it was, Santos Vega never recovered from his defeat. He died of a broken heart a few days later. To this day, on dark moonless nights a solitary horseman with a guitar across his back rides slowly and sadly across the great flat space between Dolores and Tuyú enveloped in an echoing cloud of song.

Another of the great *payadors* and gauchos became Argentina's first dictator, a blueprint for the years to come. An infamous singing cowboy, he sang better, he rode better, he threw the *bolas* better than any other gaucho. He was unstoppable. He was Juan Manuel de Rosas, the Blue-Eyed Gaucho.

After all these years there is still controversy about Rosas. Most see him as a bloodthirsty, self-serving despot, which he undoubtedly was. There are others, however, who feel he was an early saviour of the Argentine, a nationalist when everyone else was selling the country down the River Plate.

Rosas was a real cowboy in all the senses of the word. For a start, no one could match him for horsemanship. He rode horses, broke horses, lived on horseback. He liked to beat all comers at a gaucho game called *maroma*. This involved standing on a bar over the gate to a corral. The gate was opened and the gaucho would leap through the air on to a wild horse's back as it raced out underneath the bar to freedom. He would ride it, hanging on to its mane, and stay with it until it was broken or exhausted.

Another of Rosas' favourites was *pialar*, marginally more dangerous and foolhardy than *maroma* and therefore a bit more exciting. The word meant 'to lasso an animal by the legs', which is exactly what the game was about. A rider would gallop at high speed down a battery of gauchos twirling lassoes over their heads. As he rode past, the gauchos would lasso his horse's flying legs. The animal would suddenly be pulled crashing to the ground and the rider would be thrown off violently. The idea was for the rider to land sweetly on his feet with the horse's reins still in his hand. A survival game, it was based on skills a gaucho needed to survive out on the empty pampa. The plains were honeycombed with burrows from owls, *vizcachas* and hares and even the most sure-footed horse was bound to trip now and then.

To know how to fall is as important as to know how to ride. Gauchos say that you have to fall at least eleven times before you can consider yourself a horseman. Just as important out on the pampa, the gaucho needed to know how to hold on to his mount. Lost in the tall grass without a horse, he was a dead man.

Juan Manuel de Rosas knew how to fall. Brought up on his family's estancia on the pampa in south Buenos Aires province, he learned the gaucho ways better than any. He became a powerful *caudillo* and one of the first in his province with a new meat-salting plant. A stench rose from his *saladero* as every last bit of the horses and cattle that went into it was processed into salted meat, hides, hair, tallow and melted hooves. The products were sent straight to England. Rosas became very rich.

Since independence there had been constant fighting, mostly between the Federalists out in the country and the Unitarists holding the profitable reins of power in Buenos Aires. Being a country boy, he stood with the other Federalists, fighting the monopoly of Buenos Aires. Ironically, it was the *porteños* who asked Rosas to be governor in 1829 even though he had already led troops against the city. By this time the chaos of anarchy and civil war was too much for them and they needed the iron hand of a strong *caudillo*. They got it.

He became all powerful very quickly. He ran the country like it was his own estancia. He was the blue-eyed gaucho and all the gauchos idolized him. He was larger than life, a hero to many of the country people. But he became less of a Federalist as he became more powerful, though he paid lip service to his country roots and forced everyone to wear a bit of red, the Federalist colour.

He is most remembered and damned for his tyrannical despatch of his enemies. He silenced his opponents and critics by intimidation, torture, exile, jail and death – but always singing and looking sharp in the gaucho way. It was the most personal of tyrannies.

He always dressed gaucho. He met Lord Ponsonby, England's finest and the man who created Uruguay, wearing his smartest striped *chiripa* pulled nappy-like over his broad white-laced and fringed linen *calzoncillos*, his under-trousers, and his open-toed boots with spurs on. He had his broad gold-coin-covered *rastra*, a big rosista jacket and open shirt and his red rosista cap, like a French revolutionary tam. He was charming and probably offered Ponsonby maté. He certainly offered it to Charles Darwin.

Darwin had been up and down the Argentine coast in the *Beagle* once too often. He got sick, hated sea travel anyway, and decided to strike out across the pampa and meet the boat back in Buenos Aires. Some might have called him foolhardy. The pampa was full of hostile Indians and he went without a guard and with only one companion. Out in 'the space' he stumbled across Rosas' camp:

General Rosas is a man of extraordinary character; he has at present a most predominant influence in his country and may probably end up by being its ruler. He is moreover a perfect gaucho; his feats of horsemanship are very notorious. He will fall from a doorway upon an unbroken colt, as it rushes out of the corral, and will defy the worst efforts of the animal.

He wears the Gaucho dress and is said to have called upon Lord Ponsonby in it, saying at the time he thought the costume of the country the proper and therefore the most respectful dress. By these means he obtained an unbounded popularity in the Camp, and in consequence despotic power.

A man a short time since murdered another; being arrested and questioned he answered, 'the man spoke disrespectfully of General Rosas and I killed him', in one week's time the murderer was at liberty. In conversation he is enthusiastic, sensible and very grave. His gravity is carried to a high pitch.

While Rosas was out in the pampa entertaining naturalists and slaughtering Indians, clearing the land for more estancias and more *saladeros*, his wife Doña Encarnacion had organized the first death squads, the hated *mazorca*, and was piling on the pressure to have him brought back with greater powers and ultimately supreme dictatorship. It worked, and it was then the Argentine had its first lesson in brutal governmental repression and murder. He closed schools and banned books. Executions were now much more in favour than exile, and carried out in the gaucho way. This sort of brutality may have been happening for years with the far-flung *caudillos*, but Rosas' regime institutionalized it.

The *mazorca* called at night. They played the violin, cut throats, cut out tongues, castrated and lanced their victims. The lancing was done by two men, one on each side of the prisoner, running their lances into the victim simultaneously from opposite sides. One is enough to kill a man. The second pushed the message home. This primitive and ritualistic gaucho blood-letting created such a climate of fear that Rosas rode supreme through the Argentine for more than twenty years. The blue-eye gaucho.

Some say he is reviled not by the people but by Britain and the *porteño* elite. He brought protectionist tariffs back to promote home-gown industry and break the British stranglehold on the country. What stuck in his craw more than anything was that everything the ordinary gaucho out in the *camp* was wearing at that time was manufactured in England.

The British Consul in 1837 was Woodbine Parish. Describing the gaucho, Woodbine writes: 'Take his whole equipment – examine everything about him – and what is there not of rawhide that is not British? If his wife has a gown, ten to one it is made in Manchester; the camp-kettle in which he cooks his food, the earthenware he eats from, the knife, his poncho, spurs, bit, are all imported from England.'

By this time Britain had the continent sewn up. They took all the raw materials and sold back the manufactured goods. They were so good at it they even managed to sell ice-skates to Brazil, no mean achievement in a tropical country. They sold paving stones to the whole continent, brought back as ballast in the ships come to collect all the cheap raw materials.

Agents from Manchester, Liverpool and Glasgow toured Argentina and copied ponchos from Cordoba and Santiago del Estero, leather goods and wooden stirrups from Corrientes. Native industries were struggling to establish themselves. They were systematically destroyed by the British. Ponchos from Cordoba cost seven pesos, from Yorkshire three. And the same went for shirts, bandanas, boots, spurs, *bolas*, *chiripas* bridles, *facóns* from Sheffield, *calzoncillos* from Manchester. England could undercut everybody.

So Rosas' heresy was to introduce protectionism to encourage home manufacture. In fact places like Tucuman and Cordoba started turning out textiles again, and Mendoza wines were plentiful. But Rosas was too much of a gaucho, got too interested in all the money coming through Buenos Aires, and failed to establish a unified industrial policy. In the end he stayed true to his own roots, and his own interest, which were the large beef estancias in Buenos Aires province.

The British wouldn't have it, of course, and sent in the gunboats. No cowboy was going to put chains across the river and stop them trading with the world. They encouraged other Argentines, the kind of people they could better do business with, the reasonable, urbane people who finally overthrew Rosas in 1852.

The English, on hand as usual, were only too happy to take the defeated dictator and his daughter off the Argentines' hands and give him a home in England. He spent the last twenty-five years of his life, and the rest of his fortune, trying to recreate his estancia near Southampton. He is buried there.

The ruling elite of Argentina hate the blue-eyed gaucho. They passed a law in 1857 which found him 'guilty of treason to the fatherland'. They have never annulled it. The Argentines wouldn't have the Singing Cowboy's bones back in the land for all the maté in Paraguay. They are far too superstitious.

We were getting closer to BA. It was still flat but there were more houses and more trucks on the road. It was becoming more civilized. I thought of the Buenos Aires of Mitre, Sarmiento and Avellaneda. Sarmiento had a printing press on an oxcart in the final campaign against Rosas, pumping out propaganda condemning him as a tyrant. They were the educators, the intellectuals, the ones who hated gauchos. They were determined to extirpate the barbaric elements within the Argentine, the gauchos and *caudillos*. Rosas had been more than enough, a terrible scourge on the nation. They must never again lose their grip on the reins of power. If they were going to destroy the troublesome Indians, they might as well deal with the gauchos at the same time. They were all the same anyway.

Gauchos, on the bottom rung of white Christian Argentine society, looked down on Indians as 'savages', although they were more than half Indian themselves. Sarmiento detested the gauchos and called them 'biped animals of the most perverse stripe', good for nothing but to fertilize the earth with their carcases.

They press-ganged the gauchos into the army and let them die miserably out on the frontier fighting the Indians. President Mitre led wars to exterminate them. They were never the same again – until of course they became mythologized and sanitized as the true bearers of the flame of the soul of Argentina.

Do me a *gauchada*.

Well, they managed it. They kept the riff-raff out and made Buenos Aires smart and sophisticated. Kept the country cousins firmly in their place. The only gauchos you find in BA now work as *asadors* in the best restaurants. They look faintly out of place and pose with diners in snaps for the family album.

Good breezes are gently blowing down the wide green avenues of BA as we come in. Autumn trees are in flower. Lilac chandeliers of jacaranda flowers are tinkling in the huge clouds of drooping feathery leaves high above our heads. The trees are swelling oceans of delicate waving fronds whispering to the sky, higher than houses. We drive through swaying tunnels of them, the filigree branches tickling the buildings like feather dusters.

The *palo borracho*, the 'drunken stick' tree, lives up to its name. Carrying the large star-shaped white and pink flowers are the pot-bellied, leaning trunks, lurching down the sides of the big avenues like petrified drunkards.

It is a soft day and the city lives up to its promise of good airs, even though it was named not for the gentle antipodean breezes sweeping down the wide avenues but after the patron saint of the winds that carried the European navigators safely across the wide seas. Tambien said it meant 'good tunes' and promised me some mighty tango.

Before that we needed our daily hit of black pudding, so we went on the trail to find the best *morcillas* in town. It was an enthusiast's trail, one worth following because there wasn't a bad one anywhere; it was the best black pudding in the world. We were ready for the ecstasy.

They may have killed off the gauchos long ago but the heavy meat diet gets everywhere. Tambien and I couldn't get enough and by this time in the journey were eating only meat, gaucho style. Nothing else, only meat. No vegetables. The meat is perfect organic food, so it was not difficult. If vegetables were brought we asked for them to be taken away. I couldn't stand the sight of them; they were as obscene as an unjustified *facón* in a *pulpería*. I tried a chip once and it tasted awful. Dead vegetables? No thanks. Had to go back to the nice fresh-tasting flesh.

Having been through advanced states of macrobiosis in another life, I would have expected all that dead meat to make us feel heavy, solid, full, windy, spotty, macho and aggressive. In a word, all Yanged out. Instead, to my surprise, after three weeks of wolfing down nothing but big plates of beef, pig's blood and various bits of intestine and thyroid, both Tambien and I felt light, lively, clear, fresh-complexioned, active and at peace with ourselves and the world. And never farted once.

The *porteños* are *muy gaucho* in their eating habits for people too sophisticated to drink maté in public. (It is too Pampabilly for them.) They dress up smart to go out, conscious of their appearance, quite chic – but when that lump of meat arrives, watch out!

Chow down! The tools are grabbed, the elbows go flying out to each side and they attack their meat, hacking pieces off and jamming them into their mouths. All ages, too. Three-year-olds chomp *bifes* and jump up and down on their chairs. Delicate old grannies in their eighties look like they might just manage half a poached egg – until the meat comes. Young lovers gaze tenderly into each other's eyes, holding hands, softly touching across the table – until the meat comes.

Then for lovers, grannies, mums and dads and toddlers, up go the elbows and whack! in goes the beef. So Tambien and I were not alone in our lust for flesh. Except that a lot of them would eat much later than us. When we crept out wimpishly to go home around midnight, *porteños* would be pouring in the doors to go on attacking their few pounds of steak and organs into the not-so-early hours of the morning.

When we got back from the pampa I missed the space and needed some comfort food so we headed off to eat meat. La Estancia on Lavalle is a favourite. Huge, packed with Argentines stuffing themselves, there is a big *asado* by the door with carcases, goat and beef, angled round it on cruciform spits. And there are the gauchos, two *asadors* in full gaucho gear, turning the spits, raking the coals and mopping their brows.

Inside it's cavernous, like a smart meaty Jo Lyons café, with rows upon rows of tables. It has a big primitive mural down one side of the room, of corrals, steers and gauchos out on the Estancia. Home on the ranch. It is a palace of meat.

As an unexpected bonus the staff all seemed to have been supplied by Central Casting. Arthur Lowe was working the *asado*, looking chubby and sweating over the coals. Arthur still kept on his sombrero, a surprisingly broad-brimmed black one, and had his *facón* stuck into the back of his *rastra*, and his *bombachas* tucked into his high black boots. They did not have open toes. Arthur is not that gaucho. Over on the *parilla* was Lee Van Cleef, down on his luck and taking what work he could find.

There were two maître d's in full black tie. They would walk down between the tables with new arrivals, turn, wave one arm at an empty table, allow a peremptory smile to flicker across their face, pull their hand back, drop their smile and walk back impassively to lean on the receptionist's desk and get on with their chat. The puzzling thing was, one was Stalin and the other Hitler. I know they never found Adolf in his bunker, but I'd seen Uncle Joe, or at least that's who they told me it was, lying in the orange glow of his mausoleum back in the fifties, so I wasn't sure what was going on. For what it's worth, Stalin smiled a little more than Hitler.

Harry Worth and Lionel Jeffries were two of the waiters and like the others wore short white waiters' jackets. Tambien and I were looked after disconcertingly by Norman Lamont, who seemed quite worried that he might be recognized while moonlighting. They all carried the tea cloth folded over the crooked left arm.

The action that night at La Estancia was fast and furious. With queues outside, the waiters were flying past the tables with five dishes on each arm. There are a hundred and thirty tables and forty waiters serve twelve hundred people on a Saturday night, the place packed from eight in the evening until four the next morning. People are still coming in to chow down at three. It is a gold mine.

*

The tradition of obsessional flesh eating was established in the River Plate area as soon as the conquistadors tried to set foot there. They all thought the wide muddy estuary was going to be the gateway to fabulous riches.

The ill-fated Juan Diaz de Solis, the first to set eyes on it in 1516, thought it was a passage to the legendary kingdoms of Orphir and Tarsis and all the bounty of the east. He called it the *mar dulce*, the sweet sea, and landed with six men. He was greeted and soon enough captured by some Querandi tribesmen. In full view of his chronicler back on the ship, the Indians killed Juan and his men and ritually ate them.

In 1526 Sebastian Cabot was lured here by tales of a mountain of silver. The mountain existed, but at Potosí in Alto Peru on the other side of the continent. Cabot optimistically called the murky brown waters the Rio de la Plata, the River of Silver, the River of Money. Why is the River of Money the colour of shit? Cabot and some of his men were also captured by Indians but not eaten this time. Ten years before the Querandi had found Juan and his men tough, stringy and indigestible, not to their liking at all. The word had got out that these white men were very poor quality meat.

Cabot got some silver trinkets from the friendlier Guarani tribes upriver and went back to Spain convinced he was on the verge of a major discovery. He built a settlement, the first on the River Plate. It was immediately attacked, razed to the ground and the inhabitants slaughtered.

It did not get easier. The Spanish were still convinced that the Money River would hit the jackpot sooner or later. They sent a nobleman, Pedro de Mendoza, with the biggest force the New World had ever seen, 1600 soldiers in fourteen ships. He also brought thirteen mares and three stallions.

He built another settlement but still found no trace at all of silver or gold. His men abused the Indians and their women, and forced them to bring them food. The Indians, who had started by being friendly, were outraged.

In eighteen months two-thirds of the settlement had been wiped out by war, starvation and disease. Survival was not easy. A foot soldier wrote: 'The situation was so terrible that it was not enough to just eat rats and mice, reptiles or insects. We had to eat our shoes and leather and everything else.' 'Everything else' turned out to be other members of the settlement. Three thieves who had stolen and eaten a horse were hanged in the main square. In the carnivorous spirit of the times, other settlers hacked off their calves and thighs and took them back home for an *asado*. Meat was top of the menu right from the beginning.

Soon after, twenty-three thousand Indians attacked with flaming arrows, setting fire to the houses of the settlement and destroying four ships. They had

had enough and so had Mendoza. He gave up and retreated to the remaining ships, sailing upriver to calmer waters. They left their horses which escaped into the wild and started to spread over the pampa.

The Spanish settled at Asunción in Paraguay, where the Guarani, who had given Cabot the silver baubles, were much friendlier and the women more compliant. Unfortunately, Mendoza caught syphilis and died before he got back to Spain. They say his body was thrown into the River Plate and that the only gold ever found in the muddy waters of the Money River was the rings on Pedro de Mendoza's syphilitic fingers.

Nowadays, the average consumption of meat per head is around four pounds a week. Not surprisingly, heart attacks are more common here than anywhere in the world apart from Glasgow.

The day after our carnivorous frenzy at La Estancia, disturbing figures were published showing a decrease in national meat consumption during the previous week. It had slipped to a worrying low of three and a half pounds. Within hours a state of panic had swept across the country. We watched as President Menem appeared on television, looking smart, slim and younger than ever. Concerned, brow furrowed, he sincerely urged his fellow Argentines not to hold back and to eat more meat.

He brushed aside any misgivings anyone might have had about saturated fats, cholesterol and health risks as irresponsible scaremongering.

'Look at me – I'm looking good. Why? Because I *eat a lot of meat*.' He stared straight into the camera, not a wrinkle in sight, not a rogue hair out of place. 'It's good for you, not bad for you. Look at me.'

Divorce has been legal only since 1984/85. But now the divorce rate, like meat consumption and heart attacks, is the highest in South America. Even Menem himself is separated from his wife. Could this be a coincidence?

The Presidential Palace at one end of the Plaza de Mayo, where Menem now lives on his own, is called the Casa Rosada or 'Pink House'. It is a beautiful classical European-style building in keeping with the *porteños'* sense of sophistication. It has always been pink, a colour originally achieved by mixing whitewash with fresh bull's blood from the city's slaughterhouses. The veneer of *porteño* civilization is very thin.

The Columbus monument, just down from the blood-tinted Casa Rosada, is a grand affair. At the base of the column, in front, is a group of heroic mariners struggling, muscles rippling, to push the prow of a ship towards the New World. Atop the column, looking out over the River Plate, Columbus scans the horizon.

The blindfolded statue of justice sits, an afterthought hidden behind the column. The law comes later.

We talked, inevitably, about the Falklands-Malvinas war. Our taxi driver said it was a 'stupidity'. Just '*Una tonteria*, but I guess you beat us. You won.' He looked vaguely hangdog.

Jo Tambien swung into action.

'What do you mean, we won? In what sense? The war? The battle? The stupidity, the *tonteria*? After the war you got rid of your dictator and the repressive regime. The Brits were stuck with theirs for another ten years. It all depends on what you mean by winning and losing, my friend, it all depends . . .

I went out to Mataderos, the big meat market in BA. I wanted to see those legendary stockyards, the biggest in the world, where forty-two thousand head of cattle pass through every week. That's fourteen thousand a day. I wanted to see how the gauchos worked out in town. I wanted to see what chaps they wore, what sombreros they had, the size of their *espuelas*. I wanted to see all those *bifes* on the hoof.

It was Thursday and drizzling. On the way to Mataderos we passed the Sanatorio Guëmes, which I presumed must have been a Cowboy Clinic for Diseases of the Terminally Gaucho. I decided to check in later.

When we got to the stockyards they were closed. All I saw inside was a spavined old nag festering in a lone corral. It was all very gloomy. How could the people respond to their President's TV appeal if the main meat market itself was closed? No wonder meat consumption was going down. This was a damning indictment, a sign of the times.

'*Estoy infermo como un papagallo*,' I muttered to myself and decided to find a *morcilla* as a consolation prize.

The stockyards were open, they said, Monday, Tuesday, Wednesday and Thursday, excluding Thursday . . . excluding Thursday? Was this the old South American hand-jive that Jo kept telling me about, where one hand gives you something and the other takes it away before it's even in your pocket?

It was then I realized it was 17 March, St Patrick's Day. It wasn't drizzle in the air, it was Irish mist. Paddy's Day in BA.

A. F. Tschiffely's trek from Buenos Aires to Washington DC with his two Argentine horses Mancha and Gato in the 1920s was one of the great impossible journeys. No one thought he could do it. He was an effete Swiss schoolmaster from the upper crust St George's College, the alma mater of the Anglo-Argentines in BA. On the face of it, he should never have even dreamed of leaving his books and his pens, his pupils and their essays to go on his lunatic sabbatical. He should never have attempted to ride with two horses across deserts, pampa, bogs, mountain ranges and jungles, from freezing cold to tropical heat, from sea level to fourteen thousand feet, from quicksands to poisonous insects, from vampire bats to snakes.

He was a teacher, not an explorer. He was no gaucho either, but a man with a gaucho's dream. So he did it. He travelled the length of the continent, took his dream to North America and showed them what 'gaucho' meant. He got a hero's welcome in America, and wrote *Tschiffely's Ride*, which became a classic adventure story. Our parents and grandparents were brought up on it.

His success was due to his single-minded perseverance and the strength, stamina, resilience and intelligence of his two criollo horses. They were two mustangs, two *baguals* caught by Tehuelche Indians out on the Patagonian steppe. They had learned to be tough fending for themselves in the wild winds down in the far south. They became so famous in their own right that Tschiffely wrote *A Tale of Two Horses*, a children's version of the epic ride as told from Mancha and Gato's point of view.

Jo Tambien had discovered that the two horses were in a museum in Lujan. Far from being buried under a rock by pasture land like John Evans's mighty vaulting Malacara, they were apparently stuffed and standing in a glass case. We had to go.

We decided to join the pilgrimage to Lujan. It is the holy city of Argentina. Most pilgrims were going to see and speak to the miraculous Virgin of Lujan, but we had Mancha and Gato on our mind. On the trip out Roy Rogers and his miraculous horse Trigger crossed my mind. When Trigger died, Roy had him stuffed. The story, some say apocryphal but I can believe anything in this strange New World, is that when he died he wanted to be stuffed and put to rest back in the saddle, riding his old friend for ever.

The Virgin of Lujan is everywhere in Argentina. She is their version of the Virgin of Guadeloupe in Mexico, and makes Lujan the most visited city in the country. The miracle that her reputation rests on is not on the face of it all that miraculous. No miraculous tears or side-stepping of an earthquake like Salta, just a cart stuck in the mud.

The story goes that in 1630 two small statues of the Virgin were being carried in a cart from Brazil to Peru. The cart got stuck in the mud crossing a river. However hard they tried, nothing would shift the cart. Horses, mules, oxen – nothing. It was stuck. Then someone took one of the statues off the cart to put it in another, and as if by magic the cart moved. They decided it meant the statue wanted to stay where it was and had shown this in a miraculous manner. A shrine grew up around the Virgin.

Now she stands high above the altar of an absurd gothic basilica whose twin spires shoot into the sky over the pampa and can be seen for miles around. It is a shrunken version of St Pancras Station and was probably designed by the same team. It took fifty years to build, with British help, and was finished in 1935 when the Virgin finally took up residence. It is completely, magnificently out of place. To call it an eyesore would be over-generous. A sore thumb would be more accurate.

We arrived to find that Mancha and Gato had been moved from the historical museum to the museum of transport. It made sense but the trouble was, the transport museum was closed. Once again, all of Tambien's best efforts had been blocked by the old hand-jive. It was a hot day and I left him to try and blag our way in while I went to pay my respects to the miraculous effigy in its grotesque Victorian gothic box.

The shops round the square in front of the basilica were called *santerias*, saint shops, where you get all your religious artefacts and blessed necessities. They are *santerias* in the same way *sandwicherias* are where you get your sandwich. The square itself was packed with stalls selling Virgin of Lujan souvenirs of every imaginable and unimaginable kind.

Lucky for us, Tambien observed tartly, that I had no money with me that day, otherwise my bag would be full to bursting with Virgin of Lujan bumbags, matés with built-in *bombilla*, pendants and earrings, ashtrays, sanctified wall plaques, gloves, World's Smallest Bibles in Spanish, Lujan notebooks, Christian pens and pencils, holy *bolas*, plates, holy water dispensers, holy Kleenex dispensers, bandanas, sacred sunhats, religious Thermos flasks and Virgin of Lujan toilet-seat covers . . . I was in holy tat heaven but twitching in frustration.

I could buy nothing. Here I was, the perennial tourist, in the Nashville of the religious world, the Knock of Argentina, without a penny to my name. I hadn't even brought my Jesus Christ credit card ('Bank on Christ: Valid thru Eternity') that I'd got years ago in a God shop in the Smoky Mountains in Tennessee.

The basilica, defiantly incongruous, a last shake of the British fist at the pampean skies, was built of a dark-pink sandstone. A sign at the door forbade the wearing of shorts or low-cut dresses and the use of cameras. Inside it was packed with pilgrims in shorts and low-cut dresses queuing with their cameras to file past the Virgin, a little Barbie doll in a spotlight wearing a pale-blue-and-white gown with golden shafts radiating from her head, perched over the altar. Flashlights popped as relatives took snaps of their nearest and dearest prostrating themselves in their shorts before the Holy Mother.

On the walls were collections of little silver effigies of human parts from grateful or hopeful supplicants just like Salta, though not in such glorious profusion. My guess, as a medical man, is that the Virgin in Salta delivered the goods more reliably than her stick-in-the-mud sister in Lujan.

The Virgin of Lujan is known only for coming to a complete halt and refusing to budge an inch. In one of the finest of ironies, she is the patron saint of the Argentine railways.

Once again Jo shook me out of my reverie to say he had fixed it for us to get into the transport museum. He had said we were from the BBC, always a good card to play in faraway places. Outside the basilica we passed a tourist bus like a fairground trolley with Bugs Bunny and the Virgin herself painted on the side.

A nice lady with keys opened up the museum and explained that torrential rains had damaged the roof and it was wet inside. We went in past *carretas*, oxcarts used by the early pioneers, train carriages and early automobiles into a big hall.

In the centre was a magnificent amphibious aeroplane, a huge grey water bird, the *Ne Plus Ultra*, which had made the first transatlantic flight from Spain to South America. It had been flown in 1926 by Ramon Franco, the future dictator's brother. It filled the hall, but what I had come for was in a case in the corner of the room, just beyond the *Ne Plus Ultra*'s tailplane.

My heart stopped a moment. This was stranger than seeing Stalin in Red Square. I remembered Mancha and Gato on the pampa, in the Andes, in the desert. A glass box? I wanted to see the horses but I didn't. I kind of wished they might have escaped, ridden off one stormy night to Trapalanda, and not be stuffed and in some case. But there they were, as large as . . . life? I winced. They didn't say a lot, naturally. Up close you can see the joins.

Mancha means stain, and he is piebald, pinto, a black and white *tobiano*. He is carrying the pack and has a leading rein. Gato, which means Cat, is a lighter brown than the darker bay I expected, with a dark tail. He has lost his mane somewhere along the trail. He is saddled with a *recado* and stirrups in the gaucho way.

You can see a determination of stance and of look, Mancha a little more skittish and uncertain, Gato steadier and more reliable. Their ears are pricked forward. They are standing at rest looking straight ahead. Their gaze is very direct but, of necessity, vacant. Their eyes are glass, after all.

Cynically I told myself it was just their hides, that they were sad stuffed shells, but of course it wasn't as simple as that. Roy Rogers must have known something if he wanted to be set on Trigger to ride his last eternal trail.

If they could survive all the rigours of their legendary trip, surely their spirit could survive the taxidermist. And what happened when they died? Had anyone eaten them? I remembered that the Indians ate their dead chief's horse to get some of *the chief's* power as well as the horse's. What happened to Mancha and Gato's power? I have no doubt that they are both grazing peacefully in Trapalanda right now, but did they leave any of their spirit in this old glass case under the flying boat?

Before they died, Tschiffely sent them back to the pampa. Mancha remembers the last time the old schoolteacher came to visit them:

For a long time he sat with us; and when the sun was beginning to dip into the vast ocean of the pampas, he quietly rose, and, having patted our necks, went up to his horse and leapt into the saddle . .

With a wave of his old battered sombrero, out of which we had had many a good feed, he swung his horse round again, and galloped towards the setting sun. As he went away he looked smaller and smaller, until we could only see a speck at the horizon; and when the last after-glow of red had faded away, Master was but a memory . . .

Some day, when we shall have seen our last sunset, we hope to be re-united with all our old friends, and that you will come and visit us – in Trapalanda.

Until then, farewell!

Like most stuffed animals in dusty glass cases, the two horses looked pretty wistful. The good old days. Hmm.

By making his epic journey, Tschiffely had taken the gaucho tradition to North America, where they had already claimed the cowboy for their own.

He was tapping them on the shoulder, reminding them gently about the first cowboys, the lost cowboys, the ones who spoke Spanish. The ones who taught the Americans all they know.

10. Monte Vi Eu – I See a Hill

'I can't bring my children to see this any more. It's too sad.' The taxi driver had soft, sorrowful eyes. 'When I brought my younger son the first time he was six. He cries every time he sees it. He asks me how could we do such a thing. I have no answer. I can only say it was us who did it.'

We were standing in front of a bronze monument in a Montevideo park. Tambien had discovered that, unlike sophisticated Buenos Aires, there were several monuments to the gaucho and frontier life in Uruguay's capital city. We found a taxi driver to take us round the cowboy statues. With oxcarts, stagecoaches, sweating beasts of burden and battling gauchos, they did not disappoint. Near the end of the trip he asked if we knew that there was a statue of the Indians done by the same man. He warned us that it was very sad. We said we could cope. And there they were.

Four life-sized bronze Indians are gathered in a semicircle round a fire. On the fire is a little pot of boiling water. Three are sitting on the ground, one with his maté in his hand, one staring out over the horizon, his brow furrowed, not understanding. A woman is suckling her baby crossed-legged. Her name, scrawled into the bronze ground in front of her, is Guyunusa.

For these four figures are real people, not just unknown warriors or mythical noble savages, but real people. They are the last four Charrua Indians.

The two seated men, Senaca and Tacuabo, have long hair and headbands, as the gauchos did. Standing at the back is the cacique, Viamaca-Piru, a short *chiripa* with a belt and his *bolas* wrapped round his waist, and a poncho of sheepskin over his shoulders. He stares silently ahead, his sightless eyes looking out at a non-existent future with bitter resignation.

The Charrua were the main tribe in the area that is now Uruguay. Along with the Minuanes, Chanaes and Arachanes they were wiped out at the end of the nineteenth century when the white men, the Christians, were clearing the way for progress throughout the whole continent.

In this part of the world, though, they did not just kill most of the Indians and put the rest on reservations. This time they exterminated the lot.

'I cannot tell my sons that someone else killed them. It would be a lie. No one did. Not the Spanish. Not the Portuguese or the Brazilians. Not the English. It was us, only us. We exterminated the Charrua. It is our terrible shame.'

I could see why the little boy cried.

After the fierce struggle and toil of the gaucho statues, this had a terrible stillness and silence. The tragedy is palpable as the last four Indians on their bronze plinth stare extinction in the face.

A man called Prati made most of these wonderful bronzes. The Indians were the last he did, in 1931. The others – some by another sculptor, Belloni – celebrate the spirit of the gauchos, the pioneers out on the last frontier, with incredible movement. These are not bombastic heroes, but flesh-and-blood frontiersmen. Not just life-sized but living, they are statues you want to climb on, to join in with.

On the main drag in Montevideo is 'The Gaucho', high and proud on his horse, his three-pronged lance raised to the sky. He is at an intersection, surrounded by high-rise office blocks and with trolley-bus cables whistling past his ears. On the plinth are scenes of gaucho life, riding and lassoing, playing guitar, struggling with a broken cart-wheel during the great Exodus and joining up with the Liberator Artigas. Surrounded by patient and grateful women bearing his children, he is seen on the front as St Sebastian, martyred, bare-chested and exhausted from his noble efforts.

At the bottom it says:

TO THE GAUCHO
IN THE FRONT LINE OF FREEING THE COUNTRY
THE NATION THANKS YOU.

In a fountain in the centre of the city is a battle scene. Gauchos, Indians, a Negro and their horses are fighting for their lives, galloping round in a murderous circle. *Boleadores* are flying, lances waving, bows and arrows taking aim. A dead horse is being trampled as others rear over it.

'La Carreta', out in a park, is a bronze oxcart lurching dangerously to one side with a wheel stuck in a mud hole. A team of six huge oxen are straining, sinews snapping, necks bent to the ground, to pull it out. A mounted gaucho beside the cart urges them on while two fresh oxen come up behind.

In another park, 'La Diligencia' is a stagecoach being pulled out of water by a team of horses. The bronze coach actually has its wheels in a pond. The horses are pulling hard, sweating and rearing, their nostrils flaring and eyes dilated with fear as they struggle. A gaucho on horseback in front of the team is calling them on. Another, with his *china*, his woman and her child, is standing on the driving board of the stage whipping the horses to get the coach dragged out of the pond.

These monuments show clearly that Uruguay is much closer to its past, prouder of its country people, more aware of the role of the gaucho, the cowboy, in the building of the country than Argentina or Chile. The cowboy, for Uruguay, was absolutely central. The gaucho was never far away from the city. In the days when wild cattle were hunted for their hides and tallow and the rest left to rot in the sun, carcases littered the ground for a two-mile stretch outside Montevideo. But this does not mean that the city is overrun by cowboys. Just cowboy statues.

Some say uncharitably that the whole of Uruguay is just Montevideo with a ranch. As with Buenos Aires and the *camp*, there has been an age-old battle and deep suspicion on many levels between the two factions. Here, instead of the Unitarists and Federalists, it is the Colorados in the city and the Blancos in the country.

If a gaucho carries a flag it will always be white. But although there is a clear political division which has grown out of an old power struggle, country customs are not as taboo in the big city as they are the other side of the river. The country, though still separate, is closer to the city. Montevideo is not so self-consciously European as the city across the muddy water.

There is no statue, no monument to the gaucho in Buenos Aires. Maybe the blue-eyed gaucho, Rosas, gave them too much of a roasting. Maybe they still can't forget and they despise their gaucho heritage for what they think it is – wild, dangerous, cruel, barbaric and unpredictable. No, they look to Europe too much and only show their own traditions cleaned and sanitized – the noble gaucho myth.

Underneath it they know the darker truth and are ashamed of the gaucho, the gypsy of the Argentine, in spite of their gaucho clubs and societies. So it will be until the day they drink maté without shame in the street outside the Recoleta in the city of fine airs and graces.

*

Having got a taste for maté in Salta and on the pampa, the first thing I noticed in Uruguay, even in the city of Montevideo, was that everybody drinks the stuff wherever they are. I was in maté heaven. The main drag, the 18 July Avenue, is lined from one end to the other with stalls selling maté paraphernalia. The street of a thousand matés.

Most are made from gourds, calabashes, of different shapes and sizes. The commonest style is a composite breast-womb shape. Some have a silver or tin ring round the mouth. Some have a natural lip that curves out. It makes a good collar for holding in one hand while the steering wheel is in the other. This shape is called the *camionero* style, the truck driver's maté.

They have wood matés, aluminium matés, horn matés, leather-covered matés, matés covered with scrotum skin. The scrotum has a delicate, wispy fur covering. Gauchos like it for obvious reasons. And symbolically, wrapping the breast-womb in the bollock bag is one hell of a mixed metaphor.

There are leather stands for holding the matés called *posa-matés*. They have Thermos flasks, leather-covered with gaucho scenes, rearing broncos and flying *bolas*, burnt into them; pourers shaped like horses' heads; *bombillas* of metal or of cane; shoulder bags for carrying the Thermos, maté, *yerba* and *bombilla*; combined *posa-maté* and *posa-thermo* with heavy base for setting up the kit up in the car or truck and drinking your favourite tea in your *camionero*-style maté.

The street became my second home. If ever he couldn't find me, Jo Tambien would trawl the avenue and the chances are he'd come across me by some stall, drifting off into another world, having a religious experience, lovingly fingering some leather-covered matés with football team badges painted on them, a mini-*bombilla*, a maté keyring or an atrocious leather 'Martín Fierro' wall pennant.

Montevideo feels like an amiable, affectionate city.

Jorge Luis Borges said:

> You are the Buenos Aires we once had,
> That slipped away quietly over the years . . .
> False door in time,
> Your streets contemplate a lighter past.

In a lot of ways Uruguay is more like Ireland. It has a few odd parallels with the Emerald Isle. Same population, three million – except that though Uruguay is the smallest country in southern Spanish America, it is the size of England and Wales with the population of Ireland. They prefer to say you can fit

Holland and Belgium and Wales into Uruguay and still have room for Andorra, Monaco and a swinging cat. Makes it sound bigger.

Same emigration. A lot of Uruguayans leave for richer pickings. Same sad songs of lost love and lost home. Same heroes who lose their final battles. Same trouble with a big bossy neighbour – but for Uruguay it's two, Argentina and Brazil. And after all this, in Uruguay as in Ireland, they make great black pudding.

It needs to be said, in the way the monuments to the gaucho around town say it, that Uruguay actually invented the cowboy.

Now this is a serious claim. They say that gauchos first came from the River Plate area, from their side of the river which used to be the Banda Orientale. They say they gave the gaucho to Argentina and Brazil. They spread west from their lands through the pampa and beyond, and spread east across into the flatlands of southern Brazil.

This does not go down well in Salta, in the province of La Pampa, or in the southern gaucho state of Rio Grande do Sur in Brazil. The Uruguayans don't care.

Strange to tell, the word 'cowboy' was first used in Ireland a thousand years ago. More recently Dean Swift used the word in 1705 to describe a boy tending cows. Can't fault him on that. He had his eyes fixed on the New World, too, for the Patagonian Tehuelche Indians were the inspiration for the amiable giants, the Brobdignagians, in *Gulliver's Travels*.

Early this century Uruguay disestablished the Church, which made it unique in all of Hispanic America. It means that since then the Church has had nothing to do with the state or with governing the country. So though the majority of the Uruguayan people are Catholics, it is not a Catholic state like all its neighbours, but a secular state.

This has had a few bizarre consequences. Being secular, no street or building could be named after a saint. The word for god – *dios* – had to be printed in lower case, no capitals. Christmas Day became Family Day. Easter Week, Holy Week, became Tourist Week, Criollo Week or *Gaucho Week*. It was the last week of autumn before school starts and winter sets in, so it was the last chance for a week's holiday. A lot of the city folk go away to the country. So it is Tourist Week. At the same time, because it is Gaucho, Criollo Week, the celebration of all things creole and country, from meat to gauchos to horses and back again, the country comes into town.

For eight days they have *rodeos*, *baguals*, *payadors*, bucking broncos and *asado con cuero*.

Walking down one of the leafy streets of Montevideo at nine one morning, I saw flames pouring out of the top of a small brick structure in front of a building site. They weren't delicate little flames but big, crackling, lick-the-sky roaring flames. They were coming out of the chimney of this little hut, built right in front of a sixteen-storey block that was under construction.

A man came round a corner and went into the hut. He was carrying a whole side of ribs over his shoulder. They had a light coating of cement dust. He must have been the *asador* for the day and I figured he would be getting the mid-morning snack organized. I found out pretty quick that they eat as much meat this side of the river as in Argentina.

The meat was the priority for the working men. Before they start laying foundations for the block behind, the *asado* and *parilla* must be built. First things first. If the average consumption per head is four pounds a week, what do these guys put away? It must be phenomenal.

I fell to chatting with a friendly security guard who said his name was Paco. We talked of the flames and meat and gauchos. He spoke a kind of pidgin Australian and said he'd spent twenty years out there. Came back with his wife and son a year ago, to see if they could make a living back here.

His son Rodolfo spoke perfect Oz, he said. When we started talking about Gaucho Week, he said Rodolfo – Rod – was going to the rodeo and could take us. Then came the best bit: Rod's uncle was the chief judge at the rodeo. YIPPEEE!

We are standing on Plaza Independencia beside the old city gate, a gate without walls, to and from nowhere. A Dacia comes screaming to a stop an inch from my shoes. Paco's son Rod, ebullient as any Australian, sticks his head out. 'G'day, mate.' A Dacia? A Dacia is a Romanian Renault. A Dacia here in Uruguay? 'Hell, yes, it's all right and the cheapest I could get.' How much? 'Fifteen thousand dollars.'

Fifteen thousand dollars? For a Romanian car? Yep, and it's because of very high import duty. Only the wealthy can get new cars. So everyone drives old ones, very old ones – or Dacias. The Dacia is the cheapest. They don't sell the Trabant down here any more.

Two big rodeos come into town for La Semana Criolla. The main one, more gaucho, more country, is out in Roosevelt Park; with their lazy pronunciation and habit of dropping s's in mid-word down here in the

Southern Cone this becomes Parque Roo-vel. We drive out there in Rod's
Dacia, through the suburbs to the big eucalyptus woods on the edge of town.

Rod is twenty-four and acts younger. He looks dark and Uruguayan and
sounds like Brad from *Neighbours*. He talks of Oz and how Uruguay seems
primitive by contrast, but he's glad to be back.

'Shit, yeah, mate.' He talks about the security business and asks if we like
guns. He's got some at home if we'd like to see them. Shit, no, mate. What
about bayonets? No thanks, mate.

We drive right into the eucalyptus forest, park up and go to find the Judges'
Ranch. It is early in the day but already the air between the trees is hazy with
the smoke rising from a thousand fires carrying the smells of morning *asados*.
The forest floor has a crisp brown carpet of dead leaves and papery strips of
bark from the tall ghostly trunks of the gum trees.

Cowboys are everywhere, in their criollo best. Pretty duded up, they look to
me like the gauchos from the other side of the river. Same *bombachas*, *fajas*,
rastras, *facóns*, *pañuelos* and boots. There are different kinds of sombreros,
though.

The common gaucho sombrero, a small, narrow-brimmed pork-pie style of
hat, often with a very low crown, sits like a peanut on top of the head. It's a
tester – only if you're *really* gaucho can you look cool in something as silly as
this. Then there is a conical, and let's be honest, comical, sombrero with a
small brim that looks like an old country bumpkin's hat. The kind the village
idiot would wear, sitting in the stocks grinning. Like a bigger version of Chico
Marx's hat, it is probably from Entre Ríos where Gaucho Marx is reputed to
have settled. It would make a Morris dancer look good.

Some men have very wide-brimmed sombreros with a high pointed crown
and raised back in the Mexican style. These turn out to be Brazilian gauchos
from the southern *campanha*, flat cattle country, of Rio Grande do Sul. Like
many of the original cowboys in North America, several of them are black.

More common here than in Argentina, many are sporting the broad-
brimmed flat black sombrero in the Chilean or Zorro style. In cowboy terms it
is easier to relate to.

Some of the gauchos are walking through the woods, some riding. Other
horses, hitched to trees or the back of pick-up trucks, have the same sheepskin-
covered *recados* as in the Argentine. The horses are brushed but not manicured.

Smoke from all the *asados* is seeping and curling round the pale peeling
trunks of the slender eucalyptus trees, making them seem wispier and more
anorexic than usual. Everyone is very relaxed. Families are camping out, mums
and dads sitting in their folding chairs under the drooping leaves of the gum

trees. Kids canter bareback, cutting a swathe through the haze of the smoky forest.

And everybody, absolutely everybody, is carrying a Thermos flask in one hand and a maté gourd in the other.

Parked by two white-washed thatched shacks is an immaculate, shiny, burgundy-coloured 1949 flat-screen Ford pick-up truck with a grille like a gummy kid with braces on his teeth pulling his gob open with his two fingers. It is sitting under the trees beside a long, low metallic gold Oldsmobile Delta 88 from the sixties. The cars are facing the log fence of some recently erected corrals. Two gauchos are leaning on the fence, looking over a new troop of colts, mustangs, *baguals*, *potros*, wild horses that have just been brought in.

The colts are shifting around in the corral, their coats, a lot of bays and chestnuts, glowing in the morning light that suffuses the forest of tall skinny gum trees. Blue hazy prismatic smoke from the fires is soaking through the woods, drifting through the delicate pendulous leaves and making the whole scene seem mystical and suspended in time. I pinch myself. It is all in soft focus.

It is possible I might be in Trapalanda already.

Beside the corral fence, the two shacks are set at right angles to each other, making a kind of yard, a home space. There are two fires in the centre of the yard, with logs as stools, a long trestle table and benches.

One fire has a big bucket of stew sitting on it and a crucifix-shaped *asado* holding ribs angled over it. The other has an old sprung mattress base with a winch to move it up and down over the fire as an improvised *parilla*. A skewbald pinto is tethered, saddled up, near one of the shacks.

We're on the Judges' Ranch.

Sitting by the fire, a sight with sore eyes, is Uncle Roberto. He is a bit dishevelled. Last night he slept in his clothes and out of his skin. His eyes are soft and drunk. He offers us some whisky, some MacPay, a Uruguayan national whisky, the gauchos' favourite. I refuse – too early yet, need food in the belly. He agrees strongly and shakes his head fiercely.

'That's right! I only drink morning and evening. Never when I'm working. Only morning and evening.'

It's still morning, half eleven, so he takes another whack of MacPay. He stands up and sees I'm wearing my Bermudas. He gets a *faja*, winds it laboriously round my middle, under the picture on my T-shirt of a steer wearing cowboy boots, sticks a *facón* in the back. He stands back, claps his hands and cries, 'Ah! Gaucho!' He takes us round the ranch, into the bunkhouse where he and all the old boys collapse every night after a hard day's judging and drinking.

Six palliasses, camp beds and straw bales with blankets and ponchos are ranged round the bunkhouse. Clothes and sombreros, bridles and other tack hang from the rafters and roof posts. Bottles of wine and MacPay lie by the beds. The other shack is the shithouse and bath house with a classic bucket-with-holes-in-it shower.

There are half a dozen judges, between forty and sixty-five years old. Uncle Roberto would be in his late fifties, dark haired with tanned arms and the face of a horseman. All the judges are in gaucho clothes but not duded up yet. They are still moving slowly, dealing with the tail end of last night's hangover. This must be their summer camp, all the lads together for Cowboy Week. They ride into town every year and set up camp in Roosevelt Park.

Some of the wives appear with supplies, clean shirts, *bombachas* and food. They are out looking after their boys. Then the meat comes over from the *asado* on the fire and is thrown on to the table.

Chow down! We eat the meat gaucho style with *facóns* and our hands. The big bucket of mutton stew – called *puchero*, it is an on-the-trail special – is brought over. As well as the MacPay to drink there are a couple of *damajuanas* of wine and some *caña* so no one goes short.

Roberto reaches into a bucket and fishes out some ice for our glasses. His wife chides him.

'What are you doing with the ice? Have you washed your hands?'

His watery eyes look aggrieved. 'Yes, yesterday.'

When he's finished, Roberto wipes his hands on his pants, and cleans the dirt out from under his nails with the end of his two-foot-long *facón*. Then he gets up and walks slowly, tentatively, stepping on splinters, into the bunkhouse. Ten minutes later he comes out dressed top to toe in his clean, smart, freshly pressed gear. He moves carefully and methodically, as if talking himself through the process, over to the pinto tethered patiently by the bathhouse and swings up into the saddle.

Then a remarkable thing happens.

As he settles into his dark sheepskin *recado* his back straightens, his jaw juts out purposefully and his eyes rise. He grows perceptibly taller. He is wearing his broad, flat-brimmed, black sombrero, crisp white shirt and black *pañuelo*, *faja* and *rastra*. His *facón* is stuck in the back of his belt. He has his fresh black *bombachas* tucked into his shiny black boots. Sitting astride his horse he is regal, he is massive.

From a sore-eyed shambling drunk he has been transmogrified in one single extraordinary flowing movement – the mounting of his horse – into *Don Roberto*.

HERE COMES THE JUDGE!

It is the most phenomenal transformation I've ever seen. As Don Roberto rides slowly out of the judges' corral and into the rodeo ring he is a king.

His back is ramrod straight as he surveys his domain. He is riding high in the saddle. Suddenly, and for the first time, I understand the meaning of the phrase 'sober as a judge'. The fumbling fool is a distant memory. He is the Judge of Judges. He is *the Don*.

Jo Tambien slaps his leg and shouts: '*Don Roberto! Jefe de Jefes! Maestro de Maestros!*'

Don Roberto turns and nods almost imperceptibly in acknowledgement, taps the pinto's quarters twice with his *rebenque*, and goes to work.

There are three big *palenques*, hitching posts, in a line in the rodeo ring. They are ten foot high and a foot wide. In relays, and clouds of dust, two riders gallop through a gate into the ring bringing fresh broncos up to each *palenque*. Two or three *domadors*, horse breakers, work at each post.

They take each colt and snub it to the *palenque*. They usually blindfold it. Then, however hard the horse protests, pulling back, shaking its neck, kicking, bucking, throwing itself in the air, falling over and thrashing, they force a bridle and bit on it.

Each rider, each contestant in the rodeo, fixes his saddle to the horse. The *domadors* twist the horse's ear, hang on to its tail and pound on the horse's quarters with a closed fist as the rider gets into the saddle. They wear long thick leather aprons skewed round to the left to cover their *bombachas* as they struggle with the animals.

Don Roberto and another judge make sure it's all in order. They have already checked the rider's tack and particularly his spurs. They see that at least the vicious rowels, here about three inches wide, have not been bent so that they can't spin. The gauchos can do this to hurt the horse more. Fixed spurs can cut into his hide, make him buck more. Not allowed. Makes him bleed more too.

The bell is rung, the blindfold pulled off and the mustang released. The gaucho digs in his *espuelas* and rides the horse for seventeen seconds. He has to hold the reins with one hand and wave his poncho around his head as high as he can with the other.

Points are awarded, mostly on style. The higher the horse bucks, the better. If he just gallops round, however fast, or spins like a whirlwind in one spot, however difficult it looks, the rider loses points. What is ideal is a high bucking horse, which spins and gallops and bucks all at the same time, while the gaucho waves his poncho high, keeps his hat on and gets the crowd whooping and hollering.

It's very different from the Chilean rodeo, but just as closely based on work practices. 'Martín Fierro' described the breaking:

> The breaker-in with a lissom stride,
>   Unbarred the stockyard gate,
>   And while he was fresh, picked the wildest flesh,
>   And threw him deft with the lasso's mesh,
> And the colt would thrash in the swirling dust
>   Like a thing of living hate.
>
> And there the gaucho edged him in,
>   And pinned the plunging head;
>   They saddled him quick and gave him a lick,
>   And the breaker swung to the saddle slick, –
> Ah, those were the times when the gaucho showed
>   The craft that is in him bred.
>
> And through the gap of the open gate
>   Went thundering horse and man,
>   A batter of hoofs and a cloud of dust,
>   A flurry of fight and rage and lust,
> And thrashing leather and raking spurs, –
>   Till he stretched his neck and ran.

At the rodeo the riders are doing what gauchos have always done to break horses. They do it like the conquistadors. They like to fight the horse, to conquer the animal, break its spirit. It is not friendly and it is not kind, but it leaves the horse half-tamed, half-wild, just how the gauchos like them. They have always relished the liveliness of a wild horse which is why they are so sneeringly dismissive of the kind of fully trained mount they give me – *manso como para un Ingles*.

However similar and interbred the gauchos and the Indians became over the centuries, however much the gauchos learned from the Indians, their very different approaches to the horse showed that in the end they remained worlds apart. The gauchos' matter-of-fact cruelty in the breaking of horses came from their dominant, macho Andalucian blood, unlike the firm but friendly, brotherly approach of the Indian.

While the gaucho grasps and twists the horse's ear, the Indian talks, whispers and grunts encouragingly into it.

I remember the scorn Eduardo Halliday, the Scottish gaucho with the red Rob Roy beard we met in the deep south of Patagonia, poured on bronco busting. No special skill was needed, he said. All it took was an athlete with good balance. Training a horse properly, now *that* was a real art.

Martín Fierro, although he's a gaucho, agrees with Eduardo and prefers the Indian way:

To train his mount for the hand-to-hand
  Is the Pampa warrior's pride,
    He is off at a pat of the Indian's hand,
    In the length of a stride he'll come to stand;
At a twitch of a rein like a top he spins
  In the space of a bullock's hide.

Every day as soon as the sun is up
  His paces he puts him through;
    He trains him to run where the going's rough
    On the moving sand and the bog and bluff,
If you look for a horse that's better trained
  You'll find there's mighty few.

When you're forking a mount that's Indian trained
  You needn't fear a roll,
    La Pucha! and as for doing a bolt
    There's none can outpace or outlast his colt,
He doesn't tame it with quirt and spur
  But with word-and-hand control.

He handles it softly for a start,
  Its neck with his hand he slicks,
    He doesn't care what time he'll spend,
    He strokes it there for hours on end,
And he only stops when it drops its ears
  And neither jibs nor kicks.

Not a single blow he gives it there
  With whip or yet with hand;
    There's no patienter thing in the universe
    Than the way of an Indian with a horse,

When he's finished with it his every word
  The beast can understand.

Though at breaking a colt in our Christian style
  I don't waste sentiment,
    It's better I like the Indian way,
    And the horse, once rid, the very next day,
You'll see with the reins across his neck
  At the flap of the Indian's tent.

As the seventeen-second target approaches, if the rider hasn't been thrown, two gauchos gallop up either side of him, one taking the colt by the bridle, the other lifting the rider off. If a *potro* gallops riderless round the big rodeo corral a gaucho rides up behind, leans down casually, grabs him by the tail and steers him out of the ring.

Some of the gauchos get thrown, most landing agilely on their feet. As gauchos had told me before, a rider must fall eleven times, and falling on the feet is as important as riding:

To know how to fork a colt ain't all,
  You've got to know how to take a fall;
And where the gringo breaks his back,
  The gaucho finds his feet.

Almost all the competitors are tiny guys, just like athletic jockeys. A lot of the *potros*, even those that look wild and spirited as they are brought in at the gallop, seem to get tamed in some way by the *recado* and the cinch, the tight girth, so they just canter disappointingly around. Some do a quick and violent corkscrew spin and throw the rider off right at the *palenque*.

The gauchos who ride the buckingest broncos and twirl their poncho the best for the full seventeen seconds get to ride a lap of honour round the ring waving a bottle of *caña* at the crowd.

After their turn, the gauchos strip their *recado* from the colt. Then comes the long walk, the loneliest and most poignant moment in the rodeo. The small-built, bow-legged gauchos waddle sorrowfully like melancholy alligators across the rodeo ring to their enclosure carrying their bulky saddles and tack before them. A fish out of water is more comfortable.

They have always hated being out of the saddle and I can see why. In the old days when the gauchos held the wooden stirrups between their toes, which stuck out of their open-toed boots if they weren't barefoot, their feet became so distorted that they could hardly walk at all. W. H. Hudson said the gaucho on foot 'waddles in his walk; his hands feel for the reins; his toes turn inwards like a duck's.'

After the first session there is a tea break. This of course means maté and for the judges a bit of a *whicky* break. The MacPay comes out and Don Roberto reminds us that he never drinks while he's working. Except today, of course, which is special.

I take another rain check on the *whicky* and instead get a quick maté seminar with Chiquito, the oldest judge, who has snow-white hair flying out from the side of his head, a fine white handlebar moustache and sparkling white *bombachas*. His white poncho seems to confirm his Blanco political affiliations. He gets out his maté, an old thick gourd, polished and carved, with a silver collar. He shows me how the Uruguayans pile the *yerba* in, leaving a dry pile of it on one side, digging around in this bitter mass of maté for the strongest hit. He looks at my kit, my Argentine *bombilla* and maté. He pours some spectacular scorn on the inferior foreign gear.

'Well, that's shit, I mean, how can you expect to drink maté with shit like this?'

The Argentine *bombilla* does in fact look straight and weedy, not like the sturdy spoon-shaped Uruguayan utensil.

'The Argentines don't know what kind of maté to drink. All Argentine *yerba* is filled with useless *palo*, sticks to give it bulk and stop it clogging. If you know how to drink maté properly it doesn't clog anyway. *Palo* means less *yerba*, so it's not so strong, not strong enough. You only need *palo* if you're so dumb you don't know how to drink maté properly.'

No wonder they like to beat the Argentines at football.

The second session was the same as before but bareback. Many of the gauchos changed from hard to soft boots. Several wore *botas de potro*.

This session was much more exciting. The horses bucked much higher and more readily, unrestricted and untamed by a cinch. The rides were wilder, the falls more balletic, the flying and whirling more consistent.

One of the black Brazilians did really well and got a lap of honour. No Argentine gaucho managed this. One got thrown spectacularly.

The commentator announced with a massive rolling of r's:

'THE BRRRRRAVE ARRRRRRRRRGENTINIAN was not quite good enough for the URRRRRRRRRRRRRRRRRRRRRRRRRRUGUAYAN POTRRRRRRRRRRRROOO!!!'

Sitting up there in the saddle like Don Roberto, riding high and magisterial out in the rodeo ring despite the MacPay, that too is an art in itself. Sober as a judge.

Many say, particularly in Uruguay, that there was in fact very little interbreeding between gauchos and Indians. Certainly the gauchos hated and despised the Indians. However low on the social scale, the gauchos always had the Indians conveniently on the bottom rung, below them.

They called them 'savages'. The Indians, with equal contempt, called gauchos, and any westerners, 'Christians'. The Guaycurus, particularly ferocious tribes from the northern part of the pampa and the hunting grounds of the Chaco, were 'the most turbulent of heathens, who extract their eyelashes to better see the Christians and slay them'.

Nevertheless, the gauchos absorbed a lot of the Indian way of life and often looked identical. A Mapuche Indian in southern Chile, described here in 1838, looked almost indistinguishable form a Uruguayan gaucho: 'He wore a dark coloured poncho, and seated with bare legs upon a rude kind of saddletree above and beneath which a couple of sheepskins were strapped, his great toes alone being thrust into the tiny wooden stirrups. A red fillet or headband worn around the forehead confined in part his long black hair.' The Uruguayan gaucho might have a small-brimmed hat over his headband, and a beard, but would otherwise look the same. His *chiripa* would leave his legs bare and he would hold his stirrups with his big toes like the Indian.

While the gaucho adopted many Indian ways, like the *chiripa*, *boleadores*, poncho, maté and long hair and headband, the Indians took the horse, the Moorish *recado* and the European lasso. In fact, the lasso had originally come from Rome. Roman gladiators using lassoes were *laqueatores* or *enlazadores*. In South America it was always a two-way mix, which is how a Mapuche and a Uruguayan could look so similar with a mountain range and hundreds of leagues between them.

Rosas was not the only gaucho Darwin met on his trip across the pampa. He wrote in 1839:

At night we stopped at a pulperia, or drinking-shop. During the evening a great number of Gauchos came in to drink spirits and smoke cigars. Their appearance is very striking; they are generally tall and handsome, but with a proud and dissolute expression of countenance. They frequently wear their mustaches and long black hair curling down their backs. With their brightly coloured garments, great spurs clanking about their heels, and knives stuck as daggers (and often so used) at their waists, they look a very different race of men from what might be expected . . . Their politeness is excessive; they never drink their spirits without expecting you to taste it; but whilst making their exceedingly graceful bow, they seem quite as ready, if occasion offered, to cut your throat.

Darwin's only attempt at being a gaucho was disastrous. When he tried to throw *Las Tres Marias*, the *bolas*, he ended up catching himself. As he whirled the long rawhide ropes around his head one ball caught in a nearby bush, another whipped across and wound round his own horse's legs. How the gauchos laughed as the eminent naturalist tumbled to the ground.

Cunninghame Graham, as a would-be gaucho himself, and certainly a more successful one than Darwin, painted a more romanticized picture of the 1860s:

Nothing could be more typical of the wild life upon the plains than was the figure of a Gaucho dressed in his poncho and his *chiripa*, his naked toes clutching the stirrups, his long iron spurs kept in position by a thong of hide dangling below his heels, his hair bound back by a red silk handkerchief, his eyes ablaze, his silver knife passed through his sash and belt and sticking out just under his right elbow, his horse with its mane cut into castles and its long tail floating out into the breeze, as, twisting his bolas round his head, he flew like lightning down a slope which a mere European horseman would have looked on as certain death, intent to 'ball' one of a band of fleet *ñandus* all sailing down the wind.

Montevideo even has a Gaucho Museum. Significantly, it is directly above the Museum of Money. One day when I visited, the background music was great epic movie themes from *Chariots of Fire*, *Lawrence of Arabia* and other gaucho masterpieces.

I met a small, dapper academic gentleman with sleeked-back grey hair and a suit and tie. He was Professor Assunçao, Uruguay's greatest living gaucho expert and cowboy professor. He told me carefully how the gaucho was of prime national importance, how Uruguay was built by them.

He confirmed that Hernandez had written 'Martín Fierro' whilst in exile in Uruguay. Yes, he said, Hernandez had taken local myths about a Uruguayan folk hero called Martín Fierro ('Martin Iron') and woven them into his masterpiece. He was very happy for the Argentines to share the Uruguayans' local hero, no problem.

Yes, Guëmes had seen the Uruguayan hero Artigas besieging Montevideo with his gaucho cavalry and was so impressed he took the idea back, formed his own troop and won the decisive battles against the Spanish in the northwest. Assuncao didn't begrudge Guëmes his victories, especially as his inspiration was so clearly from the *banda orientale*. As icing on the cake, he maintained that Guëmes had taken the word 'gaucho' back with him, that Uruguay had given the very name of their national hero to the Argentines.

The Uruguayans, always with a slight, knowing smile, like nothing better than sticking it to the Argentines.

The Professor had a great knowledge of other cowboys of the Americas. I explained that I was on a journey to find the lost cowboys, the gauchos, the *huasos*, the *llaneros* of Venezuela and Colombia and the vaqueros of Mexico, who seem to have been working horses and cattle for centuries with little acknowledgement from the West. Hollywood had given us a deeply flawed and chauvinist view of cowboy history and I was determined to set it right.

He agreed enthusiastically but pointed out that almost all history as taught is one-sided. He said my journey was especially fortuitous because I had an opportunity to observe and learn a *comparative history* of the cowboy and thus get closer to the truth. As a small example of this comparative approach, he told me how American cowboys warm the bit with their coffee on winter mornings to avoid freezing the horse's mouth. The gauchos at the far end of the continent do the same with their maté.

He said the only way to understand the truth of history was to compare, to study parallel developments, and he called this approach 'historiography'. I might not have been blazing a trail, but at least I was on the right track.

I asked the professor about the gaucho and Indian statues. He smiled and said they were very good, very close to the gaucho. He said they captured the life and fire and struggle of the gaucho. And the death of the Indian.

I asked him about stallions and mares. He said that gauchos preferred dark horses. Black – *moro* – was the best. White horses were fit only for whores, which made me wonder about Lady Godiva. To ride a mare was worse than useless. It was shameful, 'the last grade of poverty'.

The professor told me that Uruguay, the Banda Orientale, was the last frontier, not just because of battles with the Charrua and other Indians, but because of the decades of fighting with the Argentine and Brazil. Across the last frontier, Uruguay was teeming with herds of cattle and horses, more than anywhere else, and Brazil wanted the land.

The frontier had always been a problem. Large-scale rustling and slaughter of horses and cattle went on constantly. The countryside was littered with the bones and carcases of cattle, and the Orientales and their armies were starving. This was where José Artigas came in.

Artigas was the son of wealthy landowners. He had lived out in the country with gauchos for fifteen years. Sent to study at the Sorbonne in Paris, he had been deeply affected by the teachings of Thomas Paine. Back at home, he did more than any other to foster the idea of nationhood in the Orientales.

For years he commanded small, mobile groups of gauchos that patrolled the hinterland and the frontier with Brazil. He was a great horseman, a great leader, and knew the country intimately. He and his cowboy cavalry were so successful, and his reputation as a saviour and gaucho so strong, that he was revered throughout the land as the guardian of the frontier.

Larger armies could not operate here and Artigas and his gauchos alone secured the safety of the territory. He fought in Argentina, too, and his dream was of a Great Fatherland, which would take in much of Argentina, from the north-west of Salta and Córdoba, right across Corrientes, Santa Fe, Misiones and Entre Ríos, all of Uruguay and the southern cattle-raising flatlands of Brazil. He wanted all this free from the stifling grip of Buenos Aires.

He was the first to have the classic dream of the Americas – land reform. He wanted to split up the great estates and give the land to the poor people. He even wanted to give land to the Indians and the gauchos, to change the gauchos' nomadic, predatory ways and turn them to working the land and raising cattle.

This was not on. It was an impossible dream and was crushed very smartly by a pincer movement between the Portuguese and Buenos Aires with the English in the background.

The whole country took up arms and followed Artigas in an epic exodus; men and women, ragged gauchos, Indians, old people and children, an endless caravan of people, horses and wooden-wheeled oxcarts. The pampa was aflame with a cowboy revolution.

They followed him all the way, crossing the River Uruguay and camping on its west bank. There he built up the gaucho army and, returning to the other side of the river, established the first cowboy government in Paysandu. Here, in 1815, he enacted his first reforms – free men, free land. As well as attaining Christ-like status, Artigas was now the most powerful of all the River Plate *caudillos*.

An English traveller called Robertson stumbled on Artigas' camp-fire government: 'What do you think I saw? His Excellency the Señor Protector of half the New World sitting on the head of an ox beside a bonfire on the muddy soil of his ranch, eating barbecued meat and drinking gin from a cow's horn! A dozen ragged officers surrounded him.'

Soldiers, gauchos and scouts galloped up to the camp fire constantly from every direction. Artigas dictated the revolutionary decrees of his gaucho government to two secretaries.

America's first land reform lasted only a year, then the Portuguese invaded again. Artigas was finally defeated and deserted by all his friends and allies. Many of his *caudillos*, realizing they would lose power and privileges in Artigas' scheme of things, went over to Portugal. His dream was shattered.

All the poor patriots were violently evicted. The only land they kept was just enough to be buried in. Gauchos were never again given the chance to own land and were systematically destroyed throughout the rest of the century.

Artigas, vilified by everyone, went into exile in Paraguay. He saw Uruguay become independent, but as a single small country, a buffer zone and not part of his grander scheme. He never went home. A melancholy man, he lived out the last thirty years of his life surrounded by a few slaves and some of his gauchos, sitting under a tree on a *yerba* maté plantation.

Artigas died disillusioned, but his spirit is not limited to a heroic statue in Independence Square or a mural of the pioneering exodus along a post-office wall. Some of Paine's socialist teachings that had inspired him have carried over into twentieth-century Uruguay.

As well as disestablishing the Church, it was the first country in the Americas to start a welfare state. This survived military dictatorship and, despite a top-heavy and creaky bureaucracy, is still in place. But are market forces gnawing away at the tattered edges of this socialist institution? Will it withstand the onslaught of efficiency and all its demands?

'No, there is no gaucho in my music. My music is only from the city, with no country influence.'

We were sitting in Bar Los Beatles (pronounced Beat-less), a scuzzy little place in the red-light district of old Montevideo port, with Jaime Roos. Jaime, Uruguay's biggest rock star, was talking about the music of his home town.

On the grimy yellow-gloss-painted wall of Bar Los Beat-less were two faded posters of the Fab Four, one clean shaven, with the smart high-button Epstein suits and moptop haircuts, the other with long flowing hair, beards, moustaches and shades, post-Sgt Pepper. Before and after the acid.

On the wall-mounted TV was a Spanish-dubbed Ninja film. Loud. Stuck right in front of it, wedged into a kidney-crusher of a chair, was an enormously fat young man who made Billy Bunter look anorexic.

The only other punter, also pressed up against the TV, was a rubber-faced older man in a beret whose whole head moved as he chewed. Waves and ripples flowed from behind his ears over to the top of his forehead and down to right below his third chin. He had the thick-lipped mouth and baggy eyes of a carp and looked like Uruguay's champion gurner. We were drinking MacPay, but the two locals favoured Gregson's, the stockbrokers' choice if the hoardings are to be believed.

I was trying to find some urban cowboys on the city scene. It was not to be. Like BA, Montevideo is a tango city, entirely separate, musically and politically, from the country. It is easier to find tango records than gaucho music in the record stores. The gauchos are hidden in the folk sections, but there are entire rooms of tango.

Jaime's music owes more to Africa than to the gauchos. He was born in Barrio Sur, the Southern Quarter, which is mostly black. This was different from Argentina. Africans, brought over during the slave trade, disappeared from Argentina, but had put down roots in Montevideo. Their musical roots were mostly rhythmic and came, like Cuban music, from the Congo.

In Uruguay it is called *candombe*, fast drumming on conga-like drums. Though it has a different rhythm, *candombe* mixes well into Cuban music. It mixes well, too, in Jaime's music.

Murga, the other distinctive side of Montevideo music, is extremely bizarre. It is basically a European form, brought in by turn-of-the-century immigrants, which has mutated along the way. Fourteen men sing, almost shout, close harmonies very loudly while three percussionists – a bass drum, a snare drum and a cymbal – bash and crash away. It is the manic music of exile, laughing and longing at the same time. *Murga* surfaces at Carnival time and for a month each barrio, each area of the city, battles to produce the best *murga*. The men dress in absurdly surreal carnival costume, leap around and perform a forty-five-minute satirical piece with parodies of known songs, anything from Beethoven's Ninth to the Platters' 'Only You', as well as original music. It is a cappella on speed.

The *murga* always ends on a sad song, a goodbye song for the homelands. The immigrant history and the sense of exile is confirmed at the end of the *murga* madness. It has roots in the songs of the troubadours, like the country's *payadors*, but it is strictly urban. There is nothing of the country *chamaritas* or *milongas* in it. There is no gaucho in it at all.

When Jaime took us to see a *murga* I was completely bowled over by the energy and the rampant craziness of it. In the end, I showed no sign of understanding truly what *murga* and *candombe* meant. Jaime explained, just as Don Tito had said of gaucho in Salta, that, like tango, they were a *feeling*. And however hard I tried, they were resolutely part of the city and not on the cowboy trail.

We had one more MacPay, left Billy Bunter and Rubberman to the Ninja

film in the Bar Los Beat-less, and went to eat some meat. That's definitely
more gaucho.

Though I'd had testicles in BA, I was greedy and wanted to see how they were
in Uruguay. Were they the same? Would they look like new potatoes with
veins again? I figured that out on the gaucho trail it was impossible to eat too
many testicles, but it was all wishful thinking. As usual they were off.

'*No tenemos criadillas ahora, pero tenemos choto.*' The waiter let me guess
what *choto* was, but was giving me heavy hints by poking the air with his
clenched fist and waving his eyebrows up and down his forehead lasciviously.
Surely he wasn't serious with his x-rated *What's My Line?* Surely it couldn't be
bull's dick?

I jabbed suggestively back at him and pointed at my trousers in the
wedding tackle region.

'*Que, de toro?*' I couldn't believe my luck.

'*Si, si, choto de toro.*'

I ordered some, with *sesos a la tela*, brains cooked in a cloth. They arrived
on the same plate. The brains were soft, very tasty and heavily herbed and
seasoned. The bull's dick was, as you'd expect, chewy and fatty and richly
flavoured in a strangely familiar way. Some would call it funky. I'd call it a day.
Once was enough. But together on one plate, the two were inspirational.

A plate of dickhead.

In 1791 a dashingly handsome young English aristocrat was strolling down
Rue St Honoré in Paris in the middle of the French Revolution. A little
foolhardy perhaps, or just mightily self-assured? Not surprisingly, he was
recognized as an Englishman and the mob fell on him.

'*Voilá – c'est un agent de Pitt! Un sacré anglais – à la lanterne!*' they shouted in
their witty Picardy patois.

At that time, lights were hung across the street on cords. If a lynching was
in the offing, they would be brought down and the victim strung up. The
young Englishman had the cords tightened round his neck, was strung up and
hanging in the air when they looked up at his face and realized just how
stunningly good-looking this boy was.

Several women rushed forward.

'*C'est un trop joli garçon pour être pendu!*' They cut him down, carried him off
and gave him some tender loving care.

John Ponsonby was too handsome to be hung. He was also much too
handsome to stay in King George IV's court. This was good news for Uruguay

which would not have existed but for John Ponsonby.

The first I heard of this was over a plate of *chinchulines* and sweet *morcillas* with a Uruguayan friend. We were in the Central Market in Montevideo, another fine example of English Victorian ironwork. The English monopoly once again. I'd seen it all before, but it still surprised me.

Uruguay, my friend claimed, had not just been funded or encouraged by England like the other countries. Uruguay had actually been *manufactured* by England. In fact my friend said that it should have been called Ponsonbyland as it had been entirely the creation of an Anglo-Irish artistocrat, the man whose good looks had saved him from the noose: John, First Viscount and Second Baron Ponsonby.

The eldest son of the Postmaster General of Ireland, John Ponsonby was so reticent about speaking in public that he got out of politics and went into diplomacy. He had been a member of the Irish House of Commons for Tallaght and Dungarvan but never made a speech.

'God forbid – it is all I can do to find the nerve for "yes" or "no" when there is a question in the House, and that is in a whisper.'

Later, when Ponsonby was Ambassador to Constantinople, he had to deliver a speech to the Sultan. He had the speech translated, to be read out to the Sultan and his court as he addressed them. One of the embassy attachés tells what happened:

Advancing with great dignity to where the Sultan stood, and putting out occasionally his hand as an orator might do, Lord Ponsonby with a very grave expression commenced counting 'one, two, three, four, five, six, seven, etc.' up to fifty, modulating his voice as if he desired to make an impression upon the minds of his hearers, putting emphasis upon some numbers and smiling with satisfaction when he reached the higher numbers of twenty to fifty. Of course, His Excellency knew that the Sultan and his ministers were not acquainted with the English language. On concluding, he turned to the interpreter and motioned him to speak. I hid my face and pinched myself sharply to check the outburst of laughter which inwardly convulsed me.

On another occasion, the Sultan had been complaining he wasn't getting enough respect from the Ambassadors, particularly Ponsonby. Maybe somebody had told him about the numbers game. He built an extremely low arch over the entrance to his reception room to force the various diplomats to come in on their hands and knees.

The diplomats arrived with Ponsonby at their head. When he saw the arch he didn't hesitate. In one smooth, glorious motion he turned round, crouched down, parted the tails of his blue tail coat and solemnly walked bent double backwards under the arch. He emerged stern-first with a fine display of white silk breeches into the Sultan's imperial presence.

Ponsonby was a womanizer, but being so devastatingly handsome and charming he would have had to be a saint to avoid all the beautiful women who dropped their handkerchiefs at his feet. He had serious love affairs with, among others, Lady Conyngham and the Princesse de Lieven. This was fine, but when a certain lady at court, the object of the King's affections, began longing for Ponsonby's arms, it had gone too far.

Something had to be done. The King was getting jealous. It was decided that Lord Ponsonby should be given a high diplomatic post a long way away and for a very long time.

They made him Envoy Extraordinary and Plenipotentiary to Buenos Aires. That seemed far enough. It was difficult enough too. The eastern side of the River Plate had always been thought to be part of the larger area which is now the Argentine. This was the Banda Orientale and by 1826 it wanted full independence.

Brazil was laying claim to it as it had done for years, keen to get a foothold on the River Plate. Buenos Aires, as the senior city on the other shore, wanted to keep control. But the Orientales, the people from the Banda Orientale, wanted their independence. Most of them were gauchos, more gaucho than the Argentines. Artigas, the liberator if not the architect of Uruguay, had gaucho cavalry, his *blandengues*, long before Guëmes.

Hell, hadn't Artigas gone over with his cowboy cavalry and helped the *porteños* recapture Buenos Aires from the English? Hadn't the Argentine gauchos been too scared to come back over and help out the Montevideans when they needed it? No, the Orientales were the real gauchos. They could stand on their own feet.

That was exactly what Lord Ponsonby wanted them to do. He knew that an independent Banda Orientale was best for Britain and her trade. Merchants from all over Britain had lobbied the government to do something about the terrible state of that area. With wars, hostile navies and pirates, trade was not good. And everyone remembered those days, so full of promise, after Popham had paraded the chest marked 'Treasure' through the City of London.

The English got so excited that they sent a second invasion. This was only a year after Guëmes and his gauchos had galloped into the river and captured the *Justine* with little more than rocks on ropes and a cowboy attitude.

This time the English headed for Montevideo first. The warships and the soldiers captured the fortress city. Following in their wake came *sixty-six* merchant ships loaded to the gunwales with goods, ready to do business. Two thousand merchants, some of them 'a dubious crew', set up shop wherever they could find space and 'it soon had more the appearance of an English colony than of a Spanish settlement'.

The English cut the customs duty from 50 to 12.5 per cent and made the citizens offers they couldn't refuse. They sold three quarters of a million pounds worth of goods for a million and a quarter, a profit of half a million pounds – a lot of money in 1807.

The English got even more excited. We can do business with these cowboys, they thought. They published the first bilingual newspaper, the *Southern Star*, to tell the Orientales how enlightened and liberal they were, but they still got kicked out by the gauchos. They didn't understand, they couldn't see that though the Orientales were happy with free trade, they were building an identity of their own and wanted independence, not colonization.

Lord Ponsonby, however, knew this well. He had more than two years of difficult and patient diplomacy as the mediator between Rio de Janeiro and Buenos Aires, each of whom laid claim to the territory. Even though he was patrician, supercilious and disdainful of foreigners and the lower classes, he had great skill and forthright charm.

He finally managed to get the two combatants, wearing each other down in a useless war, to agree. Most of the time during the negotiations he was in Buenos Aires and hating it. He missed the good life: 'Never did a place displease me so much . . . I always have Italy in my thoughts, to increase my mortification in this district of mud and rotten bones . . . Nothing good except meat.'

He stayed long enough in the district of mud and rotten bones to carve out the beginnings of the map of Uruguay. He helped them write a draft constitution. Then as soon as he was done, and not a minute later, he left Woodbine Parish in charge in Buenos Aires and went home.

He knew that the mad gauchos would soon be at each other's throats, city against country, *caudillo* against *caudillo*. So he went back to civilization and perhaps to pick up a few handkerchiefs. He crossed the seas to tell the English merchants they could come back.

We found a little hotel in the old town. Our rooms were right over the Bonanza! night spot. The girls did an extremely dubious cowboy-gaucho medley. The star and choreographer of this extravaganza was Miss Rita Mustang.

11. Fray Bentos

'Jesus Christ, it's a place! It's a place, goddammit, a fucking place!' Jo was jumping up and down and jabbing wildly at a map spread out on his bed. 'Fray Bentos is a goddamn place. Here, look! Where's the bible?'

Not a man given to sudden physical exertion, Tambien was leaping about and beating the map as if he'd seen a rattlesnake on his bed. I came over, gave him the *South American Travel Guide,* and looked where he was pointing before he drilled a hole in the map. There it was, clearly marked on the eastern shore of the Uruguay river, *Fray Bentos.* Jo's frenzied prodding was called 'research'. A bit late, perhaps, as we were already in Montevideo. Nursing hangovers, we'd been back to the Judges' Ranch at the rodeo and were trying to shake off last night's MacPay. Tambien was feverishly flicking through the pages of the guide while I stared mutely at the map. *Fray Bentos.*

All kinds of post-war images came flooding through. In the late forties and early fifties, while there was rationing in London, we ate what we could get hold of. I remember the banana that an American friend gave us from a bunch she had been sent. It sat on the dresser in the kitchen for three weeks before we shared it out between the four of us. Not a question of being poor, there just weren't any bananas.

One thing that always seemed to be around was corned beef. I loved corned beef. I could eat it all the time, hot or cold, I didn't care. On the label was a big, fat, meaty bull's head with a thick, solid neck. It seemed unscarred by the rigours of post-war austerity, grazing contentedly on thick green juicy pastures before it leapt into the tin with a carefree snort. Over the bull were the words 'Fray Bentos'.

It was one and the same. The town of Fray Bentos grew up round a meat packing and processing plant. The plant was dead and gone now, an industrial ghost town, but we had to go. Cowboys must have raised and driven a lot of cattle there to put a tin of corned beef on my table so regularly.

Tambien went into research overdrive. His fingers hardly touched the dial, but he managed to out do the usual telephone hand-jive and get to the heart of it in a flash. 'Right. We go tomorrow morning. It's the Anglo meat packing plant and it's enormous. It's derelict now but there's a guy there wants to make it an industrial museum, part of the country's heritage, he's writing a book about it. He says it's like Frankenstein's laboratory and he'd be pleased and proud to show us round.'

We grabbed a car and hit the road. It was going to be about seventy long leagues and a hot day. Though it was nearly a week since I'd been riding, my *medallones* were still sore. I obviously hadn't kept the *bifes* on for long enough. So I wore my baggy airy Bermudas and propped myself sideways in the back while Tambien took the wheel. I knew now I'd think twice about ordering two medallions of beef . . .

It was River Plate country. It was pampa, tilled and grazed pretty much how it is in Argentina. Near the city there were more smallholdings and as we moved out towards Mercedes the estancias and the fields got larger, and the herds bigger. They were growing maize, alfalfa and sorghum under a sky that was broad rather than enormous. There were eucalyptus and *calden* trees. My medallions throbbed in painful recognition.

The main difference between here and Argentina seemed to be the number of maté billboards – La Mulata, Campeon, El Arabe – along the highway. The other clue was the astonishing number of old cars driving down the road. It wasn't just American cars, either. They were there, naturally – the Buicks, Chevrolets, Chryslers, Pontiacs, Cadillacs, and from the forties and thirties as well as the almost standard fifties Bel Airs or sixties Impalas. No, out in the country there were Hillman Minx's, Morris Oxfords, Humber Super Snipes, Ford Populars, there were Nash Metropolitans, Citroën Traction-Avants, Renault Dauphines. They all appeared to be wonderfully restored and looked like perfect museum pieces. There were a surprising number of Ford Tin Lizzies. They were sparkling. And a thousand Ford and Chevvy pick-up trucks.

Out in the middle of the pampa, where the sky is biggest and the land widest, an immaculate 1940s black Daimler Gestapo staff car purred along ominously behind us. Just someone out for a spin, I'm sure, but it still looked dark and threatening. It's so smooth it doesn't look like it's moving, the old Daimler. It looks still, like it's crouching, ready.

There seemed to be more 1930s Ford flat-bed trucks than anything else on the road. Many had the wood-frame sides and Tambien said the whole place looked like Oklahoma. The old trucks were straight out of *Grapes of Wrath*. It was almost a surprise they were in colour. Tambien talked of a film about itinerant Mexican workers getting skin diseases from picking fruit and grapes that had been heavily sprayed with insecticides. It was called the *Wrath of Grapes*.

The reasons there are so many classic cars are simple. New cars are monstrously and prohibitively taxed. Old cars cannot be exported. There is no MOT. Uruguayans are fantastic and resourceful mechanics.

Instant museum.

Out in the middle of the country, on a bridge crossing into Rio Negro province is painted 'SEXO, DROGAS Y ROCK 'N' ROLL'.

We had arrived.

The Intendencia, the Town Hall, is on Fray Bentos' small town plaza. In the centre is a filigree iron bandstand like the one in Kensington Gardens. We go in and find Eduardo Irigoyen who is to take us to the plant.

Eduardo has jet-black hair and a neatly trimmed beard vaguely of the French student type. He is wearing a white short-sleeved shirt under a blue V-neck pullover. Behind his glasses his dark eyes get very intense when he talks in a soft but precise voice about Fray Bentos and the Anglo plant. He loves the Anglo plant and all its gory history and I want to hear every word.

We drive down past old tree-lined terraces of low workers' houses, part of the original Anglo workers' ghetto round the plant. We turn a corner, come out of the trees and suddenly we are on the edge of a wide river and underneath a gigantic building. We walk out on to a rickety jetty and right there on the shore is a towering concrete monolith of a building, a hangar, a massive, brutish stone box sticking right out into the bright-blue Uruguayan sky beside the wide, slow-flowing, yellow-ochre river. Across the top of this huge block, in gigantic faded black letters roaring across the Río Uruguay, the beautiful River of Birds, is 'ANGLO'. This monstrous box is the cold-storage building for the plant, the end of this particular line for carcases waiting to be shipped directly from the shores of this muddy yellow river across the Atlantic Ocean to Europe.

It needed to be this big. The Anglo plant was the biggest meat-processing plant in the world. This gargantuan fridge used to hold enough meat to feed the whole of Britain and free Europe during the Second World War.

I wanted to know more.

*

Legend has it that centuries ago a monk called Fraille Bento, Brother Bento, lived here as a hermit in a cave near the river for a hundred years. He built his own bed and table, spoke to no one, never lit a fire and called his hideout Caracoles, 'snails', either as a tribute to his neighbours or the pace of life. His name appears on sixteenth-century Jesuit maps as Fray Bento.

The area was wooded – *monte* – and wood-cutters moved in and set up as charcoal-burners servicing the river traffic. The spot was ideal and was called Puntas de Fray Bentos after the two natural deep-water moorings where even the biggest ships could tie up.

An Argentine trader of French-Basque origin called José Hargain crossed over the great river and opened an inn and a general store, to be nearer the busy charcoal-burners who owed him increasingly large sums of money. With heavy and regular river traffic, business boomed. It expanded so much that very soon, excited by the intercontinental possibilities of the deep-water moorings so high upriver, deep in the heart of cattle country, a group of hard-nosed entrepreneurs moved in on Hargain. Disenchanted, and usurped as the town's founder, the Basque moved out.

Despite some whining pamphlets from Hargain, who was presumably looking for a piece of the action, the big guys stayed put. In 1862, five years after the town was officially founded, a German company called Liebig started to set up a meat-processing plant. They had developed a meat-extract process and Uruguay had a lot of beef on the hoof out on the pampa.

As if by magic, up in the very heart of beef and gaucho country, was a river deep enough to take the biggest ocean-going cargo ships. Sometimes God is good.

In his wisdom, god (as he is known in Uruguay) decided that the world's greatest slaughterhouse should blossom on the oriental shore of the sedate River Uruguay. In the beginning meat was salted but soon the Lord created refrigeration, in buildings and boats alike. So it came to pass that El Frigorifico Liebig de Fray Bentos became the greatest meat-packing plant yet to have been built.

For more than one hundred years afterwards, cattle were slaughtered, butchered, packed and processed round the clock and shipped around the world. A lot of Uruguayan beef was rendered down to 'Liebig Extract', a cheap beef spread sold primarily to the British working class. Corned beef, the canned trimmings, followed. As early as the 1880s, 150,000 head of Uruguayan cattle were slaughtered in a year at Fray Bentos. That way the name and that stocky bull's head appeared on kitchen tables everywhere.

We thought Fray Bentos was Spanish for corned beef.

*

Jorge Luis Borges's mother was Uruguayan. He claimed to have been conceived at Fray Bentos and thus had a special affection for the place. The community that gathered here to work the plant was unique. Gringos and criollos flocked to the town. Here, gringo meant any foreigner. It had to because they came from everywhere: Russians, Basques, Poles, Germans, Bulgarians, Italians, Ukrainians, French, Czechs, Spanish, Austro-Hungarians, Greeks, Slavs, Peruvians, Bolivians, Argentines, Paraguayans, Japanese, even Mongolians. There were Chinese too. They were the cooks. But there were no English workers.

'It was a completely unplanned social experiment – the United Nations.' Eduardo's black eyes sparkle as he beats the table and harangues Tambien and me. We are sitting in the Wolves' Club, the old workers' club, eating gnocchi and looking out over the river at the green shores of Argentina on the other side.

'And the experiment worked. Everyone got on with everyone else. They all intermarried, French with Bulgarians, Germans with Slavs, criollos with Poles. All except a group of Manchurians who arrived much later, in 1966. They were conscientious objectors, were persecuted and came here because they didn't want to fight. They lived outside town and have no contact with the outside world except when they come in to buy sugar and noodles. But they are the exception.'

Eduardo has more than warmed to his subject and is ready to autocombust. Certainly his eyes are aflame. 'It was the first cooperative in Uruguay. There was no management class, no bourgeoisie. They had no class structure – the doctor would dance with the daughter of a labourer. There was no unemployment – seven thousand people lived in Fray Bentos, men, women and children, and three thousand five hundred worked at the Anglo. There was a peculiar harmony.'

That was in the 1920s. After Germany's defeat in the First World War, Liebig had money problems and sold out to the Vestey family interest in BA. The plant became El Anglo.

For more than forty years the Vesteys, a Liverpool family, had been big in beef. In 1876, the same year the first refrigerated ship, *Le Frigorifique*, brought an 'edible' shipment of beef from Argentina, the eldest Vestey son, William, was despatched to the USA to buy and ship home anything the family could sell. He was seventeen.

He made a fortune canning the massive trimmings from the Chicago stockyards – 'Corned Beef' He went to Argentina and was once again shocked by the enormous waste. The Argentines, it seemed, were still more interested in hides and tallow than in flesh. They still had the old gaucho attitude and left the meat to rot. Why shouldn't they? When young Vestey arrived, there were *thirteen million* head of cattle on the Argentine pampas alone. As well as beef, William found an abundant stock of partridges, which the locals ignored. So he set up a trial shipment of frozen partridges and business boomed. Union Cold Storage, now Union International, was born.

By the turn of the century, two hundred and eighty refrigerated ships were regularly crossing the Atlantic taking Uruguayan and Argentinian beef and extract to Liverpool and Europe.

The Vestey family began the Great War with cold stores in Britain, Russia and China and four large refrigerated ships. In 1915 the British Government introduced draconian tax laws. To finance the war effort they were going to tax companies which made profits abroad. The Vesteys, fiercely protective of their money, packed up and left Britain, setting up the heart of their operation in Buenos Aires. At the same time they began converting a large meat plant at Las Palmas on the Río Parana. The total slaughter of cattle for export in the Argentine doubled between 1914 and 1918.

By the last year of the war, the Vesteys had built cold-storage facilities at Boulogne, Dunkirk and Le Havre. Allied troops were consuming *one million pounds* of beef a day. The gauchos were working overtime. A year after the war, as well as their previous holdings, the family had ranches, plants and cold stores in Australia, New Zealand, South Africa, Madagascar, France, Spain and Portugal. They now had nine refrigerated ships. Bigger in beef.

Once they had bought the Liebig plant at Fray Bentos they became the biggest. William Vestey bought himself a peerage from Lloyd George and got a nasty, truculent letter from George V.

The Vesteys had undoubtedly helped the war effort but had helped themselves even more. The Inland Revenue was furious. They were investigating the family, in one of many frustrating attempts at wresting money from them.

The Vesteys had woven an ingenious web of holding companies that made it very difficult for anyone, especially the taxman, to get near their money. Their empire by now was built on meat, wood mills, property development, grocery wholesaling, insurance, shipping and travel. And more meat.

I began to understand why the cold store at El Anglo was so huge. I began to grasp the scale of this operation and to see why they needed to control the wild gauchos to get them working on the big ranches and driving those steers to slaughter.

It had been inevitable that the Vesteys should wrest control of Fray Bentos from Liebig. Everything else was British-run. They had improved the livestock with heavy imports of British animals, moved the stock on railroads built and owned by the British to plants equipped and financed by the British. The products from these plants were shipped on British ships to England, the monopoly export market for many decades.

I began, too, to understand Eduardo's fascination with this bizarre charnel-house out in the middle of nowhere. An odd aspect of the place, especially to one like myself who has dabbled in macrobiotics and advanced vegetarianism, was why a society like this, sustained by the wilful and unceasing slaughter of dumb animals, can have been so peaceful, self-contained and free of rancour or aggression. Surely butchers are butchers? Surely on a negative scale of karma from one to ten, eviscerating animals dangling on a conveyor belt must score a high nine? And yet the facts speak for themselves.

For fifty years, Eduardo Irigoyen's 'unplanned social experiment' was a resounding social and spiritual success. People lived in extraordinary harmony.

What are we to conclude from all this? That all the workers' aggression was burnt out by the incessant slaughter? Or that man has an innate need to kill which, once satisfied, leaves him at peace? If so, then the slaughter of vegetables, which do after all have feelings – beans and lentils are *pulses*, remember – is no substitute for killing animals. It might be a difficult bullet to bite on, especially for those of a herbivorous frame of mind, but perhaps killing animals is good for the soul. I wonder how seven thousand workers in a tofu factory in the middle of nowhere would cope? I foresee terrible problems.

Not only did this utopian community exist by butchering animals, they also ate the meat they produced. The work didn't put them off their food at all; in fact, the two kilos of meat each worker was given to take home every day was not enough for some. In addition they would hack off strips from the fresh carcases, and lay them on the hot steam pipes that ran through the slaughterhouse to cook and eat while they worked. Others would wrap layers of beef round their bodies and put their clothes back on over them to smuggle them home.

One time a worker on his way out of the plant saw people ahead of him being stopped and searched at the factory gates. With remarkable presence of mind, he quickly loosened his clothing enough to pull out the large strip of beef he had wrapped round himself. He threw it high in the air just as he got to the gate. The strip of meat twisted and spun through the air like fleshy *bolas*.

'Hey!' he shouted as the beef whistled back down and slapped on to his head, 'Don't throw that meat at me.'

History doesn't record whether he got away with it and was allowed home wearing his beefy beret.

Another over-confident worker was caught with a whole leg of beef. It was strapped to his belly under his belt but started to slip down the wide leg of his overalls just as he got to the gate. Desperate to stop the incriminating evidence from spilling out on to his boot, he bent down suddenly to grab the runaway joint. *Ping!* A disc slipped in his back and he was left bent double at the factory gate, one hand holding his agonized back, the other flailing impotently at his trouser leg as the meat slipped out.

Others would take home meat extract in the same Thermos that they had brought to work to make their maté. Though they weren't on horseback, their diet was that of the gauchos who drove the cattle into El Anglo – meat, maté, tobacco and occasional wine.

Only once did relations sour in this carnivorous utopia. Unions had never been allowed, and any sign of union activity was snuffed out by instant dismissal. The one and only strike came in 1929. There had been a wage demand which the management were ignoring. Communist militants picked the gates, waving flags and urging the workers to strike. One morning, as the night shift was coming off, the incoming shift gathered at the gates and an instant strike meeting took place. The communists founded a strike committee in their offices in Fray Bentos.

The management called the Vestey offices in BA who agreed to settle the workers' demands immediately. It looked as if it would all be resolved in the usual easy-going Fray Bentos way, but the deal broke down when the communists insisted that the agreement should be signed in their headquarters under the Party banner. The management refused and wanted to sign it in a neutral place – a bar in town. The deal was never signed, the strike dragged on and the peaceful mood in the town disintegrated. There were ugly scenes.

One day stones were thrown at a *carnero* – a blackleg – going into a plant, but it turned out to be the blackleg's brother. They'd got the wrong man. A lone policeman rode up to his assistance, but also got stoned. He went to get help and police returned in force to ride down the strikers. A major battle followed, the police chief was knifed in the lungs, many strikers were beaten and injured and the strike was crushed.

Eduardo's soft eyes cloud over as he tells us this story, the one stain on his tale of an industrial paradise on the peaceful shores of a lazy river. He brightens up again when he tells us of the only other time in over a century when El Anglo shut down.

'The whole community had great sympathy for the Allies in the Second

World War. The people had their feet in Uruguay but their hearts were always in Europe. They had always worked round-the-clock shifts but stepped up production during the war. El Anglo was feeding all of Britain and the Allies.'

He is warming again, closing his copybook on its solitary blot. 'When the news reached Fray Bentos in August 1944 that Paris had been liberated, there was a huge fiesta. The whole town celebrated hard for three days solid while El Anglo stayed silent. Bulgarians, French, Russians, Chinese and Czechs, they all danced tangos and *paso dobles* and waltzes in the streets, they were so overcome with joy. They still talk of it today.'

El Anglo was finally closed in 1979. The military government that ruled Uruguay in the sixties had nationalized the plant with disastrous results. A combination of reasons – lack of investment, outdated equipment and increasingly stringent EEC regulations – meant that El Anglo could not operate in the world of the late twentieth century. It was an industrial dinosaur and collapsed under its own weight. Now it stands rotting and glowering over the empty river where the big boats used to come. A monument to the time the Industrial Revolution sailed right up the Río Uruguay, it is still and silent apart from the wind off the river whistling through the broken windows and whipping under loose sheets of corrugated iron which flap and crash mournfully. Vesteys went into receivership early in 1995.

Eduardo Irigoyen wants to turn El Anglo into an industrial museum but there are no funds to repair the acres of broken windows, roofs and walkways. He pushes his chair back.

'Come and see. Come back to the nineteenth century.'

He takes us first to the office. It smells of warm dry wood. Rows of broad desks and old typewriters sit in the typing pool. On the wooden walls, painted pale green, cream and brown, are pictures of the plant at the end of the last century.

The records room is a gold mine, packed with inventory ledgers, pristine bound copies of the local newspaper *El Litoral*, 'The Shore', and pamphlets from suppliers of machinery from Bolton, Sheffield, Manchester, Rugby, Glasgow and Liverpool. The plant's whole history is documented in this room, ready for Eduardo's would-be reconstruction: photographs, accounts, posters and labels, original artwork for the tins we all saw on our tables some time in our lives, in many different languages and perfectly preserved.

Dust hangs still in the shafts of sunlight that stream in through the office windows. The dust motes stampede after us as we walk through the shafts of light and break the thick, silent stillness. Behind the enormous entrepreneurial desk is an old Chubb wall safe.

At the door is a punch-card machine. I clock in and its bell rings. Just before we go out I notice a round-topped display jar catching the sunlight, glinting at me, calling me from a desktop. Something green and murky is inside. When I get close I realize it is the two heads of a double-headed calf, a young Siamese steer. Welcome to paradise in a pickling jar.

The sloping alleyways between the warehouses, offices, slaughterhouse, cold-storage and engine rooms shine and sparkle in the afternoon sun. They are floored with five-foot-long, two-inch thick iron plates with stamps like 'Glasgow 1866'. This colossal weight of iron pavement was brought over as ballast by the big ships that came for the meat.

Eduardo guides us through the plant, following the route taken by the cattle, from freedom to fridge, from corrals to cans. We walk up a narrowing channel and tiptoe gingerly along rotting planks by the side of a concrete chute, hanging out over a forty-foot drop.

Each steer was isolated by a door and killed by a blow to the head from a man called the Hammerer. The side wall opened and the dead animal fell out into the beginning of the slaughterhouse hall, the *plaza de la faena* or *matadero*. Its throat was cut and it was hooked up on to a conveyor belt that runs along the ceiling, twisting and turning through the abattoir. It runs slightly downwards all the time, so the carcases were simply pushed along by the workers, helped by gravity.

On their journey through this killing room, the animals were skinned, dismembered and gutted, each part of the process carried out by a separate worker. There were specialists for each organ – heart, kidneys, liver, guts, lungs and glands such as pancreas and thyroid. The organs were tossed separately down chutes and holes in the floor to be processed below while the stripped carcases swung along, snaking though the slaughterhouse in their last dance, a final bizarre conga on their way to the cold storage.

The desolation in this murderous hall is palpable. It is a cold light grey, all metal and stone, clinical and industrial at the same time. There are broad butchering counters and huge weighing machines from Avery of Birmingham and Toledo of Ohio. The metal is rusting and redundant. The only softness in this bleak room is the spiders' webs which drape every corner and beam, anchoring machines to the ground and shrouding piles of chains that lie on the floor. The webs shake as the corrugated-iron sheets flap and crash over the bridge to the cold storage, reverberating through this cold, deathly place.

This dilapidated abattoir is where hundreds of thousands of animals were slaughtered and butchered, hung, drawn and quartered twenty-four hours a day without stopping. It is hard not to imagine the noise, the blood, the heat and, worst of all, the smell.

Nothing was thrown away. William Vestey would have been proud. Horns and hoofs were boiled down for glue. Even gall-stones were exported to Japan where they were used as aphrodisiacs. The bits, the trimmings and some organs were rendered down for beef extract in enormous vats.

Worst of all, the smell.

The refrigeration block – the concrete monolith with 'Anglo' along its gable that it seemed I had first seen a lifetime ago – had five floors of cold storage and seventy kilometres of refrigerant piping.

'Welcome to the nineteenth century – after the apocalypse,' says Eduardo as he opens the door to the machine room. 'My dream is that they will come and make Alien 4 here one day.'

We go in, out of the bright Uruguayan sunlight, and peer through the gloom. As our eyes accommodate to the brown half-light, we see enormous rusting driving wheels, chains, steam engines and pistons, rotting in pools of oil and muck. It is a Victorian vision of the future, post-apocalyptic indeed, something from Jules Verne via Fritz Lang's *Metropolis*. I shudder. The *matadero* is still with me and these gigantic driving wheels gave muscle to the killing floor above. The boilers have long since stopped working and the lagging sags from unused cylinders. This was the powerhouse of El Anglo. The big wheels are generators for electricity, the first one a steam generator which drove the first electric lights in the whole River Plate area early in the 1860s. It was the most advanced technology of its time.

'Now from the Brave New World,' says Eduardo, 'to Frankenstein.' His gentle black eyes are gleaming, a child showing us his toy fort and soldiers.

We slip out of the shadows, blinking, and into the control room. High, grey and metallic, its wall is covered with switches, dials and the kind of levers the good Baron F. would slap down as the lightning flashed above and his monster started to twitch. On the dials and plaques on the walls are written:

ERSKINE HEAP & CO. Ltd
Lancashire Switchgear Works,
Broughton, Manchester

EVERETT EDGCOMBE, London

The BRITISH THOMSON-HOUSTON Co. Ltd
Rugby, England

They are real dials, these, big bulky things that stick right out of the wall, dials you can tap and believe in. Under them are written 'Office', 'Cold Store', 'Slaughterhouse'.

We haven't finished. Eduardo takes us breathlessly down to a circular brick structure built into the edge of the river with a walkway across to it. He unlocks the padlock, opens the door and motions us in with a shining grin of anticipation lighting up his whole face. He is getting younger and younger through the afternoon and now is about five years old. As soon as we go in we see why.

Perched on blocks, every little boy's dream, shining brass and steel and red-painted metal, is a Merryweather Holt steam fire-engine. Now stripped of its wheels and the horses that used to pull it through the streets for the London Fire Brigade, it sits placidly and contentedly, ready to draw up river water and pump it out to any part of El Anglo that might burst into flame. It is perfectly restored and a thing of gleaming beauty. More than thirty plaques round it lay claim to its excellence: 'London First Grand Prize Patent Steam Fire Engine', says one.

Down a short way from the Merryweather 'Holt' is the jetty. Very rickety its gnarled and twisted planks have more gaps than substance. A narrow-gauge rail track runs out of the bottom of the gigantic cold store, through a little wooden shed and on to the jetty.

Like a backdrop from *Cannery Row*, it looks far too insubstantial to have carried millions of frozen carcases brought out of the cold store, smoking cold in the Uruguayan sun, to be loaded on to the great cargo ships parked slap bang against it. Two cranes stand forlornly like broken-necked storks. The ends of this matchstick jetty are frayed and slipping into the swirling ochre waters. It seems inconceivable that this frail little dock could have handled everything the monster killing-machine behind it belched out, but it did.

Over the years, drawn by stories of a high-cholesterol El Dorado, the immigrants kept on coming for a chance to work in El Anglo. In the mid-twenties, a large group of Georgians arrived from the Caucasus. In 1929, three hundred illiterate Bulgarian peasant boys turned up in one day. A colony of Germans came in the fifties. And, of course, there were the inscrutable Manchurians in 1966. They are still there, holed up in the country outside Fray Bentos, and still only know the Spanish for 'sugar' and noodles'. Two German colonies, one Russian and one Bulgarian are still intact in the town.

Among all these different peoples working and playing together, intermarrying and living in carnivorous harmony, one nationality remained aloof. They built their own mansion, their own garden, their own tennis courts and made do with just a nine-hole golf course. They were the managers of El Anglo.

They were, of course, the English.

Their mansion, grand colonial style, stands imperiously alone, above and behind the plant. The garden is more of an arboretum, with rare trees from all around the world. A sign says 'Absolutely No Dogs Allowed In This Garden'. The word for 'Absolutely' is *Terminamente*.

The clubhouse at the golf course is as English as the Hurlingham in Buenos Aires. In El Anglo's ghetto an old man told us how to find the golf club, stroking his fat belly with a gnarled brown hand and scratching his dark tanned Uruguayan neck. He looked typically criollo until, that is, he turned to look at me.

His eyes were a very pale, limpid blue.

United Nations.

We decided to stop over at Colonia on the way back to Montevideo. My medallions were grateful for the break, and Tambien assured me that Colonia would not disappoint on the historical front. I was ready for more history, happy to go along. I lay propped up in the back seat, looking up at the blinding full moon with its upside-down smile, wondering if my lover across the seas was looking at the same smiling moon the right way up.

Colonia delivered. It is very historical, with charming old cobbled streets of white . . . er . . . *colonial* buildings. A smell of mimosa hung in the air. It is a museum town. There is a Portuguese and a Spanish museum, a civic and a natural history one. They were closed that night so we trawled them the next day. The history of the seesawing between Spain and Portugal, the British invasions and the role of the gaucho cavalry was all there. The natural history museum was full of stuffed birds and animals and prehistoric remains of *Glyptodon*, giant coral-backed armadillos.

I was most drawn to an early eighteenth-century cattle-herder's outfit, the best I've seen yet. It was, basically, a giant haystack. The man had a conical straw hat, straw jacket, big straw coat, a bulky straw skirt and straw moon boots. He was Thatch Man, a walking winter feed.

The cattle he was tending must have thought he was wearing their dinner. Maybe he was.

But the night we arrived, instead of looking for history, Jo and I went out and hit the *whickerias*. Whisky is as popular here as in the Argentine, maybe more so. We'd seen it with the MacPay at the rodeo. I'd seen shop windows and *whickeria* shelves packed with obscure Scotches as well as national whiskies. We found a gold mine in Colonia. We stumbled into the Meson de Whicky, Whisky House. Some of the lesser-known Scotches ranked along its shelves were Mansion House, Usher's Green Stripe, Black Cock (with a black turkey on the label), Sandy Mac, Old Angus, Ye Monks ('A Curious Old Whisky'), Old Parr, Scottish Leader, King George IV, King Edward I, The Real Mackenzie, House of Peers, Old Smuggler ('Scotch with a History'), Pinwhinnie Royale, Grand Macnish, Doctor's Special (from the House of Macnish), Black Prince (Special Old), Passport and Lord & Lord ('Very Rare, Very Mellow' – very cheap?).

We got stuck in. We mixed nationals with Scotches. Then I saw a bottle which said 'DRUNK' in white block letters. It called to me. It claimed to be gin. The label was a stroke of marketing genius. On a dark blue, suitably naval background, it said:

DRUNK

London

OLD TOM

Dry Gin

Guaranteed by

(indecipherable)

London

On the back it said reassuringly 'Concentrated in glass deposits'. And of course, the clincher, 'Made in Uruguay'.

It was industrial spirit.

So was 'Old Scotch', but fair play to them. For when I tasted it and realized it was banana-flavoured meths, I saw there was no mention of the word 'whisky' on the label. It is just Old Scotch, and that's as far as it goes.

Although this seemed like being spoiled for choice I couldn't find my favourite whisky. Last time I saw it was in Romania. It had a simple black label. On it, joyously welcoming the poor wretches blinking like moles as they emerge into the glorious dawn of capitalism's free market, is the mocking name Johnny Worker. Johnny Worker Black Label. Hmmmm . . .

We got so whickied up we giggled all night at the thought of Alan Whicker doing a programme on *whickerias* – 'Whicker 'ere in the *whickeria*'. Oh, how we laughed.

Sitting in the *whickeria*, we thought of all the *-erias* we had seen so far. The *panaderias*, *licorerias* and *confiterias* were everywhere. The *whickerias* and *cocktelerias* were old hat, as were the *sandwicherias* and even *frankfurterias*. I'd seen *pollerias*, chicken shops, and *corseterias*, lingerie stores, though Tambien thought they would have been more euphonious as *lingeri-erias*. We'd coped with *santerias*, holy relic and graven image shops, in Lujan, *bombillerias*, *bombilla* specialists and even *putarias*, whorehouses.

I had seen the best, though, from one of the old Leyland troop-carrier buses that rumble through Montevideo. I told Tambien that I had passed a *flipperia*, a video-game and slot-machine arcade. Pinball machines are called *flippers*.

I was sitting in the sun on the end of a jetty sticking out into the River Plate with the whitewashed walls of Colonia's old town glaring out behind me. I was nursing a Drunk London Old Tom kind of hangover. Not literally, for one shot of Drunk was already too much, but Tambien and I had compared and contrasted a lot of whiskies in minute detail. My head hurt. I kept my shades firmly strapped over my eyes and avoided looking too hard at Colonia's white walls.

Colonia del Sacramento was founded in 1680 by the Portuguese, directly opposite BA, attempting to get a foothold on the River Plate and to challenge Spanish supremacy. One way to do this was by breaking the Spanish trade monopoly by smuggling. So right from the beginning Colonia was a smuggling centre.

It is a living tradition. As I sat on the jetty a police launch was being washed down and refuelled. They had just busted a man trying to slip in with a boatload of contraband cigarettes. Old habits die hard.

As I watched the muddy waters moving out to the sea, my thoughts started to carry me out of Uruguay. Soon enough we would be heading up to Venezuela. There is a whole other cowboy culture up there in the tropical north. They share the *llaneros* – the plainsmen – with Colombia, but Jo Tambien said everything pointed to Venezuela as more important to the cowboy trail.

I kept on flying further north in my mind, jumping the jungles of the isthmus, and thought of Mexico, of the vaqueros, the horsemen who taught the Anglo cowboys the tricks of the trade.

More than all of these, as I watched the eddying terracotta waters and nursed my aching head, I kept thinking about the Alamo. It must have been a song I'd heard last night, a cowboy song about a gaucho general who died in a siege. I had been down in the Southern Cone for a long time now, maybe too long. I knew I was heading ultimately for San Antonio, across the final Rio Grande, to try to understand what really happened at the Alamo. The siege, the heroes, the winners and losers.

Davy Crockett is not alone. In Uruguay, Leandro Gomez was besieged by a hated Brazilian army for much longer than the thirteen days Crockett and Bowie were holed up in the Alamo. He was under siege in Paysandu, the place where Artigas set up his ill-fated cowboy government. Like Crockett, he had a song written about him.

He held out for months, a heroic last stand with his gaucho army a quarter of a century after the Alamo. Like the Alamo, the fort was finally overrun and all the defenders were killed.

There is a gaucho *milonga*, a sad Uruguayan country song, full of dark power, about General Leandro Gomez. If a siege mentality exists, it is there in the defiant melancholy of this *milonga*. In the heart of the song it breaks into a deep-voiced *payador* recitation. When I heard it the night before, whisky or no whisky, it sent shivers down my spine.

General Leandro Gomez is with us
General Leandro Gomez has a star
General Leandro Gomez, your country needs you
General Leandro Gomez shouted 'Independence or Death!'

From the birth of mystery
General Leandro Gomez
   signed the death warrant of the Empire
General Leandro Gomez
   had a boat of lights made for him
General Leandro Gomez
   is sailing over the country high above Paysandu,
   high in the heavens in his boat of lights.

Señors! When this story is sung,
The General Leandro Gomez rises again
The General Leandro Gomez lives forever.

On the bus out to the airport, driving past the never-ending white sandy beaches that edge the hem of Montevideo, I fell to talking with a Uruguayan about politics and football. I asked why so many of the national heroes – Artigas, Leandro Gomez, O'Higgins, San Martín – were killed or died in exile.

He didn't have to think. He answered immediately.

'Because they were too idealistic. They were too honest for this continent.'

12. Pass the Maté, Mate

'Pass the maté, mate.'

There was a tap on my shoulder. Sitting behind me was a stocky fair-haired man of about thirty with a heavy Aussie accent. Somehow Jo and I were on a plane heading north to Venezuela, leaving the Southern Cone, a bit of a wrench after such a long time. Maybe I was hanging on to Uruguay by drinking maté. I knew it didn't exist up in the tropics. From now on, any cowboys we might see would drink coffee.

I passed him the maté. He didn't wipe or twist and dig the *bombilla* round in the *yerba*. He just drank it and passed it back without a thank you. He'd drunk it before.

'Keep it coming, mate, I don't think they've ever seen maté on this plane before – scored a first there. Come on, mate, what you waiting for, pass the maté over.'

He'd been drinking it for six years against my two weeks.

'Great stuff. You know it's addictive, of course, mate, but what the hell. Just keep it coming.'

Tim Young was a salesman. It turned out he wasn't an Aussie, and I could hear the clipped tones of a Kiwi. He'd been coming to South America for ten years on and off.

Originally he had been a cattle trader and had done government work.

'Between '86 and '89 I lived in Venezuela, dealing on behalf of the New Zealand Government. In that time we shipped thirty thousand head of dairy cattle live from New Zealand to Venezuela. It was a huge, humungous business. The Venezuelans were committed to improving the genetic base of their herds; it meant the odd New Zealander had to come over, had to learn to ride a horse, now there's a lot of New Zealand cattle out on the *llanos*.'

Sheep?

'Sheep? No, mate, We tried, but it turned out they couldn't adapt to the tropical conditions. They all died. We brought cross-bred cattle that could cope, that had some resistance to the tropics.' He talked fast and didn't stop for breath. I wondered whether he played the didgeridoo and had mastered the circular breathing technique. I watched to see if he snorted air in through his nose while talking simultaneously with his mouth.

'Biggest cattle haul, biggest shipment ever placed on the water so far in the history of mankind was in '87, three thousand cattle, shipped on a leased Saudi-Arabian cattle ship, from Hamilton New Zealand to Maracaibo. Went through the Panama Canal, took us five weeks, had four New Zealand vets on board, only lost three head of cattle.' He settled back, pleased and proud.

He rattled on and kept on reaching for the maté. He was a bit of a wide boy. He got out of cattle when he saw the market shrinking, and into whisky.

'I decided that cows had gone a bit quiet on us, so I moved into Scotch whisky which is a great business down here. Much more secure, mate.'

A whisky dealer – just the man I needed to see. Are Argentina and Uruguay as big whisky consumers as they seem? Nothing compared to Venezuela, he said.

'They're a bunch of crazy fuckers. They have nowhere near a third of the population base, but they get through more than a third of all the whisky in South America. Look, on top of all those national whiskies, Breeder's Choice and the like, they import seventy-four million bottles of Scotch into South America every year. Biggest market in the world. And the Venezuelans chug twenty-five million of those bottles of Scotch whisky a year, mate. They pour it down their throats as fast as they can. But just remember, the country is built on cattle and oil, and fuelled with whisky, that's why they're so crazy.'

'*Barbaro!*' I muttered. Wicked.

'Ah, that's what they say down south, mate, but up in the tropics these crazy bastards say *Machete*.'

Tim took it on himself to warn us of the dangers of Caracas. Warnings, where to stay, what to do, advice on how to deal with these bandits, it all poured out of him like stream-of-consciousness stuff.

'Dangerous place, mate. You're going into bandit country now, it's nothing like down south any more. There's a lot of money around and a lot of very poor people would like to get their hands on it. You got to watch out. I told you they're crazy. They're all looking for a buck. Pass the maté, mate, don't hang around, hey.'

He didn't stop for breath, just reached over and tugged the maté out of my lifeless fingers. By now my mouth had dropped open and I was staring at him like a slack-jawed schoolkid.

Tim enjoyed being a flash bastard, a bit of a rogue, and telling wild stories of high and low life in the worlds of oil, of cattle and whisky. The cattle were still important.

'In spite of all the oil noise that comes out of Venezuela, mate, don't forget there's a huge cattle sector and a huge cowboy population there, a bunch of cowboys who've been around long before John Wayne got his mitts on any six-guns.'

He told us of a cattle deal he did in Medellín where the guy asked if cash was acceptable. Of course, no problem. It was a thousand head of cattle. The man came back with one million two hundred thousand dollars in a paper bag. 'Bandit country, mate, bandit country.'

He checked where we were staying and said that it was safe. And that he'd come by later and show us round Caracas.

He was right. It felt like bandit country straight away, a place where a lot of easy money has been creamed off by a few fast people and no money goes to the rest of the poor buggers. It was in the air, the whiff of the fast buck. It was completely different from the more restrained European style of the Southern Cone.

It was a long drive into Caracas. The city sprawled out all over the encircling hills and mountains. It engulfed them with tar paper, breeze block and corrugated-iron shacks. The poor people were up there clinging to the hillsides, watching the rich folks down in the valleys. More than it ever did down south, the poverty and the threat of violence crackled like static in the air.

It was like any American city. Caracas chews gum.

Out on the roads were motorcycle cops looking moody in khaki cloth caps and shades. Belching, wheezing and wallowing around them were a lot of sleazy old American cars with cracked windscreens.

It looked like every low-slung gas guzzler built before 1980 had been driven down the old Pan American highway and dropped off in Venezuela. They were noisy and dirty and had burgundy crushed velvet or sky-blue nylon carpet lining the dashboards. They were in the right place for their age and their condition, with petrol only twenty pence a gallon in oil-rich Venezuela.

It was a limbo, a purgatory for old Yankee cars to wallow through with the remains of their marshmallow suspension, until they were allowed to die peacefully, cough out their last dark cloud, their last polluted gift to the world and slip off to the great Motown in the sky.

The centre of the city was swamped by skyscrapers topped with *parabolicas* like giant fans facing the onrushing sunset. Caracas is Dallas and Tijuana mixed together. Our hotel was a high-rise souvenir of the sixties well past its use-by date. Its weary carpets bore the battle scars and blemishes of an exhausting life. No pain, no stain.

Tambien and I went to meet our mate Tim the whisky rep in Weekends, an American potato-skin bar. His friend Homero, an advertising man, was as flash and speedy as himself, with a new leather jacket and a shiny new Camaro.

They took us out on the town. On the thin pretext of selling his whisky, Tim took us from bar to bar, the low life getting lower at each turn. Red and black leather, on the walls, the furniture and the people, was the universal decoration. The bars got darker and the hookers moved towards us faster as we got drunker and the night wore on. Leather basques, high-rise tights, peek-a-boo bras, suspender belts, stilettos, French knickers and the rest all passed before our eyes like an adult funwear catalogue from the *Sunday Times*.

Tim was enjoying the role as tour guide to the nether world. One bar felt dodgier and darker than any of the others and was filled with androgynous looking women with broad shoulders and big feet in red and black leather basques and fishnet stockings. We walked six paces into the darkness, Tim spun on his heel, said 'No!' curtly and walked straight out. No questions needed, we knew the answer.

For someone who lived in Soho for years I am pretty naive. We found ourselves in what looked like the bar of a smart hotel having a quiet drink from Tim's bottle of whisky. Men and women kept constantly appearing and disappearing. The women had changed out of their street clothes and were relaxing. I thought they must have been hotel residents.

We were quickly joined by several beautiful young women who seemed to like us a lot. Maria Eugenia wanted to be my special friend. She was tall and dark skinned with simple clear eyes. I told her as usual that I was from the other side of the moon.

Maria Eugenia stuck her tongue in my ear. Still the penny didn't drop. I thought she was just friendly. Even a hand on the thigh and a lot of leg squeezing didn't give me a clue.

I guess I'm just plain stupid. I thought either my pulling gear was working or that after the *criadillas* the other day she could still smell the testosterone on my breath. Ah, the vanity of man . . .

'You want to fuck?' No, not really, thanks.

'Sure you do. Everyone want to fuck.' No, thanks I'm engaged. I have a fiancée back home.

'That don't matter. We can fuck, I won't tell her anything.' No, really, nothing personal, I'm OK.

'Why not – I have clean bed, I am clean girl. I give you massage.' I was pretty knotted up after the long journey and pointed at my neck. 'Oh, lovely, yes please. My neck's really stiff and painful. It'd be great if you could sort it out for me. Would you mind?'

That did it. Within one minute all the girls had evaporated from our group and started stroking thighs at another table. We finished the whisky and Tim paid the bill. Two hundred dollars for the four of us to sit in the bar, get our legs felt, drink our own whisky and fuck nobody.

We crammed back into the Camaro, Tambien and I folded up into the tiny rear seat space, Homero racing through the streets of Caracas, all of us drunk. As we tore the wrong way up a one-way street, Tom Jones on the radio assured us that 'It's Not Unusual'.

Tom must be big in Venezuela, because three times that night in the Camaro 'It's Not Unusual' came over the airwaves.

They dropped us back at the hotel.

'I could take you deeper into the twilight zone,' said Tim, getting back into the Camaro, 'but I don't think you guys are quite ready for it.'

The car roared away with a smell of burnt rubber and a screech of the wheels as they disappeared, laughing, round the corner.

I was keen to hear something other than Tom Jones while we were in Caracas, so Jo got in touch with some musicians the next day. I had a friend in Mexico City who was part of the South American leftie folk music scene. He had told us to go and see Lilia Vera, one of Venezuela's great singers. So we did.

Lilia turned up trumps. She had recently had a baby, her fourteenth child, and looked radiant. We met her with her *compañero*, her companion, Romulo, and a lot of other musicians, in a youth music project in a community centre. A big sign said that it had been funded, presumably as a guilt-minimizing exercise, by the Bigott Foundation, a big tobacco corporation. Bigott Corp. The musicians were stunning. At first I thought it was Caribbean music, with the harp rolling and chopping over the rhythm from the maracas. Then I realized, and it was soon obvious, that they were playing high-octane tropical cowboy music. The maracas galloped like horses' hooves. The *cuatros*, the four-stringed small *llanero* rhythm guitar, a kind of ukulele, pushed everything along.

When the harp wasn't playing, the *bandola*, an instrument peculiar to the *llanos*, took over. It comes from the Arab *oud* which became the lute and came over with the Spanish. Coincidentally, one tune explored an Arabic scale, similar to flamenco, with astonishing virtuosity. The *bandola* from the eastern *llanos* had four sets of double strings like a madolin.

They played a lot of *joropos*, the fast *llanero* dance music. Lilia said that most Venezuelan music was fast and happy, that it wasn't generally as mournful and sad as a lot of the gaucho songs. She did, however, sing us a sad *tonada*, a slow song about a canary.

The harp player was something else. He wrestled with the harp, cursing it. It wasn't his own.

'This harp is SHIT!' he shouted, beating its frame with both hands. 'I've got one at home that could slice a mango in two!'

Shit or not, he still got a mighty sound out of it. I never realized what an aggressive instrument the harp can be in the right hands. The other musicians were mesmerized, shouting '*Machete! Autentico!*' at him as he chopped his way across the tunes.

José Antonio de Armas Chitty's forebears came from Kent. He is one of Venezuela's foremost historians, and an expert on the *llaneros*, the horsemen of the *llanos*, the high tropical plains that spread through Venezuela and Colombia. Another cowboy professor, and a *llanero* himself, he shared my passion for the horsemen of the Americas just like our friend Assuncao, professor of gauchismo in Montevideo. He had been widely quoted in cowboy literature, so it was a thrill to see him in the flesh. He was going to give me my first history lesson on the region.

We met Professor Chitty in an old Franciscan covent, now the National History Academy. White, cool and spacious with airy patios and peaceful cloisters, it is in the heart of the old town, ringed by the air-conditioned madness of the oil culture.

Chitty was a very short, intense man with a huge shock of thick white hair swirling round his head like a wiry turban. For a small man he was wearing a very long tie which reached down to just above his knees. His hands flew in great sweeps through the air, catching his tie which he waved round his head like a battle standard as he threw his stories at us and opened our first door on to the *llanos* and the *llaneros*.

He spoke of Bolívar the Liberator, of course. Up here the Plaza San Martín becomes Plaza Bolívar. We came through Bolívar Tunnel, cutting through the highlands, into Caracas. The money here in Venezuela is bolivars. An important man.

Chitty told me that General Paez was just as important to Venezuela as a liberator and, with my search for the lost cowboys, probably even more important to me. Paez became Venezuela's first ruler. And he was a *llanero*, the greatest cowboy of them all. He destroyed the Spanish with his *llanero* cavalry, who were so savage, so wild, they made the gauchos look civilized.

He talked of the differences between the *llaneros* and the gauchos, how *llaneros* tie their lasso to their horse's tail, how they catch bulls by grabbing their tails and turning them over. How these differences derived from the different terrains, the *llanos* and the pampa.

The *llanos*, said Chitty, are severe and inhospitable. They lurch between drought and flood. *Llaneros* raise cattle on the harsh tropical plains in impossible conditions. Once again the great Robert Bontine Cunninghame Graham is there with the plainsmen:

Upon the Llanos, snakes abound. The buzzing of an infinity of insects is always in the air. Alligators haunt the rivers. These and electric eels make all the waters dangerous. Tigers abound in all the woods, taking a continual toll of foals and of the weaker full grown animals.

The poisonous vampire bat sucks the blood of the horses when they venture into the woods. For half the year the plains are under water. For the other half calcined and dry under the fierce rays of the tropic sun. Thus horses all their lives fight with conditions unpropitious to them. That they survive in such considerable numbers speaks volumes for the resisting powers of the old Spanish breed.

Chitty, his arms and his tie waving and flapping in the air, spoke of superstition. He told me about Guardahumo, 'Smokescreen', an Indian bandit who escaped his persecutors a hundred times in a puff of smoke. He mentioned, in passing, General Daniel O'Leary, Bolívar's aide and biographer. And Gregor McGregor, another of Paez' generals, likely to be a Scotsman. He talked glowingly of the British Legion which had helped Paez destroy the Spanish army at the decisive battle of Carabobo which clinched Venezuela's independence – an independence which they effectively lost to America as soon as the first black gold gushed out of the ground in 1914. He kept using the word *cimarron*, which means 'wild', 'savage' or 'crude'. On those 'calcined and dry' days out on the *llanos* it also means 'all you can see is dust'.

It was as if the professor was waving an enormous quilt, shaking out a counterpane of stories and history at me. As each panel of the counterpane, each story, fluttered past, he could see he had caught me hook, line and sinker.

The story that got me most, that made me want to get out to the *llanos* as soon as possible, was a *llanero* battle cry that survived into this century.

Because of the shifting sands of politics, because dictators and governments came and went like snowstorms, said Chitty, they often didn't know who was in power, who the hell it was they were fighting for. So as they charged screaming into battle, the *llaneros* would shout, '*Vive Fulano de Tal!*' 'Long Live . . . Whoever!'

Outside the old Franciscan convent the streets were packed with hundreds of police, all in shades. The first coup in twenty-five years, by a bunch of ambitious *llanero* army officers, had taken place three weeks before. That'll keep the world's press happy, I thought.

Journalists think the only things that happen in this continent are earthquakes, football riots and coups. They've never heard of the lost cowboys in this land of exiles. They've never met José Antonio de Armas Chitty. And I doubt if many have gone out to the *llanos*.

13. The Plainsmen

It may have been hot in Caracas and near the coast, but up in Barinas on the *llanos* it was much hotter. Hot and flat. As we stepped off the plane the horizon, the old straight line, stretched off to nowhere, and the hundred-degree heat hit me right between the eyes. The air was heavy and humid and the sun burned down on to the palms and banana trees. This may have been another dead flat plain, but it was completely different from the pampas or the prairies. It is savannah like the flatlands of central Africa but it felt more like Texas than Africa.

Just like Texas, on the outskirts of town was a radio station, a bright-pink and sky-blue bungalow with a big antenna among the palm trees in the yard. It looked like one of the border radios of the fifties in Mexico that used to beam country music right across Texas and the South. It wasn't surprising because Barinas was wall-to-wall Cowtown.

It was full of dusty four-wheel drives and battered pick-up trucks cruising into town from the outlying countryside. The cars were rattling shells, ghosts of Pontiacs, Buicks and Chevvies scraping the ground and making the hulks in Caracas look like this year's model. They were all driven lazily by dark-skinned mestizo *llaneros*, with dusty old straw cowboy hats on the back of their heads and their arms hanging out of the rusting remains of their open car windows.

Cowtown all right, built on a grid like all prairie towns. The narrow one-way streets between the low-slung houses had a black oily line running down the middle from all the leaky transmissions of the ancient heaps farting and squittering their way through. The town was full of saddle and grain and feed shops, boot shops and hat shops. Not a tourist shop in sight. Real Western stuff.

In the central plaza was the compulsory statue of the pint-sized Liberator Bolívar. A small thin man, he is immortalized in bronze as he always was in life – on horseback. In Barinas his horse was prancing high, rearing up on its hind legs for extra elevation. Tropical bird droppings were smeared down his noble forehead. Butterflies the size of his fist fluttered past him through the palm trees.

They generously called a dilapidated, peeling church the cathedral. Beside it was a bar called El Arriero – The Muledriver. It had a picture of a mule, some cowboys and some cattle on the outside. It looked promising.

I went in to escape the molten sun and to get a bite to eat. I stood there blinking in the dark. Everything was red and black but I didn't take the hint. They laughed when I asked what food they had and where I could hear some cowboy music tonight.

'*¡Ai chicas aqui, nada mas a comer!*' Girls were the only thing on the menu there. I had chanced on one of Cowtown's whorehouses, right next door to the cathedral.

Knocking on heaven's door.

I stumbled back out, cursing, into the thick white heat. I got thrown out of another café on the plaza by a chubby waitress in a microskirt because I was wearing shorts. I argued with her but it did no good. She didn't understand when I pointed at her bare legs and asked whether this was the café or the cathedral. I passed on another restaurant called The Temptations of Adam & Eve, '*un restaurant Criolliiiiiiiiisssimo*', figuring my chances of getting a plate of rice were zero.

I finally struck oil in Ristorante Gladismar, Gladys by the sea. There were posters for cockfights and last week's rodeo on the walls. It was festooned with Christmas decorations, either last year's or next year's, hard to say which in March. Under the glass table tops was a hand-written notice which said in English, 'Please Don't Sit Down If You Are Ordering Nothing.'

I sat down and ordered something. On a long wall on the other side of the street was a brightly painted mural in a naive style. A huge curly-haired mestizo sun shone down on an assorted crowd of Venezuelans, black and white, men, women and children, workers, farmers, doctors and mothers all standing shoulder to shoulder and staring out.

Sitting on their heads was a bloated, smug caricature capitalist in top hat and tails, with vampire teeth, a glass of champagne and waving an American flag. The slogan said '*Primero El Pueblo . . . Despues La Deuda*' – first the people, then the debt.

Sitting there in Cowtown waiting for my order and looking at the mural I spun back to 1807 in Uruguay and the British invasion. I remembered how the soldiers were followed by the merchants, with the British bankers hard on their heels, giving out the first of the huge loans, bankrolling the fight for independence from Spain and setting up the start of the continent's massive debts.

The grinning vampire-toothed capitalist may be more recent, but the roots of the debt came from the beginning of the nineteenth century when the Old World made sure that most of the New World became the Third World.

Just as the British destroyed the manufacturing base of Argentina, Chile and Uruguay nearly two hundred years ago, so the American-based multinationals annexed all the Venezuelan oil fields. Oil had been discovered in 1914, but as soon as the La Rosa well exploded in 1922 and started gushing 100,000 barrels of oil a day, the orgy was on and the oil men from the North moved in.

The dictator of the time, a cattleman from the *llanos* called Juan Vicente Gomez, was only too happy to let the American oilmen draft the 1922 petroleum laws, to fence off all the oilfields and to patrol them with their own army of police. He was happy, for a consideration, to let them take all the crude oil and the profits out of the country, leaving the enormous national debt behind for the people. Venezuela was potentially one of the richest countries in the world, but stayed one of the poorest.

Gomez was busy doing deals and making lots of babies and needed all the money he could get to pay off his generals, his bodyguards and his friends. He needed money for his personal physician who looked after his overworked prostate gland. He needed more money to pay off the Archbishop he found to give him special dispensation to eat meat on Good Friday. He needed all the protein he could get and these things don't come cheap.

A plate of fried plantains, rice and refried beans came out. As I ate it I watched the pick-up trucks cruising lazily past Gladismar, leaving their trail of black gold down the middle of the road. They were on their way back home or off to check Los Tentaciones de Adan y Eva. Cruising through Cowtown.

Searching for the local cowboy music, the *llaneros'* C & W, we found Barinas had six radio stations pumping out tunes to the boys in the boondocks. At Radio Continental a dead-faced woman blanked us and said she knew of nowhere to hear the *llaneros'* music. Not a lot of it about. As she said this, cowboy music was blaring out of a radio set directly behind her head.

In the street right outside the radio station was another mural, bright and glowing even in the gathering dusk. It had a *cuatro*, a harp and some maracas, surrounded with shining stars, treble clefs and musical notes dancing up the wall and off into a hole in the dark purple *llanos* sky. We tried unsuccessfully to find live music that night. At the Casa del Llano a man put both his hands through the fence and made a twat sign.

'No music. Fucky fucky? Nice girls.'

Mañana. We found the one hotel in Cowtown that wasn't a knocking shop, like a Tex-Mex motel with rooms round a central patio filled with palms. I switched on the rattling air conditioning, the soundtrack for the heat, and settled down for the night.

The next day we found some musicians sitting in the shade of a mango tree playing their cowboy music. The maracas galloped across the *llanos*, the *cuatros* raced alongside them and the harp soared above them like a sparrowhawk. The *bandola*, this time just the four-string one, wove in and out in its fierce Arabic way.

Not surprisingly, as the *llanos* are one of the richest areas of the world for birds, a twitcher's paradise, many of the songs were about birds, with titles like 'The Hawk', 'Little Bird' and 'The Parakeet'. A round-faced, high-cheekboned young girl, Yurbeli, scarcely fourteen years old, played harp. She had only been playing for a year but was a natural. They were all proud of her.

Before we left them, Yurbeli's teacher grabbed the harp and played us a Venezuelan cowboy version of 'Hey Jude'. The Beat-less again, just to make us feel at home. Inspired, we left them under the mango tree and went to find some cattlemen.

The Barinas Ganaderos' (Cattlemen's) Association clubhouse walls are lined with pictures of prizewinning hump-backed bulls, proud ranchers and past presidents in full *llanero* gear. The main room is heavy, solid, almost meaty. In the centre is a long dark wooden table. Around it are heavy wooden chairs with high dark-brown cowhide backs; branded into the cowhide is their motto – 'God and Us'.

You can't say fairer than that.

We found that a rancher known to the mad Kiwi Tim was out on his *hato*, his estancia, and that he'd be happy to pass a day or two with us. Tambien found a four-wheel drive and we hit the dust.

There was plenty of it. Last night the temperature had gone down to a cool eighty degrees, but was up to a hundred again. The air was thick and humid but the land was dry. Cracked and dusty. Calcined.

You could smell the heat.

Llanos are the plains. Up in Texas the High Staked Plains of West Texas are the *llano estacado*. On the *llanos* of Venezuela the cowboys, the *llaneros*, are the plainsmen.

Venezuela has always been a slow developer, especially on the *llanos*. Even today life on the *llanos* can be primitive. During the wars of independence the *llanos* were the main battle ground and the battles were rougher and tougher than anywhere else. And if the life of the early gauchos as wild cattle hunters was primitive, the *llaneros* were prehistoric.

For all the difficulties of life on the pampas, the dangers of getting lost or killed, of drowning in the vast sea of grass, it was nothing to the murderous conditions out on the *llanos* where everything is hard for man and beast. The conditions on the pampas were perfect for the explosion of wild cattle and horses, as if they had been invented as a forcing ground – unending grasslands and pastures, few predators and a temperate climate. On the *llanos* it was astonishing that anything survived at all. Right into the twentieth century, the *llanos* have been backward, underpopulated, unchanging and harsh.

Although often called a desert, the *llanos* are honeycombed with rivers and streams and – unlike the treeless pampas of Argentina or the North American Great Plains – covered in places with forests and groves of trees and shrubs called *matas*. The *llanos* are huge and occupy a third of the national territory.

There are only two seasons: no spring or autumn, only a hot dry summer and a torrential winter with mass flooding. In the six months of winter, Barinas gets nearly eighty inches of rainfall. Cunninghame Graham waxes lyrical in his florid Edwardian way:

A very sea of grass and sky, sun-scourged and hostile to mankind. The rivers, full of electric eels, and of caribes [piranhas], those most ravenous of fish, more terrible than even the great alligators that lie like logs upon the sandbanks or the inert and pulpy rays, with their mortiferous barbed spike, are still more hostile than the land.

Islets of stunted palmtrees break the surface of the plains . . . The sun pours down like molten fire for six months of the year, burning the grass up, forcing the cattle to stray leagues away along the river banks, or in the depths of the thick woods. Then come the rains, and the dry, calcined plains are turned into a muddy lake, on which the whilom centaurs of the dry season paddle long, crank canoes dug from a single log.

So the climate was vile and the conditions as inhospitable and extreme as you can get. All the major battles, even after independence, were fought there and the *caudillos*, the crazy warlords, came out of the *llanos* to disrupt the country. The *llanos* were a violent melting-pot that spilled over bringing chaos and anarchy to the rest of the Venezuelans, shaping the country's political destiny.

Professor Chitty warned us of all this in Caracas. 'The *llano*,' he said cryptically, 'is the enemy and the explanation of Venezuela.' He explained that, as usually happens, the land moulded the men. '"The life of the Llanero",' he quoted, '"is of the rudest it is possible to conceive."' Leading such a rude life, *llaneros* were harder than most, but the constant struggle for survival meant that the *llanero* was not the smartest cowboy to be seen:

Any old saddle, any clothes, content the dweller on the plains of the Apure. His horse is almost always thin, often sore-backed, and always looks uncared for, while the ungainly pace at which he rides, a shambling *pasitrote*, or tied camel waddle, moving both feet on the same side at once, deprives him of all grace. Still few can equal, none excel, him for endurance. Nothing daunts him, neither the peril of the rivers, with all their enemies to mankind ever awake, to tear or numb the unlucky horseman who may come near their fangs or their electrically charged bodies, or any danger either by flood and field.

He, of all wielders of the rawhide noose, alone secures it to his horse's tail, fishing for, rather than lassoing, a steer, playing it like a salmon with a rope a hundred feet in length, instead of bringing it up with a smart jerk, after the fashion of the Argentines or Mexicans. Abominably tedious in his methods to the eyes of the commentators; still it is never wise, in matters of such deep import, to criticize customs that use and wont have consecrated.

The *llaneros* had little of the gaucho dandy in them; they didn't have the same sense of macho style. No time to get duded up when you're dodging spiders and snakes, scorpions, vampire bats, piranhas, crocodiles, electric eels, drought and drowning. And with your spavined saddle-sore nag shambling along with its tied camel waddle, you don't look too smart.

It is small wonder that Sir Robert Ker Porter, a British diplomat, was driven to exclaim in the 1830s: 'Their manners were the most unpolished and almost uncivil I ever met with.' Almost uncivil they certainly were. They didn't have the hooded-eyed formality, the threatening velvet-glove politeness that Darwin had noticed in the gauchos. They didn't have the clothes or the traditions of the gauchos. But they always carried a knife or machete, like the gaucho and his *facón*. The ever-diplomatic Porter called the machete 'an appendage no *llanero* is without, and which amongst the poorest classes, answers likewise for a spear head'.

Like the laws governing the *facón* in the Argentine, there were restrictions on the *llanos*. A *llanero* could never wear a shirt outside his pants. It had to be tucked in so a machete couldn't be hidden under the shirt. Often they didn't have a shirt; many *llaneros*, like the early gauchos, were close to the Indians and wore no more than a loin cloth or a torn pair of pants. If they could afford more, like the son of the liberator, Ramon Paez, they would wear what he did in 'Wild Scenes in South America' in 1860, where he adopted:

the less cumbrous attire of the *Llaneros*, consisting mainly of breeches tightly buttoned at the knee, and a loose shirt, usually of a bright checkered pattern. Shoes are altogether dispensed with in a country like the *llanos*, subject to drenching rains, and covered with mud during a great portion of the year, besides the inconvenience they offer to the rider in holding the stirrup securely when in chase of wild animals. The leg, however, is well protected from the thorns and cutting grass of the savannas by a neat legging or *botin*, made of buffskin, tightly buttoned down the calf by knobs or studs of highly polished silver.

Another characteristic article of dress, and one in which the wearers take great pride, is the linen checkered handkerchief, loosely worn around the head. Its object is ostensibly to protect it from the intensity of the sun's rays; but the constant habit of wearing it has rendered the handkerchief as indispensable a headdress to the *Llaneros* as is the cravat to the neck of the city gentleman.

The classic llanero cowboy hat is a wide-brimmed, long-napped felt, made originally in Austria, called *pelo de guamo*. The nap of the hat is supposed to look like the inside of the fruit of the guamo tree. But not many of the *llaneros* fighting with Bolívar and Paez could afford to wear hats.

A crucial item for both rich and poor out on the *llanos* was the universal poncho, the *cobija*:

It is fully six feet square . . . and its office is twofold, viz., to protect the rider from the heavy showers and dews of the tropics, and to spread under him when there is no convenience for slinging the hammock. It also serves as a protection from the scorching rays of the sun . . . a thick woollen covering keeps the body moist and cool by day, and warm by night.

It is made double, by sewing together two different blankets, the outside one being dark blue and the inner one bright red, which colours are differently acted upon by light and heat. By exposing alternately the sides of the poncho to the light according to the state of the weather, those modifications of temperature most agreeable to the body are obtained. Thus, when the day is damp and cloudy, the dark side, which absorbs the most heat, is turned towards the light, while the reverse is the case when the red surface is presented to the sun.

Landowners, ranchers with big *hatos*, would dress up more, with trappings like the gaucho *calzoncillos*, the white linen short trouser, and white linen *mantas* that reflected the sun perfectly and were highly and expensively embroidered. The *manta* was like the Chilean *huaso*'s small poncho that I had seen Pope Juan Pablo wearing with pride in Santiago.

Like all other cowboys and frontiersmen, *llaneros* had a very limited diet of meat, coffee and sugar:

Beef is the staple, almost the only food of the *Llanero*; his ordinary drink is the muddy water of the neighbouring stream or lagoon. His luxuries, coffee, and the rough brown sugar full of lye, known as Panela; his bed a hammock, that he carried rolled up, behind his saddle . . . He who had a hammock thought himself fortunate. This hammock most likely was made of cords of the wild pineapple, or else cut out of a raw hide. The bed most used was a dried horse's hide. The *Llanero*, like the Gaucho of those days, had but one regular repast. The hour was sunset, and throughout the day he probably chewed a piece of jerked beef steeped in water. The Gaucho was more fortunate for he had Maté, a most sustaining beverage.

Rarely, on special days, they might eat *arepa*, maize bread. Otherwise it was constant beef. Never mutton; like the gauchos, *llaneros* used to say, 'Mutton is not meat.' They cooked large pieces of beef, at least ten pounds each, on a wooden spit; between the lumps of meat they stuck pieces of heart, liver (which the gauchos never seemed to like) and suet. All this they barbecued over a fire of bones, thistles and dried bullshit. Just like the gauchos and *huasos*, they cut strips off the lumps of meat with their long knives or machetes. They held the meat between their teeth. They cut off the piece nearest their teeth with their knives and worked their way down to the bone held in their other hand.

One thing I had never seen gauchos or *huasos* do was 'tailing'. The *llaneros* would ride up behind a steer, lean over and grasp the bull's tail and whip it off balance. Looks impressive but it's easy when you know how. Sir Edward Sullivan in his classic Victorian *Rambles and Scrambles in North and South America* was impressed:

The *coleador*, mounted on a good horse that knows his business, gallops close up to the bull, when catching hold of the tail he clenches it under his knee, and the horse darting off at right angles pulls the bull's legs from under him, and he comes to the ground with crashing force. This art of throwing bulls by the tail is all knack, and the slightest men generally make the best *coleadors*. They say that, as in bull fighting, there is a certain fascination in the danger, and though many lose their lives every year, it is a favourite sport amongst the wild riders of the plains; and the reputation of being the best *coleador* of a district, ensures the happy possessor the admiration of his comrades and the prettiest partners at the fandangos. An expert *coleador* will by himself throw and brand fifty wild cattle on a day.

The prettiest partners at the fandangos, eh? Hmmm.

Some *coleadors* are so dexterous they can whip two bulls over, with both hands, at the same time. If the man can't pull the bull over, he throws himself off his horse at full speed and the momentum as he crashes to the ground never fails to bring the bull down. Then he draws the tail between the bull's hind legs and waits for his partner, or for the applause.

In early *coleadas*, tailing rodeos, the *llaneros* worked in pairs. As the first whipped the bull over to the ground, the second leapt from his horse and neatly sliced of the bull's balls with his knife while the hapless beast was still winded from the fall. Get that unkind cut right and all the pretty girls would want to dance with you all night long.

Like all cowboys, the *llaneros* loved gambling. The cockfight poster in the Gladismar showed that nothing had changed. A good cockfight on a Sunday will still pull in two or three hundred *llaneros*. Better than going to church. A game of cards, too, is still hard for them to resist.

What else is money for? Well, judging by the numbers of whorehouses we kept tripping over in Barinas, any win on a cockfight will pay for a visit to the soiled doves of the plains. No need to impress there, no need to tail a bull to dance the night away.

The *llanos* were always the most primitive of the prairies and plains of the Americas. They were further away than any others from any civilizing influences, from any sense of law and order. Of all the frontiers cowboys have lived on, the *llanos* were the wildest. *Llanero* implies 'frontiersman' as much as it does the more literal 'plainsman'.

They were so far away from anything, that life changed far less on the *llanos* than on the Argentine pampas. Don Roberto went back for a nostalgic visit in 1925, when the oilmen were flooding in and the oil flooding out, and he could have been talking about the middle of the previous century:

His well-greased *lazo* ready coiled in front of his right knee, his brown, bare toes sticking out through his *alpargatas*, clutching the light *llanero* stirrup with its crown-like prolongation underneath the foot, the *llanero* scans the horizon as his horse paces rapidly along, leaving a well-marked trail upon the dewy grass. He sits so loosely in the saddle that one would think if his horse shied it must unseat him, but that he also shies. High in his *vaquero* saddle, so straight and upright that a plummet dropped from his shoulder would touch his heel, he reads the *llano* like a book.

Above all else, more than gambling, singing, dancing and whoring, the *llanero*'s greatest love was sitting on horseback. He passionately clung to his life riding high in the saddle. He wasn't in the least interested in the world outside the *llanos*. They were a hellish kind of heaven but seen from the saddle they were paradise. The *llanero* wasn't remotely interested in religion, politics, philosophy or any other form of culture. Quite simply, the *llanero* lived to ride.

'Calcined' means consumed by fire and reduced to dust; now I understand why Cunninghame Graham used the word so much. While the air felt thick and humid, the land looked cracked and dry as a bone. It looked so parched that if a drop of water hit it, the fissures would grow, the cracks open and the earth explode. More water, and some strange chemical reaction might occur and the ground burst into flame or dance around like phosphorus. We were constantly reminded that we were on a tropical plain. One moment we were rolling across a desiccated expanse of empty scrubby desert, the next we were passing mudholes and speeding into the jungle.

Jo was at the wheel, patronizing as usual – 'Don't worry, Hank, I know how to handle these four-wheelers on this kind of terrain. You just look at the birds.'

I gritted my teeth but was grateful for the chance to sit and stare.

The staring was well worth it. Even Tambien, who always claimed to have seen everything, admitted he had never seen anything like it. Birds were everywhere. Round the occasional water- and mudholes were flocks of white long-necked herons, storks and showers of dazzling snow-white egrets. In the trees canaries were singing and parrots were screaming. Tambien had told me of a bird called a goatsucker, but I wouldn't know it from a hole in the ground unless I saw it sucking my goat. Great red, blue and yellow macaws soared like Technicolor hawks above the trees. A solitary crane stood apart at the edge of a dry mudhole, watching impassively while a wild boar wallowed scratchily in the caked-up centre.

The trees, and some long grass, seemed to flourish along river banks, but gave way all too easily to the hungry desert and the patchy grass. The biggest trees were the wide-spreading *samaans* and the massive swollen-trunked *ceibas*, the West Indian silk cotton trees. In the bulbous shade of a towering *ceiba*, and in spite of the crushing heat, a determined goat was urgently fucking another. Doing what it knew best and, I guess, keeping a weather eye open for any goatsuckers.

We raced past mango, banana and grapefruit trees, past tamarind, palm, guava and vanilla trees, past cassia trees with their threatening, purgative senna pods hanging like the *chinchuline* trees of the pampas, past trees bursting with red and orange and yellow and violet flowers defying the all-consuming heat, past trees I had never seen before. Tambien, as usual, was right. We had never seen anything like it. There were hawks like the *caranchos* of the pampas, called *caricaris* on the *llanos*, soaring through the humid skies. Big carrion-eaters, most likely vultures, *gaviluchos*, were riding the thermals over grazing cattle hoping one might drop down dead. It looked like they could do. The grass tufts they were searching for appeared harsh and abrasive rather than nutritious.

The cattle looked severely dehydrated, like drought victims. Humpbacked and emaciated, they had big floppy pink-veined rabbit's ears waving round their skinny necks and their white skin hung alarmingly from their jagged hip-bones. They stood skinny and still, hiding under trees from the midday sun.

It was hot enough now, well over a hundred degrees. All of a sudden the trees slipped away and the sky rolled itself right out. In the blink of an eye everything stretched off into the far distance. All lines, all roads got straighter and led out through the shimmering expanse to the horizon. Moving out of the trees and on to the bare plain was a sudden leap from the finite to the infinite. It felt like leaving this world for another, but another with no limits. The horizon was no kind of boundary, but simply a way of attaching the sky to the earth.

I could understand why the *llaneros* never wanted to leave this place. It may seem like a hellish kind of heaven to us but it was heaven all the same. You didn't need to look up; it was all around you. And God was there, squatting on the horizon like the vast burning blue sky. Amid all this space and the shimmering thermals were ancient oil-rigs, the nodding donkey rockers like in the old movies of Texas, stuck out in the middle of nowhere, rocking and pumping away. Oil and money the *llaneros* would never see was being sucked out of the ground, bound for foreign parts.

We were still on paved roads, but cracked, calcined dirt roads flew straight out into the flat scrubland, racing for the horizon. In the distance a troop of riderless horses, manes and tails flying, galloped across the plain kicking up a tornado of dust.

We passed cotton fields. Cotton fluff that had fallen from trucks had lined the road for some time, snow in summer. While the cattle were hiding under the trees, people were out picking cotton. Breaking their backs, baking their heads and slicing their hands in the midday sun. Maybe they're the ones the vultures were watching.

Llaneros often watch the vultures. They watch everything in the sky and on the ground. Rising dust will tell them of people or cattle moving. A big cloud will tell them the size of the force or the herd. Flocks of birds could be signs of other riders. Vultures, of course, talk death. On the ground, tracks and trails can speak volumes by the way the grass is bent and by the foot and hoof prints:

Nothing escapes his sight, as keen as that of his Achagua Indian ancestors. Signs on the ground, almost undiscernible, he marks. Pointing with his whip he says, 'Three horses passed along here early in the night. One is the big cream colour that always strays, for he is a little lame in the off hind foot, see where he has stepped short upon it.' With an unerring eye he sights a steer with a strange brand. 'That is one of General Atilio Pacheco's animals,' he says, and turning to his companion, smiling, remarks, 'If he stays too long in these parts he may stay for ever, for God is not a bad man, anyhow.

Just as suddenly we crossed a river and we were in jungle. A lot of moriche palms, mango trees and all. There were some shacks in there, mostly *caneys*, the traditional *llanos* homes, thatched roofs on wood stilts without walls. Some had corrugated-iron roofs, but most were thatched with dried brown palm leaves. Don Roberto – his heart still longing to be back in the Argentine pampa – described an original *caney*:

The straw roofed hut, open on all four sides, stood upon an island in the vast pampa, a sea of grass whose waves flowed up almost to the door. A line of bones of animals that had been slaughtered as near as possible to the house, to save the trouble of carrying home the meat, lay amongst thistles and filth of every kind. This was known as Los Escoberos and corresponded to the midden that in old days adorned the entrance to Scottish cottages. Inside the house there was no furniture; the skulls of horses or of oxen formed the seats, on which the owners squatted, with their knees up to their eyes.

It sounds just like Artigas in Uruguay, except that he was drinking gin from a cow's horn, an unknown luxury on the backward *llanos*.

We stopped at one of the shacks and asked directions. A brown-eyed girl was putting shirts, pants and jeans out to dry on a fence. When we asked her, she went over to check with the boss, taking his siesta with his wife in hammocks under a mango tree. She came back and pointed down the road: turn left at the little school, the *escuelita*, then another left at the mango grove, indicating each left turn with her right arm.

We got lost pretty soon. There were a lot of mango groves. Exploring hopefully down a rutted track we were surprised by a rising, flapping cloud of a dazzling, electric, blood-orange red.

'Red ibis,' muttered Tambien in a non-committal, ornithological kind of way, 'common in the *llanos*.'

He found a man who said he'd heard of the *finca*, the farmhouse, we were looking for, but had never been there in his life. It was only another three miles away.

By now we had left the paved road and were beginning to kick up a bit of dust. There were some trees around but the jungle had gone, elbowed aside by the inevitable expansive flatness. Barefoot men in straw hats were fixing fences in the blazing sun, their skinny horses hitched up beside them.

And then we hit the Dust.

This was dust I was not prepared for. This was mega-dust. Scholarship-level dust. Even Tambien was taken aback, hard put to stay cool, and we couldn't have wound the windows up faster if we had hit a hornet's nest or run over a skunk. Neither of us had seen dust like it and it got lighter and finer the further down the track we went. We couldn't escape it.

Driving faster simply made the cyclone of ochre dust rise up higher. We couldn't leave it behind. The faster we went, the quicker it caught us up, swirled over the top of the wagon like an Atlantic roller, broke on the bonnet and engulfed us. Waves of it shimmied and settled on the back window, sucked in by the slipstream. Then it started to seep into the inside of the wagon. With all the windows and air inlets tight shut, the ethereal dust sought out every little crack and cranny to slip through. A speck of this dust was so fine it would make an average particle look like a boulder.

JT got the wipers scratching a path across the windscreen and we could just make out the sides of the track to aim the car between them. Soon the cloud of a million motes swirled so thick and sulphurous round the interior that we could hardly see each other across the front seats. Then, just in time, we glimpsed a sign which said Mata Oscura, Dark Wood. We had arrived.

We hurtled through a gate and coughing, sweating and spluttering we leapt out of the wagon. As the swirling typhoon settled I could feel the stillness. We were standing in the yard of the *hato*, the ranch, and the settling dust was the only thing that seemed to be moving. A two-foot salamander watched us lazily from the trunk of a palm tree, wondering what the fuss was all about. A mule, with a fancy silver-inlaid bridle, saddled up and hitched to another tree, wasn't about to get excited either.

The ranch yard was a shaded oasis of green in an ocean of dust and scrubland that stretched away to join the distant sky. It was a large enclosure surrounded by white wood fencing. There were several open-sided stables and cattle stalls, farm machinery buildings, and a large single-storey ranch house with a long open verandah with protective netting. The ground was dry and grassy, regularly watered, and there was plenty of shade under moriche and coconut palms, grapefruit and mango trees. Not a breath of wind ruffled the leaves or whispered through the sultry air.

A subdued chatter of parrots and parakeets in the trees, with cattle and horses in the background, was punctuated every now and then by a thud as a coconut fell through the thick silent air to the ground. Tropical ranch noise.

Iacobo Obadiah had the belly, Texan cowboy boots, Rolex watch and spotless straw Stetson of a wealthy rancher. He had four thousand head of prime Zebu cattle, some of which were gathered in corrals round the central ranch enclosure. He was tanned, had dark rings round his brown eyes and smiled as he welcomed us and invited us into the cool of the ranch house. His amply built wife brought us iced tea and slipped away into the shadows of another room.

Like a true cowboy, Iacobo kept his Stetson on. Going to bed to sleep is the only reason to take it off; going to bed for sex the sombrero is optional, depending on the position. He sat at the dark wood bar at one end of the living room and talked about life on the *llanos*.

'On the *llanos*, just as day turns to night with no dusk, so summer turns to winter, dry to wet in a flash. There is no announcement, no introduction on the *llanos*. Everything just happens, like the shock from an eel. Suddenly it starts to rain, then it goes on raining solidly through April and May. And the *llaneros* have to be as much at home in canoes or swimming in the water as they are on horseback on dry land. It is a hard life.' He smiled a little half-smile. 'But they're used to it, they know it. They live with the alligators and jaguars and snakes and *la plaga*.'

La plaga is the plague of insects that comes out at night. Mosquitoes, sandflies, 'and all the flying devilry of the whole insect world', waits for nightfall to attack. Striking a match, or even shouting to a friend, could cause a swarm. Something else to toughen up the *llaneros*.

Iacobo was surrounded by all the trappings of a cattleman. The furniture was dark-stained heavy wood and leather, high-backed wooden chairs with dark cowhide seats and backs. A light high-backed saddle and a harness were on a stand beside the bar. On the walls were lariats, bridles, harnesses, quirts, and a long coiled horsewhip. There was both a rawhide and a horsehair lasso.

Ashtrays on the tables were fashioned from steers' feet and horses' hooves. They didn't seem to cater for the vegetarian smoker in these parts, but it was still recycling, cowboy style. Can't deny it was ecological.

He kept reminding us of how backward the *llanos* have been, how slow to change. 'Our ranching ways changed only about thirty-five years ago. Up till then it was man against animal or sometimes animal against man. Originally there weren't rodeos, the cattle were hunted. They were wild. The way they were rounded up in the beginning was, they were hamstrung. Their tendons were cut with machetes when they needed to be rounded up. Then they skinned them.

'So it is very recent, really, that we have started to organize our herds, to look after them, to get roads and fencing out on to the *llanos*. The spread of ranching methods that happened more than a hundred years ago everywhere else didn't happen here until well into this century. Things had not changed here for hundreds of years. Of all the frontierlands on this continent, the *llanos* is the most static. Only in these last thirty-five years have we brought in new blood from all over the world.

'The first livestock was from Spain, breeds like Casanareño and San Martinero. Now I raise Zebu cattle, the white cattle you've seen here, an Indian-Pakistan breed that came from the States, like everything in Venezuela. Ha! But the Zebu are good, very hardy, with thin skins that are good for the tropics. They have adapted well to the *llanos*. Come and see my prize bulls.'

They say the first livestock was brought in by Cristobal Rodriguez in 1548. Some cattle had already been driven across the Andes from Colombia seven years before. A shipment of eight hundred head was brought in from the island of Margarita in 1569. Horses and cattle multiplied and spread wild all over the *llanos*.

Ranches, *hatos*, were well established by the end of the sixteenth century, but ranches for the hunting of wild cattle for their hides. The cattlemen didn't breed the cattle or care for them. Recently, a *llanero* rancher said, 'God nourishes the cattle and I sell them. It's a profitable deal.'

*

I asked about saddles.

'We don't have a special one. The *llanero* will ride on anything. Everything else is so harsh, his saddle is the least of his worries. It's the same with his clothes – what does it matter? All he needs is a poncho, and a hat and pants if he's lucky. So we never had anything as specific as the *recado* of the gauchos. Anyway, most *llaneros* rode bareback. Certainly the ones who beat the Spanish with Paez in the wars had no more than a loincloth, a lance and a primitive bridle – no saddle. So when we do have saddles we have several different kinds. Some came from Colombia, high backed, some from the US Army, some English saddles, even Spanish. All types. Except with the heat and wet we've mostly gone for light saddles.'

I still didn't know how *llaneros* were with their horses, whether they went the Indian or gaucho way. Iacobo tried to maintain that they loved all animals as their brothers, but Sir Edward Sullivan, rambling and scrambling in the 1850s, didn't see a lot of brotherly love: 'An active man and a good horseman will jump on a wild horse without bridle or saddle, armed with nothing but his spurs, and gallop across the plain kicking the poor beast until he begins to flag, when he slips off, and catching hold of the tail gives the horse a heavy fall. A few falls of this kind will tame the wildest horse, and convince him that the thing upon his back is his master.'

In the end, though, *llaneros* seemed to take better care of their horses, and would tend to them before themselves. After a day's round-up they would unsaddle and water their mounts first. This was not entirely altruistic; horses were scarcer than on the pampas. The horse population was always threatened by the ravages of war and epidemics, and day-to-day survival was more difficult on these harsh plains. As with the gauchos, the horse meant survival for the *llanero*. As horses were not two a penny as on the pampas, the *llaneros* were never quite as careless or as pitiless as the gauchos.

They could be even crazier, though. They play a version of the gaucho *maroma* that the murderous blue-eyed gaucho Rosas did so well, the game where the horseman stands on the bar over the corral gate and as the mustang races out he drops on to its back and rides it bareback into the ground. This isn't hard enough for the *llaneros*, who leap on to the colt's bare back *backwards*. That means they ride it backwards, galloping around holding on to the horse's tail until they have broken the horse. Backwards.

They lived in a wilder place and they were a wilder mixture than the gauchos. First it was mestizo, Spanish and indigenous Indians. Then mulatto, Spanish and Negro. Then zambo, Indian and Negro. The differences were very important in the eighteenth and nineteenth centuries, especially down on the coast. The hierarchy was carefully worked out and observed. Out on the wild *llanos*, though, it was Indian and Spanish and Negro all mixed up together in one big stew.

Native plainsmen, Spanish freebooters and African slaves were in the make-up of the *llaneros*. Their blood was a mixture of Spanish, Barbary Moorish, American Indian and African – wild men. The educated elite from the northern coats and valleys called them the 'mongrel breed'. They thought of them and treated them as a race apart.

Riding a long trail had its own peculiar problems on the *llanos*. The *llaneros* faced at least two major trail drives every year. In the dry summer they would drive cattle down from the parched high northern *llanos* south to the Apure river. Then once the rains had started but before the floods took hold completely, they would drive back up to the high places.

The floods made all *llaneros*, unlike any other cowboys, great swimmers. They were also expert in getting a herd across the river. Cattle often refused to cross the hundreds of rivers that flow across the *llanos*. *Llaneros* would have to leap in the water in front of the cattle to guide or pull them through:

If the stream is narrow he sits upon the horse's back, taking care not to touch his mouth with the bit, for that would almost certainly make him turn over on his side. The rider guides his horse by splashing water in his face, at the side he wishes him to turn, or if he has taken off the bit as a precaution, so that the horse may have a better chance to breathe he strikes him gently with the halter that he holds in his hand. In wider rivers he slips off and grasps the horse's tail and is pulled over easily enough, although he has to face the danger of the alligators, the *caribes* and the electric eels.

Sometimes, without his horse, a *llanero* would tie a set of horns on his head, ignore the cuckold jokes, and leap into the water mooing. This would usually fool the cattle, which would come thundering in after him. He would also take a stick, for hitting alligators on the nose. They weren't fooled either by the horns or the mooing.

We went out and looked at Iacobo's bulls. They were in the open-sided shed closest to the house. Big and white, they were much beefier than the famine victims we'd seen on the way. They still had prominent hip-bones, a big Brahman hump, a long head with high brown-tinged forehead, the huge flapping rabbit ears and waves of treble chins hanging down their fronts. Their horns were circular and pointed backwards like a gazelle.

They glowed, whiter than white. Spoiled and pampered, they looked at us indolently, heavy lidded, as peons in working shirts and jeans, cowboy hat and *alpargatas*, brushed and groomed them constantly. They had the air of a bunch of overfed bishops getting full body rubs before an ecumenical council meeting.

Above their heads, hanging from the rafters by string, were large clear plastic bags, two foot in diameter, full of water. They ran the length of the shed. Shafts of sunlight sparkled through them. They are there, Iacobo said, to keep the flies away. To keep the flies away? How can hanging plastic bags of water keep flies away? The stables, and kitchens, of the world need to know.

Iacobo said they used them because they worked. He thought it was something about the light reflecting and refracting through the water that the flies didn't like. In the end they didn't know, but they wouldn't waste time putting up bags of water if they didn't get results.

Remember where you heard it first.

That evening the sun set when my back was turned. It was too quick for me. The first I knew that the sun had gone was when I heard the melancholy hooting of an owl outside. They told me it was often there: *titiriji*, the great tiger owl.

By this time I was close to bird overload and asked not to be told about any more for a while. Jo said OK but before I signed off from the world of beaks and feathers he should warn me of a local bird, an *alcaravan*, a kind of long-legged plover, that acted as an alarm clock and watchman. It called out on the hour, every hour through the night. Otherwise all was quiet and still out in the middle of the plains.

When we got up at seven the next morning, Iacobo had been up for four hours. He worked through the cool of the night and early morning and slept through the heat. He worked hard, too, which must explain the dark rings round his eyes.

Outside the day had broken and some of the men were driving a herd of Zebus into the big corral. They all had light high-cantled saddles on a couple of small bits of blanket or hide. They rode quite straight-legged, long in the stirrup. Almost all of them were barefoot, feet in the small iron stirrups with the triangular point hanging below. A couple were wearing *alpargatas*. None had spurs. They had short sticks with a piece of rawhide for cattle goads. The horses looked the same Arab-Barb mix, small horses, a bit finer than the stocky Argentine criollo. They were stringier and rangier than the *pingos* down south, but not the spavined nags I had read about.

They rode into the herd, cutting out a few selected bullocks and moving through the cattle without thinking. Easy and natural. The horses seemed born to the life just as the *llaneros* were to the saddle. No wonder the original Indians thought the first men on horses were one animal.

The cattle were a bit skittish. Their skin looked like a shroud, white and holy, hanging off them in folds, and their strange circular antelope horns glinted like haloes in the early morning sun. Holy cow . . .

None of the peons I saw had braided their lasso into the horse's tail. All carried them on the left side of their saddle. One was attached to the cantle. A couple had their lassoes tied to the horse's mane. None used their lassoes that day, especially not the way Sir Edward Sullivan saw in 1852:

I could never believe this till I saw it. It always struck me that it would either pull the horse's tail out by the root, or else throw him down; and so it would, but the horses become so cunning, and so fond of the sport, that the moment the lasso leaves the hand of the rider, instead of stopping short, as I always imagined was the method, they gallop off at a slight tangent as fast as they can, when if the lasso is round the leg, the slightest jerk brings the bull to the ground. So little actual force and so much knack is there in it, that many men will throw bull after bull with a mere jerk from the shoulder, without laying any strain whatever on the horse.

Several of the *llaneros'* horses that morning were white like the cattle. Down south, some had been scathing about white horses as fit only for whores. Not up here. The *llaneros* love white horses. Beyond superstition, they believe and maintain objectively that white horses make better swimmers. The great Paez believed it so much he and his entire *llanero* guard of honour rode white horses. Don Roberto had one in Paraguay, El Blanco, which was renowned for its swimming prowess. El Blanco swam with his back well out of the water and his head erect, like a water snake.

When we left, about midday, I asked Iacobo if, even with his sharp boots, new Stetson and horse's hoof ashtray, the life didn't get him down.

'No, not at all, because every day there's something to learn and every day there's something beautiful out there.'

14. The Greatest Llanero of Them All

José Antonio Paez liked to ride a white horse. He was a *llanero* and he knew all about horses. Of all the South American heroes he was the most charismatic. He didn't have the genius, or the education, of Bolívar; San Martín was a greater general, a better and more experienced soldier; but Paez had more personal magnetism, more cowboy charisma, than any. Apart from, perhaps, the other cowboy *caudillo*, from down south, the crazed Argentine Rosas.

José Paez was a seventh son, a redhead and an epileptic. He was born in a thatched shack by a small lost river out in the middle of nowhere near Barinas. He was educated at a hedge school by an old woman as illiterate as the children.

Under Spanish rule there were no official schools outside the main cities because it was their policy to prevent the spread of education in the colonies. Paez, like many others was illiterate right into adulthood. If this sounds a bit like the early life of a Country and Western star, Paez was no rhinestone cowboy. Though not as blood-crazed as Rosas he was a hard man, a true *llanero*.

Paez was born in 1790, about the same time John Ponsonby was nearly strung up in revolutionary Paris. He had a fair complexion, and reddish hair. He was called El Catire Paez, *llanos* slang for the fair one. Unlike most *llaneros*, Paez was 'white on all four sides', meaning all four grandparents were white. Like all *llaneros* he was a born horseman.

He learnt his horsemanship from a Negro slave, a big man called Manuelote. Big Manuel was the foreman, the *capataz*, at the Hato de La Calzada, the Highway Ranch, where Paez found himself when he was seventeen. This was not unusual in the Spanish colonies. Slaves who were skilled horsemen and good workers could become foremen.

Manuel, as a *capataz*, could boss around any free man he liked, Cunninghame Graham noted; 'even white men such as Paez, who had no tincture of Indian blood'. He could be left up in the *llanos*, as manager of the ranch, while the absent owners lived in comfort in Caracas. Manuel could be left looking after the ranch; as he himself was already their property, he was unlikely to steal any of their other belongings.

Given this power, Manuel was a firm believer in the school of hard knocks. In fact he was an overbearing bully. Life at La Calzada was a permanent obstacle course, like a commando training camp. And Manuelote seemed to have it in for El Catire. Maybe Paez was too white. Whatever it was, Manuelote put him through it.

' I had a capataz, a tall negro, taciturn and severe of aspect, a rough, thick beard made him look more formidable,' wrote Paez in his memoirs, 'who in an imperious voice ordered me to mount an untamed colt.' Paez had no choice but to leap bareback on to the colt. Cunninghame Graham gets excited:

As to the negro's orders there was no reply, the unlucky *peon* [Paez] jumped on the wild colt, and seized his thick, rough mane with both hands. Hardly was he well seated, when the wild beast began to buck and try to catch the rider's legs between his teeth, in his efforts to get rid of the unaccustomed load. Then, with fire blazing from his eyes, he set off at a furious gallop after his companions in the plains, as if to ask their help to free him of his burden.

The wretched rider felt as if borne by a hurricane; the wind whistled in his ears; he hardly dared to breathe. If he kept his eyes open it was only to look for help, or to try and convince himself the peril was not so great as it appeared. The ground that to a man on foot looked level, to the frightened rider seemed full of precipices down which the wild colt must plunge.

At last the agony was over when, quite exhausted, the colt came to an involuntary halt. However as a smith only becomes a master by working at his trade, so the young Llanero, by degrees loses his terror, and at last he finds no pleasure greater than that of training a wild horse.

Manuelote never let up. He made El Catire work the cattle on a wild horse all the time; made him stand guard against the predators at night; made him do night watch amid *la plaga*. He pulled a classic one on Paez when they came to a river one day:

As all the Llanos are intersected with rivers and with streams, and cattle on the march often refuse to enter them, a man on horseback swims in front to give them confidence. Should the man not be a swimmer, he holds the horse's mane, and puts one arm across its withers as a support.

One day, Paez and Manuel and the other peons came to a river of tolerable width, Manuel shouted to him to jump in and guide the cattle, and when the miserable youngster said he could not swim, answered, 'I didn't ask you if you could swim, what I said was jump in and guide the fucking cattle to the other side.' In such a school it is to be supposed that swimming soon was one of the young man's accomplishments . . .

In that rough school he graduated, and so his constitution gradually hardened, his strength increased, his body became as hard as iron, and the whole man emerged from rude trial able to endure the hardships of the years of war in which he was called upon to take so great a part, and to preserve his vigour quite unimpaired, till eighty years of age.

When Paez was twenty, news arrived in Venezuela that Napoleon had installed his brother Joseph on the Spanish throne. The Spanish Cortes, the government, expelled from Madrid, were patronizing and blind to the confusion and the demands of the colonies. By ignoring them, hoping they would go away, they only fanned the flames of revolution.

Getting no support from the Cortes, a revolt in Caracas set up a junta to govern until a Spaniard was reinstated on the throne. Many of the Venezuelans were Royalists and wanted to stay loyal to Spain. The old country didn't listen:

Reading the account of the negotiations that went on before the revolution actually broke out, the case of Ireland rises to mind. The same intolerance and the same blindness to events, the arrogance in dealing with the people's representatives, the pride of race and above all the insolence of office, were shown in Spain by the government of Cadiz towards the Creoles, as England manifested in days gone by to the extremely moderate advocates of self-government in Ireland.

The truth was that Spain did not take the creoles seriously. The whole of Venezuela at that time, including the *llanos*, had a population of only 800,000, too few to threaten Spain. But men like Paez and Bolívar deserved to be taken seriously. Spain's condescension certainly made an impression on Paez. Hardened by Manuelote's tough regime, he was now a superlative horseman, horse breaker and handy with the lasso, lance and sabre. He was also still illiterate.

He joined the cavalry in Barinas. Nothing much happened up on the *llanos* for a couple of years. It was a backwater as always and the *llaneros* remained royalists simply because that's how things were. All that politics had little effect on life on the sweltering plains.

While Paez was learning his military craft in Barinas, the politicking went on in Caracas. The junta sent three men to London for help. One was Simón Bolívar, a wealthy young creole who had been educated in Europe and, like Artigas and San Martín, had caught the revolutionary fever there. They got no help from the British but made contact with the Venezuelan revolutionary Francisco de Miranda and the patriot network he had built up in London.

The circle is unbroken, they do say.

It was the same Miranda who had been Bernardo O'Higgins' maths teacher some years before. It was Miranda who had written the revolutionary diatribe that the young Bernardo had sewn into his coat when he went back to his native Chile.

Miranda already had the flag for the nascent republic. Touting for help, and looking for troops, he had visited Catherine the Great in Russia. She had troubles in the Crimea so couldn't spare the soldiers, but gave the tall handsome Venezuelan money. As a special favour, she gave him the Russian flag and Miranda adapted it for his country. He changed the white – the colour of surrender – to gold. So the Venezuelan flag is blue, red and gold.

It was Miranda who had mounted an expedition to Venezuela in 1806. He brought with him the first printing press seen in the country, to break the Spanish stranglehold on education and propaganda. In the Caribbean he borrowed fifteen more ships.

On their return to Caracas, Miranda and Bolívar convinced the rest of the junta to drop any pretence of loyalty to the Spanish crown. The next year they proclaimed independence. Miranda was in charge but there was a lot of rivalry and infighting amongst the elite, and most of the ordinary people were either Royalist or indifferent. The Church was fiercely Royalist.

When an earthquake occurred early the following year, the Church said it was divine retribution for the heresy against Spain. Many went back to the Royalist cause and joined a bloodthirsty wave of Spanish retribution that swept the country. Miranda was deposed, the First Republic collapsed, and Bolívar handed Miranda over to the Royalists, saying he was a traitor.

It was not Bolívar's proudest moment. Miranda died miserably in a Spanish dungeon four years later, three years after Bolívar was proclaimed the Great Liberator.

From here on the wars that raged, mostly across the *llanos*, were bloody and barbaric on both sides. The creoles were slaughtering each other. More and more bloodthirsty commanders, men like Boves and Morillo, came out from

Spain and the killing reached epic proportions. Two thousand civilians hiding in a church were hacked to pieces. Another commander, coming on a *llanos* town after a victory in the field, would slaughter a third of the population just to celebrate his victory. Decapitating enemies and frying the heads in oil was a favourite gesture.

At this gory time Paez was given a cavalry command. He led a charmed life. He had been imprisoned several times by the Royalists; twice he spent a night in the condemned cell. He got away each time, by bribery or cunning. This made him the stuff of legend, because prisoners were slaughtered at that time. Neither side kept prisoners for long. But El Catire, the Fair One, seemed to have nine lives.

The carnage went on unabated. The Royalists routed the Patriots for a while. Bolívar crossed over to Colombia to regroup, then came back for more.

Paez' fame grew. He became a master of guerrilla warfare with his bands of screaming cowboy marauders, his flexible light cavalry. He took part in more and more spectacular skirmishes and battles, always personally leading his wild *llanero* cavalry into the fight. He had no fear. He showed astonishing personal bravery and was a wizard with a lance, the best man in the whole of South America.

Once, out scouting alone, Paez found a troop of Goths, which is what he called the Spanish. The Royalists called the Patriots *chocutos*, or 'skinheads', because they shaved their heads. He ambushed the Goths and killed a sergeant. The rest of the troop ran off leaving two cannon and a man. The man was Sanchez, a famous *llanero* strong man. They say that once he saved a cannon, carrying it over his shoulder like a musket from the battlefield. He stood firm and faced Paez down.

Paez had his lance and Sanchez had only an empty gun. He grabbed at the lance and pulled Paez off his horse. Paez was too strong even for Sanchez. He wrenched his lance free and ran the man through. Let Paez tell us himself:

Seeing him stretched upon the ground I tried to take off a handsome cartridge belt that he wore round his waist, and as he broke out into ill-considered words not fitting for the situation in which he found himself, I began to exhort him to make a Christian ending, and reciting the Creed aloud to stimulate him to repeat it. Luckily for me, I looked down by accident and saw that instead of accompanying me in my prayers he had half drawn the dagger that he carried in his belt.

I confess my charity was completely chilled and as my indignation did not allow me to waste more time as to my adversary's future destiny, I freed him from the rage which was choking him, even more than the blood he was losing, with another lance thrust.

Paez was said to be the last great lance fighter before artillery finally took over. On the *llanos*, he won many battles against guns with his lance and his *llaneros*. Paez always used a standard ten-foot-long Alvarico palm lance, sharpened at one end. Even as a general, he needed nothing special.

To the *llaneros*, the lance was a second arm. As children they all rode horses and used long canes with metal and rawhide rattles on the end as goads to drive the wild cattle. When driving a herd, and later in battle, they knotted their reins short, dropping them on their horses' necks to leave both their hands free. Major Flinter, an English officer, thought they were fearsome:

In the charge they lay their hands close along the right side of the horse's neck with the lance poised in the right hand ready to plunge into their antagonist. At a distance the rider is not discernible and on a nearer approach it is very difficult to take aim at them so close do they crouch to their horses' backs. Their charge is furious, nor will the most dreadful fire deter them from approaching. During the charge they make the most horrid yells.

Instead of a troop of *llanero* cavalry, Flinter could have been describing Comanche or Apache war parties who charged in exactly the same way. Indians of the southern pampas of Argentina, too, fought alike, lying along the horse's body. So the line between the *llaneros* and their Achagua Indian forebears, the line between cowboys and Indians, so simple and so clear in Hollywood, gets increasingly blurred out on the *llanos*.

The *llaneros*, most of whom were originally Royalists, defected to the patriot cause out of respect for Paez. They loved him. As the brutal wars ground on, more and more *llaneros* came over to fight with Paez and demanded that Paez be their commander. They turned down another of Bolívar's generals, Santander. A good man, but only El Catire Paez would do. To the plainsmen, he was the greatest cowboy of them all.

Hippisley was an English officer who had served under Wellington. He came to Venezuela at the head of a regiment that he had raised, to fight the Spanish. He hated everything about Venezuela, though, and failed to see the genius of Bolívar.

But he was impressed by Paez:

Paez is self taught and sprang up all of a sudden from nothing during the revolution . . . His courage, intrepidity, repeated successes and the number of his followers speedily gained him a name. His followers too were all so many Paezes, looking up to their general as a superior being. On the parade or in the field, he was their general, and supreme. In the hours of rest from the fatigues of a long and rapid march, or from conquest over the adversary, and the retaliation rigidly executed, Paez would be seen dancing with his people in the ring formed for that purpose, smoking with them, drinking from the same cup, and lighting the fresh cigar from the one in the mouth of his fellow soldier.

Paez's victories mounted up. One which secured his place in the Cowboy Hall of Fame was at Mata de la Miel, the Honey Grove. It was the first time *llanero* cavalry with lances had routed regular soldiers with artillery.

Paez had been left in the lurch with a small army of five hundred *llaneros* by his general, who was worried by news of the approach of a heavily armed Spanish force. Late in the day Paez went to investigate a dense cloud of dust hanging over a palm grove. He came on an enemy outpost and shouted insults at them, challenging the commanding officer to a man-to-man duel, in the cowboy way. Before he could get down to business his horse was shot dead beneath him.

'Friends,' he shouted, 'they have killed my good horse. If you won't help me to revenge him, I'll go alone.'

The battle began. With no twilight on the *llanos*, night fell quickly and Paez' officers urged that they wait until dawn. With his instinct for guerrilla warfare Paez would have none of it, figuring the artillery would be useless in the dark and that now was the time to attack.

So with Paez at their head, the reckless half-naked cowboys, with only a loincloth and a rawhide headband for clothes, hunkered down bareback over their horses in the Apache style and charged straight at the big guns.

As they swept down on the artillerymen and infantry, a shot struck Paez's horse, which at once plunged violently and broke the girths. Paez, with the saddle still between his knees, found himself on the ground and the whole of his own squadron passed over him with a thunderous noise. Mounting another horse that a friend offered him, he hurried to rally his second squadron that had been thrown into confusion by the artillery fire.

By that time night had fallen and the charge of the Llaneros was so impetuous that the Royalist cavalry broke and fled into the dark. Many were lanced by their pursuers before the darkness shrouded them from pursuit.

It was a stunning victory. With his small band Paez had killed four hundred men, taken five hundred prisoners, artillery pieces, stores and ammunition and, most important, had captured three thousand horses. This meant the

Royalists were stuck for horses for a long time and their cavalry were effectively immobilized.

Paez did not kill his prisoners, unlike all the other Patriot commanders. Bolívar himself had declared 'War to the Death – Take No Prisoners' and never stopped the massacre of prisoners. Paez preferred to release them. Coming up from the ranks himself, a man of the people, he did not want to murder fellow *llaneros*, and thought that if he spared them, many might join his ranks later. He was right.

The three thousand horses Paez' cowboys had captured were, of course, wild and had to be broken. A man called Baralt watched the taming of this army of horses:

The horses were tamed in the Llanero fashion by squadrons. It was a curious sight to see five or six hundred soldiers struggling at the same time with these wild animals out on the sweltering plains. All round the place where the breaking was going on mounted men were posted riding tame horses, not to assist the rough riders who fell, but to pursue the horses that had thrown them to prevent their escaping with the saddles, although these saddles were but a wooden tree, with a few strips of rawhide hanging from them.

Daniel O'Leary was Bolívar's biographer and another of his generals. He took an immediate dislike to Paez, preferring the more educated and ascetic Bolívar. He may well have been jealous.

Paez was far too popular with his men and had too much fun. At the feast of St John, O'Leary saw Paez and his cowboy crew painting the town. They rode about in their shirts playing guitars and singing and calling on everyone to come out and dance. Paez was, even into his eighties, a great singer and dancer. Those who refused to come out that day were pulled out and rolled in the muddy streets. The joke was to get everyone as muddy as themselves. Good ol'-fashioned cowboy fun. O'Leary didn't get the joke.

In the evening, Paez and his men rode into the river to wash themselves. A gargantuan banquet followed, a *llanero* special. They had ribs of beef, wild boars roasted whole, venison from the nearby woods, wild ducks, fish from the river, wild pheasants, cheese, corn bread, *arepa*, and *guarapo*, fermented sugar juice. It was too much for O'Leary, who described Paez in these words:

He was of middle height, robust and well made, although the lower portion of his body was not in due proportion to his bust. His chest and shoulders were broad; his thick, short neck supported a large head, covered with dark, crisp, chestnut hair; his eyes were brown and lively; his nose straight, with wide nostrils; his lips thick and his chin round. His clear skin showed his good health, and would have been very white had he not been sunburned. Caution and suspicion were the distinctive traits of his countenance. Born of humble parentage he owed nothing to his education.

In the presence of those he thought better educated than himself he was silent and almost timid. With his inferiors he was loquacious, and not averse to practical jokes. He was fond of talking of his military exploits. Entirely illiterate, he was quite ignorant of the theory of the profession that he practised, and he would have never been a first rate captain, for the slightest contradiction or emotion brought on convulsions that took away his senses for the moment, and were followed by fits of physical and moral weakness.

It was not unusual for Paez to have an epileptic attack before or even during a battle. Some writers, like the mealy-mouthed O'Leary, suggested it was just nervousness, but the descriptions sound like full-blown grand mal epilepsy.

His men knew to support him in the saddle when he twitched and foamed. If he fell unconscious from his horse, the horse would know to stay beside him until his soldiers came to lift him up. They would take him to the rear and throw water in his face or even dunk him in water and shake him until he came to. Once he had regained consciousness, his men would put him back in the saddle and, even if he had not regained his speech and his head was away on some other sun-scorched plain, he would be off into the thick of the battle. Like many epileptics, he could be weakened for days after a severe attack.

Paez had great success with two particular guerrilla tactics. One was a kind of Parthian manoeuvre. If the first charge was unsuccessful they would retire and reform. As the enemy, thinking they had retreated, came out, the *llaneros* would ambush them with another charge.

The other was to get upwind of the enemy and start a brush fire which would power down on the opposing forces. They got burned, asphyxiated, and would panic. Ranks broke, and as the fire almost reached them, the *llaneros* would come screaming through the wall of flame and spear down the coughing, blinded enemy.

Carabobo is a sun-scorched windswept plain up on a high plateau. A battle could be decisive, and Bolívar wanted Paez there with as many men and horses and cattle as he could bring.

On 10 May 1821, Paez set out for Carabobo with a thousand infantry and fifteen hundred horsemen, driving two thousand horses and four thousand steers. Cunninghame Graham warns of the dangers of such a massive drive across the *llanos*:

No one who has not tried to take large bodies of semi-feral horses or cattle over the plains, can have the least idea of the enormous difficulty of the task. The animals cannot be driven quickly or they all lose condition and become footsore. They have to stop and graze at intervals, and drink where there are places suitable, for steep descents to rivers, or muddy water holes, are dangerous for them. On every one of these occasions for the first two or three days there is the chance they may stampede and break away.

The peons who are in charge of them sit on their horses, in the burning sun, the rain, or icy wind, with an eye always on the animals they drive. They must not shout, wave whips or ponchos, and above all avoid putting their horses into a sudden gallop. At night they must not light a match, for the flicker of it might alarm the herd, and alarm quickly turns to flight. If a man wishes to speak to one of his comrades he must not call to him, but ride up to his side and almost whisper in his ear.

Those who sleep round the camp fire must keep it low, never throw green wood, or boughs with leaves upon them into the flames, for they are apt to crackle and flare up, and then the herd with a loud snort is off into the night. When it stampedes, at the peril of their lives the watchers of the herd must ride like madmen, no matter how rough the ground may be, or dark the night, waving their ponchos and their whips, shouting their loudest, stretched out upon their horses' necks, endeavouring to head off the cattle, and so to stem the rush. The horses bound through the darkness and in the moonlight strain every nerve, under the whip and spur.

If at last, by dint of hard riding the rush is checked, the herdsmen ride slowly round the mob of animals, raising a melancholy chant that seems to have a wonderful effect in soothing them. At any moment they may begin to run again; but if they once begin to go round in a circle, a phenomenon that cattlemen call 'milling', they will not take to flight again, at least on the same night.

Paez arrived at Carabobo in July 1821, two months after he set out. The battle of Carabobo decided the fate not only of Venezuela but the whole of South America. If the Spanish lost Venezuela, the nearest of their colonies, they had little chance of keeping Chile and Peru. The battle was decided by two armies of barely six thousand men each. Paez had fifteen hundred *llaneros*. And there was the British Legion.

The British Legion were there to fight the Spanish and that is exactly what they did. Largely between them and Paez' cowboy cavalry the battle was over in less than an hour. After a decade of brutality, it was won with relatively little loss of life.

Around two hundred Patriots and a few more Royalists died. The Patriots' losses came mostly from the British Legion: 'The British Legion ceased to be a corps like all the others, but having rooted themselves in the ground, became a granite wall.' It was a triumph of British discipline.

They took everything the Spanish could throw at them, sacrificing themselves manfully row after row. It was true British rugged-jawed glinty-eyed stoic bravery and monumental stupidity but it turned the tide. Men fell like corn before the reapers and their chums stepped in to close up the decimated ranks and to get theirs. Most of their officers, Like Colonel Farrar and Major Denny, were mown down shouting orders to their men to 'Stand firm!'

And then Paez and his wild half-naked, lance-wielding, horse-hugging screaming cowboys came charging down on the Royalists with their 'most horrid yells' and scared them shitless. All resistance evaporated. The Spanish gave in, gave up or ran away.

Bolívar and the Patriots took two thousand prisoners, a mountain of ammunition and all their artillery.

It was all over. Bolívar's problems had just begun.

If it seems that Paez and his *llaneros* won the war on their own, it must be remembered that Simón Bolívar was the genius behind it all. He made the plans, he motivated everyone, he was the orator, the politician and the Commander-in-Chief. He had the dream just like Miranda. He prevented all attempts to wrest control away from him during the battle for independence. He was the Great Liberator.

Daniel O'Leary, his Boswell, adored him as much as he disliked Paez, but other writers paint a more severe picture of the great man. He was always on horseback, partly because of his lack of height and partly because he loved riding. His soldiers called him Culo de Hierro, old Iron Arse.

Once the battles for independence were over the real battles began. Chaos and rebellion broke out. Attempts to impose democratic constitutions on old colonial societies built on slavery, *encomiendas*, subjugation and a ruling elite failed as they were bound to do.

Bolívar's dream was to see a single unified America.

'For us the fatherland is America!' he proclaimed.

He fought to create a state of Gran Colombia – Venezuela, Colombia and Ecuador – joined with Peru and Chile to form a greater Confederation of the

Andes. In his vision he was the supreme ruler of all this land. But too many people were suspicious of his dreams of empire and he lost more and more credibility.

Those already in power under the old system did not want to lose their grip; the British were jealously guarding their hold on the ports and the trade they had annexed and monopolized. They certainly didn't want a single powerful state. In the face of all this hostility and suspicion the dream evaporated. Gran Colombia split into three countries almost immediately. The Venezuelan Congress branded Bolívar a tyrant and a danger to his native country.

Deeply wounded, he fell into a black depression. His health got worse. 'We will never be happy, never,' he said. 'Spanish America is ungovernable,' he went on, and 'All we have gained by the revolution is our independence.' Such comments did not endear him to his compatriots. Rejected by everyone, he saw his life's work fall apart. He died penniless, in obscurity, in a small house in Colombia. All he had was his sword, his clothes and some books. In the depths of his despair he cried out: 'After Jesus Christ and Don Quixote I am the third biggest fool in history.'

So the winners were losers again. Like Bolívar, San Martín and Artigas, the other two great American idealists, both died in obscurity, San Martín in Boulogne and Artigas on a maté plantation in Paraguay. Like Bolívar, they had the same American dream, a unified continent free of nationalism and exploitation, with land and rights for everyone. All were rejected by their homelands. All saw their aspirations swept away. The dream was over.

George Laval Chesterton was one of the British Legion whose number did not come up on the plains of Carabobo. He wrote later of Paez:

When I served with him, Paez could neither read nor write, and until the English came to the Llanos, had never used a knife and fork, so rough and so uncultured had been his former life; but when he met the officers of the British Legion he copied their way of living and their dress, modelling himself upon them.

Nature has endowed Paez with surprising strength. Sometimes, and only as an exercise, when his men are catching wild cattle with the lazo, he will single out a bull, and pursuing it on horseback seize it by the tail, and with a sharp jerk bring it to the ground.

His character is ardent, generous, and affable, and his intelligence, though it has not been cultivated, shows all the virtues that adorn human nature. Sincere, frank and simple, he is a perfect friend, and as he is a stranger to all mean passions, a generous enemy.

A stranger to all mean passions and a generous enemy, Paez was more successful in seeing his dream realized than the other liberators. But he had no grandiose schemes. He was a simpler man, at heart a *llanero*, a cowboy, who did what he liked doing, and who enjoyed life. He enjoyed it so much that late in life he got educated. He learned to read and write and speak French and English and a bit of Italian.

He became President of Venezuela for two terms. The first in the continent to champion the emancipation of slaves, he travelled and was given state welcomes by the crowned heads of Europe. He became the world's favourite South American cowboy dictator. He had his problems, was rejected, imprisoned, but always seemed to bounce back. He lived in New York for many years and once paraded down Broadway on a fine charger, showered with flowers.

Unfortunately the horse slipped and smashed his leg. But even at seventy he had an iron constitution. A broken leg never stopped an old cowboy. He recovered and went on dancing and singing until the age of eighty-three, when he rode off into his final sunset on the celestial *llanos*.

15. Sunset on the Llanos

The dust didn't last too long. Passing through some jungle we drove alongside a river. We stopped to watch some children swimming. Jo talked to an old man and asked about the *caribes*. Sure, he said, there were *caribes* in there. Visions of *Jaws*, a river of blood, foaming water, feeding frenzy, innocent children thrashing about screaming, dismembered limbs waving as they are stripped to the white gleaming bone by the most voracious of all animals flashed in front of our eyes. The old man watched us and grinned. No, there was no real danger, he said. But *caribes*, piranhas for God's sake, surely . . .

No, no problem. Sure, if there is a fair bit of blood, it can alert them, but they are dangerous only in a confined space. Boxed up they feel threatened and they attack. Then it's not nice. But in a free-flowing river like here, no problem. What do you think, we'd let the children play in there if they're going to get massacred?

The children looked lively.

We drove back to Barinas.

I'd got it in my mind to buy a *cuatro*, the deep-bodied *llanero* ukulele. A good travelling instrument. Marcelino, the fine *bandola* player from the other day, told me the best *cuatro* maker on the whole *llanos* was in Barinas. He was Misael Montoya and his workshop was in front of Barinas jail.

I thought of Paez – damnit, I couldn't get Paez out of my mind – and the times he'd been thrown into the jail in Barinas. Was it the same jail? Ask the *cuatro* man.

'No se, señor.' He couldn't help me. But he could sell me a *cuatro*. Misael, stripped to the waist, had a huge round belly that he stroked and slapped a lot.

It was golden brown, smooth as a baby's and hung carelessly out over his pants. He poured with sweat. His sleek black hair was oiled back over his head.

Two toddlers peered at us round his legs. A ten-year-old girl and two teenage boys came out of the workroom asked papa something, clocked the gringos, and went back. His heavily pregnant wife came out carrying two babies, looked at us and smiled. Hold on: that's seven already and one on the way and still counting. Misael wiped the sweat from his face while the kids kept staring at the gringos. I had a feeling somehow he was going to take all of my money. He looked like he was positioning himself, sitting behind his counter, right in front of my wallet.

It turned out that Misael was Marcelino's godfather, but what the hell. Someone had to be. Anyway, his instruments sounded good. I played some. It was easy, they were tuned almost like the top four strings of a guitar. The kids kept staring and his wife stood watching behind his shoulder. Misael stroked his face and his belly. I chose one.

We haggled. The price we agreed was more than I had in bolívars. Forget plastic on the *llanos*, but the hard stuff should be all right. They like it in Russia. I got dollars out but he didn't look happy. He didn't care about the rate, he just wanted bolívars.

His wife peered at the dollars over his shoulder. She kept shaking her head, looking puzzled. He argued with her. He might be losing a sale. I didn't have enough bollis and could just walk out of the shop. Two gringos and no sale. She still didn't look happy and kept on shaking her head.

It turned out that although we were in a fairly big town, we were still out on the *llanos*. Though we were at the end of the twentieth century, dollars come from outside – not to be trusted. She couldn't believe in them. The thing was, she had never seen dollars before.

I got the *cuatro* anyway, but still only with bollis. Tambien had to dig down and see if he could make up the balance. As it happens, the cost of the instrument was, magically, exactly all the bolivars we had between us. The lot. Montoya cleaned us out of every note and every coin, down to the very last bolivar.

I was full of admiration but could not work out how he knew exactly how much local currency Tambien and I were carrying, and then to settle on that amount for the *cuatro*. It can't have been sleight of hand like the three-card trick. X-ray vision is the only possible explanation. We had nothing for a taxi, they wouldn't take dollars either, so we walked back to the hotel.

He gave us a key ring each, though. Key rings are very big in South America. I was still carrying one from the tip of Patagonia, from Río Gallegos.

His was a combined key ring and bottle opener, had Misael Montoya and some *cuatros* on it, and his address – 'Frente al Penal', ' In front to the Jail, Barinas'.

It's a great sounding *cuatro*, though.

Llaneros are as superstitious, or have as many un-Christian beliefs, as all other cowboys. Professor Chitty had told us of the most powerful novel of the *llanos*, *Doña Barbara*. The protagonist was a witch out on the *llanos* in league with a wizard, a *brujo*, and the Devil. Lights glowing in the swamps. Real Cowboy stuff. He had told us, too, of Smokescreen, the Indian with nine hundred lives.

Before we walked back to the hotel, we found a bar close to the prison that would give us a drink for a dollar. It was the prison that reminded me so I asked the *dueño*, the owner, about Guardahumo.

He was taken aback that the gringos knew about him. Yes, he was a real man, not just a legend, who lived at the end of the nineteenth century. Guardahumo was an Indian bandit who escaped the law a hundred times and more. His trick, when in a difficult situation, was to assume the form of a cloud of smoke and simply blow away.

He disappeared like this in front of gunmen, bounty hunters, posses, soldiers, even a battalion of heavy field artillery. They said he was a *brujo*, a witch-doctor, a man of magic. He was a thorn in the authorities flesh. It was all-out war. Time and again they'd have him surrounded and *poof*, old Smokescreen would evaporate once more.

They managed to catch him several times. He was in Barinas prison twice, but somehow he'd always assume his ethereal form and wisp out between the bars before the day of execution arrived. One day, they finally caught him unawares and he was murdered in his cell a week before the official execution.

They had to bring in a hitman from Caracas, a city boy who didn't believe all that supernatural nonsense, to despatch Guardahumo. No one from the *llanos* would do it for fear of old Smokescreen creeping into their dreams and haunting them for the rest of their lives.

No one heard any more about the executioner from Caracas. They haven't stopped talking about Guardahumo.

Our man said his grandfather had seen the fugitive Indian in real life. Well, he thinks he did, but the crafty old bandit had already changed into his nebulous, mystic fog form. As usual, old Smokescreen had been too quick for him.

Walking back to the hotel through Cowtown the evening hung heavy. We passed an undertaker carefully easing his ancient asthmatic Cadillac hearse into the courtyard of his funeral parlour beside a grain and tack store on an old street. It was wide and low and it looked like the fins wouldn't get through the gateway.

But he'd done it before. After a couple of wheezing reversals it slid in. He slowly closed the black wooden double doors of the courtyard, shutting the doors on the day. They creaked in a convincingly funereal way. On the doors was written in large white prophetic letters

CAUTION
UNEXPECTED EXITS

After the undertaker, we saw the death of the day, a short but spectacular sunset. I still wanted to hear more music, so later that night we went back to the Casa del Llano. They offered us girls again but left us alone when we said all we wanted was rum and the *joropo*.

It was amateur night. Good amateurs, and more fast, galloping cowboy tunes. The sound was *muy amplificando*, heavily amplified with loads of reverb. Wa-wa-wa-wa-wa. A young boy, about twelve, looked nervous but sang well. He was wearing the standard *llanero* evening gear, a glowing white acrylic Nehru suit, buttoned up to the neck.

The star, or so he seemed to think, was known as 'The Professor'. He was a tiny old guy in his sixties, very dark with crinkly greying hair, gold-rimmed glasses and flashing gold rings and teeth, a sprightly walk and the air of the Guvnor. He made an entrance, dressed to kill, full tuxedo, black tie and two women on each arm.

He had a regal, condescending air, giving his blessing on the evening, gracing us with his presence, acting as if he was the main attraction and this was Madison Square Garden, instead of amateur night at the Casa del Llano. Everyone leaned over to us and whispered that he was the Maestro. I was expecting great things.

He was terrible. After pushing the women who came in with him to get up and play maracas and sing, he joined some other musicians on a *joropo*. He opened his case and pulled out a saxophone, and played free-form, or rather, form-less, jazz, way beyond Ornette Coleman, over the happily thrumming *cuatros* and racing maracas. Nothing he played had any relation whatsoever to what was going on around him but he didn't care. He was the Maestro, he was looking sharp, he was strutting his stuff and he was going to blow his sax whatever happened.

Everyone seemed to love him, and didn't act as if the Maestro had blown it this time. They applauded and shouted '*Machete!*' and '*Autentico!*'

They looked over to the two gringos to see how we liked him. I nodded encouragingly.

Was there something I was missing? Were these *llaneros* into some kind of tangential modern jazz that makes Sun Ra and His Solar Arkestra seem like Dixieland? I gave him one more tune, but no, he was just really bad. A stinker.

Still, what the hell. I admired him for his self-confidence. He was the Professor, the Head Bollocks. Big in Barinas.

I woke up the next day with a head full of *llaneros*, Paez, Bolívar and rum. I suddenly realized we were about to leave the southern part of this continent.

I drank some strong coffee. Tried to get Paez and the rum out of my head. There was a tune, too, that wouldn't leave me alone. Among all the galloping *joropos* and the Professor's free-form *llano*-jazz there were some heroic *galerones* and one great *tonada* which stirred up love and food together, a timeless mix. With the rum, it kept trotting round my mind:

Corn for the chicken,
Fish for the goose,
And pretty girls
For the love-sick man.

A woman should have
Two things to be good;
Much desire to work,
And very little to eat.

More coffee. Must clear my mind. I remember Professor Chitty's warning that the *llaneros* and the rum could become addictive. Sure, the *llaneros* didn't have the same political or mythic stature as the gauchos, he said, and the only piece of *llanero* literature was *Doña Barbara*. There was nothing like 'Martín Fierro'. But they did have the poetry of 'much desire to work, and very little to eat'. It went with the primitive life of the *llanos*. Though the cattlemen were wealthy, they never had the political weight or the dizzying power of the cocoa and coffee planters of the coastal valleys. It was they who did the big deals and kept the *llaneros* in their place. But far from being poor second cousins, said Chitty, the *llaneros* and their unforgiving home would still be hard to forget. He was right.

Kept pouring the coffee down. Much as I'd have like to stay, I had to get this rum and these plainsmen out of my head. Like Chitty, I was hooked.

But now it was time to go to Mexico. Another coffee should do it. Time for the vaqueros.

I remembered the intense sunset the night before. I pulled out my copy of Don Roberto, Cunninghame Graham, to read his florid, pre-psychedelic painting of the end of a *llanos* day. It was the best way to say goodbye to these tropical plains:

Then comes the miracle; the miracle of miracles, unknown to those who have not journeyed on those interminable steppes or sailed upon the Apure or the Orinoco. No words can paint the infinite gradation of the scale of colour that leaves the spectroscope lacking a shade or two. Green turns to mauve, then back to green again; to scarlet, orange and vermilion, flinging the flag of Spain across the sky. Dark coffee-coloured bars, shooting across a sea of carmine, deepen to black; the carmine melts into pale grey.

Castles and pyramids spring up; they turn into cities; the pyramids to broken arches, waterfalls, and ships, with poops like argosies. Gradually pale apple-green floods all the heaven; then it fades into jade. Castles and towns and ships and broken arches disappear. The sun sinks in a globe of fire, leaving the world in mourning for its death.

Then comes the after-glory, when all the colours that have united, separated, blended, and broken up, unite and separate again, and once more blend. A sheet of flame, that for an instant turns the Apure into a streak of molten metal, bathes the *llano* in a bath of fire, fades gradually and dies, just where the plain and sky appear to join as if the grass was all aglow.'

16. Mexico City

It's easy to see from the map why Mexico needs soul and a good sense of humour, living in the shadow, groaning under the weight, of its overbearing neighbour. It brings Uruguay and Ireland back to mind. Maybe the Alamo was the last time, or the only time, Mexico ever bullied the Americans.

We Europeans usually come into Mexico from the north, from the States, and perceive it through American eyes. Crossing the border becomes a step from clean sterility to dirty soul, a step up or a step down depending on your point of view.

Coming from the south, though, from the top of Patagonia through the lands of the lost cowboys, gives a different perspective. It is more of a step across, from one cowboy culture to another. Without setting a foot in the Wild West I had now seen horsemen down south who could out-cowboy anything that ever galloped across the silver screen.

I knew already that Hollywood was not to be believed. They had only borrowed cowboys, not invented them, hijacked them from the guys who are now south of the Rio Grande. In an effort to cover their tracks, if not their guilt, they had turned them into bandits or snivelling peasants.

It's time for the rewrite.

The original men who rode the horses and herded the cattle across North America spoke Spanish. After the gauchos, *huasos*, and *llaneros*, the wild orphans and the plainsmen, up here in the north the cowboys are, literally, the vaqueros.

Hollywood's celluloid conscience has begun to rehabilitate the Indian, but to admit the debt the Anglos owe to the vaqueros would be to accept that the Anglo cowboys are pale shadows of the real thing. And as the cowboy is as important to America as apple pie, that would be a hard Hispanic bullet to bite on.

Customs at Mexico City's airport is like Caracas, a kind of bingo game. After an initial search we stood in line to hit a button. In front of us was Sergio, an Argentine. His grandfather, a Russian Jew from an old theatrical family, went to Argentina and became one of the Jewish gauchos of the Entre Rios.

He became a great rider and, with the theatre still in his blood, a film star. He made a film about the Jewish gauchos and with the money bought land for an estancia. He raised Jewish cattle and slaughtered them in the orthodox way, supplying kosher *bife de chorizo* to the burgeoning Jewish population of the pampa between the rivers.

He taught Sergio to ride and was still playing *maroma*, jumping from the gate-post on to an unbroken colt's back into his sixties. Sergio left Argentina when he was twenty and was now a drug company rep in New Jersey.

It was our time for the lottery. I hit the button. If a green light comes up you walk free. If it is red, you go over for a second customs search. Mexican Roulette. We hit red.

The customs man got very interested in the green herbiness of my maté and kept sniffing my maté pot. He took no notice of my bleating 'tea' and 'herb, related to the holly bush' and called a colleague over. I wanted to ask why the fuck we would be smuggling marijuana *into* Mexico but kept quiet. The colleague went on sniffing at the maté pot, opened my *cuatro* case and his eyes lit up. He's scored.

'Ha, musician?' He peered up expectantly, smirking. I could feel a rectal examination coming on. But Jo Tambien was in there quick as a flash and with the right officious tone.

'No, musicologist.' That did it.

'*Bueno. Pase.*' Through, and no more buttons to hit.

This was not the first trip to Mexico City for me or Tambien and there were a few favourite spots. Plaza Garibaldi was one. Named after the great freedom fighter and biscuit inventor who fought from Uruguay to Italy, Plaza Garibaldi is Mariachi Central. You'd be hard put not to notice.

It is the market for a hundred bands. Every night they rub shoulders with each other and with the punters strolling through. They play for money and wait for someone to commission them. Busking to order. It could be anyone from elderly American tourists to young Mexican couples. Far from just a tourist trap, there have always been more Mexicans than gringos on the plaza.

When Tambien and I arrived it was early, about nine. The square was already packed with musicians, but not all playing yet. Most of them were mestizo. Some were standing around, some chatting, some looking forlorn, all dressed up to the eyeballs in their impressive *charro* suits. These are the classic mariachi suits, mostly black or grey, some red, a couple sky blue. They were extremely sharp, as they should be, for the suit is the dress of the gentleman horseman, the *charro*. He would be the landowner, the hacendado, flashing his wealth as he rode.

So the mariachis were wearing the boss's trousers.

They had a short bolero jacket, the *chamarro*, heavily embroidered and carefully tailored, full white shirt and waistcoat, a broad sash round the belly like the gaucho *faja*, and the skin-tight pants, tight at the knee and split over the boot. These were the serious trousers, the tight, clanking strides with the silverware all the way down the leg. Many of them were threatened by advancing bellies they hadn't quite bargained for. The mariachis wore cowboy boots, some with spurs. Each one had his broad Mexican sombrero. Several went all the way with a folded serape, the poncho, over the shoulder. They made a lot of noise as they walked around, carrying a lot of loose change down their legs.

Most of the bands were mariachi, but some played *Norteño conjunto* music. *Norteño conjunto* as a name sounds full of exotic promise, but loses in the translation to 'Northern Group' music. It is border music, from Rio Grande country, and is also called Tex Mex over the border. In Plaza Garibaldi it was played by musicians in less flamboyant cowboy hats and shirts and ponchos. Not *charro*. More vaquero.

There are two equestrian traditions in Mexico, the gentlemanly *charros* and the working cowboys or vaqueros.

The charros were the descendants of the Spanish landed gentry who had been given *encomiendas*, gifts of land with free local Indian labour. They had always ridden horses, and used *la gineta*, a short-stirruped saddle, riding with the knees bent in the style of the Moorish cavalry who invaded Spain. In battle the Moors would stand high in the stirrups, above the enemy, and slash downwards with the scimitar. The Spanish word for horseman, *jinete*, comes from *la gineta*.

In Spanish society the horse had always been a mark of class – so much so that the word for gentleman is *caballero*, the man of the horse, the knight. This class-consciousness was exported to the New World. Originally the Spanish would not allow non-whites to ride horses. The ruling creoles thought the Indians and mestizos were born stupid, lazy, criminal and untrustworthy. It was too democratic, too dangerous to let them sit on a horse. It would give them ideas above their station. It would also give them the magic.

This was, of course, all true. The trouble was, there was work to be done, and one thing the Spanish hated was work.

As the ranches expanded they needed workers on horseback. So the hard-working vaqueros emerged and the poor Indians, mestizos and blacks started to ride and to develop cattle-handling skills. The landed elite liked riding, looking good in their *charro* gear, but a brief talk with the ranch foreman was enough. You don't want to get the jacket dirty.

The snobbery the vaqueros got from the ruling Spanish was nothing to the virulent racism they were to suffer later from the Anglo cowboys. And from Hollywood, where all Mexicans were shown as stupid, lazy, criminal and untrustworthy.

Overwhelmingly the Plaza is mariachi. In the centre was a statue of the Saint of Mariachi with its own fountain. Round the square were bars, clubs and restaurants like the Mariachi House, El Rincon Mariachi (the Mariachi Corner), El Barco de Mariachi (the Mariachi Boat), Los Mariachis in the Salon Tropicana.

Mariachi is part of Mexico's musical tradition, not just nightclub music. It comes from the southern part of the state of Jalisco, not far from the home of tequila in the south-west of Mexico. The trumpets are not a traditional ingredient, but to the rest of the world they are the trademark of mariachi. This is because every mariachi band we ever saw on the silver screen used trumpets.

In fact it was Hollywood itself that introduced the trumpets, giving them the parts previously played by violins. They thought the violins couldn't be heard well enough on the soundtrack, so, with their usual attention to authenticity, they changed them to trumpets. And the trumpets stuck.

The great Eddie Santiago was packing them in, his tour bus ostentatiously parked by the square. It was still early; you could walk across the square without pushing. Knots of musicians stood around smoking, their instruments in their cases or out sitting on the edge of a flower bed.

An occasional strangled early-evening version of 'Guadalajara' wafted through the air. A man pushed a wheelbarrow filled with a mountain of peanuts but sold none. It was all still waiting. Time to eat.

I felt out of place. The Argentine was still sticking to me, let alone Venezuela, and the best way to get in touch, to feel Mexico, was to eat it then listen to it. Gauchos and *llaneros* were still galloping across my own personal prairie. I had to shake free of those southern cowboys and start to find the vaqueros. Say goodbye to *bifes* and hello to chilli. Jo and I went in the back of the square where there was a long gallery of food stalls – like the central markets down south, the best place to eat.

We went to a *pulqueria* where they served cactus beer, frothy fermented cactus juice called *pulque*. That started it. Then I got a good big pre-Columbian bowl of *pozole* to sort me out. It worked. It was all-the-way Indian, a corn soup with shredded lettuce, onion and meat; you add hot salsa, guacamole and dried mint to taste. It put a whole new light on the mariachi.

When we went back to the square it was hotting up. It was eleven, most of the bands were playing and the noise was winding itself up nicely. Dozens of mariachi bands were playing different songs on top of each other. In a great distorting bedlam of sound, the tunes changed constantly as we walked between the bands. The most bizarre moment was standing between two fairly bad versions of 'Guadalajara', the chestnut of all mariachi chestnuts. It has lots of dramatic stops and there were bravura climaxes from the lead tenors out of tune with themselves and each other.

Yes! With the chilli and *pozole* in the belly, the lurching attacks on 'Guadalajara', one for each ear, and shrill twin trumpets battling it out into the purple night sky, I knew I had arrived. In a flash the south was forgotten.

We were most definitely in Mexico.

Throughout the conquest the Spanish hated work and appropriated the native Indians on the *encomiendas* as debt slaves. Spanish *caballeros* rode horses but never hunted or tended cattle. They left that to the non-whites, the *castas*. The missions were much more humane, and as they spread up through north Mexico the Franciscans taught Indians to herd the wild and semi-wild cattle.

There were a lot of cattle, too. In 1582, less than ninety years after Columbus brought the first livestock to the New World, only sixty years after Cortés arrived in Mexico, there were one hundred thousand cattle, two hundred thousand sheep and ten thousand wild horses grazing the range near San Juan de los Ríos in northern Mexico. Ranches appeared there in the next twenty years. And the cowboys that worked the cattle were Indians. Then mestizos and blacks became cowboys. A rotten, dirty, stinking job, no white man would touch it.

In Mexico in the late sixteenth century, the first cowboys didn't just look or ride like Indians like the *llaneros*, or learn Indian ways like the gauchos. The first cowboys *were* the Indians.

*

There is, of course, good and bad mariachi. There were one or two good ones that night. They are the ones you need for that special occasion. For these *charros*, these dudes, are available not just to play to you there in the square, but will come and serenade your young lady outside her bedroom window at four in the morning for the right price. So it pays to be careful: the choice of a cheesy mariachi band could seriously threaten the relationship, or even nip something rather beautiful in the bud.

Several times that night I saw cars drive up to the pavement, call musicians over, agree a song and a price, and get a drive-in serenade. I watched one. The band grouped round the side of the car, the singer bent over and leaned his arm on the open window. The harmony singer crouched behind him. Then they both sang a heart-wrencher, full blast and total vibrato, with those great oily tramline harmonies straight into the car to the man's girlfriend at the other end of the front seat. The trumpets played their Western movie in the background and the singers slithered across the beat. Pesos passed and another satisfied customer roared off into the night, his girl turned to jelly.

Many authorities say, and I had always believed it, that the word 'mariachi' came from the French *mariage* because it was often wedding music. A musicologist friend said this was not true, there was no connection. He offered no other explanation, though, so I am inclined to keep an open mind.

Walking down the Reforma, the big main boulevard, I crossed paths with a very drunk shoeshine boy. I was wearing unshineable dirty trainers. He saw his trade swept away by a relentless wave of fashion, the universal Reebok.

He ran twenty yards ahead of me, and stood stooping with his stool under one arm and his box of tricks in his hand. He watched me walking towards him. As I got nearer to him on the sidewalk he stared and kept pointing at my trainers, muttering, 'Fucking shoes. Fuck fuck you shoes.'

Praying for brogues, boots, slip-ons, anything in leather, anything to shine, his voice got louder until he was gibbering a hopeless litany, a desperate prayer to stem the inexorable tide of canvas and plastic.

'Fuck shoes. Fuck fuck fucking shoes. You fucking fucking fucking shoes you fuck. Shoes you fucking fuck shoes.' With his stream of unconsciousness he never once looked me in the eye, nor accused me in any way for wearing the trainers. He just shouted at the shoes.

They were the enemy, the trainers themselves.

I understood. Five million Mexicans had no shoes at all, so a gringo with unpolishable trainers was the last thing he needed. It was them that he hated, but he knew it was hopeless. He knew it was all over. The trainers had already won and he was just a lone voice in the wilderness.

He stared at them and went on hurling invective at them as they bounced past his eyes. 'Fucking fuck shoes. You shoes fucking fuck fuck you fucking fucking fuck fucking shoes . . . '

They still make VW Beetles in Mexico. A lot of the yellow cabs in Mexico City are Beetles. The front passenger seat has been taken out and there is a strap from the dashboard to the offside door so the driver can reach over and snap the door shut once the customers have crammed into the back seat.

Tambien and I would both stick our legs into the space left by the absent seat; JT, like me, is well over six foot. Lying back like this, relaxing in stretch limo style, the doctored Beetle is good and intimate for a cosy political discussion, but this time the driver wanted to discuss broader, more philosophical issues.

'Why couldn't it have been you?'

'What?'

'Why couldn't it have been you?'

'What do you mean?'

'I mean why couldn't it have been you came and conquered us, you or the Germans instead of the Spanish?'

What was this guy on about?

'Look,' he nodded at the four lanky legs stretching across the empty space in the front, 'look at the height of you. You're tall. So are the Germans. My ancestors, the Aztecs, the Toltecs, the Mixtecs, they were all tall like you. Big guys, that's my true heritage. Then what happens? The Spanish, all small men, a bunch of squits, come and take us over. They fuck our women. What happens? Look at us, we're all shortarses. Little people, and we didn't deserve it. Why couldn't it have been you?'

He shook his head at the pain of walking so close to the ground. We gave him an extra tall tip at the end but I don't think it helped a lot.

When the conquistadors were on horseback they didn't look so small. Hernando Cortés rode a black horse from Cordoba, El Morzillo, the Black One. Among his five hundred fighting men he had only sixteen cavalrymen. They had eleven stallions and five mares. One had foaled on the way.

'Next to God,' said Cortés, 'we owe our victory to the horse.'

The horses they brought were similar to the criollos down south. A Barb-Spanish cross, they were Andalucian horses. That was in 1519. The Andalucian horses ran wild. Four hundred years later there were twenty-five million horses in the States, creole, thoroughbred and Arab, one horse for every three people.

A *mordita* is a little bite. The British would call it a bung, but bungs don't fly around as much as little bites happen in Mexico. The *mordita* is like a generous tip, a good drop of oil to keep things running smoothly and sometimes to get authority, and possible retribution, off your back.

Y para reglar, señor? – How would you like to sort this out, to regulate this, sir? – could apply to anything from a parking ticket to an embarrassing lump of the best hashish found in the pocket by the customs man. The extent of the *mordita*, of course, can vary infinitely.

Call it bribery and corruption if you will, but that is just gringo-speak. The little bite is just a piece of the action, like *baksheesh* in the east. It makes the world go round.

That is not exactly how we felt about it when we were fined one day for going round a roundabout the correct way. We had foolishly hired a car, a sure thing to mark you out for a *mordita*, and were waiting at a red light by the base of a column with an Indian cacique on the top. It might have been Cuahtemoc. It was at the intersection of the wide Reforma with several other boulevards.

Two motorcycle cops drew up beside us. They were both wearing mirror shades, riding breeches, high riding boots and *spurs*. Spurs on a motorbike. I was impressed and pointed encouragingly. '*Espuelas! Autentico! Barbaro!*' If I knew the word, I might as well use it. The cops impassively asked for our passports. We handed them over.

JT translated from then on. The cop kept calling each of us '*joven*', young man, though he was at least fifteen years younger than either of us. He was saying that we were going round this roundabout in the same way as the rest of the traffic. Right. And we were waiting at a red light, waiting for it to go green. Right. So the law was the law and there was nothing he could do. In what sense? He had to fine us. What? We were going the right way, surely, following the direction of the arrows painted on the road? Sorry, that's not good enough. The light was red so we stopped at it, yes? No, you'll have to pay the fine.

'*Y como puedo reglar, joven?*'

He'd got us. He had our passports, we could collect them in a fortnight . . . ah, but you want to leave the country in a week. Hmmm, then, how would you like to regulate it, young man? A simple fine will clear it up and I can give you your passports back right now. Special consideration.

He scribbled something on a piece of paper and held it out to us. It said thirty dollars. Fair enough. The standard fine for driving below the speed limit round a roundabout in the right direction, not drunk, and stopping at a red light. Cash. We paid. Sorry, no receipts.

They roared off and their spurs shone brighter than their chrome exhausts in the sunlight.

We drove on warily, baffled. We had just been legally mugged, the carpet pulled from under our feet. Fined for following the rules? We were still clinging to a British sense of logic, far too linear for Mexico.

Then I remembered, reassuringly, one of the cries of South America, '*No hay reglas fijas.*'

There are no fixed rules.

Just testing, we drove through two red lights. It seemed safer. No one took any notice. At the third, a big intersection, we stopped. Suddenly flames were everywhere.

Trade at traffic lights has boomed in recent years. Armies of youths mugging windscreens with suds and squeegee have been part of a growth industry of the eighties that the New World has exported successfully, like tobacco and chocolate, to the Old. In Venezuela, traffic lights are a market, with pigs and turkeys dangled in front of waiting traffic.

Here in Mexico it was flames. Amid the washers and clown-faced jugglers were the teenage fire-eaters.

A boy stood in front of us stripped to the waist. His face and hands blackened and scorched, he swigged at his bottle of alcohol and put a torch to his mouth. WHOOOOFF! The jet of flame shot up just over the car roof. He came to the window, his lethal bottle still in his hand. We didn't argue. It wasn't washing liquid in the bottle and we all knew it.

Tambien tried to talk to the lad. His chest was scorched and hairless and he had no eyebrows or lashes. The fire had gone from his empty black eyes. When he tried to speak, a desiccated croak was all he could manage. His voice had been burnt out, consumed by fire.

These street children are called *milusos*, a thousand uses. Under the volcano.

On Cortés' 1524 expedition into Honduras El Morzillo damaged a foot and was left in the care of an Indian chief. Keen to do right by Cortés and overawed by the great black horse, the chief had him stabled in a temple where garlanded maidens cosseted him and served him spicy chicken dishes and exotic fruits.

It was all too much for El Morzillo who keeled over and died. He went into rigor mortis as the Indians prayed over him and worshipped him as a god. They erected a statue of him in death. The statue showed him sitting on his hindquarters with his four legs stretched out stiff and straight in front. The

Indians continued to worship him as the god of thunder and lightning, Tziunchan.

They prayed and made sacrifices to him until the next century when Spanish priests came and tore him down.

The ancient obsessions of time, timing and ritual death that drove the old civilizations are still alive.

In the Mexican highway code one of the most quixotic of rules concerns two cars approaching a narrow bridge from opposite directions. *The first car to flash its lights has the right of way.*

JT said it would make an interesting argument as to who flashed first if there were any survivors.

Ever since 1959, Café Habana has been the best café in Mexico City. It says so in gold right across the window: 'Desde 1959 LO MEJOR!'

It's true, too. A giant step up from a *lonchería*, it is a Mexican Lyons Corner House. Coffee is roasted and sold at the door. When you smell it halfway up the street first thing in the morning your pace quickens. Inside, the metal trestle tables are formica covered with tubular metal plastic-backed chairs. The place mats are orange plastic with a drawing of a steaming cup of coffee and 'La Habana'.

The waitresses were of an age, all mums, buxom, wearing white aprons and black skirts. The morning light shone through the gilt letters on the wide window and lit up the shadowy high-ceilinged room. The place smelt homely. Our waitress came and mothered us into the morning.

After eggs with extra chillis and coffee to kick the day in, Tambien and I sat and stared up at the ceiling, trying to see the bullet holes. *Desde 1959*: that was when Fidel Castro and Che Guevara were mapping out their insurrectionist dreams. It's said they met regularly at the Café Habana and plotted over coffee. It's said, too, that once or twice they shot off their pistols, and you can still see the bullet holes.

We couldn't see them, so we went to find a cab to take us to the pyramids.

Mexico City is on a broad high plateau ringed with volcanic mountains. Bullet holes in the café were not the only thing we couldn't see that day. The sulphurous bouillon that passes for air in the city blocked out the great snow-topped volcanoes Popocatepetl, 'smoking mountain', and its female partner Ixtaccihuatl, the 'sleeping white lady'. It was a bad day for breathing and I was beginning to gasp a bit as we searched for a taxi and a way out of the soup.

Many of the city streets, far from being boulevards, have narrow pavements, giving the walker the feeling of being right on top of the traffic. The fumes from two or three rows of snorting machines stuck in the narrow one-way streets choke up the already oxygen-thin, thermally inverted, highly polluted air. Everything they say about the air in Mexico City is true: there's not much of it around and what there is, is shite.

On one of those streets I saw a fat man. The sun was hot, the traffic was heavy, and a mountain of a man stood hunched over, propping himself up on a shop corner, sweating and wheezing heavily. He squirted a puffer into his mouth continuously, chain-puffing, sucking terminally at it. Things were looking desperate when a friend came up to him and started chatting. He didn't seem worried, and the fat man talked to him between gasps and puffs as if nothing was happening. If this was the fat man's normal state, I'd hate to see him sick.

This was the site of the earliest American city. As the Aztecs crossed the rim of the great valley they saw an eagle on a cactus with a snake in its talons by a great salt lake. It was a sign. They built their fabled city of Tenochtitlán in the centre of the lake within the ring of fire.

Mexico means Navel of the Moon. Standing on the corner with the fat man gasping hopelessly at the miserly, mephitic air, it was hard not to think it meant Arsehole of the Universe.

More than twenty million people live in Mexico City now and it feels as if all of them have cars. Getting out of town can be punishing, even in a taxi. Unlike Caracas, where it is perched out of the way up on the mountainside, shantytown is much closer here, running ragged along the edge of the road.

The slums go on for ever on the Navel of the Moon. Sad dirt roads, rusting cars and coaches, high wire fences, adobe, breeze block and corrugated iron shacks. Kids kicking balls round dusty, pock-marked, rubbish-strewn patches of ground. Occasional shiny cars and flower-filled gardens, and endless long painted walls with slogans and posters for political parties and bands.

The walls, like Mexico, are dominated by PRI, the Institutional Revolutionary Party, which has ruled for more than sixty-five years. Another clue: this is the only country where a party can be institutional and revolutionary at the same time, where the two words are strangely compatible instead of openly antagonistic. The wall says, with carefree ambivalence, '63 YEARS OF DEEDS'.

Los Babys appeared to be in town. So, too, were Manfred y los Chicharrones, Manfred and the Fried Pigskins.

I recognized Los Pinguinos del Norte, the Penguins of the North, a fine

Norteño, Tex-Mex group. Did I see Victor Hugo and the Bengalis on their North American tour, or was it just lack of oxygen?

'I take you to see the drunken donkey.'

'No, thanks. Just the pyramids, thanks.'

'No problem. It's on our way anyway.'

'No, just the temple of the Sun and Moon, thanks. Just the pyramids. Teotihuacán, no drunk donkeys.'

'Okay, no problem. And I show you a hundred things you can do with cactus.'

'No, thanks.' It was no use.

He drove us a little way off the main road to a clutch of tourist stores. A couple of large maguey cactuses had been hacked about. One had the heart removed. We were given a lightning lecture on the uses of the plant.

The fibres are used for shoes, textiles, ropes, lassoes and hats. The spines can serve as needles, and with a fibre for thread you can carry out sewing repairs on the trail. You can make paper like papyrus from it. Best of all, the heart and juice is used for *pulque* and mescal . . . I began to fade in the heat.

Halfway through this seminar I noticed him. Standing morosely beside us, hitched to a scrubby bush, a daft straw bonnet stuck on his head with his ears poking through, was a drunk donkey.

'*¡El burro borracho!* Buy him a beer! Go ahead, buy him a beer, he will drink it.'

I was a bit hesitant, but then figured that drinking was probably the only way for him to deal with it all. Standing there with the silly hat on, ogled by the tourists day in day out, would make a saint, let alone a donkey, turn to the bottle. We bought him a beer. The driver opened it for us.

'Put it down in front of him!'

I stood the bottle in front of the donkey. He leaned over and picked it up in his mouth by the neck. He raised his head until the bottle was upside down and glug glug glug, the beer was gone. He opened his mouth and the bottle dropped lifelessly to the dusty ground. The driver was jubilant and just for the hell of it took us to the pyramids at Teotihuacán.

I stood on top of the pyramid of the Sun, looking down on school kids clambering up the steep unending steps. Earlier, from the ground, they had been like so many flies crawling up a wall.

Their teacher, a young man, arrived puffing and sweating at the top. We talked. No, he didn't know what civilization built these massive cairns on the navel of the moon long before the Aztecs arrived. We talked of cowboys and Indians. He had been a vaquero himself when he was younger. He said I would find cowboys further north, but there were Indians everywhere.

Did I know that the first cowboys had been Indians anyway, even though the first Spanish wouldn't allow any non-whites on horseback? Yes, I had heard about the Franciscan missions. He urged me to go and see some of the different Indian races still surviving all over his great country.

Two of the best places, where the Indians were strongest, were to the west and south, Michoacan and Oaxaca. He pointed with his arm. In these areas, however Christianized, he said, the indigenous Indians had resisted the worst depredations of the conquistadors. To understand where the vaqueros came from, he said we should follow the cowboy trail through Indian heartland.

Huejotzingo (*Hwey-xhot-zingo*) is a village near Cholula, south-east of Mexico City in Puebla State. They hold a carnival every year to celebrate the battle of Puebla, where they beat the French. One of the few battles Mexico won, it was worth celebrating.

The British, French and Spanish armies regularly docked at Vera Cruz and invaded Mexico demanding payment of debts. In 1861 all three came together, an unholy alliance of repo men, until Britain and Spain realized that France had bigger ideas and wanted the whole country. They left France to it. The French Army marched directly on Mexico City but against the odds they were beaten, stopped in their tracks near Puebla by General Zaragoza's Mexicans.

Victory! A taste so sweet to a Mexican, and so rare. The paradox of winning and losing is never so acute as with the Mexicans. They are winners and losers combined, a confused mixture of aggressive Spanish, the eternal conquerors, and proud but passive Indians, the eternal victims.

Success at last! Little matter the French came back later and beat the Mexicans. They had still won the first battle, and in effect held up the French advance for the best part of a year. Victory indeed, and well worth a fiesta.

We lost ourselves on the way out of Mexico City. It's easily done. Once Ejes 2, 3, 4, 5, 6, Division del Norte and Chapultepec get hold of you and twist you round, and rusting cars weave unknown, dizzying patterns around you, and you can't find Avenida Ignacio Zaragoza to save your life, you start to think: Battle? What battle?

Tambien said not to expect too many cowboys in Huejotzingo. It would be a carnival of soldiers but what the hell. And he did have a lead for some cowboys and a *charro* association in nearby Cholula.

We found the autopista and finally dragged ourselves out of the stale smog in Mexico's giant ashtray and crawled up the crater's edge, the ring of fire.

Popocatepetl and Ixtaccihuatl shone out white topped and massive over to our right as the road came up to the pass. Seventeen-thousand-foot-high volcanoes, invisible through the city soup. You didn't even know they were there until you were upon them.

The traffic came to a standstill on the freeway just outside Puebla. A cloud of bright orange chemical smoke rose over the cars and glared in the sun. More white smoke blew up. A red flare dropped into a field the other side of the road. The day-glo orange could kept billowing up into the sky. Was it a chemical fire? Had a tanker blown up? The holocaust?

Then we saw the people running scared.

The freeway curved down and round and we could see beyond the stoppage. Hundreds of people, men and women, young and old, were running across the autopista, leaping down an embankment on our side, and scattering out across the fields. The apocalyptic sun shone through the orange and white smoke hanging in the air. The red flare kept on burning.

Then we saw the police and the dogs.

There were hundreds of police, in full riot gear, shields, helmets and batons. With their dogs they chased the people across the road and down into the fields. Tear gas was fired. People were clubbed down and dragged away.

It was the new battle of Puebla. And it was the oldest battle in Mexico's history, the battle for land. The new battle of Puebla involved land, corruption, rich industrial landowners and poor *paisanos*. So what's new? It is the beginning and the end, the whole story of Mexico.

Eight years previously the district governor had appropriated a big patch of peasants' land and sold it to the Volkswagen car factory which needed to expand. It was clearly illegal and the *paisanos* fought back. They took him to court and won their land back.

Trampling on the irrelevancies of law, the present governor had just done the same thing, taking the land back again for the VW factory. For each square metre they were paying the *paisanos* compensation of five hundred pesos, the price of a small bottle of Coke. An insult. The people didn't want to sell any land, and the governor's men had already taken fifty acres more than they said they would. So they were demonstrating and the police were throwing them into jail, beating them down in the fields and taking them away.

Huejotzingo is out the other side of the volcano, east of Popocatepetl. The sun was high, it was hot and very dusty. There was gunfire cracking through the shimmering air. A drunk man, cursing and with his head bleeding, smashed a truck window with the butt of what looked like a musket.

Walking into town, everyone was carrying crude home-made muskets. The gunfire got louder and nearer. More and more people were dressed in bizarre caricatures of soldiers' uniforms. All were wearing expressionless pink full-face masks, vacant and haunting.

Each was a different army, a different country. There were members of the Russian Imperial Guard, all with the same pink face and bushy black beard pointing straight out at a surreal forty-five degrees. Their headgear was a towering black beehive with gold, red and white ticking and braid, gold tassels like curtain pulls and a gold eagle on the front. A huge samovar cosy, a kind of rastafarian bearskin, it would have been hot on a cold day and suicidal today.

The French Army were cartoon Foreign Legion.

Shiny blue jackets with gold epaulettes and silver braid, baggy white Zouave trousers, gold-braided oriental hats – part turban, part fez – long pink, red and blue ostrich feathers and white gloves. They had hard blue backpacks filled with ammunition. Their masks had long pointed black beards that curved upwards like the toe of a Turkish slipper, or Moroccan Mr Punches.

The Mexican Army wore broad straw sombreros covered with a shredded, shimmering mass of rustling red, white and green dreadlocks. Mighty corn-cob sideburns poked out from under these shaking, swirling great pompons. They had satin cloaks of many colours with gaudy embroideries of Conan warriors and breasty nude Indian pin-up princesses surrounded by hearts and flowers.

There were other armies, too, but more difficult to identify. The Carabinieros de Cristo, Jesus' Fusiliers, had the strangest beards of all, long white straggling goatees, big white moustachios and bushy white eyebrows.

On children these outfits looked even stranger, more grotesque, because big or small, the uniforms, hats, masks and beards were all identical. They looked like moving primitive wall paintings. A woman walked down the street dressed like a Zapatista rebel, white peasant clothes, dark sombrero and gun belts crossing her chest. She was stooping, holding hands with a small child in the full Jesus' Fusilier gear, white beard, moustache and eyebrows. He was a Lilliputian effigy, one of the little People, a walking cartoon ghost.

By now battalions of these extra-terrestrial troops were hopping and shuffling down the streets, merging into some kind of parade. Muskets boomed out regularly.

A soldier would stop, pull out the ramrod from his flintlock, get a pack of gunpowder, load it down the muzzle, tamp it down with the ramrod and prime the flint. He would dance down the street, holding the musket vertically, butt to the ground, stock and trigger in one hand, barrel in the other. Then, BOOOMM!! *Zingo-Zingo!* The musket would explode like a cannon and the deafened reveller would skip and spin round on his heels, whooping and shrieking. The guns were ear-splittingly loud. It was a real battle.

Then one group would turn on another, French v. Russians, Mexicans v. the Carabinieros, and act out the battle with lots of banging, yelling and spinning. They didn't really attack each other, just hopped and spun and exploded a lot more. It was all very stylized, quite unreal and completely mad. It went on – *Booomm – bang!* – all day and all night long.

For a while I had no idea what was going on. Neither, for once, did Jo Tambien. Nor, as it turned out, did anyone else.

'What's the battle?'

'I don't now.'

'Is it the Russians?'

'I don't know. I'm not from here.'

It reminded me of the war-cry of the cowboy cavalry out on the Venezuelan *llanos*: '*Vive Fulano de Tal!*'

Long live . . . whoever!

Only later, over a *mole poblano*, chicken in chocolate sauce, and a *coco con ginebra*, a fresh coconut with mescal added to the milk, did we find out the whole story. We were in Cantina El Convento where big primitive murals of French and Mexican soldiers looked more real than the people dancing and whooping around us.

El Convento in Huejotzingo was the first Franciscan monastery in all the Americas, founded in 1524, only three years after Cortés' destruction of the Aztecs. The twelve friars, full of the utopian ideals of the Renaissance, came to found an ideal society and to put behind them the sins and crimes of Europe, perhaps also to mitigate the sins and crimes of the conquistadors.

In front of the church and monastery is a large, peaceful, cloistered square with fine old trees and a processional open chapel at each corner. The Franciscans quickly and astutely noticed that the Indians did their worshipping in the open air and didn't like going into buildings. So they preached from the open-sided chapels to the Indians gathered in this serene walled garden.

Quiet it may have been once, but today the serenity of the cloisters was broken by the explosions and gunfire of the raging, dinning battle outside and the shrieking delirium of the whooping, whirling souls with the powder-blackened hands. The precise uniformity of each army, each soldier a mirror image of all the others, with exactly the same face, beard, hat and outfit down to the smallest detail, created not a togetherness or any sense of belonging, but a surreal loneliness.

Unseen dark mestizo faces, unknown hopes and fears were buried deep behind those blank melancholy masks. And through all the detonations and explosions, the salvos of whooping, howling spinning and shrieking was a sadness, a separateness as they blasted away their eardrums and all vestiges of memory. It was a victory no one could really bring themselves to believe.

Cholula had always been a holy place, not just to the Aztecs, but to the Olmecs, Zapotecs and Toltecs before them. The word Cholula means 'place where life begins, where water flows' in the dominant Nahuatl language. All the gods were there at Cholula. Most important was Quetzalcoatl, the plumed serpent. This was the Mecca of Central America, a spiritual crossroads with four hundred temples.

At the centre of this sacred city was the Great Pyramid. Not called Great for nothing, it was the biggest in the world. In fact there had been six pyramids, five smaller pyramids from previous civilizations under the final one. It was more than twice the size of the pyramid of Cheops in Egypt.

When Cortés was here with his Tlascalan allies, it became the place where blood rather than water flowed, where death, not life, began. Waiting for the word from Montezuma to move on Tenochtitlán, the Aztec capital, Cortés discovered a Cholulan plot against him. The Spanish massacred almost the entire population, a hundred thousand people, and destroyed the city.

Cortés razed the temples, including the temple to the rain god on top of the great pyramid. In a move designed to hit at the heart of the chronologically obsessed Indians, the Spanish built churches on top of most of the temples. Three hundred and sixty-five churches to be exact, one for every day of the year, completed this sacred spot's degradation and conversion.

Some say that Quetzalcoatl, bearded and fair-skinned, was a lone white man from way back who somehow happened on Mexico. In any case, the arrival of bearded strangers who resembled the plumed serpent god had been prophesied. The Aztecs' Ancient Books of Memory said: 'Prepare yourselves, oh my little brothers, for the white twin of heaven has come and he will castrate the sun bringing the night, and sadness, and the weight of pain.'

Morality, it seems, was relative. Cortés, like all the conquistadors, was forbidden to kill Indians in cold blood. Before any battle, he would have to read a long speech to the Indians in the presence of a notary public. It was in Spanish and there was no interpreter.

The conquistadors' equivalent of a police caution, it was legally necessary because enslavement of Indians was formally outlawed. This *requerimiento* exhorted them to convert to the Holy Roman Church:

If you do not, or if you maliciously delay in so doing, I certify that with God's help I will advance powerfully against you and make war on you wherever and however I am able, and will subject you to the yoke and obedience of the Church and of their majesties and take your women and children to be slaves, and as such I will sell and dispose of them as their majesties may order, and I will take your possessions and do you all the harm and damage I can.

They could kill the Indians if they didn't convert but they couldn't have sex with them. They had principles after all. Certain things a gentleman wouldn't do. With the Tlascalan girls, the Spaniards would baptize them first. Then they would fuck them. Like a biblical plague the Spaniards brought smallpox, with its festering, exploding flesh and burning fever. Then came typhus, leprosy, tetanus, yellow fever, trachoma, lung, gut and venereal diseases, and tooth decay. The Indians gave the Spaniards syphilis.

The Great Pyramid still stands, buried under a mountain of earth and topped off with the gleaming white baroque basilica of the Virgen del Remedios.

We went to Cholula, leaving the hopping, skipping and jumping armies to go on blasting their brains out with gunpowder and mescal through the night. Climbing the white stone staircase that zigzagged up the pyramid hill to the basilica, we saw Cholula spread out below us, all peeling yellow ochre and grubby whitewashed walls, filled with churches everywhere.

Inside, the basilica was white and gold, wealthy and glittering. But as I looked closely at some of the mouldings and carvings, I saw, among the saints and crosses and conquistadors, what looked like occasional Indian faces, native flowers, palm trees and corn cobs.

Were the Indian gods still there, disguised and concealed amid the flurry of European images? Was the fair-skinned Quetzalcoatl still up on top of the pyramid with his bearded cousins? Was Christianity destroying or preserving the old Indian beliefs? Had something survived through all this bloodshed and destruction?

Tambien hit the phones. He tried to follow up the lead on the *charros* but there was no one back on the ranch. We drew a blank on every other cowboy connection we had in Puebla. They'd all ridden off into the sunset.

So, heads full of history, ears still ringing from the frenzied cannonades, we slunk back over the pass to the acrid familiarity of the big smoke.

17. La Charreada!

We seemed to have been drawing blanks everywhere we looked. It felt as if the cowboy trail was fading out before we reached the end of it. After all the promise of vaqueros in Mexico, we still hadn't found any. Plenty of pyramids but not a cowboy in sight. Then we heard of the *charreada*.

We had travelled up north from Mexico City to San Luis Potosí to meet Guillermo Velazquez, a troubadour, a *payador*. If we couldn't find any cowboys, we could at least hear some cowboy songs.

We drove out across the Bajio, Mexico's central plateau, with endless fields of maize and rolling hillsides. As we passed Queretaro, Jo pointed up to a hillside on our right. He said that was where the Emperor Maximilian had been executed. The French, who had installed him, summarily abandoned him to his fate. Maximilian was the original innocent abroad. Giving each of the gunmen in the firing squad a gold coin, he said, 'Mexicans, I am going to die for a just cause: the liberty and independence of Mexico. May my blood be the last shed for the happiness of my new country. ¡Viva Mexico!'

They shot him. His blood was far from the last. He was out by several oceans.

As we went further north, the land became drier, flatter and harsher, scrubby desert with occasional maguey and prickly pear plantations. Over to the left, in a blue haze, the mountains of Michoacan called quietly.

The miles rolled past. The road itself was lined with endless car, truck, paint and cement factories. Ford, Kenworth and Chevrolet had taken advantage of the unique opportunities for cheap labour so close to the borders.

So far from God, so close to the United States, said Porfirio Diaz. But it was the dictator Diaz himself who had welcomed all the foreign investors with open arms. It was he who had brought Mexico into the modern world, or rather, sold Mexico to the modern world. It was the *porfiriato* which showed the way finally to help Kenworth and Ford make the drive up north such a scenic joy.

Twenty years before the well-meaning, confused Maximilian paid his executioners to cut short his dreams, Queretaro saw the signing of the treaty which gave half of Mexico's territories to the United States.

With a gun at their head and an army at their throat, the offer of fifteen million dollars was one the Mexicans were in no position to refuse. In one tranche they lost California, Arizona, New Mexico, Utah, Colorado and Nevada, barely a decade after they had destroyed the Texans at the Alamo. Winners or losers? They make tacos in Texas but they don't build Mexican trucks.

When they were taking the gun to Mexico's head, a young American officer was having qualms about the annexation of Mexican land. Texas used to stop at the Nueces river, and didn't extend as far as the Rio Grande. The young officer was Ulysses S. Grant, later General, then President Grant.

He wrote: 'I do not think there was ever a more wicked war than that waged by the United States on Mexico. I thought so at the time, when I was a youngster, only I had not the moral courage to resign.

'Texans had no claim beyond the Nueces River, and yet we pushed on to the Rio Grande and crossed it.'

The Motel Azteca had its name in rocks on the nearby hillside. It had computerized bills, a modern polystyrene model of how it would look as a conference centre, but the old slow traditional service. Mañana.

It was lined with grotesque murals of dancing Aztecs wearing G-strings, painted by a buttock fetishist. On the menu, among the familiar Aztec soup and *pozole*, was something new, *sopa de medula*. *Medula*? Sounded strangely familiar, a memory flickered ineffectually but didn't light up.

'*Qué es, medula?*' I needed to know.

'*Es muy rico* – it's very rich.'

Why not? As I waited patiently for my rich soup, I thought of the story of the Mexican and the Irishman discussing the concept of mañana.

'Mañana means you don't do today what you can put off until tomorrow.'

'Oh,' says the Irishman, 'we don't have a word with quite the same degree of urgency.'

My *sopa de medula* arrived.

The old cowboys always said, 'Take a good look at what you're about to eat. You don't need to know what it is, but you better be damn sure you know what it was.'

I took a good look and suddenly everything slotted into place. A satori. I shrieked. Tambien looked over.

'It is. It is. I knew *medula* meant something. I knew it. It's *medulla oblongata*, *medulla* fucking *oblongata*, Tambien, this stuff is brainstem. It's brainstem broth, it's fucking spinal soup.'

It was. There in the brown liquid were floating little-finger-sized white tubes, firm and rubbery. Spinal cord. Yes! Mexico had outdone the visceral excesses of Argentina in a single, almost Zen, bowl of cow soup.

The soup? Not quite as rich as I'd been led to believe. The spinal cord? Not as chewy as I expected, but all in all fairly bland. I got nervous eating it.

No backbone, that's my trouble.

San Luis Potosí was an old silver- and gold-mining town. It was once the seat of government for the whole of the north of Mexico, including Texas and Louisiana. Now it was just the state capital and a town of a hundred plazas, a great place to sit down and watch the world.

We found Guillermo Velazquez and his wife Chabé in a smart hotel. They were a striking couple. Chabé, her pet name which means 'beautiful girl', had high broad Indian cheekbones and black eyes and hair – a classic Mexican beauty. Guillermo was handsome in a dark Iberian way. He spoke perfect New World Spanish, with the voice and enunciation of a poet and orator. He excused the surroundings – not his normal lifestyle, he said, but they had just done a TV show. He and his group the Lions of the Sierra were usually more street- or sierra-wise than this.

The lions came in, three *campesinos* in jeans and workshirts and straw cowboy hats. Two, cool and taciturn with moustaches and shades, were the fiddle players. A younger man had his *jarana*, a small five-string ukulele-style guitar. We all shook hands. They mumbled '*Encantado*' and slunk off to the back of the room.

I understood Guillermo's embarrassment. It was a flash hotel, the kind a TV company would put you in. Not his style, as a socialist and a man of the people. This was no hollow pretence either. He was clearly sincere. When he said that they often got paid for a gig with a chicken I could believe him.

One of the Lions of the Sierra lived in such a remote place that he picked up news of forthcoming gigs on the local radio. There was no post or telephone. The announcer would say that a truck was due to pass at a certain time and

Eusebio of the Lions should be there. It was a three-hour walk from Eusebio's house to the pick-up point on the road.

Guillermo sang *huapango*, a mixture as always of Spanish and Indian traditions. It came initially from twelfth-century Spanish troubadours, just like the River Plate *payadors*. The singers, the *huapangeros*, sing and improvise long narrative songs, telling news and commenting on life. They sing in *decimas*, archaic ten-line troubadour verses.

They involve the life of the *campesinos*, the country people. Songs of love, of revolution, of wars, of the church, songs of landowners, dictators, foreigners and oppression. Songs of day-to-day life. Songs of the constant battle for land. The classic long Mexican story songs are called *corridos*. They can go on for ever.

'Americans drink to forget,' Guillermo told me, 'Mexicans drink to confess.' He didn't drink. He didn't want to forget and his songs were his confession.

Within *huapango*, said Guillermo, there is always a confrontation of ideas. An actual confrontation occurs when two troubadours and their band line up face to face and play against each other. It is exactly the same as the *payadas* down in the Southern Cone. Here in Mexico they are called *topadas*. Guillermo was playing at one tomorrow. At a *charreada*.

I liked the idea of a *charreada*.

I love Linda Ronstadt singing 'La Charreada'. A *charreada* is a rodeo, with the emphasis on the *charro*, the looking good, the performance, the showing off. In the song she sings of wanting to mount the big bull, hold on to its horns, and ride it to show her lover what she can do. Proud to have her lover watch her as she rides the bull. Dark and erotic, it is sung with a disdainful, passionate flourish. It is very Mexican.

We arranged to meet the Lions of the Sierra at the *charreada* at a place called Río Verde the next day. It's not too far, they called as we went out, just past the Valley of the Ghosts.

I went to buy a new hat. Mexican sombreros are just like cowboy hats but the crowns are often higher and the brims fly up at the sides at a more exuberant angle, racing towards the sky. A nice touch on many, and I went for one, is a small tassel hanging like a vestigial horse's tail from the back of the brim. Good for the rodeo.

The drive to Río Verde took us through the mountains. More hard, dry, stony land with hot little scrubby trees and forests of candelabra cactuses, frozen arms grasping for the sky.

As we curved and twisted through passes and round mountain slopes, crosses appeared at the side of the road. Each precipitous bend had its own clutch of crosses, *animitas*, little spirits, marking someone's last grasp at the steering wheel.

The broken-backed wreck of a tanker lay belly up far below us. Long gone, perhaps, but were its wheels still spinning? It was the nearest thing to a ghost we saw in the Valle de Los Fantasmas.

At the dirt-track village outside Río Verde things were getting ready. Guillermo and the Lions were there, getting their instruments out and tuning up. An unpaved, dusty central area – a *plazoleta* – was surrounded by single-storey adobe and breeze-block houses with corrugated iron roofs and porches.

Either side of the *plazoleta*, the finishing touches were being put on two wood and scaffolding structures. They were facing each other and had only a ladder up to the top.

A man was hacking the PA system into the electricity supply by sticking a safety-pin through the overhead cable to the local district court building. He bulldog-clipped another wire to the pin and a string of lights hung round the enclosure stuttered tentatively into life.

A bang told us the PA was ready for testing. The basic principle seemed to be to see how much reverb could be cranked up before the echo multiplied so much it turned back snarling on to the original sound and gobbled it up.

'*Si-si-si-Sssi*', setting those high sibilant sounds on to brain slice, then '*Sssi-si—bueno-bueno-Provando-Provando-ando-ando-Ando-ANDO-O-O-OO-OO-OOO-OOOO.*' Wah-wah-wah-wah. When the great rolling rock of echo was long and loud enough to just avoid terminal speaker-splitting feedback that was it.

Bueno.

People stood around. Now and then a young man would ride through casually, back straight, horse impeccably groomed, brushed and shiny. A truckload of horses rolled through to the *charreada* round the back. Dust rose from the ground.

Every man and boy was wearing a straw cowboy hat. I was relieved I'd got mine. Guillermo had got a new hat too, his a low-crown flat-brimmed style, more in the riverboat gambler mode.

Los Leones de la Sierra wore the more common Mexican high-crowned cowboy hat and shades. They were still pretty cool, and said very little – more like nothing. They had tuned to Guillermo's big-bodied *huapango* guitar, an eight-string monster, and were easing into a song. A crowd of *campesinos* milled around.

The song was '*Mojado Desobligado*', the Useless Wetback. *Mojado* means moist, and a wetback is an illegal immigrant who crossed into the States by swimming the Rio Grande.

In the song he comes back to his wife and family with nothing in his pockets. His wife has to contend with him trying to wheedle his way back into her affections as he makes his excuses for bringing home no bacon at all.

It was a commentary on the relationship of Mexico with the States, the exploitation of cheap Mexican labour, and the trials of women having to put up with their useless men. Guillermo was the wetback. Chabé played her part to the hilt, spitting out her words, nostrils flaring, lip curling and eyes ablaze. The audience gathered round close, still and silent. Now and then a drunk would wobble.

There were long recitations. The troubadour's song was a story, a bulletin a comedy and a lesson with a moral. The *campesinos* were transfixed.

HE:
I've been away but now I'm back again,
'*Good evening, how are you?*'
You see, I speak like them now – I'm a different man,
I'm civilized now
I'm mixed like a cocktail, English style, '*my darling*'.

I'm back from over the river
From those great northern lands,
The people are all well bred there
But I went as a wetback.

SHE:
Don't Start on me with this '*Yes, my darling*'
I'm Juana Jiminez
I don't care where you've come from –
Keep your English to yourself
Don't use your tricks on me
Keep them for the gringos, your '*darling*' and your '*OK*'.

Save me, Holy Saviour, he's back again
Don't let it be like the last time.

Carlos Fuentes writes of the Americanization of Mexico, the United States' influence on all aspects of Mexican life. He calls it the Pepsicoatl culture.

I've seen it myself, down at the *lonchería*.

*

I slipped out to the edge of the village. It was nestling in the hills, part of a huge hacienda. The hillsides were sparsely wooded and had more of the transfixed many-limbed cactuses reaching for the clouds. The sun was still up, shadows were short, but it was getting to be late afternoon.

In a large circular corral full of milling horses and steers, young boys were riding around wildly, leaning down low from their saddles and grabbing at the steers' tails. None managed properly to tail a bull and bring him to the ground, but they leaned over well. They were showing off, conscious of the ring of silent spectators. I stood by the corral fence and watched for a while.

Then finally one lad managed to reach down, grab the steers' tail and whip it under his leg as his pony veered off to the right. The steer twisted right over on to his back with a thump. An old man leaning on the fence beside me grunted appreciatively. As the teenage vaqueros heaved their horses one way and then the other, and wild-eyed steers charged about, young boys on a dare pushed and danced their way through the heaving snorting mass.

Then, inevitably, there he was.

Waving his cowboy hat clumsily over his head with anaesthetized bravado, a drunk weaved his way through the flurry of dust and hooves, horseflesh and beef, miraculously unhurt by the nervous young bulls as he staggered blindly from one side of the corral to the other. I thought about the nature of invisibility. I wondered if he was a drunken *brujo*.

The old man beside me cursed. I looked at him. He was wearing an old pale-grey *charro* suit, the *chamorro* bordered and picked out in silver, a white shirt and red cravat and *faja*. The *conchos*, the silver rosettes down the outside of his trouser legs, were glinting and gleaming from a recent polishing, but the suit was past its best and a little on the tight side. He had a broad, flat-brimmed, low-crowned sombrero like Guillermo's on the back of his head.

He must have been seventy or so. He had white bristly hair and stubble, and the dried creeks and gullies of the hills were etched into his dark leathery weather-beaten face. His black eyes were as shiny as the *conchos* on his pants. He saw me looking at him.

'*Gringo?*'

I drew myself up in mock indignation. Here was the chance to use my one joke in Spanish that I'd learned from Jo Tambien.

'*Gringo?*' I said, eyebrows raised disdainfully. '*No, señor, no soy gringo. Soy hijo de la Grannnn . . . Bretaña.*' The joke is they think you're going to say *hijo de la gran puta*, son of the great whore, and you say son of Great . . . Britain.

Goes down well in Latin America. The old man laughed.

'*¡Hijo! ¡Inglés!* English.'

No, I said, Scottish, but how did he speak English?

'*Mojado*. Many times I am *mojado*. I learn English in Texas.'

He turned back and watched as the corral was cleared and a steer prepared for riding with a rope around its neck. There didn't seem to be much finery around. It was all very low-key, a little local show.

Two vaqueros, in jeans, working shirts, cowboy boots and hats, held the steer by the fence as a young man in a fringed leather waistcoat balanced himself standing on the second rung of the corral fence. I winced as the young bull rider, scarcely fifteen, launched himself into the air, his legs splayed wide, and forked on to the steer's back like a clothes-peg.

The steer looked more surprised than the lad did and tore away from the fence. It leapt off the ground and went into a twisting double spin. Then, shaking and tossing the young rider, the steer jumped into the air, back arched, all four feet off the ground, and crashed down again juddering. Each time it did this, the lad left the bull's back, flying right up into the air. He hung on desperately to the rope as daylight showed between his legs, then crashed back on to the beast's spine with a contraceptive thump.

This went on – jump, crash, jump, judder, crash – until the lad's testicles must have been rammed up to his ears. But he kept his cowboy hat on, and his eyes wide open, waving his free arm, until the steer whipped his hindquarters round viciously and he toppled off to one side. He fell on his back and the steer charged round the corral on a lap of honour.

The old man clucked and shook his head.

'Ride like a Mexican, fall like a gringo.'

I looked at him quizzically.

'No good just to ride. More important to fall good.'

About twenty young men tried their luck. Three stayed the distance. A couple were tossed overhead on the first turn. Most slipped sideways off the bull. Only one hurt himself and limped off. Several fell nimbly on to their feet.

One, a brash, stockily built young vaquero in his twenties, was somersaulted backwards off the steer, landed on his feet and in one scything motion of his right arm, using the momentum of his jump, he grabbed the steer's tail and whipped it across. It was beautifully done. The animal left the ground, dumbstruck, and crashed on to its side.

'*¡Hijolé! ¡Hayy! ¡Coleador tambien!*' The old man did a little skip, slapped the corral fence and looked round. The gullies at the curves of his eyes deepened into ravines, his face cracked into a grin and his eyes blazed.

'Good boy, this one *¡Vaquero de verdad! ¡Autentico!* He do the way we do, in the old days. *¡Prodigio!*'

'You are vaquero?'

'Now I look, only.' He slapped his silver-jangling leg. 'Old legs now. I ride only *mansos*, now no *toros*, no *mesteños*. Old legs.'

There were different styles of vaquero dress in the different parts of Mexico. Up in the north in 1891. 'Our Chihuahua vaquero wears white cotton clothes, and goat-skin *chaparejos* (chaps) with the hair left on, naked feet, and *huaraches*, or sandals, and big jingling spurs. A gourd, lashed to his cantle, does the duty of canteen.'

The *Californios* of Spanish California wore a bandana round their heads, with a flat, wide-brimmed hat on top of it. They were long-haired and bearded. They wore a wide-cut shirt, a broad *faja* or sash, short pants to the knees buttoned up the sides, with long white drawers tucked into leather leggings, *botas*, like the *polainas* of the Chilean *huasos*.

Like most vaqueros who didn't wear sandals, they wore soft, low-heeled shoes, not the high-heeled boots of the Anglo cowboys. These low-heeled shoes resembled the small, courtly shoes I had seen the *huasos* wearing down in Chile.

Just like the gauchos, they would wear a *tirador*, a wide-hipped leather belt they used for working on foot in the corrals with their lassoes. They carried a long knife inside the garter of their right leg. The most important item for most vaqueros was their poncho or serape, used against the cold, the rain, the sun and for sleeping at night. The colonial vaqueros even attached large leather wings to their saddles just like the *guardamontes* of the Salta gauchos, to work the thorny, cactus-ridden brush country. They called them *armas*.

The similarities the vaqueros shared with the lost cowboys of the far south were greater than any differences.

It was getting late in the day. The sun was dipping over the hills and the air was closing down. Shadows were creeping across the ground. Noises from the corral, and the checking and re-checking of the PA round the corner seemed to intensify in the still air. The steers had been cleared from the corral.

'Were you a *domador*?'

'No. Not a *domador*. *Amansador*. I tame the horse. I teach him. Not just break him.'

His name was José Leon Rincón. His full name, he said, drawing himself up with pride, was a bit of a mouthful, but he'd tell me anyway. It was Don José Leonidas Rincón de las Casas. I was impressed. And he was eighty-five years old. I was more impressed.

'Seventy? Ha! I told you my legs are old now. When I had seventy years I still ride *mesteños*, I still tame wild horses. But now . . . ' He trailed off and tapped his leg again.

Why did he call himself *amansador* and not *domador*?

'I am mestizo, we all are mestizo here. Some conquistador, some *indigena*, Spanish and Indian mestizo. I – I have more *indigena* blood, more Indian. The horse is my brother. Yes, I must be *domador* first, I must break him, I must show him it is no good to fight, I must show him he will not win over me. Then I train him. But to train is *primero*. The bronco busting in gringo rodeos is nothing. *Espuelas, nada mas.*'

Don José was only repeating exactly what Eduardo Halliday, the gaucho Rob Roy in Patagonia, had told me a long while back about bronco busting. He had said it was just balance between three points. No skill.

I told the old man about my journey, that I wanted to find out all I could about the unsung lost cowboys of the Americas. He clapped his hands.

'¡*Hijolé!* I will tell you all I know. You are in very good place here. *Son muchos vaqueros aquí.*'

Gradually the penny began to drop.

The old man, even with his faltering English and my moribund Spanish, was painting a clearer picture of horse breaking than any I'd had so far. I understood now that everything in front of the cinch belongs to the horse. A rodeo rider gets points for spurring in the shoulders, for it makes the horse buck more. It hurts and he doesn't like it.

A trainer like Don José would never do this. He would lose his job. The rodeo rider has no time or place for kindness but a good trainer relies on it. He encourages the horse to do the right thing and discourages him firmly from doing wrong.

'One part is conquistador, I know. We must overtake the wild horse. But we must have kindness, to be the friend.'

I remembered the ear twisting the *domadors* did in Uruguay while the blindfolded bronco was being saddled.

'No! Ear is for hearing, not for pain. When I have roped the horse with my *reata*, and put on the cloth to make him blind, then the *jaquima*, I talk, sweet, nice, *abajo* – low, to him and put on the *silla*. All the time it is good to talk, to sing to the horse. This is the *indigena* way.'

Everything to do with horses and herding cattle up here in North America came from Spain, just as in the south. You see it in the clothes, the language, the techniques and the equipment. Everything the Anglo cowboys do, wear, use and describe on horseback is Hispanic. Everything they do they have learned from the Mexican vaqueros.

Some historians may tell you of cowpens in the east, and particularly Carolina, as a purely Anglo ranching tradition. They will say that the men who worked there were called cowboys. So they were. There are those who believe that these eastern cowpen skills moved west with the Anglo cowboys.

This is a fiction. The Carolina cowboys had nothing to do with the Western cowboys at all. They rarely used horses. They worked their cattle on foot and used dogs and long thick whips, 'Georgia crackers', to move them around.

The *jaquima*, the hackamore, for instance, is a long way from any Anglo tradition. It comes from Spain, and ultimately from the Arabs, who called it the *haqma*. It is a bitless bridle that puts pressure on the horse's nose. Patience and gentleness are crucial in hackamore training. The hackamore was used all over the West by those who knew how.

It survived in California. The *charros* all over Mexico had prided themselves on the use of the hackamore; while gentlemen *charros* were thin on the ground in Mexico after successive revolutions, the *Californios*, the *charros* and vaqueros of the West Coast, survived. Texans on cattle drives to the West Coast a century ago were astonished at the *Californios'* skills with the hackamore. They used the *haqma* the way the conquistadors had learned from the Moors.

Don José used the hackamore when he moved around Texas as *amansador*. He was also a king of *la reata*, the lariat. The vaqueros are the greatest of all cowboys with the lariat, he said, and he taught many Anglo cowboys all the different Mexican throws.

'If you are here tomorrow, I can show you working with *la reata*. We have good vaqueros here on the hacienda. You will see better work with *la reata* here than United States. They only know what we tell them. But they are not *charro*, they are not vaquero. They are not proud like us.'

Then why, I asked, do the Anglo cowboys always win? Why are the Mexicans we see on the screen wicked bandidos and poor cringing peons if they are all so proud? Where are all the *charros* and vaqueros? The old man pointed at the ground.

'They are here, here in Mexico. Not in Hollywood. There it is stories they make for the gringos. They are also conquistadors, the gringos, but conquistadors to us. They think they are our *domadors*, they break us.

'They steal everything from us, our horses, our saddles, our cattle, our land, our country, and say they were always the first. First with horses, first with cowboys. Ha! They say we are only fools. But inside they are ashamed. I teach gringos, *Tejanos*, to catch horses, to train, to throw *la reata*, and *colear los toros*, pull over with the tail the bulls.

'They learn from me then throw me back over the Rio Grande. They break me but they do not tame me. They do not know how. But they take my work, they learn, then call me Little Joe, *mojado*, wetback, greaser, and throw me off like a dead horse. But I still live and I am here in Río Verde and I am still Don José Leon Rincon de las Casas.'

He couldn't have stood taller if he were standing in seven-league boots.

Far from being cowardly, the vaqueros thought the Anglo cowboys themselves were unmanly. Like the gauchos, vaqueros disdained the use of guns. They were only for cheats who couldn't face a fight. Far better to outwit your enemy than pull a gun on him.

They were contemptuous of the pistol-packing Anglo who couldn't defend himself like a real man.

The denigration of the vaquero had its roots in racism. They were described as lazy, treacherous, drunken, untrustworthy and unskilled by people like Theodore Roosevelt. Hollywood was merely painting the prevailing picture.

Frank Dobie, in 1931, thought differently:

He is full of stories about buried treasures which are guarded by ghosts, clanking chains and eerie lights. If he does not know a witch, he knows of one. If he does not fear the evil eye, he respects it. If he or any of his family become ill, he wants a doctor, but at the same time he yearns for a *curandero*, a folk healer. He is familiar with the habits of every creature of his soil. For him, every hill and hollow has a personality and a name. He regards the stars; he watches the phases of the moon. He knows the name and virtue of every bush and herb. He is a child of nature.

Either despite or because of his nearness to nature, he is as insensible to the sufferings of nature's progeny as nature is herself. He will run his horse into thorns and then have no thought of pulling the thorns out; he will ride a thirsty horse within fifty yards of a water hole and unless he himself is thirsty will not turn aside. He will sit all day in the shade of his hut and never offer to carry a bucket of water for his over-worked wife.

For all that, the vaquero is kind to his family, sets no limit to his hospitality, and probably goes beyond the average human being in faithfulness. He will divide his last tortilla with any stranger who happens by . . . The reputation he has somehow acquired in literature for being treacherous is altogether undeserved.

The sun was way behind the hills and dusk was rolling down the valley. The steers were back in the corral, milling around, and the young horsemen were cutting in and out of them, swinging down and trying to tail them again before the night called time on them. Don José kept telling me what they were doing and how they managed it with their saddles.

He pointed out the vaquero saddles they were using and told me in half-English, half-Spanish, where they came from. And how the gringos took them over.

He said that the Western saddle, deep-seated, high-cantled and long-stirruped, came from the Mexican. The Mexican saddle is close to the conquistadors' which in its turn derived from the Crusaders' saddle.

So the Mexican *silla* comes from the people who fought the Moors, unlike the Argentine sofa of the gauchos, the multi-layered, sheepskin-covered *recado* which is the typically Moorish saddle, the *enjalma*. But both came over with the Spanish.

I wondered how this could be.

It was simple, said the Don. The Spanish who came across were not a pure race at all. They were mestizo long before they even set out from the Old World. Iberian, Greek, Roman, Goth, Arab, Jew, Christian and Gypsy – all these cultures and traditions went into the Spanish mix. The Iberians, masters of incorporation, not exclusion, were always absorbing new cultures. Forty per cent of Spanish words are Arabic. A lot of different blood ran, not just down their lances and sabres, but through their veins.

It happens that the horses they brought with them were all the small Moorish Arab-Barb mix from Andalucia. The Spanish also brought two distinct riding styles. With their mixed ancestry, it is a surprise that they didn't bring more.

The European, northern style, the Christian way, was *a la brida*, sitting in a heavy saddle with a high pommel and cantle, legs straight and sticking forward, the horse on a severe curb bit.

It was based on the obsolete battle tactics of knights in cumbersome armour on big, ponderous horses. Charging with a shield in one hand and a massive lance in the other, the rider braced himself between the stirrups and the cantle for the crunching impact when he hit someone trying to do the same to him. He needed the severe bit to control his lumbering, heavyweight horse as it charged forward like a tank carrying a ton of armour.

All this had nothing to do with the conditions in the New World, where unarmoured men rode on small horses. Yet *a la brida*, riding straight legged, sitting well back in a high-pommelled and cantled saddle was the way in

Mexico. And because they taught the Anglos, it became the way of the Western cowboys.

The Moorish way of riding, by contrast, was *a la gineta*, a short-stirruped cavalry style. They stood in the stirrups, scything down with the scimitar. *La gineta* was a ring-bit, named after the Moorish tribe who introduced it. After becoming the name of the riding style, *jinete* became the Spanish word for horseman. Some of the gauchos, the Indians and the *llaneros* rode *a la gineta*, but the North Americans rode almost universally sitting back in heavy saddles like knights of old out on the Crusades.

Stirrups came from the Asian hordes of Attila the Hun and Genghis Khan. The Mongols introduced short stirrups on small ponies. Probably the greatest cowboys of them all, the Mongols were able to cover immense distances because each rider had three or four spare horses with him and changed mounts frequently.

There is little new in this world. This practice was adopted both by the American Indians and the Mexican vaqueros on long trail drives. The US Cavalry hadn't learned that lesson. Always one man one horse, they wondered why the Indians out-ran them so frequently.

There were saddles for the rich and saddles for the poor. *Charros* had heavily ornamented, finely tooled symbols of wealth and power. Vaqueros had working saddles. They developed from hard, rawhide-covered wooden trees, uncomfortable for horse and rider, into more comfortable seats with an added leather covering and saddlebags. High-cantled, they had a pommel with a prominent horn but a flatter base and were called the *mochila* saddle. The Pony Express used the *mochila*, and switched the leather over-seat and saddlebags when they changed mounts.

The early Mexican and Texan stock saddles were like the *mochila*, with a flatter seat. The McLelland was the simplified US Cavalry saddle, flat seated and with no pommel. They did no roping so needed no horn. The Mother Hubbard was like the *mochila* but the leather covering with saddlebags was permanent.

Variations developed but the stock saddle always had a high pommel and cantle, bracing the rider between the cantle and stirrups. To modern eyes the cowboy was very unbalanced, right off the horse's centre of gravity. He sat too far back in his seat, which stood too far off the horse's withers, and with his feet too far forward. This made poor riders feel more secure and less likely to fall off. Not all Anglo cowboys were the great horsemen that we were led to believe; unlike the Hispanic horsemen, they were not brought up in the saddle.

The Brazos tree, a basic cowboy's saddle, was cut deeper and more circular than the vaquero rig, and really enclosed the cowboy. The Texas and Cheyenne saddles had flatter seats, more like the vaquero. They all had big leather skirts which spread the rider's weight over the horse's back. Although the stock saddle was a heavy one, it was surprisingly easy on the horse for long rides.

For extra security, many of the big Western saddles had two cinches, front and back. This was the 'rim-fire' rig, common in Texas, Montana and Wyoming. The vaqueros used a single central cinch, a 'centre-fire' rig, the Spanish way, which spread as far as Oregon and stayed popular there and in California.

For work among the thorny bushes and scrubland of the brush country, vaqueros added *tapaderas* or 'taps', leather pouches that hung over the stirrups and protected the feet from the thorns. Taps also stopped vaqueros from getting their feet trapped in the stirrups if they fell.

In the nineteenth century, the Hawaiians were building up cattle-ranching, as the vaqueros went out there to train them as cowboys. The Hawaiians favoured taps as well. They developed huge 'mule-ear taps' for an extra bit of show. The Hawaiian cowboys, like the Anglos of the West, owed all their horse sense to the vaqueros; they were more grateful and less racist than the gringos. As a tribute to their mentors they call cowboys in Hawaii *paniolos*, a lazy Pacific version of *español*. But that is another story.

Vaqueros kept a Spanish prejudice against light coloured, yellow or pinto horses. They preferred dark colours, greys, chestnuts and black horses. This was passed on to Anglo cowboys who didn't like paints (pintos), palominos or Appaloosas. They thought, like the vaqueros, that dark mounts worked better, especially as cutting horses.

Like the other lost cowboys of South America, no self-respecting vaquero ever rode mares. That would have been unmanly.

Suddenly, in the middle of Don José's rambling dissertation on Mexican and Western saddles, a shining vision of *charro* woke me from my Hawaiian reverie.

'El hacendado, Don Raimundo,' hissed Don José. The owner of the ranch, el hacendado, was all duded up. The night was falling fast and what little light was left seemed to have been soaked up by Don Raimundo and was radiating out of him. He was riding high in the saddle, back as straight as a ramrod, loose reined, moving slow and regal. His legs were slightly bent, his stirrups short.

'¡Mire! Look! He rides *jinetea*. You see what I tell you? The *charro* way is *jinetea*.'

The hacendado sat perfectly still in his saddle, exuding *charro*.

The horse walked slowly, grandly, stepping quietly from the shadows of the valley up on the right and towards the light spilling out from the *plazoleta* in the village. He hardly seemed to be moving.

Ha! W. H. Hudson's great line, 'There is no mode of progression so delightful as riding on horseback,' took on a different veneer.

The Don was definitely *progressing*. In a *charro* mode.

I could see now, the horse was a beautifully glossy black stallion, a *moro*. It looked to have some thoroughbred blood. I followed them into the light. Don Raimundo shone like the sun. I squinted.

His suit was impeccable. Pale, sky blue with filigree silver and black edging and silver clasps on the short *chamarro*. Ornate embroidery in a strip round the silver medallions running down the outside of his pants. Black Cuban-heeled boots and silver spurs with two-inch rowels. White shirt and floppy black bow. A classic wide-brimmed, conical-crowned dark sombrero with intricate silver and gold working round the rolled-up edge.

If his *charro* suit and his bearing were regal, the saddle, his *silla charra*, was imperial, almost papal. No one but the Pope himself could have anything richer or more ostentatious. It was beautifully tooled, covered with roses woven through with leaves. Silver was worked into the edges and gold swirled around on the lattice of intertwining leaves. Leather thongs with silver tips hung from silver *conchos* and the priapic bragging of the pommel horn was inlaid with gold and silver. A finely woven ornamental *mecate* hung from the right side of the saddle.

The horse had a breast band, almost a plate, dripping with silver coins and chains. Even the reins shone and had silver *conchos* on the horse's cheeks. The saddle, the whole *charro* rig, radiated money, power and class.

The horse's mane and tail had the flow and shine of a thousand brush-strokes. There was not a hair out of place, not a speck of dust on his coat. You could eat out of his hooves.

My eyes adjusted to the glare off the silverware. Don Raimundo was a striking man in his early forties, with a thin black moustache and sideburns. No one made a great fuss over him, and despite his regal air, he nodded casually, acknowledging greetings. His eyes deferred to no one.

My eyes were still acclimatizing. I had to keep blinking. It was not just the light shafting off the silver *conchos* – I had never seen *charro* like this before.

There was a tap on my arm. It was Don José, my vaquero professor. He was grinning ear to ear.

'¡*Hijolé*! You never see like this, huh? You never see nothing like this in the United States. Only here. This is *charro*! *Real Charro*!'

*

The lights were on in the *plazoleta* and the bands were about ready to start. They had each climbed up a ladder and were sitting, four in a row, on two lengths of scaffolding, like boys on the top rung of a high fence. Two long poles, stripped saplings, stood in front of each section of scaffolding. Each pole had a microphone strapped to it, one for the Poet, one for the fiddles.

Guillermo was on one side of the little square. Facing him on the other side was Adrian Turrubiartes and Conjunto Río Verde, with the same line-up as the Lions of the Desert, big *huapango* guitar, *jarana* and two fiddles.

People stood silently around the sides of the square and some milled about in the middle. Young men on horseback rode through now and then, nothing rowdy, all quietly waiting. It was early times. But here in the heartland, barely twenty miles from Cardenas, the Nashville of *huapango*, the poets were ready to do battle.

Guillermo started. He started to beat at his big *guitarron huapangero* as he welcomed everybody. For the next twenty minutes he welcomed everybody, greeting the audience and laying out his programme.

'We are the Lions of the Sierra. We are the best. You are all welcome tonight. We will tell you stories like you've never heard before. We'll tell you things about the government and your landlords that will open your eyes. This will be the best *huapango* you've ever heard and you will wonder how we can make it all up as we go along.

'Nothing you've heard before, or that you will hear from the band across the way, will prepare you for the night of music and stories you will get from us. You will dance and laugh and cry and we will touch your hearts as we sing you secrets about your lives.'

Then Guillermo stopped and handed over to the local heroes. Adrian was hoarse and croaky, but regaled the audience with promises, exhorting them to listen to him, the true poet, and not to the opposition.

Again it was an extended meet and greet, laying out his wares, insulting Guillermo in a poetic and gentlemanly way, and promising the best songs, the fastest wit and the best dancing they had had in years. After each verse, a kind of shouted recitation, the fiddles would strike up a lively instrumental dance chorus. Then the poet would be back.

The crowd watched and drifted, bemused, for the first few hours. By midnight it had warmed up and there was dancing and stamping of feet as people circled around each other, arms high above their heads. Dust was rising, skirts flying, arms waving, heels clicking and stamping, drunks weaving. *Huapango* means 'the booted dance'; there are strong echoes of flamenco.

For the poet, the idea seemed to be to draw the crowd over to your side. If everyone finished up standing and dancing around your bit of scaffolding, and none on the other side of the arena, you could see very graphically who was the winner. The loser would sit in a lonely place, on the edge of the shadow, away from the action, a sad discarded sideshow.

By two in the morning Guillermo was well in the driving seat, with only a few stragglers supporting the local band. Tambien and I were both getting a bit worse for wear. The mescal helped me *huapango* but with critically rubber legs. By that time I needed all the legs I could stand on; it definitely takes two to *huapango*, and I was in trouble.

The district judge, hooting and hollering with the best of them, saw me wobbling and said he could put down a couple of mattresses for us in the courtroom. My head said no but my legs said a grateful yes. I left the poets to their battle.

The sun hit me full face, streaming through a crack in the shutters. I eased myself slowly off a straw mattress and crept over to the window. I pulled the shutter open, felt the pain and shut it quickly. Then I opened it again, inch by gradual inch. JT was still spark out on his palliasse. I looked round.

The room was plain and sparsely furnished. Pale green walls, a wood floor, a long table at one end with two large armchairs behind it, and rows of bent cane chairs down the other end. A Mexican flag hung over the table. Bare necessities.

I staggered outside, squinting, into the glare and drank a gallon of water from the pump in the street. I poured another gallon over my head. Blurs coalesced into real people, still standing around the *plazoleta*. Guillermo hadn't stopped playing. The Lions of the Sierra were still roaring. It was eight o'clock.

'¡Hola! ¡Hijo!' It was Don José, bright as a button. 'You sleep good, huh? You drink good last night.' He peered close. 'Hmm. *Hijo*, you have mescal eyes, eyes of the moon. Come.'

I waved at Guillermo, who seemed to have the whole village round his scaffold now. He sang something, nodded at me, and the crowd looked over and grinned. I followed Don José round the corner. He turned to me.

'Remember for ever. Never get out before *desayuno*. What you call *desayuno*?'

'Breakfast. Get *up*.'

'Bueno. Never get *up* before . . . breakfast, yes? If you must get up before breakfast, eat first. Come.'

He took me into a small house which smelt of cooking.

'Sit. ¡Hola! *Jefe! Revueltos!*'

A woman brought out a plate of scrambled eggs with chilli sauce, whole chillies and a side plate of chillies. With it were tortillas and a jug of water, a large and a small glass. The Don gravely and gingerly poured some drink into the small glass out of a big old petrol can.

'Mescal. Just little one. No more. Then you feel better. Eat and drink.'

I ate and drank, burst into flames from the ferocious chillies, tried ineffectually to douse them with another gallon of water and riveted myself to the ceiling with the small shot of fiery medicine. In half an hour I was a different man. Not sure who, but different. The Don clapped me on the back.

'¡Vamos! We go.'

Jo was still out cold. The Don had two mules and we rode about a mile out of town. It was my first ride on a mule. The animal was surprisingly docile and very sure-footed.

In a large enclosed field with a stream running alongside was a herd of about three hundred young steers. Five vaqueros were working the herd. Two had built a fire and had irons in it. It was branding time.

Two were cutting into the herd, riding straight in, driving out the animals they wanted and roping them. Another vaquero was roping steers on the edge of the herd. They knew what they were doing. It seemed like second nature.

I watched the way they were roping. They looked like they were throwing in different ways, and catching the steers by the forefeet, hindlegs or round the neck. They all wound their ropes round the large saddle horn and let it slip off as needed when the animal struggled.

They would guide the steer close to the fire and then bring him down. Leaping from their horse, they hobbled all four legs with their lariats and held the steer as the man came over from the fire with the branding iron.

What kind of lariats were they using, I asked Don José.

'*Bueno*. They use all kind. This man has a *mecate*. This man there has *cuero*. You say rawhide. They are all kinds. This one is from maguey.'

The maguey fibres stiffen in the wet so these ropes are used only on the dry ranges. Rawhide is more versatile. I remembered the drunken donkey and the milk and honey, ropes and sandals that flowed from the maguey cactus beside it.

The Don took a *mecate* – the Anglos called this fine horsehair rope a McCarty – and showed me some throws. If the animal was running fast, he said, a figure eight was the way to bring him down. The *piale* was an underhand toss which caught the hindlegs, and the *mangana* an overhand throw which opened to catch the forefeet. He caught a lazy-looking steer with a *mangana* to show me, and his old arm still swung in a single fluid movement.

'*Dar la vuelta, dar la vuelta!*' He nudged me and pointed to the vaqueros on horseback as they wound their ropes round their saddle horns. 'Best way, strong, to let the *toro* run and not pull off the saddle.'

With the heavy Western or vaquero saddles there was somewhere to tie the lasso instead of using the horse's tail like the *llaneros*. Some Anglo cowboys, especially those with the double cinch rim-fire rigs, would tie their ropes firmly to the saddle horn if they were long-roping.

Vaqueros, often working in brush country with shorter ropes, taught many of the Anglos to *dar la vuelta*, to 'take a turn', which the Anglos corrupted into 'dally' or 'dally welter'. Like the vaqueros, they became 'dally men'. It gave them leverage but they had to be careful as they wound the rope round the pommel. A mistake could be costly and painful, for the whizzing rope could catch the thumb on the saddle horn and amputate it in double quick time. But done well, dally roping was the best way.

A cowboy would wrap a few turns round the horn, let the rope slide through and 'smoke the pommel!'

Anglo cowboys adapted the vaqueros' ways. As well as the *mangana* and the *piale*, by the late 1860s they had developed the 'Hoolihan', swinging the noose only once over the head before tossing it. This was a fast throw, good for catching corralled horses.

'Vaquero always make his own *reatas*, his own *lazos*,' said the Don, 'maguey, *mecate*, *cuero torcido* or *trenzado*. Just the same we make our own *maneas*, *correas*, *frenos*, you say bridle, even the saddle. Anglos never make those things, always they buy them from the *tienda*.'

It was true. By the nature of things in the States, everything was manufactured. A few cowboys learned to make rawhide lariats and horsehair McCartys, but most bought rolls of Manila hemp rope, cut them to size, and treated them with tallow and paraffin. Certainly the stock saddles were never made by the cowboys themselves.

The *mecate* had a bonus. Many vaqueros would open it into a circle and sleep inside it. It kept rattlesnakes away – a wise thing to do.

I never saw what brand they used on the cattle. My brain was still not connected enough to read. I only smelt the burning cowhide. Then suddenly, in a cloud of dust, JT arrived, driving down the trail from the village. He had come to take me away.

Don José said he could take both mules back to the village. I felt sad. I had grown fond of the old man.

'Will we meet again?'

'No, not on this earth. It is possible with God up in heaven. *Quien sabe?* Go with God and do not forget these two things. These I learned from a *Tejano* friend many years before.'

He paused for full dramatic effect.

'Speak your mind, but ride a fast horse. And remember, young buckaroo, wherever you ride to, that is where you are.'

My head jangled with saddles, *frenos*, *la gineta*, *mochilas*, *la reata*, *tapaderas*, *mecates*, McCartys, lariats, rim-fire rigs, high cantles and pommel horns as we rattled back round the mountain bends.

The old Don had sure thrown a lot of rawhide at me and I hadn't quite taken it all in yet. I was still reeling from the discovery that the vaqueros were comprehensively the forerunners and godfathers of the Anglo cowboys.

I couldn't either remember when I was last called a young buckaroo. Probably never. Then another penny dropped.

Buckaroo is the Anglo for vaquero.

18. The Land of Fishermen

Forty leagues to the west of Mexico City is a land the Aztecs called Michoacan, the 'Land of Fishermen'. Fishermen they may have been, but the Purepecha empire that ruled from Michoacan was strong enough to resist the Aztecs. They controlled most of western Mexico.

They were a race apart. The Purepechas' fighting prowess, their language, music, art and culture were very different from other tribes. Why? One clue is that they cultivated their land in terraces. Many believe they originally came from Peru and built their empire round the magical Lake Patzcuaro, where the Blue Gods of Water lived. If this is true, then they are closer to the Incas, or the Huancas, than the Aztecs.

Their language is still alive and they sing sweet songs in the old way, the way the Indians did before the conquest. This, as much as anything, excited me. The promise of real Indian harmonies was one of the few things that would get me out of the saddle and off the cowboy trail for a while. Even if it had been one of the first parts of Mexico opened up to cattle in the sixteenth century, it wasn't known for vaqueros now. But if the word was that Michoacan had great Indian singing, that was good enough.

Many say that the Indians always sang beautifully. Linda Ronstadt, who is half Mexican, told me once that when the Spanish came over, there was already a very strong vocal tradition, and that this, added to the Spanish guitars and lutes and troubadours, went to make Mexican music. We had been talking about the influence of Mexico on the United States rather than the other way round. We wondered about the influence of Mexican music on country music – and some cowboy music. We wanted to see how far back we could go. Could some cowboy music be Indian? What she called the 'tramline harmonies', the oily Mexican harmonies that slide impossibly over any backing, might even owe something to the Purepecha.

As harmonies were at the heart of a lot of American country and western music, was it possible that pre-Columbian Indian vocals lived on in the music of Buck Owens and Merle Haggard? It had to be investigated.

We headed for the land of the fishermen.

Morelia, the capital, is a dark-pink city, named after Morelos, Michoacan's favourite son. He was a creole priest who led the insurgent forces to victory in the wars of independence, only to be captured and shot. He became the ultimate hero and most poignant symbol of Mexican independence. Another winner, another loser.

The city was full of exquisite pink Spanish colonial and baroque architecture. The rosy glow came from trachyte, a local pink stone which gave a softness and warmth to the old buildings, although it stained a nearby lake a lurid orange. Walking through the city, courtyards peered out of doorways in baroque façades. Rosy cloisters echoed to footsteps. Fountains pattered. It had all the trappings of money, a wealthy city, and that wasn't just from fish. I went to the cathedral.

Morelia's cathedral was large and confused, baroque in one part, sparse and plain in another. All paled into insignificance, though, before the statue of Jesus. Here, in the massive temple of the Christian god, in the centre of the city manifesting Spain's authority and dominion, was an Indian fifth column.

El Señor de la Sacristia had been made by Purepecha Indians in the sixteenth century. They made El Señor out of very un-Christian materials. He was sculpted out of ground corn cobs and orchid juice.

I decided to get a shoeshine. The sun was up, Morelia was looking good and I felt like joining in. I dug out my black Texas needle-point cowboy boots, a pair of Noconas that I loved.

An older, traditional Texas style, they are called 'roach crushers', sharp enough to get into the corner of the room where the *cucurachas* are cowering and *splat*! Crush those roaches! These days folks go for the snub- or square-toe boots, technically known as 'shit kickers'. Designed for the job – just as these couldn't get to the cockroaches, the needle-points would simply impale a cow pat. Then you'd have to pull it off. Serious loss of face.

Don't forget the old cowboy maxim: 'Never kick a fresh turd on a hot day.'

The boots were pointed enough for Mexico, too, sharp enough to go *pachuco*. *Pachuco* is cocky streetwise, Mexican flash, a shiny sense of taste.

Reminded me of the stainless steel trousers I'd got in a black shop in Nashville. Mmm, *pachuco*.

I went out walking tall, looking for a maestro. I found an old man with his box open, his rags, brushes and polish laid out and a full podium chair outside a *lonchería*. Uniquely Mexican, a *lonchería* is where you go for your lonch break, to eat your lonch.

The old man looked at the boots. '*Todo?*'

'*Todo.*'

He gave me the ultimate shoeshine.

It took nine separate stages. Or ten. First the boots were washed and scrubbed with soap and water, stripping off inferior layers, getting back to the leather. Then the rinsing and drying. Then he painted the boots, using a clear liquid put on with a paint brush. After a short wait for absorption he rubbed and polished the paint with sponge and skins. Then, with his fingers, he rubbed a little grease with a smell of beeswax into the leather. Next he rubbed hard with a cloth and brushed for the first time.

The all-important seventh stage was the actual black polish, put on with a rag. Everything before this was preparation, relatively leisurely and relaxed. Short bursts and flurries of brushing now and then, but even those were laid back. Now it was different.

Once the polish was on, it was like coming out of the pits for the last time. He went into overdrive. His hands disappeared in a blur, rags flapped, a leather whistled and the broad-backed brush flew round the rear of the boot and surfed back magically on to the front. Slap! Slap! Slap! It rocketed from hand to hand, skimmed over the toe, barrelled round the heel, shot along the sides. Slap! Slap! Then back to a rag, then a leather, another rag and over to the brush again. And with each leather, each cloth, each brush and duster, the shine on the boots became more and more like a mirror. Something nagged at me. Was it obsidian? Why obsidian? Were the boots going glassy? I started to panic, too shiny, too shiny, too *pachuco*, but I managed to control it.

I watched the *jefe*, the maestro, finish the job in a whirlwind of arms and hands. Whistle! Slap! Blur! It was the shine of a lifetime.

For the rest of the day – for the rest of the week – I kept looking down at those glass boots. They couldn't have had a louder, more sparkling shine if they had been solid gold. It was a shine that roared.

They were blinding. Without sunglasses I could only look at them for a few seconds. A shine like this in England, way beyond a hot spoon, spit-and-polish Army job, would raise eyebrows. In Mexico it meant simply that I melted into the background. Boots this shiny had to be Mexican. Never gringo.

Did this Mexican passion for shiny shoes come from way back? Why not? So much still came from pre-Columbian times. The evidence was all around. Sometimes it was clear; other times it was just echoes, shadowed and distorted by conquest. Always the cultures were mixed. So why not shiny shoes? Could it be possible that the Mexican passion for glassy footwear comes from obsidian mirrors?

Obsidian is volcanic glass, lava which has turned to glass with rapid cooling. There is a lot of it in Mexico, Hungary, a Greek island and Yellowstone Park. It has had magical and religious uses in the Old and the New Worlds. Pharaohs' statues have had obsidian eyes. The ancients thought it was life-giving.

The big Mexican mines were at Hidalgo. They made curved obsidian mirrors. Like a crystal ball, the obsidian would reveal the will of the gods. It was the eye of heaven, looking up at the sun.

The god Tezcatlipoca was the first to popularize the use of concave obsidian mirrors in religious ceremonies. He used them to focus the sun and start sacred fires in the temples, guarded by the vestal virgins, brides of the sun. His statue is always carved out of black obsidian.

Obsidian related to women, fire, god, sex and the sun. They also made sharp-edged sacrificial knives of obsidian.

I remembered the stories of men putting mirrors on the toes of their shoes so they could look up women's skirts. I tried it with the boots as they were and blushed bright red. They worked. Beware of men with shiny shoes. For a while I went back to the trainers and scuffed the boots up a little until they were safe to wear again.

Right opposite the hotel entrance was an undertaker. Another tatty 1961 Cadillac hearse similar to the Barinas one stood outside. No doors to open, ready for unexpected exits. It was the most positive, if not cheerful, funeral directors I had seen.

FUNERALES BRAVO!
'La Mejor Casa en el Ramo de Inhumaciones
Los Precios los mas Baratos'
The best house in the field of Inhumations
The cheapest prices

Apart from the corn and orchid juice effigy, not much was Indian in Morelia. We went to the culture institute and met a one-eyed architect who told us to go straight to Lake Patzcuaro.

In truth, the architect had two eyes, but one of them was glass. I thought people with glass eyes shouldn't build houses. Unless they were obsidian eyes.

He told us of the best musicians and the sweetest singers. We left that minute for the magical lake and the Blue Gods of Water.

Where Morelia was rich and colonial, Patzcuaro, sitting on a hill overlooking the magical lake in the mountains, was gently run down and Indian: organic. The Spanish colonial buildings – churches, convents, colleges – were tatty and peeling. They had all gone back to the Indians long ago. They had all been Purepecha'd.

Patzcuaro had belonged to the Purepecha in the first place. The Purepecha were also known as the Tarascans, and before the conquest, Patzcuaro had been the capital of the Purepecha or Tarascan empire, ruling most of western Mexico, for centuries.

There was a lot of action in and around the Basilica, big crowds, people crawling on their knees, a brass band, candle sellers. The Basilica was enormous for the size of the town. With a big domed roof, it had five naves like the fingers of an outstretched hand, and had been racked by earthquakes, rebuilt, shaken again and rebuilt once more. Three hundred years after they started building, it still wasn't complete.

Inside, it was packed with Indians and mestizo faces. They were all staring at a grandiose altar under a high vaulted roof with frescoed arabesques.

In a glass box with gold Corinthian columns was the object of their adoration, Nuestra Señora de la Salud, the Virgin Mary. She was again made with *tatzingue*, the paste from ground corn cobs and orchid nectar, a symbol of the Purepechas' embrace of Christianity.

Salud is health, which explained all the pilgrims crawling on their knees down the aisle, right up to the Purepecha image of the Christian mother. I followed the line out of the church, and saw it stretching across the courtyard, off down the street and out of sight.

In the courtyard in front of the Basilica, surrounded by holy relic stalls, penitent Indians in the throes of mortification, and a brass band blasting out a few French marches, I bumped into José Dimas.

José was slim, smooth-skinned and fit, handsome with soft features, a small pencil moustache and wearing a smart square-shouldered sports jacket. He didn't look fifty. He was one of the singers and had heard from our monocular architect friend that we were coming.

Was he performing soon?

He said we could talk about it if we wanted to eat lunch with him in an hour. Before he left I asked about the corn and orchid Virgin.

'Aha!' he said. 'That's all because of Tata Vasco.'

Tata Vasco's name was everywhere. He seems to have been one of those great
and good men who sometimes arrive in the wake of the holocaust. Luckily for
the Purepecha and their integrity through the following centuries, Tata Vasco
arrived in the nick of time to mitigate the worst ravages of the conquistadors.
Single-handedly he managed to cherish and protect the people around the
magical lake.

That is why he is *Tata* Vasco. Vasco de Quiroga had been a lawyer all his
life. He came out to the new world and in his late sixties he gave it all up to be
ordained as a priest. He became a bishop five years later, at seventy-five. He
was inspired by the idealism of Thomas More, but seemed more like a saint
than a mere humanitarian.

Like Moses in the desert, he struck the ground in Patzcuaro and a freshwater
spring burst forth and flowed for the next four hundred years. It dried up in
1940. Right beside the spring, he founded St Nicolas, the first college in all the
Americas. Then he built a basilica and asked the Purepechas to fashion a Holy
Virgin for him in their own way. But instead of a virgin, instead of an ascetic
Christian mother, she was to be a goddess of health, Our Lady of Health. The
Mother.

Tata Vasco was bringing them in, acknowledging their customs and their
beliefs. He was a holy rather than a purely Christian man. He knew that his
religion would only be taken to heart if it gave some kind of space to the
conquered people, a space where they could disguise, mask and protect their
ancient beliefs. Kindness, not the *encomienda*, was Tata Vasco's way.

He protected the Purepecha from ruthless landowners and miners looking
for slave labour. That's why they called him Tata, a combination of protector,
godfather and uncle. They loved him then and seem to love him now.

José Dimas came back to take us to his friends for lunch. Tambien had
discovered the Dimas were stars in Patzcuaro. Yes, said José, we've done some
radio and TV and a foreign TV team is coming to film us soon.

He sang with his sister Angelita, and Nestor her nephew played lead guitar.
Yes, they'd sung together all their lives. The Purepecha call their songs *pirekuas*
and they are mostly love songs. Were they sad? Yes, many. Good.

We got lost in the backstreets of Patzcuaro trying to find José's friend's
house. Dirt roads, red-tiled roofs, poor houses and grubby whitewashed walls.
There were people watching us out of little doorways, an occasional mule,

a lot of dogs, old women and young children on the streets.

We passed the Licoreria Jesu Cristo, Jesus Christ's Liquor Store. How would that go down in Nashville? I tried to go in but José wouldn't let us buy a bottle for lunch.

Just as well. When we finally found the place, there were five priests, already very drunk on mescal and beer. We joined in with them, ate oxtail and ribs, rice, tortillas, beans, salsa and dumplings, and mescal and beer.

It was more like a business lunch. The priests were discussing the Dimas' fortunes as if they were managers and PR men. Maybe they were. It got heated.

Some thought Nestor, the nephew, was not a very good guitarist or road manager when they toured. Others thought the Dimas were going down the wrong road. They thought artistic changes were needed. The drunker the priests got, the more seriously they took the discussion.

It seemed that the Dimas were having some success, so they needed spiritual guidance. They had a record out, had done radio and a foreign TV crew was on its way. Now they were on the edge of international stardom and the hit parade, everybody wanted to put their oar in. Money was talking.

They should get rid of Nestor. He was just an opportunist, jumping on José and Angelita's bandwagon. The priests grew more and more heated. Father Augustin, fired up by mescal and oxtail, kept beating on the table at very mention of Nestor's name. For a priest he was more than a bit uncharitable. Eaten up with envy. Downright covetous, I'd say.

Wearing a green baseball cap which he never took off during the whole meal, Father Augustin maintained that he had been usurped by Nestor, and that he was more important to the group than Nestor (*thump*). He could make much better introductions and announcements than Nestor (*thump*) ever did. How many introductions had Nestor (*thump!*) made? And anyway Nestor (*thummpp!!*) couldn't bless anyone.

They got interested in us, obviously thinking we were talent scouts or agents. I explained about the cowboy trail. I said that I was a musician and had heard that *pirekuas* were beautiful and historic and the Dimas' harmonies were the best. No TV, no radio, I was just a fool for harmonies. That seemed to satisfy them.

On the way to the Dimas' house on the other side of the lake was Tzintzuntzan, the 'place of the hummingbirds', which had become the Tarascan emperors' seat of power before the conquistadors appeared. Just outside Tzintzuntzan, standing on its own overlooking the lake, was a temple of Tarascan pyramids, the *yacatas*. We drove off the road and got out.

Only the bases of the pyramids and lower parts of the *yacatas* remained but they were impressive enough. Each pyramid represented a different bird. Dark-stoned, with high steps upwards, circular and square ruins, they were in a breathtaking position. This morning it seemed particularly heavenly, with a silver mist still clinging to the lake and a haze shimmering through the mountains like a Japanese watercolour.

There was a tap on my leg. I had seen no one around, and the Tzintzuntzan pyramids were out in the open, away from any habitation. There was another tap.

It was a young Indian boy, six or seven years old. Would we like him to look after the car, to protect it while we looked over the pyramids? Jo Tambien hooted.

'Protect us from what?' We looked around and the place was deserted. Tambien asked the boy who would damage the car. He shrugged. The penny dropped.

'Protect it from him, of course. Ha! There you go, an embryonic protection racket. A few pesos, or he'll let the tyres down. Or worse.'

Fair play to him, I thought. A well-deserved *mordita*. I went all wishy-washy, liberal and concerned about the oppression of the Third World, but JT was hard. He gave the lad just enough to keep his hands off our tyres.

We climbed up the pyramids. What made them unique was that the *yacatas*, built of dark volcanic rock and shingles, were elliptical and not triangular – just like the Huanca, or Wanka, citadels in Peru. Most of the *yacatas* were ruined, but the view made up for any missing history.

As we clambered along the pyramids, the sun had burnt the mist off the surface of the lake which was shining out a preposterous blue. Those blue gods again. The mountains were still oriental, softened in the haze to a pale greenish grey. Their reflections in the glassy waters of the lake were sharper than the mountains themselves. It was easy to understand why the Tarascans settled on this side of heaven, even if they had come all the way from Peru.

It was equally difficult to believe, in this vision of perfect beauty, that the blue gods of water had abandoned the lake, that the magic had gone, that the exquisite *laguna* was dying, poisoned, drying up and throttled by an explosion of waterlilies, beauty killing beauty.

Santa Fe de la Laguna is the first place Tata Vasco came to in this paradise. There was a Purepecha settlement here and he moved in. He built a hospice for the Indians. He encouraged all the Purepecha round the lake, from here to Patzcuaro, to learn various skills and trades.

He wanted them to be self-sufficient, able to trade and to augment their fishing. He got each village to learn a different craft: weaving, carving, pottery, delicate ceramics, mask making, copper work and toys. They carry on all these to this day.

Tata Vasco's hospice was still there. It had a four-sided porch, a cloistered, whitewashed walkway with rust-brown columns, running round a central square. It was the centre, the heart of village life. Nothing had changed.

All day long women came to take water from a well in the centre of the square. The Tata again, water and health. A town drunk was arguing with one of the columns. Rooms off the covered walkway round the square were lived in or storerooms. One of them was a shrine to Quiroga. There was a painting of him, and in a big glass case were his robe and his chair.

In or out of the hospice, everything moved very slowly. As they should in this part of the world, dogs lay stretched out sleeping in the middle of the road.

Right inside the door of a small dark church by the hospice were two dark-skinned life-sized and very lifelike Jesuses.

One was on the cross and, like most Spanish Señors, was very bloody. He was so realistic I jumped backwards out of the church into the sunlight. When I went back in, there was blood everywhere, pouring out of the holes in his sides, dripping down his face from the crown of thorns, seeping out of his hands and feet. It was blood you could believe in, blood you could taste.

Worst of all, and what made it so ghoulish that I leapt back out of the doorway, was that it had real human hair. I felt like doubting Thomas as I went up close just to be sure that it was only an effigy after all, though I didn't actually go as far as feeling the chest wounds.

Then I got to the gloom. Further in, behind the bleeding Señor, was another, even darker-skinned Jesus. If the one on the cross looked Mexican, this one was pure Purepecha. Even the donkey he was sitting on was from these parts. It was more a *burro* than a donkey.

El Señor was sitting on a simple vaquero saddle. He was wearing a broad-brimmed Mexican sombrero and, thinking ahead, had a spare sombrero tied to his saddle. A lost cowboy. He couldn't have looked more local if he tried.

To the Coptic Christians, black Africans in Egypt, God and Jesus are black. The Devil is white.

Who could argue with them?

The courtyard of the Dimas' house was bursting with flowers and tropical bushes. José, Angelita and the much maligned Nestor were there. They were rehearsing for the imminent foreign film crew. José and Nestor were wearing flat-brimmed straw sombreros just like the Chilean *huasos'* hat.

I told them of this and they said they weren't surprised; down in the *tierra calientes*, the hot lands by the Michoacan coast, they play dance music called the *marinera*, the sailor's dance, or the *chilena*, the Chilean dance. Along with the terracing, this would confirm the cultural movement up and down the Pacific west coast over the centuries.

As well as the sombreros, they were all duded up, trying out their costume for the filming. Nestor and José were both wearing their best serapes and Angelita a long dress with a bright tropical-blue blouse with white lace daisies around the collar.

Angelita was a big, reserved woman. She had a large, inscrutable Indian face, far more Purepecha than José or Nestor, who looked much softer and more Hispanic. Her face was timeless and, with her sober, severe look born of shyness, could have been carved out of stone.

Then they sang, and I was as bowled backwards as I had been by the slaughtered Jesus in the chapel.

Although Angelita's face stayed impassive, even her lips hardly moving, they sang sweet, simple, tender harmonies, their voices caressing the poignant little melodies. I had never heard harmonies so fluid, so silky before. And just like primitive country music or blues, there was no regard to bar length or structured lines. Their voices just slid across the backing guitars, always gentle and pensive, always serenading.

It was sweet Indian Everly Brothers, and I could hear the roots of *Norteño* and Tex-Mex music in there. It was captivating, true pre-Columbian harmonies at last. I got very excited. This was the missing link. Here in this overflowing garden by the magical lake lived the roots of all the great south-western harmonies of country and Mexican music.

Hummingbird harmonies? Could be. They'd be bound to say that's what they were in Tzintzuntzan.

Sitting by the lake on an uprooted tree trunk I watched two fishermen. They had long, slender boats, almost canoes, with huge butterfly-wing nets curving out like sails on bamboo poles either side. They dipped them under the water to catch the fish.

When they brought them up they more often than not brought out great green streamers of weed. I could see them struggling to clear the surrounding water of the choking plants before dipping again. I could feel their frustration as they battled hopelessly against this throttling greenery.

Back in Patzcuaro a small *conjunto* – a very old fiddle player, two guitars and a double bass – were playing in a little square under a tree. It was lively stuff, different from the pensive, silky harmonies of the Dimas family.

Tata Gerbasio, the fiddle player, was a wizened old man of eighty-three. The rest of the group, the Sunset Band, were his sons and a grandson. They played a *marinera* and a little girl hopped and skipped around them. They played a fandango which promised a '*fantasia de contrabasse*'.

This must have been a day for jumping, for I leapt back again. The '*fantasia*' was a break for a bass solo. The bass player started to beat at his strings, snapping and slapping them mercilessly on to the fingerboard. Here, in the middle of the Michoacan mountains, this Purepecha Indian was playing perfect rockabilly slap bass.

Rockabilly? He'd never heard of it.

We sat under the tree and took a rest. One of Tata Gerbasio's sons produced a petrol can and poured out a few stiffeners of mescal. I stiffened. They said they had a song about their lake. The two brothers, both fishermen, sang it in the tender, dreamy style of the Dimas. With guitars gloriously out of tune, their voices slid like velvet across the top as they said goodbye to the Blue Gods of Water:

> The song we are going to sing you
> Was written with tears in our eyes.
> Our laguna is drying up
> And the fish in it are dying.
> Now we are going to lose our laguna
> What will we do without it
> Now that it is being choked to death?

As we left Patzcuaro, I saw a sign for a dance that night in Morelia: 'ALDO Y SUS PASTELES.' Aldo and His Cakes.

It was our loss, but we couldn't wait.

> 'Teposcolula, she's my baby,
> Teposcolula, don't mean maybe . . . '

Skimming through the high sierras of Oaxaca way down south, Jo and I were in full throat. We were going to meet an old friend who we heard was at a *campesinos*' meeting in an isolated village up in the hills. It was called Teposcolula.

As we drove higher the forests opened out. The land became drier, chalky and then brick red and pink, arid and eroded like the badlands. The road wound up round mountainsides, vistas spread out across ranges further south.

It felt like Hollywood cowboy country, though we passed only an occasional *paisano* on a mule, a couple of men riding horses and few cattle.

Some lusher, flat valleys in these highlands were growing wheat and barley as well as the all-pervasive maize. At least for variety's sake there were different fields of white, yellow, blue, black and red maize.

'Teposcolula, she's my baby . . . '

Well, little things please little minds. We were nearly there. I thought of our friend. We had met two years before and we had played songs to each other through a long night of mescal. I had heard that the Oaxaca mushrooms were something special, a high-quality door to the skies above the high sierras and our friend had promised to get us some when we came back.

'Teposcolula, don't mean maybe . . . '

In the end, Teposcolula proved to be a two-cantina town up in the middle of nowhere. There were several UN aid groups in the area to help the poor, struggling and often landless *campesinos*. As we got to the centre we heard the carefree blaring of a raggedy brass band. We turned a corner and there was our friend Jaime.

Jaime Luna, like the great Benito Juarez, was a full-blooded Zapotec Indian and it showed. His name, Jimmy Moon, was reflected in his broad, round face, pitted with pockmarks like a lunar landscape. He had wide, high cheekbones, shiny black Siberian eyes, jet-black hair and a big, wide-lipped mouth. His wide nose was squashed up against his face like a prize-fighter's. He was what the French call *joli-laid*, pretty-ugly.

Tambien and I were pulled up on to the committee table at the top, as foreign correspondents, musicians and special guests. When we were introduced, two hundred *campesinos* applauded and the brass band gave a fifteen-second blast as a welcome.

Speechifying filled the next few hours. Forty-five community representatives were each to give reports. Each speaker had a good go at amputating a *burro*'s hindleg, starting off with rambling introductions and thanks, like Guillermo's introduction at the *topada*. As often as not this was all they would manage before being cut short by a quick squirt from the brass band. Very few reports got heard beyond the introductions. It was the only way as no one took any notice of the committee's repeated appeals for brevity.

Even so, several speakers managed to evade the brass band and fill the air with words. I noticed three out of four *burros* in the square had collapsed, arse to the ground.

Underlying all the speeches, the brass band and the aid workers was the fact that the poor Mexicans' battle for land is not over. It probably never will be. Every time we heard of another Zapatista uprising in the far south, it was a reminder that neither independence nor any of the revolutions since have ever improved the lot of the *campesinos* one jot.

After the meeting we went back to Jaime's village. Guelatao nestled high up in a bowl, adrift in the Papaluapan mountains. The whole *pueblito* was a monument to Benito Juarez, Oaxaca and Mexico's most favourite son. Like Jaime a full-blood Zapotec, he was the one wholly good man to govern Mexico. He led the *Reforma*, and managed to kick out the occupying French forces. With statues, a mausoleum, a civic plaza and a museum, the pueblito seemed more like a memorial park than a living village.

Jaime struggled out on to the porch with an enormous plastic jerrycan.

'I forgot the mushrooms, but will this do? This is for you and Tambien too – will it be enough?'

'Well, we're here another week. What do you reckon, Jo?'

Jo tried to lift the jerrycan. It was a struggle. It held at least fifty litres of high-octane home-distilled mescal . . . Oaxaca mountain dew . . . Papaluapan white lightning.

'Yes,' said Tambien, trying not to seem ungrateful or to wince under the weight, 'I think that should do it all right.'

Jaime's Venezuelan wife came in holding their new baby daughter. Both mother and daughter were stunning. Fuelled by the mescal, I pulled out a picture of Mat, my pride and joy, now leading a rock 'n' roll band in New York City. He's a good-looking young man. Not to be outdone by proud fatherhood, I showed him around.

Jaime looked at the picture and tossed down another good shot of mescal.

'He's much better looking than you.'

'Yes, well, that's because his mother's very beautiful.'

'Ah,' Jaime said, leaning over, his soft mescal eyes smiling conspiratorially, 'that's right. Guys as ugly as you and me, we owe it to our children to marry beautiful women.'

When France pulled out of Mexico, leaving Maximilian in the lurch, they left one big cultural footprint – the brass band. In Oaxaca every tiniest *pueblito* has a brass band. The tradition is stronger here than anywhere else in Mexico. We found one village with five separate bands. These were not just small ensembles, but big bands with thirty-five or forty people.

When we got there a funeral procession was winding mournfully along a track in the midday sun, heading for the village, carrying a coffin past fields of the broken stumps of corn stalks. The plaintive sound of six brass players marked the dead man's last journey. It was the classic Western soundtrack. A church bell tolled. Time stood still.

In the square a forty-piece band was gathering for a rehearsal under the trees. Trumpets, trombones, cornets, euphoniums, two large tubas, saxophones, flutes, fifes, clarinets, cymbals and a bass drum. They struck up a fantasia called Zapotec Dreams. A little girl danced around and a little boy in the church doorway conducted to himself, dreaming his Zapotec dreams of having a French military brass band of his own one day.

With forty musicians blaring away the opportunities for being out of tune were limitless. At first it grated, but soon it found its own level of harmony. Discord became accord. Out of tune became in tune with something beyond music.

I'd love to have heard this band backing the Texas Troubadour, Ernest Tubb, the old Country singer who sang flatter than anyone else. A collaboration between the two would have been inspirational. These guys had such a sense of expanded intonation that they would have made Ernest sound like he had perfect pitch.

All the way through Hispanic America I had seen a good many Christian visions of a lush and baroque heaven, created to entice the Indians away from their old gods. One in Oaxaca town was not a mere vision but had to be a slice of heaven itself. If a sophisticated westerner could feel that, what was a poor Mixtec or Zapotec to think?

I felt the same seeing the Northern Lights up near Hudson's Bay several years before. As I fell to the ground, I wondered how anyone could convince a Cree Indian that they were not witnessing the Great Spirit dancing across the night skies.

When I walked into the church of Santo Domingo, nothing on this earth could have stopped me from crying out loud, 'Jesus Christ!' and falling over. I blinked, and it was still blinding in its sumptuous, celestial wealth.

Everything in it was pure white and shining gold – everything, that is, except the roof of the porch with its intricately ramifying family tree. The Guzman family had Santo Domingo built, and they were all up there, the great and the good, the deceitful, the conniving and the murderous. At the base of the tree, giving life (and impeccable lineage) to the burgeoning Guzman family, was God.

As I passed through the porch, the interior of the church opened out into a white and gold baroque dream. Like Salta and Cholula, this was a vision of paradise as wealthy and abundant, rather than peaceful and spiritual.

But all the other churches were sideshows: this was the main event.

Everything in this blisteringly white and gold wedding-cake was decorated. Not a space was left unfilled, no question left hanging in the air. Arabesques of stucco ornamentation covered in gold leaf danced across the ceiling, round the altars, over the arches, down the columns and through the chapels. The whole place was drowning in its own abundance. It was perfect baroque in its gaudiness – beautiful, vulgar and grotesque all at the same time.

Another peso dropped, something to do with the nature of the baroque out here in the New World. The Guzmans were, of course, buying their place in heaven with the biggest *mordita* for God they could muster. They were also dazzling the Mixtecs and Zapotecs into submission.

There was something else, though. This place had gone beyond baroque. Ostentatious was far too puny a word for it. The filling of every space as if emptiness were threatening seemed driven by fear – fear of a vacuum, of eternity. But heaven is eternity, the great nothingness that the Guzmans could not comprehend. So they were plugging the gap between their ideals and aspirations and the gritty reality of their lives, praying to God while they conquered and enslaved human beings in the most un-Christian way possible.

We had another night of mescal with Jaime. He sang a song called 'La Martiniana'. It stayed with me all the way out of Mexico.

> Little one, when I die
> Don't cry over my grave;
> Sing me happy songs, little mama
> Sing me 'La Sandunga'.
>
> No, don't cry for me,
> No, don't cry for me,
> Because if you cry I will die;
> Instead, sing me happy songs,
> And that way I'll live for ever.

19. Adios Amigos!

Reports differ on the number of times Santa Anna was President, or Dictator, of Mexico. Historians argue amongst themselves. Some say seven times, others eleven. History is fluid in this part of the world. But one thing they all agree on: Santa Anna was the most hated and despised man in Mexico. Although he erected statues of himself all over the country, not a single one stands today – not even one of his leg.

He was crafty and unscrupulous. The great opportunist, he dominated Mexican politics for a quarter of a century. He loved power but not its responsibility. He often installed a front man to take the flak but never the glory.

His political views were . . . flexible. He followed whatever road served him best. He started with the liberals then swung over to the powerful landowning conservatives. He betrayed friends and changed sides whenever it was expedient. In a world of self-serving politicians, Santa Anna served himself more than any. He was exiled five times, and returned again and again to take power back, dissolve constitutions and trample on any fledgling signs of democracy.

He swung between hero and villain all his political life. First he was the 'Hero of Tampico', when he defeated a weak Spanish force trying to get back into Mexico. He confirmed himself a hero by destroying the Alamo. He became a villain when he was defeated seven weeks later. He was captured trying to escape in a private's uniform. An opium addict, he agreed to terms so as to get his drug supply back.

He signed a treaty never to take up arms against Texas again, a treaty the Mexican government immediately repudiated. He was sent to Washington as a prisoner, where he tried to sell the Americans Texas. It wasn't his to sell.

Several times the United States cannily sent him back to Mexico like a bad penny, knowing what a liability he was and how he was bound to weaken the country in one way or another.

When his public image was at its lowest, his leg was shot off in an unsuccessful battle against the French. Earlier that day he had narrowly missed getting caught by the French but escaped in his underwear. In the battle, prancing around on a white horse, he lost his leg to a cannonball. Nothing like it for raising the ratings: he was a hero again. He erected a few more statues of himself and gave his leg a state funeral. It was carried in a crystal urn, blessed by the Archbishop and buried with full military honours in a gilded grave. Later, when he was once more a villain, citizens dug the leg up and dragged it through the streets. When he had reinstated himself as hero, he gave the leg another state funeral.

A popular English song, 'The Hokey Cokey', was based on the saga of Santa Anna: 'You put the left leg in, The left leg out, You do the Hokey Cokey and you shake it all about . . .'

He thought he was Napoleon, and called himself the Napoleon of the West. He dressed his troops in old Napoleonic Army uniforms. He carried a $7,000 sabre and sat on a golden saddle.

Mexicans derisively called the peg-legged dictator 'The Immortal Three Quarters'.

Santa Anna said, with horrible foresight: 'A hundred years from now, my people will not be fit for freedom. They do not know what it is, unenlightened as they are, and under the influence of the Catholic Clergy. Despotism is the proper government for them, but there is no reason why it should not be a wise and virtuous one.'

Santa Anna is not the only one without a memorial in Mexico. There are no statues to Cortés.

This is understandable. The slaughter of half the indigenous population within a few years of his arrival was not guaranteed to find him a place in the hearts of native Mexicans.

There was worse. When the conquistadors first arrived there were seventy million American Indians. Seventy million.

A century and a half later there were only three and a half million left.

We met Guillermo again by chance one morning in the Café Habana. He had recovered from the *topada* better than we had. But he was a poet, and a professional.

It was getting close to the time we had to cross the last frontier, into the States. I told Guillermo about old Don José and what he'd told me of vaqueros and the Anglo cowboys of America. He said he agreed with the Don.

What about the Mexican bandits?

'Listen, there are bandits in every country of the world. This stereotype of the Mexican isn't true. Of course we do have bandits. We had rustlers that stole cattle, but the stereotype of the Mexican that you get in Hollywood films is a complete lie.'

'A complete lie?'

'Yes. They put over the Mexican as a stupid, weak, gaudily dressed man who loses all the time. Ridiculous. In reality, the Mexican bandit was strong, well armed and knew how to handle himself. A match for any John Wayne or Clint Eastwood.'

'So Mexico wasn't a savage frontier waiting to be civilized by the American cowboy?'

'Not at all. There were ranches, cattle were raised and the ranchers lived on the land. They weren't wild at all.'

'So if the wicked Mexican bandit is a fiction and the good American cowboy another fiction, what was Hollywood doing?'

'Hollywood doesn't always respect history. They're more interested in business, wealth and sales. They change history as often as they like. What we must do is think about defending life on the land. It's the same in Chile, Argentina, and in Mexico. We have to claim back the old traditions. Every day there's more technology, more compact discs, and we're losing out. We're losing contact with what life on the land was like.'

I ordered my last *pozole* with extra chilli. As I ate it I thought how often Mexico had been called 'America's back yard'. That was looking at it the wrong way.

Far from being America's back yard, Mexico is more like its front garden. We headed for the airport and Texas.

20. Remember the Alamo?

'Those people sitting in Exit Rows must fulfil Exit Row Information Criteria.'

It started even before we had left the brown rusty smear over Mexico City, climbing away, safe in the sanitized hands of American Airlines. Long before we had crossed the border between the United States and Mexico, the two-thousand-mile scar gouged across America's history, we were in the Modern World.

Tambien and I were stretching out our lanky forms in the long-leg seats by the emergency exit. The nice stewardess had given us the Exit Row Information Criteria Information Brochure. It went on: 'Please read special directions for Exit Row Information. If any passenger is infirm, with a physical disability, unable to intake the information as a result of ocular or aural inability unable to be corrected by eyeglasses or hearing aids please contact the cabin crew by pressing the button above them.'

What, I thought, if they were unable, through some peripheral or manual disability, to press the button to summon the cabin crew? Or if, through some cerebral malfunction or educational or learning disability, they were unable to read or understand these directions? Or if they were Mongolian? Do they deplane?

It reminded me of a comment from Charles Flandrau, a turn-of-the-century traveller in Mexico: 'Most gringos have an inscrutable preference in favour of the definite.'

Still, we should be thankful for small mercies. On the back of the seat in front there was a credit card phone. Maybe I should call for further clarification.

*

Later, in Dallas – Fort Worth airport – I did try to call for help on a credit card phone. I tried. I followed the information to the letter, but I don't think I fulfilled the criteria.

I dialled the required number.

A computer-generated Dalek answered: '*Please respond which service you require – person to person* (click) *collect* (click) *card number* (click).'

I stood there stunned and didn't respond in time. I didn't fulfil the temporal criteria and the dialling tone came back. I tried again, and got the same series of options.

This time I was ready.

'Collect.'

'*Collect. What name? Please respond.*'

'Er . . . Hank.'

'*Er . . . Hank.*'

There was a pause. The Daleks were discussing the merits of my response. Then another click.

'*Collect call Er . . . Hank.*'

Bugger me, the machine was asking if I would accept a collect call from myself. I tried again and went round the same futile circle, grappling with the computer. I tried a different move, to see if I could confuse it.

'*Please respond which service you require – person to person* (click) *collect* (click) *card number* (click).'

'Credit card.'

The Dalek was unforgiving.

'*Incorrect response – please repeat.*'

I repeated and repeated. The litany went on and on. I started to bang the phone box. Always used to work in the old days. Then, just when I thought I was beginning to build up a relationship with the Dalek, a human voice came on the line. A real human being. What had I done wrong? What criteria had I unwittingly fulfilled?

I explained my problem and that I had my credit card, hot in my hand, to prove that I was a bona fide member of modern society, not some hippie, organic, macrobiotic Luddite.

'I'm sorry, sir, AT&T do not accept credit cards.'

'Hold on, it says here on this credit card telephone . . . '

'I'm sorry, sir, that is incorrect information.'

'But . . . but,' I start to splutter, 'it says here . . . '

'I'm sorry, sir, that is incorrect information.'

'Could it be a lie?'

'No, sir, merely incorrect.'

I gave up.

After this the nightmare got worse. We rode on transportation systems. I went to my first American lavatory in months. Tambien asked a bewildered airport employee: 'Excuse me, where is the nice part of the airport?'

She indicated the grey concrete corridor. 'This is it. This is what it's like, sir.' There was probably an atrium somewhere but we didn't have our Airport Users Information Manual with us.

All the soul, all the warm, dirty reality of Latin America had disappeared like a turd down the instant vacuuming suck of the airport lavatories. Swirl! Slurp! All clean! All dead!

I had the feeling that if I went for self-immolation as an option, and tried a burning tyre necklace in the middle of the arrival lounge, someone would come to tell me that it was a non-smoking area. Or offer me an Airport Users' Information Manual.

Everything changed in San Antonio, which is as Hispanic as it is Texan. Not too many information criteria here.

We had timed it to perfection and arrived on the eve of the anniversary of the fall of the Alamo, the end of the thirteen-day siege. All the hotels were full, not for the Alamo but for a tennis tournament. We got a microbus shuttle into town. I asked the young driver if he knew of any Alamo celebrations.

'No, sir, I *sure don't*', he said chirpily, helpfully, what the Americans probably call a Positive Negatory response. But he found us some rooms in the Alamo Travelodge.

Lying on my big American bed I tried to gather myself. It had been a bit of a rollercoaster ride into the States, mitigated in the end by San Antonio which was like putting one foot back into Mexico. Now I was nearly at the Alamo at last; the start of the journey with the Caledonian gauchos at the far tip of the continent was not just three months but several lifetimes ago. Perspectives had changed and questions I had been asking then I didn't seem to be asking any more.

The basic question of winners and losers had not been answered as much as turned on its head. Of course in lands like Latin America, 'so blessed by nature, so cursed by history', there were very obvious losers. Sixty-six million Indians disappearing in a century and a half came to mind. There were times, though, when the nature of winning and losing became less certain. Winners, I had told myself, were just losers in disguise.

The other losers, apart from the Indians, were the working cowboys themselves. Tending cattle was never a glamorous job. It was hard, dirty, dangerous work. It had always been very low paid, with little continuity and no security. It hasn't changed.

It was seasonal, migrant work. The old image of the cowboy working hard and saving his roll for a spread where he would build up his own herd was a myth. Very few managed it.

Not surprising since three or four months' work in a year was average, three or four months at forty or fifty dollars a month. That was good pay; it could be twenty dollars a month. The remaining eight or nine months had to be survived somehow, doing odd jobs, chopping wood, getting hand-outs, doing some poaching, 'riding the grub line'. A poached steer, stolen beef, was 'slow elk'.

Most cowboys' only possessions were their saddles and ropes and the clothes they worked and lived in. They usually didn't even own their own horses, but rode mounts belonging to the outfit. They weren't quite in debt peonage but they might as well have been. They scraped a living and had no chance at all of buying any land, even if they did somehow get the money.

The cattlemen's associations saw to that. They prevented individuals from getting land and sought to maintain a ready pool of poor, cheap labour, blocking any attempts at forming unions, blacklisting union members and using strikebreakers.

Unions threatened their power and wealth more than rustlers so they stamped them out fast. It was not difficult because cowboys were never by nature union men, but lone and independent. Self-reliant, as they would like to see it.

We don't want no pension plan, no sirree! They were perfect right-wing fodder, the poor old cowpokes. They would definitely say no to a welfare state and foreigners, yes to self-reliance and guns.

The stockmen's associations drafted the laws and drew up all the rules of the range. Throughout the Americas, the powerful rich annexed the land and the poor were kept poor to work the land and the stock. In this way the United States was no different from the countries further south.

The image of the poor American going out to the West to make his fortune with the free and easy life of a cowboy was nothing like accurate. Unfortunately, this was the American Dream combined with the Manifest Destiny of the Frontier, two images essential to the American psyche. In reality the cowboy was as miserable and exploited as the Mississippi cotton-picker, the Kentucky coal-miner, or the Pittsburgh steel-worker, except for one very important thing: the cowboy was on horseback, out on the range.

That was the difference, coupled with the romance of the cowboy life, already being mythologized in the nineteenth century; riding on horseback made up for many privations. Many men chose the lifestyle of the cowboy rather than the job.

Cowboys were no different from gauchos or *llaneros* in this respect – happiest in the saddle, miserable out of it. The appearance of barbed wire across the continental ranges in the 1870s and 1880s gave them new, despised work to do. They rode the line but had to dismount to repair the wire.

Winners or losers? Ask any old cowboy. He'll tell you that even line work isn't as bad as walking behind a plough. Ploughing, the sodbuster's work, was the cowboy's idea of hell.

He would also tell you that 'Life is like pullin' on a mule team. If you ain't the lead mule, all the scenery looks the same.'

The Alamo, symbolically, was to have answered the conundrum of winners and losers. Even before getting there, though, travelling across the Latin countries had complicated the original question. Who won and who lost was often unclear.

So many of the great heroes, the visionaries of independence and revolution – Artigas, San Martín, O'Higgins, and above all Bolívar – ended their lives disillusioned and despairing. So many winners were ultimately reviled, persecuted and exiled.

So many prophets and saviours were killed by those they were liberating that lines were getting blurred. Certainties no longer existed. Maybe the victims of the Alamo could have been winners? I still didn't understand 'Remember the Alamo!' but would surely get to the answer soon.

Certainly, many times down the line, the lost cowboys hadn't been winners but had been abused and exploited. Some had been ignored by history simply because none of them wrote it. Everyone knows that winners write history. Winning and racism is a potent combination which helps justify the twisting of facts and the invention of truths. Never was this so clear as in a typically racist comparison of the shifty vaquero and the noble Anglo cowboy. Here, in 1891, Colonel Theodore A. Dodge carefully buries the Anglo cowboys' origins and debts and builds on the myth in a shockingly one-sided account in *Harper's New Monthly Magazine*:

The vaquero is generally a peon, and as lazy, shiftless, and unreliable a vagabond as all men held to involuntary servitude are wont to be. He is essentially a low down fellow in his habits and instinct. Anything is grub to him which is not poison, and he will thrive on offal which no human being except a starving savage will touch.

In his ways the vaquero is a sort of tinsel imitation of a Mexican gentleman, and very cheap tinsel at that.

Our cowboy is independent, and quite sufficient unto himself. He has as long an array of manly qualities as any fellow living, and despite many rough-and-tumble traits, compels our honest admiration. Not only this, but the percentage of American cowboys who are not pretty decent fellows is small.

One cannot claim so much for the vaquero in question, though the term vaquero covers great territory and class, and applies to the just and unjust alike.

Dodge was not alone. The notion of Anglo-Saxon supremacy had been promoted since the 1840s. If, by the end of the century, through pulp fiction and imagery of the western frontier, the cowboy was on his way to becoming the national symbol, he had to be an Anglo. History needed to be written fast.

Here in San Antonio, the first cowboys were, of course, the Indians with the missions. Then the Mexican mestizo vaqueros. Then the black cowboys. But if the black cowboys were the first American cowboys, with the vaqueros, before the Anglos came along, then who were they? Sometimes God works in wondrous ways. I flicked the TV on. The third channel I hit, there was the Gucci-clad sophisticated negro sheriff in *Blazing Saddles*. He had been a joke then, but the racism being lampooned wasn't. It was that racism that had wiped out the memory of the black cowboy, just like the vaquero. A black infantryman or a black ranch cook was acceptable in the movies but somehow the cowboy was a different kind of icon. He had to be white. But there he was, the suave smooth-talking nigger, putting the fear of God up the honky white townsfolk.

The Alamo might be the end of the Hispanic story, and I knew well the Anglo cowboys' debt to the vaqueros. I knew nothing, though, of the black cowboys' contribution. They had to be the lost cowboys of the United States.

I flicked on through the channels. A man, some kind of psychotherapist or New Age prophet or politician, was being interviewed. He was talking in that American sharing, psychobabblish kind of jargon. Then he said it: 'Winners are those people who make a habit of doing those things that losers are uncomfortable doing.'

I ran screaming from the room to find Jo Tambien.

We thought, Jo and I, that the Alamo would take a Disneyland approach to history, or at least present a one-sided Anglo vision of it all. We were feeling protective of what we had seen as the Hispanic side of things, and the airport experience had not been a good omen. Would the Alamo tell us of treacherous, drunken, cringing Mexicans again?

Our fears were entirely unfounded.

The old museum of the Alamo was now in downtown San Antonio with streets, shops and high-rise blocks around it. There was the old mission building with the famous façade just like in the movies and the Long Barracks around some courtyards. On the Alamo plaza in front was the Cenotaph, with heroic carvings of the principal players, Travis, Crockett and Bowie.

Instead of a bubblegum, leisure-park approach, we were both disarmed to find that the mission and its museum had an unexpected dignity. In its treatment of the story of Texas, the role of the Spanish and the Indians was fully acknowledged. There was no pretence that everything started with the Anglos.

Texas is Texas. Fiercely independent in spirit still, it never was heartland United States, as my 'US OUT OF TEXAS NOW!' T-shirt attested. This was especially true of San Antonio. The museum is owned and run by the Daughters of the Republic of Texas. The site had been bought early this century by some rich young Texas society women, the Daughters of the Republic themselves. So the Alamo is a sort of Texas National Trust.

In the Long Barracks museum we learned how Stephen Austin went as a land agent on behalf of Mexico to offer land in Texas free to Anglo settlers. At this time, Texas was rough territory, 'a heaven for men and dogs, but a hell for women and oxen'.

To get the land, settlers had to be Catholic. For this purpose, Austin got a priest in 1831 to convert any land-seeking Protestants. The priest was a jovial Irishman, Father Miguel Muldoon, who took special delight in marrying couples, converting them and baptizing their children all at the same time . . .

Then I heard them: Bagpipes.

A piper was passing the Long Barracks. We ran out. Young and dark, with thick black eyebrows, in full Scottish dress, the piper was doing a slow march through the Alamo courtyard.

A line of white Americans, most middle-aged, some wearing kilts and the full plaid, one carrying a tartan banner on a pole, several in Tam o'Shanters, were following in sober procession. I didn't recognize the plaid, a red tartan, or the pibroch. The piper kept playing as the line of perhaps a dozen people marched behind him and disappeared into another courtyard. Someone had pressed the surreal button.

It turned out the Scots were extremely important in the history of Texas. The people here were wearing MacGregor tartan. Today was the anniversary of the fall of the Alamo and the slaughter of the 182 heroes. A memorial service was being held in the old mission chapel.

So what was this Caledonian contingent? Why the plaid and the pipes? I thought of Jimmy Halliday in Patagonia. Would these people know about Burns' Night? Was there an Alamo Burns?

There was.

Alamo John MacGregor, the unsung piper of the Alamo, was being honoured and commemorated for the first time ever. He was being celebrated by the MacGregor Society of Texas. I had never heard of him, and he certainly wasn't in the film. There was a 'Scotty' in *The Alamo*, but he didn't play the pipes. For that matter, I don't remember Davy Crockett playing his fiddle in the film. He did in reality.

Davy Crockett had been a successful politician and businessman in the East, going from his native Tennessee's state legislature to the US House of Representatives. He promoted the populist image of a rough backwoodsman and became known as a 'coonskin' politician. He hunted raccoons and bears for sport in winter in the dense canebrakes of western Tennessee and peppered his speeches with yarns and homespun metaphors. He played the fiddle. When he was defeated in an election in 1835 by Andrew Jackson's party who were nervous about his growing grassroots popularity, he headed west to Texas.

It was there at the Alamo that he met John MacGregor. During Santa Anna's thirteen-day siege of the Alamo, Crockett and MacGregor would play fireside duets, fiddle and pipes, to keep up the men's spirits whenever the fighting died down. They played to see who could play loudest. Alamo John always won; pipes beat the fiddle every time.

On the final day, John MacGregor played the pipes over the din of battle until he was killed. The MacGregor Society was commemorating the final heroic stand of the warrior piper.

Little is known of MacGregor's life. He was a single man who had emigrated from Scotland, taking his bagpipes, and settled in Nacogdoches in east Texas. He wandered around Texas and did some farming here and there. He had a smallholding in Turkey County. He came to San Antonio to fight in the siege of Bexar, as San Antonio was known, the year before the battle of the Alamo.

The story of his wanderings was typical of many Scots looking for a better life in the New World. The MacGregors had been a wandering clan for two centuries.

They had become the 'Nameless Clan', the 'Children of the Mist', forced to relinquish their lands and their names on pain of death. They were persecuted and hunted down. They could not carry weapons. They could not meet in groups of more than four. Their severed heads became legal tender and could purchase land or pardons. So emigration was in the MacGregors' blood.

None of this highly charged legend was lost on the MacGregor Society of Texas. This was, after all, Alamo John's first commemoration service so no holds were barred.

The procession stopped round a small plinth topped with an arrangement of purple heather and bluebonnets. The Gulf Coast Commissioner of the Society, Zoe Alexander, did some speechifying and gave thanks to various officials including the Chairman of the Scottish Clan Gregor Society.

When there was an invitation to other clans, I stepped up to take my rightful place in the proceedings. It wasn't for the Clan Wangford, but for my mother, a MacKinlay. There is of course no Tambien tartan, so Jo stayed back.

The Daughters of the Republic were presented with a framed copy of 'The Last Warrior Piper', a rambling epic poem in the style of William McGonagal about the Children of the Mist and Alamo John. Members got misty-eyed. More speeches followed about pipers, Scotland and Rob Roy. Jim Bowie was acknowledged as a MacGregor.

An interesting theory, confirming the pivotal role the Scots played in Texas, was that bluebonnets – a kind of lupin which is the State flower of Texas – are so called because they were the hats the Scots soldiers always wore. The soldiers themselves were called Bluebonnets. It seemed fair enough.

There was a minute's silent meditation, as silent as it could be in the middle of downtown San Antonio, then the entire epic poem was read out with much rrrrolling of rrr's in the auld Hielan' fashion:

'But the blood is aye strong and the memories are deep,
And Clan Gregor have gathered at long last to weep
For their kinsman who died with the last gallant men;
Free the Child of the Mist, send him home back again.

'May his spirit rest light, may his soul rest in peace,
May his pipe fill the glens and the kilt brush his knees,
And the heather burn purple the bens and the braes,
As we send back his spirit to live out its days.

'For the last of the legend lies deep in the heart
Of the highlands of Texas, forever a part
Of the nation he fought for, the land he helped win,
And McGregor has won back his name once again.

'For the Lone Star and *Ailpein* are fast joined together;
May their union aye flourish, despite them, forever.'

© Zoe Alexander, MacGregor Society of Texas

After the ceremony I spoke to several of the MacGregors. The piper, Ramón Martín, was twenty-one.

'My dad is a hillbilly and my ma is Filipino,' he confided, 'but I am a MacGregor.'

Zoe Alexander ('I'm not quite a MacGregor, just an honorary one') said that the Scots built Texas. Not the English or the Americans or the Germans but the Scots. As proof, she said, sixty per cent of all place names in Texas are Scottish. I could only think of Dallas, and was struggling to justify San Antonio, but then remembered my Glasgow childhood.

'Right, of course,' I said helpfully, 'Antonio's was the ice cream van that used to come up our street.' I added, just to improve my MacGregor credentials, that I lived near Robroyston. Still a bit self-conscious about fulfilling criteria.

Whatever the truth, its relevance for our journey, starting and finishing with the Scots, was not lost on us. It didn't address our question about winners and losers, but that was on the way to being answered by now.

Tambien was still hooting when we went outside on to Alamo Plaza. He took my picture sitting on the motorcycle cop's bike. They weren't Harleys any more, but Hondas. Honda sounded Scottish to me.

I wondered if they were related to the MacGregors.

The winners and losers at the Alamo? William Barrett Travis, the young commanding officer, said prophetically, 'Victory will cost the enemy so dear, it will be worse for him than defeat.'

He was right. At five in the morning Santa Anna ordered the advance. The bugler sounded the degüello, the fanfare from the bullfight before the final killing, the traditional fanfare of no quarter. It was a nice touch. The battle was over in ninety minutes. To defeat the 182 defenders, Santa Anna lost six hundred men.

Travis's prophecy of an expensive victory didn't stop there. Forty-six days later, Sam Houston's Texan army came upon Santa Anna's encampment. Outnumbered two to one, the Texans, screaming '*Remember The Alamo!*', fell on the Mexicans and tore them to pieces. They killed half the Mexican army and took the other half prisoner. In eighteen minutes, at San Jacinto, the Texans destroyed Santa Anna's army, took the General prisoner, and assured their independence.

The battle had not been between the United States and poor Mexico, as it was to be a decade later, but between a small group of men fighting for their freedom from the tyranny of the dictator Santa Anna.

They won, and Texas became an independent republic. The black men fighting by their side lost their freedom and went back to slavery. The US incorporation of Texas, considered an act of war by Mexico, was driven not only by manifest destiny. Texas was an important market for slaves.

Consider the tragic story of Greenbury Logan, for instance, who answered the call of Stephen Austin to settle in Texas. He wrote GTT across his door. Gone to Texas, and left for the West in 1831. By the time war broke out four years later Logan had been granted Texas citizenship and a quarter-acre plot. The battle of Bexar, when the Texans beat the Mexicans and captured the Alamo, he was right in the forefront; he was the third man to fall wounded. But the Texan triumph introduced slavery and he lost everything.

There is a book called *Films of the Alamo* which discusses the merits and otherwise of hundreds of Alamo films. It is a very thorough treatment, right through from the first, *The Immortal Alamo* of 1911, to *Alamo – Price of Freedom* of 1988. It chronicles lost Alamo movies, films that have disappeared, like *The Siege & Fall of the Alamo*, not seen since 1914. As a trainspotter milestone, it even has a chapter on films on the Alamo *that were never made*. The most notable of these was a silent epic, *Birth of Texas* by D. W. Griffith.

It is a must for lovers of films about the Alamo. I've only seen one myself, the John Wayne epic. He not only played Davy Crockett but directed and financed it himself. It took the best part of a decade for Wayne to get the money. Apparently, people were not falling over themselves to finance his project – but it was the Duke's great dream and he got there in the end.

It was premiered in 1960 in San Antonio, Texas, where it all happened. The San Antonians greeted the film with a kind of religious ecstasy which the rest of the world did not share.

The Duke, undeterred as usual, said, 'I think it's the greatest piece of folklore ever brought down through history [sic]. The Alamo is real Americana. Those fellas were real heroes, and if somebody doesn't like heroes, *they'd better not come see this picture*.'

That was real cowboy talk.

21. Big Bad Juan

The next morning I had an important appointment with Paris Hatters, one of the world's great hat shops and an old family business. I was looking for a new felt and a straw. I went down to Broadway, not far from the Alamo.

It felt like I'd come ten thousand miles for this, which of course I had. The journey was worth it. The Americans do make the best hats. Behind all the Resistols and Americans and Stetsons were framed photos of the great and the good wearing their 5X beavers from Paris Hatters.

A lot of country stars were up there, from Ernest Tubb, George Jones, Tex Ritter and Hank Williams to George Strait, Willie Nelson and Dwight Yoakam. All the past American Presidents had been hatted by Paris. I only caught sight of Johnson, Bush and Reagan up on the wall.

I talked hats, sombreros and famous heads with Abe Cortez Jr, who ran the business with his father, Abe Cortez Sr.

'Here's your King Charles,' said Abe Jr after he had sorted me out with a fine tan 5X Resistol and had steamed the brim to my exact requirements. 'He took six.'

He took me over to the famous photograph of Prince Charles and Prince Andrew in happier times, all Stetsoned up at the Calgary Stampede. The hats sat surprisingly well on the royal heads. Then, as I went over to the counter to flash my plastic, there was the Man again.

Right on cue, just when I thought I might have lost the papal trail, there was Juan Pablo, Pope John Paul, near the end of his 1987 tour, the Holy Cowboy Tour.

He was sitting at a table. Behind him was a picture of himself looking infallible in the papal mitre and such, ready to get down to some blessing. Two cardinals with ear-to-ear grins were standing beside him, egging him on. In his hand, halfway towards his head, was the reason for their excitement.

He was about to put on the most beautiful pure white cowboy hat I have ever seen. The Vatican had sent his measurements over to Stetson, who made it specially in the traditional Rancher style. I was thrilled to see, from a news item of the day in the *San Antonio Light*, that His Holiness took a seven and a half, the same as me.

It had a four-inch brim and was made of 100 per cent beaver, way beyond 5X. It was SkyX, HeavenX – nothing but the best. And to top it off, a twenty-four-carat gold hatband. No wonder Juan Pablo looked pleased with himself. No wonder he stopped over in San Antone before he went on to El Paso to pick up his boots.

In the myth of the West, the white Anglo cowboy, white outlaw and white lawman dominated. He had to. It was the story of the Americas, of European victory over Indian savagery, the old story of white supremacy. But the first man shot in Dodge City was a black man called Tex, innocently watching two white men shooting at each other. The first man jailed in Abilene's new stone jail was black.

In Argentina the gauchos needed to be re-invented as pure Europeans, denying any Indian connections and especially any Indian blood. In Roca's Wars of the Desert the gauchos did this graphically by castrating the barbaric Indians and claiming payment by the pairs of testicles.

In the United States, it had to be Anglo civilization overcoming Indian barbarity – so it was the Anglo cowboys who were glorified and mythologized. Out on the frontier, on the edge of Injun country, in the forefront of the battle against evil 'redskins' and 'half-breeds' and 'greasers', was the noble white cowboy. The West was white. It was simpler that way.

Simpler, perhaps, but unjust, for by denying the black cowboy heritage, generations of black kids have been denied their heroes and their fairytales, denied the cowboy images that belong to them as much as they do to the white kids. It seems that fairy tales, just like history, are written by the winners.

In Texas, it was Anglo dominance over Mexicans that wrote the history books. By calling the vaqueros who had taught them their cowboy skills 'greasers', they denied them their place up in the pantheon. Mexicans were the villains of the Alamo, untrustworthy, feckless, drunk, treacherous . . .

There is one solitary Mexican cowboy commemorated in the National Cowboy Hall of Fame in Oklahoma City. All the rest are Anglos.

*

The story of the black cowboys has been kept quiet, lost and forgotten. Woody Strode, a tall bald black man of great majesty, had been in many Westerns. But he was the exception rather than the rule. As often as not he played a tragic part. The first real black cowboy I had been aware of was Bill Pickett. I had seen a silent clip of him once wrestling a steer. It was extraordinary.

Bill Pickett's mother was a Choctaw Indian – a black Choctaw Indian. In the decades before the Civil War, a lot of black men and women settled among the Indian tribes. Bill had horses in his blood.

Bill Pickett single-handedly created the rodeo sport of bull-dogging, wrestling a steer to the ground. He was described by Zack Miller, the owner of the 101 Ranch in Oklahoma, as 'the greatest sweat and dirt cowhand that ever lived – bar none.' He was probably right. The undisputed father of bull-dogging, Pickett became a huge box-office draw at home and abroad. Travelling with the Miller & Lux 101 Wild West Show, he often appeared on the same bill as the then unknown cowpokes Tom Mix and Will Rogers. We heard more of those guys later than we did of Bill.

Pickett would mount his horse Spradley, ride down a steer, leap on to its back and grab its horns. With his boot heels dug into the ground he would then wrestle the steer off its feet by twisting its head back with its nose pointing upwards.

Once he'd done that, Pickett would sink his own teeth into the beast's upper lip and take his hands off the horns. He would roll the steer over on to the ground *holding on to the steer's lip with his teeth alone.*

The 101 Show became a big attraction. One opening night in Madison Square Garden, Pickett's steer leapt into the stands with Bill and Will Rogers in frantic pursuit.

In 1908, during a Mexican rodeo, Pickett's boss bet $5,000 he could bull-dog a fighting bull. Twenty thousand Mexicans watched, dumbstruck, as Pickett held on to the terrifying bull Little Bean for several minutes before being forced to flee the ring.

Bill made two films, *The Crimson Skull* and *The Bull-Dogger.* He was sixty when he made those films. Finally, he got his own quarter, his own 160-acre spread, in Oklahoma, near the 101 Ranch.

At the age of seventy-one, in 1932, he was still breaking horses until one kicked him and broke his head. He died eleven days later, a slow cowboy's death.

Isom Dart was born into slavery in Arkansas in 1849. He was a born thief, not a born slave. He developed his talents as a thief foraging for Confederate troops in the Civil War. After the war he worked as a rodeo clown in Texas and Mexico before teaming up with a Mexican and smuggling cattle over the border for sale in Texas. He did some prospecting and then turned his hand to bronco busting. One observer said: 'No man understood horses better. I have seen all the great riders, but for all around skill as a cowman, Isom Dart was unexcelled. He could outride any of them; but he never entered any contest.'

Despite this success, Dart's heart was in thieving and he went back to rustling. He rode with the Gault gang until they were ambushed and wiped out. Isom survived by hiding all night in a grave beside the body of a gang member they'd been burying when they were ambushed.

There was something nice and friendly about Isom Dart, though. A lot of people said so. He was arrested many times but somehow never seemed to finish up in jail. They say he was such an easy-going man, a man who enjoyed life, despite his wicked ways, that everyone was charmed by him.

On one occasion, he was being taken in by a deputy from Sweetwater County, Wyoming, when the buckboard spilt off the road and turned over. The lawman was badly injured. Isom Dart tended his wounds, lifted the buckboard back on to its wheels, calmed the horses, carried the deputy to the wagon and drove into town. Leaving the deputy at the hospital, he turned himself in to the sheriff. That was proof enough of his innocence. They let him go again.

Isom Dart was shot dead in 1900 by the notorious bounty hunter Tom Horn.

Nat Love was born into slavery like Isom Dart. By the time he was fifteen, he was punching cows around Dodge City, Kansas. For a generation he drove cattle on the trail from Texas to anywhere north. On July 4, 1876, Nat Love entered the rodeo at Deadwood City in the Dakota Territory and won several roping and shooting contests. He was proclaimed Champion Roper of the Western cattle country and the crowd named him 'Deadwood Dick' from then on.

Then the cattle country was invaded, its spaces hemmed in, as the great iron horse tore across the prairies. In the end, Nat Love, Deadwood Dick, got a job working as a porter on the pullman cars. That was probably the best position open to a black man at the turn of the century and for a good few years afterwards.

The slave market did have its eyes on Texas. When Mexico started colonizing in 1821, there were 2,500 people of European descent in Texas. By independence, in 1836, there were 30,000 Anglos, 5,000 blacks and 4,000

Mexicans. Stephen Austin and his father Moses had been working hard.

By the time Texas was absorbed into the United States ten years later, there were 100,000 whites and 35,000 slaves. Fifteen years after this, on the eve of the Civil War, Texas had 430,000 whites and 182,000 slaves. As predicted, slavery was big business.

The slaves who had been working cattle continued to do so as free men after the Civil War. Texas ranches east of the Trinity river often worked with all-black teams. West of the Nueces river, the ranchers would use vaqueros rather than black cowboys.

The discrimination against black cowboys was more social than economic. They would get roughly the same pay as white cowhands – more than the vaqueros who were on the bottom rung – but the blacks didn't have any career mobility. A good black hand might end his days as cook, but never as ranch foreman.

A black cowboy on a huge ranch which had seven foremen for each of its divisions complained in 1900: 'If it weren't for my damned black face, I'd have been boss of one of these divisions long ago.' He had worked on the ranch for twenty years. He finished up as the cook. Like most black cowboys, he was called 'Nigger John'.

About five thousand black cowboys worked on the long cattle trails north from Texas. For the last third of the nineteenth century, increasing numbers of white cowboys came to the West. On the trail drivers there were in the end 63 per cent Anglo cowhands, 25 per cent blacks and 12 per cent Hispanics. So even in 1900 there were still a significant number of black cowboys.

Things have come around full circle. The white Anglo cowboys are drifting away from ranch work. It is still a rotten, dirty, dangerous, low-paid job with few prospects.

Vaqueros are coming back. This could be because they are cheaper. For whatever reason, more and more cowboys in the States are of Mexican descent, replacing the Anglos in a cattle culture that was Hispanic in the first place.

There are no real stockyards in the States any more, certainly not in Fort Worth. It's all on television now. Instead of yards like we walked round from Osorno to BA, selling is done on cable. It's the shopping channel, but for cattle. Instead of live animals in the yards, a video camera goes out to the ranches and you look at the herd on your TV back home. You do your buying, you go to your auction, with a video image: cable cattle.

The cable station is based in Fort Worth stockyards.

22. Home

W. H. Hudson settled in England when he was only twenty-seven, and lived there for fifty-three years until his death. He wrote and dreamed of the great skies, the space, the sea of grass out on the pampa, while his wife supported them by running boarding houses. He never went back.

Robert Bontine Cunninghame Graham, too, dreamed his quixotic dreams over on this side of the great water.

Tschiffely, the third of the trio who first enticed me on to the trail of the lost cowboys, recounts a strange coincidence. Cunninghame Graham visited him when he was lodging in North Kensington, waiting for a new book to be published.

Don Roberto was flummoxed. 'Strange, very strange,' he kept saying, shaking his great white mane. Then he took Tschiffely out and walked him round the corner.

'When you and Hudson were in Argentina, you lived near each other in that great magnitude of country. Now you are in London, you are walking the same streets as him. Strange.' He pointed with his stick at what Tschiffely called 'a most unattractive house in a side street'. This was the house in which Hudson spent his last years, where he died.

It was 40 St Luke's Road. I live nearby, and walked round to pay homage. It's a fine house on a corner, three blocks from the Portobello Road. I could see why Hudson settled here. The house had an eccentric layout, with a square tower at the top looking out over the roofs of North Kensington, where Hudson doubtless dreamed and scribbled.

He dreamed of the silence and the emptiness of Patagonia. He dreamed of the desolation, of the eternal peace he had felt out at the end of the earth. He dreamed of dying with his boots on under the great sky:

The man who finishes his course by a fall from his horse, or is swept away and drowned when fording a swollen stream, has, in most cases, spent a happier life than he who dies of apoplexy in a counting house or dining room; or who, finding that end which seemed so infinitely beautiful to Leigh Hunt (which to me seems to unutterably hateful), drops his white face on the open book before him.

I know what he meant.

Further Reading

RICHARD SLATTA, THE KEY TO THE LOST COWBOYS
Gauchos, Llaneros and Cowboys (Persimmon Hill, 1983)
Cowboys of the Americas (Yale, 1990)
Gauchos and the Vanishing Frontier (University of Nebraska, 1983)
Bandidos: Varieties of Latin American Banditry (Connecticut, 1987)

A.F. TSCHIFFELY
Tschiffely's Ride: Being the Account of 10,000 Miles in the Saddle through the Americas from Argentina to Washington (London, 1933)
The Tale of Two Horses (London, 1934)
Don Roberto: the Life and Works of R. B. Cunninghame Graham (London, 1937)
This Way Southward (London, 1945)
Bohemia Junction (London, 1951)
Tornado Cavalier: a Biography of Cunninghame Graham (London, 1955)

R.B. CUNNINGHAME GRAHAM
Pedro de Valdivia, Conqueror of Chile (London, 1926)
Thirty Tales and Sketches, ed. Edward Garnett (London, 1929)
Jose Antonio Paez (London, 1929)
Horses of the Conquest (London, 1930)
Rodeo and the Plains of Venezuela, ed. A.F. Tschiffely (New York, 1936)
South American Sketches (Oklahoma, 1978)

PATAGONIA, ARGENTINA AND CHILE
Alba, Manuel: *Guëmes, El Senor Gaucho* (Buenos Aires, 1946)
Bridges, Lucas: *The Uttermost Part of the Earth* (London, 1948)
Chatwin, Bruce: *In Patagonia* (London, 1977)
Chatwin, Bruce, and Theroux, Paul: *Patagonia Revisited* (London, 1992)
Clissold, Stephen: *Bernardo O'Higgins and the Independence of Chile* (London, 1968)
Guiraldes, Ricardo: *Don Segundo Sombra* (Buenos Aires, n.d.)
Hernandez, Jose: *Martin Fierro* (London, 1935)
Hudson, W.H.: *The Naturalist in La Plata* (London, 1892)

Hudson, W.H.: *Far Away and Long Ago: A Childhood in Argentina* (London 1918)
de Saint-Exupéry, Antoine: *Wind, Sand and Stars* (London, 1939)
Theroux, Paul: *The Old Patagonia Express* (London, 1979)
Vernon, Tom: *Fat Man in Argentina* (London, 1990)
Wheeler, Sara: *Travels Through a Thin Country* (London, 1994)

URUGUAY
Street, John: *Artigas and the Emancipation of Uruguay* (Cambridge, 1959)
Ponsonby, Sir John: *The Ponsonby Family* (London, 1929)
Vanger, Milton: *Batlle y Ordonez of Uruguay, Creator of His Times* (Harvard, 1963)
Vidart, D.: *Caballos y Jinetes (Horses and Horsemen)* (Montevideo, 1967)

VENEZUELA
Chitty, J.A.: *Vocabulario del Hato* (U. Central Venezuela, 1966)
Gallegos, Romulo: *Dona Barbara* (Caracas, n.d.)
O'Leary, Daniel: *Memorias* [a twelve-volume biography of Bolivar by his A.D.C.] (n.d.)
Paine, Lauran: *Bolivar the Liberator* (New York, 1970)

MEXICO
Flandrau, Charles Macomb: *Viva Mexico!* (1908, London, 1982)
de Gomara, Francisco Lopez: *Cortes, the Life of the Conqueror by His Secretary*, trans. and edited L.B. Simpson (California, 1964)
Lincoln, John: *One Man's Mexico* (London, 1983)
Marks, Richard Lee: *Cortes* (New York, 1993)
Marnham, Patrick: *So Far from God* (London, 1985)
Reed, John: *Insurgent Mexico* (1914, London, 1983)
Riding, Alan: *Distant Neighbours* (New York, 1989)
Thomas, Hugh: *The Conquest of Mexico* (London, 1993)

THE WEST AND THE ALAMO
Buscombe, Ed (ed.): *The BFI Guide to the Western* (London, 1988)
Katz, William Loren: *The Black West* (New York, 1973)
Thompson, Frank: *Alamo Movies* (Pennsylvania, 1991)
Milner, O'Connor, Sandweiss (eds): *The Oxford Book of the American West* (New York, 1994)

LATIN AMERICA GENERAL
Galeano, Eduardo: *Open Veins of Latin America: Five Centuries' Pillage of a Continent* (New York, 1973)
von Hagen, Victor: *South America Called Them: Explorations of the Great Naturalists* (London, 1949)

Glossary

Abajo	Down, below: 'Down with . . .'
Adobe	Sun-dried mud bricks.
Alamo	Cottonwood or poplar tree.
Alpargatas	(Argentina, Uruguay) Gaucho slippers, like espadrilles. (See *huaraches*, Mexican equivalent.)
Amansador	Horse-trainer, not breaker. See *domador*.
Anglo	White or Anglo-European. Anglo-American cowboy.
Animitas	'Little spirits': roadside shrines to car crashes.
Arepa	(Venezuela) Maize bread.
Armas	(Baja California, N. Mexico) Stiff leather skirts attached to saddle, protecting legs from thorns. (See *guardamontes*)
Arriba	Up, above, high.
Asado	(Argentina, Uruguay) Meat barbecued over open fire, stretched on cruciform spit, angled over hot embers.
Asado con cuero	Meat cooked in its hide.
Asador	Man who cooks the *asado*.
Autentico!	(Venezuela) 'Wicked!' or 'Great!' Lit. 'authentic'.
B.A.	Buenos Aires.
Bagual	*Quechua* for wild horse.
Baguala	Falsetto, yodelling style of singing, especially from mountainous regions of Argentina, also songs sung in this style. Horse-singing?
Bandoneon	Big square plangent German accordion. The sound of Tango.
Barbaro!!	'Wicked!' in the southern cone. Lit. 'barbaric'.
Bastos	Leather saddle panel or pad.

Bife de chorizo	Thick steak from underside of rib. Good for black eyes and *medallones*.
Blandengues	Gaucho militia of River Plate region in colonial times.
Bolas/Boleadores	(Argentina, Uruguay) 'Las Tres Marias', three rocks wrapped and joined with rawhide, used as offensive weapon by Indians and Gauchos.
Bombachas	Gauchos' baggy trousers. Originally ex-army Bulgarian, Turkish or Zouave.
Bombilla	Metal straw for drinking *maté*. Pron. *bom-bee-zha*.
Borracho	Drunk. See *palo borracho* and *burro borracho*.
Botas de potro	Gauchos' soft open-toed boots, taken from rear leg of young colt. Heel is formed by colt's hock.
Brujo, Bruja	Witch-doctor, native sorcerer.
Burro	Donkey.
Burro borracho	Drunk donkey.
Cabildo	Town council, town hall.
Cacique	Indian chief, Carib origin. Pron. *ka-see-kay*.
Calden	'Chinchuline tree', thorny tree on the pampas and in the *monte*, with carob-like seed pods used for animal feed.
Calzoncillos	White linen lace-embroidered undertrousers; Gauchos' underpants.
Cantle	Rear lip of saddle (English).
Camino Real	'Royal Road'; Inca road through Peru to NW Argentina.
Camp, The	The countryside or estate in *southern cone*. From *El Campo*.
Campesino	Peasant.
Candombe	(Uruguay) African-rooted drumming, close to Cuban.
Capataz	Ranch foreman.
Carancho	Large carrion hawk, *Polyborus Braziliensis*.
Caribe	Piranha, carnivorous river fish.
Carnear	To slaughter animals, lit. 'to make meat'.
Carpincho	Water hog.
Caudillo	Warlord, hence strong regional leader (Spanish tradition).

Chacarera	(Argentina) Fast, excitable Gaucho dance.
Chaleco	(Chile) Waistcoat.
Chamanto	(Chile) Medium-size dress poncho.
Chamarro	(Mexico) Short, heavily embroidered *charro* jacket.
Chañar	Low thorny tree common on dry Chañar-steppe, *Gurliaca Decorticans*.
Chapareras/ Chaparejos	Chaps, protective leather leggings.
Chaqueta	(Chile) Bolero-style jacket.
Charqui	Jerky; sun- and wind-dried strips of beef.
Charreada	Dressage rodeo, with emphasis on Looking Good. See *charro*.
Charro	Mexican gentleman horseman. Smart and straight-backed. A state of mind.
China	Gaucho's woman (historical).
Chinchulines/ 'Chinchos'	Chitlins or chitterlings; small intestines of cow. Delicious when barbecued *crocante*, crisp.
Chiripa	Gauchos' nappy-like cloth pants, pulled up between the legs and tucked into the belt. Pre-*bombachas*.
Cimarron	Wild, savage, crude.
Cinch	Girth to hold saddle secure on horse. Anglo: 'It's a cinch.'
Cobija	(Venezuela) Large poncho.
Codo	Elbow.
Cojinillo	Sheepskin saddle pad.
Colear	To pull a bull over by the tail.
Coleador	Man who pulls the bull over by the tail.
Conjunto	(Mexico) Musical group.
Correas	(Mexico) Straps on harness.
Corrido	(Mexico) Long story ballad. Can last a week.
Criadillas	Testicles of bullock. Lit. 'breeders', 'creators'.
Criollo	Creole. Of people: those born in the New World of Spanish stock. Of horses: the tough thick-necked, short-legged pony. Pron. *cree-o-zho*.
Cuatro	(Venezuela) Small four-stringed rhythm guitar.
Cucuracha	Cockroach.
Cueca	Lively *huaso* dance.

Cuero torcido	(Mexican) Twisted rawhide.
Cuero trenzado	Plaited rawhide.
Culo	Arse.
Domador	Horse-breaker.
Dulce de leche	Caramelised condensed milk in the *southern cone*. Sweet. Stunning with flan, crème caramel.
Encomienda	Royal decree giving land and Indians to work it unpaid on the pretext of converting them to Christianity. Slave labour by another name.
Enjalma	Moorish saddle.
Espuelas	Spurs.
Esquina	Bar/store out on the pampa. Lit. 'corner'.
Estancia	Ranch, farm, estate in *southern cone*.
Estanciero	Rancher, owner of estate.
Estepa	Steppe in Patagonia.
Estoy arriba de la luna, Kique	'I'm over the moon, Harry.'
Estoy infermo como un papagallo	'I'm sick as a parrot.'
Estribos	Stirrups.
Facón	Two-foot Gaucho knife, used for everything.
Faja	Broad cloth belt or sash.
Finca	(Venezuela – and Spain) Farm, farmhouse, ranch-house.
Fliperia	Pinball arcade. Lit. 'flipper shop'.
Fonda	Inn.
Frenos	Brakes, reins, bridle.
Galeron	(Argentina) Song and dance.
Galpon	Storage shed.
Ganadero	Cattleman.
Gauchada	A favour.
Gauchismo	The essence of Gaucho.
Gaucho	'Wild orphan [bastard] of the pampa'; Argentine and Uruguayan cowboy. A state of mind.
Guanaco/Huanaco	Wild pampa llama, never tamed or used as beast of burden like llama.
Guardacalcones	(Argentina, Salta) Leather leg coverings, like *chaparejos*.

Guardamontes	(Argentina, Salta) Huge leather batwings mounted on saddle, protecting horses' shoulders and riders' legs from thorny bushes. See *armas*.
Guëmes	The Gaucho general. Pron. *Goo-wem-ess*.
Hacienda	(Argentina, Uruguay, Chile) Ranch house, main *estancia* house; (Mexico) Estate or ranch itself.
Hato	(Venezuela) Ranch.
Hijo	Kid, child. Expletive greeting: Hijo! Hey!
Hijo de la gran puta(na)	Son of a whore. Lit. 'of the Great Whore'.
Hijo de la Gran Bretaña	Briton. Lit. 'son of Great Britain'.
Hijole!	Son-of-a-bitch! Lit. 'son of a rape', *Hijo de la chingada*.
Huancas	See *Wankas*.
Huapango	Regional form of Mexican *son*, folk music. Hence eight-stringed *huapango*, big-bodied troubadour guitar.
Huaraches	Mexican slippers. See *alpargatas*.
Huaso	Chilean cowboy, ranch hand.
Jaquima	Bitless bridle (Arabic). 'Hackamore' to Anglos.
Jarana	(Mexico) Small four-stringed rhythm guitar.
Jefe	Chief, boss.
Jinete	Horseman. From 'La Gineta', a short-stirruped riding style, named after a Moorish tribe.
Joropo	(Venezuela) Fast cowboy, *llanero*; also dance.
Jujuy	North of Salta, towards Bolivian border. Pron. *hoo-hooey*.
La Reata	Lariat to Anglos.
Lazo	Lassoo to Anglos.
Llama	Tame mountain *guanaco*.
Llanero	(Venezuela, Colombia) Cowboy. Lit. 'plainsman'.
Llanos	Unique tropical plains of Venezuela and Colombia.
Loncheria	(Mexico) Café. Pepsicoatl culture.
Machete	Broad two-foot all-purpose tropical or jungle knife.
Machete!!	'Wicked!' in Venezuela. See *barbaro!!* and *autentico!!*

MacPay	Uruguayan national whisky, Gaucho favourite. Pron. Mac-*pie*.
Malacara	White-faced horse.
Maneas	(Mexico) Reins.
Manso	Tame.
Manso como para un Ingles	Good enough for me. Lit. 'tame enough for an Englishman.'
Manta	(Chile) Short poncho. As worn by the Pope.
Marinera	(Mexico) Sailors' dance, brought up Pacific coast by sailors from South America.
Maroma	Reckless Gaucho game, dropping from corral gate on to unbroken colt's back and riding him into the ground. Llaneros do it backwards and hold on to the tail. Hard.
Mata	(Venezuela) Wood, forest.
Matadero	Abbatoir, slaughterhouse.
Matambre	'Hunger-killer'; cut of meat between ribs and hide, cooked flat or rolled and stuffed.
Maté	Regional caffeine drink of *southern cone*. Lit. *Quechua* for gourd or calabash. See *yerba maté*.
Mecate	(Mexico) Fine horsehair rope. 'McCartys' to Anglos.
Medallones	Saddle sores. Lit. 'medallions', round sores.
Medio Bagualon	Half broken, half wild (horse).
Meseta	Tableland.
Mesteño	Mustang, wild horse.
Mestizo	Spanish-Indian mix. Most people in Latin America.
Mexico	Aztec 'Navel of the Moon'.
Mezcal	Distilled cactus juice. Smoky flavour from roasted cactus heart. Smoky tequila. No connection with mescaline at all. Personal experience.
Milagro	Miracle.
Milonga	(Argentina, Uruguay) Slow, sad country song. Gaucho.
Mollejas	Thyroid, type of sweetbread. Popular in *southern cone*.
Monte	Arid, hard land with low, thorny bushes and trees. West and south of *pampa* towards the Cordillera.

Morcillas	(Argentina, Uruguay) Black pudding, pig's blood sausage, both savoury and sweet. Best in the world.
Mordita	Baksheesh, a bribe. Lit. 'little bite'.
Mulatto	Black-white mix.
Muy Gaucho	Very Gaucho. Hard.
Ñandu	Patagonian ostrich, *Rhea Darwinii*.
Norteño	(Mexico) Tex-Mex *conjunto* music. Lit. 'northern'.
Ombu	Large, dark-shaded, umbrella-shaped tree. Mysterious.
Overo	Piebald or skewbald horse with soft, outlined blotches.
Paisano	Countryman, peasant. In S. Patagonia, a Gaucho.
Palenque	(Argentina, Uruguay) Hitching post.
Palo Borracho	'Drunken stick', or bottle tree. Chorizia.
Pampa	The flat grasslands extending out from the River Plate, called Pampas in English. 'The Space' in Quechua.
Pampero	Wind and storm from the South.
Paniolo	Hawaiian cowboys. From 'Español', language of the Mexican cowboys who taught their language to the Hawaiians.
Panqueque	Pancake.
Panuelo	Bandana, scarf.
Parabolica	TV satellite dish.
Parilla	Grill, barbecue; meat and organs grilled over coals on a grid. Pron. *par-ee-zha*. *Southern cone*.
Paseo	Walk, stroll.
Paso castellano	Castilian pace, trotting slowly.
Pato	Gaucho chase game, on horseback, using a duck sewn into a leather bag as the ball. Many killed. Made illegal.
Payada	(Argentina, Uruguay) Poetic battle between troubadours. See *topada*.
Payador	Gaucho troubadour, derived from 12th-century Spanish troubadour tradition.
Pechada	Pushing horse's chest against cattle, 'horse-handling' cattle as in Chilean rodeo.
Pejerreyes	You wouldn't like them . . .
Peludo	Hairy armadillo.

Peon	Farmhand.
Pialar	Another reckless Gaucho horse game. Gallop past chums who try to lassoo your horse's legs and bring you down.
Pingo	Argentine saddle horse, a good, well trained mount.
Plaza	Square, town square.
Plazoleta	Small town square.
Polainas/Perneras	(Chile, Mexico) Protective leather leggings.
Polleria	Chicken shop.
Porteño	Someone from Buenos Aires, 'the Port'.
Posa maté	Holder, usually leather, for round *maté* cup.
Potro	Colt, young horse.
Potranca	Filly.
Provando	Testing, testing, testttiiiiinnngg.
Pucha	Same as *puta*, whore.
Puchero	Gaucho trail-stew, meat and vegetables.
Pueblito	Little village.
Pulperia	Bar/general store in the middle of nowhere. Also called *esquina*.
Quebrada	Gorge, ravine.
Quechua	Original Inca language, now main language of Peru, Bolivia and NW Argentina. Quichua is a dialect.
Quien sabe?	Who knows?
Rastra	Wide Gaucho belt, heavily ornamented with silver and gold coins and chains.
Rebenque	Flat Gaucho whip.
Rebozo	(Mexico) Woman's shawl.
Recado	Multi-layered, sheepskinned Gaucho saddle derived from Moorish *enjalma*.
Reduccion	Indian reservation. Lit. 'reduction'.
Reglas fijas	Fixed rules. There are none.
Rincon	Corner.
Rodeo	Roundup.
Saladero	Establishment, factory for salting meat.
Santeria	'Saint shop', for holy statues and relics.
Serape	(Mexico) Poncho.
Silla	Saddle.

Sombrero	Hat. Lit. 'shader', from *sombra*, shade.
Southern cone	Argentina, Chile, Uruguay, Paraguay, Southern Brazil. The bottom of the ice-cream cone.
Taba	Gaucho gambling game, throwing astragalus, ankle-bone, of steer.
Tallow	Hard animal fat, melted down to make candles and soap.
Tanguero	Tango singer or player.
Tapaderas	'Taps', protective leather stirrup covering.
Tienda	(Mexico) Shop, where Anglos buy all their tack; *vaqueros* make their own.
Tirador	Wide Gaucho leather working belt, used for roping and snubbing horses in the corral.
Tobiano/Tuviano	Piebald, skewbald, Pinto horse. A Paint, with sharp outlined blotches.
Tonada	(Venezuela) Slow, sad song.
Tonto	Stupid. Hence
Tonteria	A stupidity. The Falklands War.
Topada	(Mexico) Poetic battle between troubadours. See *payada*.
Trapalanda	Horse heaven for Gauchos.
Tripa gorda	Marrow gut, between a steer's two ruminant stomachs. Tasty.
Tropa	A troop of horses.
Tropilla	Small troop.
Vamos!/Vamanos!	Let's go! 'Vamoose' to Anglos.
Vaquero	(Mexico) Cowboy. 'Buckaroo' to Anglos.
Vengo del otro lado de la luna	I am from the other side of the moon.
Vihuela	(Mexico) Small four-stringed guitar.
Vive fulano de tal!	(Venezuela) Llanero battle cry: 'Long Live Whoever!'
Vizcacha	Pampa prairie dog.
Wankas	Also *Huancas*. Important pre-Inca culture in Peru.
Whicky	Whisky in the *southern cone*.
Whickeria	Bar where you drink *whicky*.
Yerba (Maté)	The Maté tea itself. Lit. 'herb', leaves of *Ilex Paraguayensis*, related to holly bush.

| Zamba | (Argentina) Slow, sad song. |
| Zambo | Mixed Indian and Negro. |